"YOU KILLE[illegible]

Larson whirled to face [illegible] as a horse, black above and white beneath. The fur of its spine and hackles bristled. Its eyes flashed red fire. Its presence seemed to fill Larson's mind.

"W-what?" Larson stammered.

The wolf exposed a mouthful of sword-sharp, yellowed teeth. "Al Larson, *Allerum Godslayer,* you destroyed Loki, my father, but you can't slay the force he represented. Soon you will die beneath my paws. For tonight, you will know only chaos and terror."

"Wait!" Larson started.

The wolf-god raised a threatening paw. For a moment, Larson glimpsed the carefully woven web of nerves which composed his own thoughts. Then white hot pain crashed through his head. His vision exploded to crimson-black. He stood in frightened awe as a chunk of vine-streaked jungle dissolved into a scorched plain. Shadowy forms low-crawled across Larson's peripheral vision. Mentally, he chased them, and his pursuit flung him into a limitless spiral of god-ruled illusion. . . .

DAW Titles by Mickey Zucker Reichert:

THE BIFROST GUARDIANS

GODSLAYER (Book 1)

SHADOW CLIMBER (Book 2)

DRAGONRANK MASTER (Book 3)

MICKEY ZUCKER REICHERT

DAW BOOKS, INC.
DONALD A. WOLLHEIM, PUBLISHER

1633 Broadway, New York, NY 10019

Copyright © 1989 by Miriam S. Zucker.

All Rights Reserved.

Cover art by Richard Hescox.

DAW Book Collectors No. 792.

Permissions and Acknowledgments

Benet, Stephen Vincent, lines from "Litany for Dictatorships" from: THE SELECTED WORKS OF STEPHEN VINCENT BENET; Holt, Rinehart and Winston, Inc.; copyright, 1935, by Stephen Vincent Benet; copyright renewed © 1963, by Thomas C. Benet, Stephanie B. Mahin and Rachel Benet Lewis. Reprinted by permission of Brandt & Brandt Literary Agents, Inc.

First Printing, September 1989

1 2 3 4 5 6 7 8 9

PRINTED IN THE U.S.A.

In loving memory:
To Gertrude Reichert
and
Ryan Boyles,
as promised.

ACKNOWLEDGMENTS

To all those deserving who were inadvertently forgotten: D.J. Miller, R. Douglas, and S. Davis who encouraged and fueled my imagination; also Cindy and Melissa Mosko who kept the sparks alive.

To Dave Hartlage for effort above and beyond the call of duty; James Hoffman and the Beths, Nachison and Hudson, who helped more than they know. To Arthur, Sandra, Steve, and Tal Zucker, Laura Newman, and Evelyn Migdol (you all know why). To Captain Kevin Randle who spared an hour (the equivalent of 8½ of his manuscript pages) to take me back to Vietnam—again.

And, as always, to Sheila Gilbert who accepts nothing short of the best . . . and deserves it, too.

But mostly, I would like to thank Tim Larson, once a bold lunatic who could never pass up a challenge, now a yuppie in suburbia.

CONTENTS

RAJARKMAR
GEIRMAGNUS' ESTATE
MIKALSBORG
SCHOOL OF THE DRAGONRANK MAGES
R. GUNNTHRA
BIFROST BRIDGE AND KIARRMAR
R. SVOL
R. GJOLL
R. LEIPTR
R. VID
R. FJORM
HVERGELMIR
ORACLE OF HARGATYR
R. FIMBULTHUL
R. SLIDR
R. HRID
MANIVOLL
R. YLG
R. SVIP
FORSTE-MAR
Skagerrak
NORTH SEA
MOONBEARS' PEOPLE
Kattegat
SVERIGEHAVN
Danwald Wilderness
Colrmar PORT
KOLDING HILLS
HAWK ROCK
KIELWALD
WYNETH
Cumsberg
R. KIEL
N
©84 GILBERT

PROLOGUE

Northern winds battered a mud-chinked log longhouse in Kiarrmar, carrying the promise of a fierce Scandinavian winter. Inside, Taziar Medakan huddled beneath his bearskin cloak, a stranger to Norway's fouler weather. The cards in his small, callused fist felt brittle. He studied the faces of his four Viking companions and smiled as Kolbyr Hansson threw his cards to the rickety table which served as the only piece of furniture. Four pairs of grim, blue eyes settled on Taziar.

Ignoring the Vikings' stares, Taziar shook a comma of black hair from his eyes. He flicked cards from his hand to the table in groups. "Two Vikings, two kings, and three dragons." He looked up. "Guess I win again." Leaning forward, he swept a pile of coins from the center of the table into a larger stack before him.

Kolbyr went silent. To his left, Torben grunted. Bothi muttered a phrase to Hamar which Taziar could not decipher. He had spent a harried month learning the Norwegian tongue from barbarian friends in Sweden. Bothi's accent and civilized dialect rendered his words unintelligible, but their intention seemed all too clear. Suddenly, Taziar felt acutely aware of being the shortest man in the room by a full head and the lightest by again his own weight. Irony seared through him. *Eight years a thief in Cullinsberg and I'm going to get killed for winning a card game honestly.* He rose. "Friends, your Fates were kind to me today . . ."

Torben opened his mouth to speak.

Taziar dropped formality and finished in a rush. "It's

not much fun spending money alone. Anyone for dinner and drinks? I'll buy.''

A tense hush followed Taziar's invitation. The Cullinsbergen waited expectantly, his hand sliding near the sword at his hip. He could never hope to best even one of the huge warriors before him, but he knew a display of crazed boldness might be his only means of regaining the Vikings' favor. He seized his hilt and twisted his face into a feigned snarl of offense. ''Too good to drink with me?'' His words rang with challenge, yet his eyes measured the distance to the door.

Bothi growled. His sword rattled from its sheath, spinning wild highlights through the longhouse.

Taziar held his breath and his ground. He kept his expression unreadable, but sweat spangled his brow.

Hamar clapped a palm to Bothi's shoulder. ''Enough. You've always preferred drinking to fighting. Don't begrudge the little man his winnings when he's offered to spend them on us, eh?'' He gave Taziar a reassuring half smile. ''Besides, Bothi, he'd probably kill you. Then you'd be embarrassed.''

Hamar's logic was lost on Taziar, but it seemed to calm Bothi. Hostility vanished beneath a rush of camaraderie. Bothi sheathed his weapon. Hamar opened the door, and the Norsemen filed through the portal into a snow-blanketed forest of evergreens. With practiced skill, Taziar flicked a handful of gold coins into his pocket and swept the remainder of his winnings into the pouch at his belt. From habit, he paused to pull his cloak more tightly about the black linen shirt and britches which had become his trademark from his days as a master thief, known as the Shadow Climber, in the southern barony of Cullinsberg. Though less fierce than the squalls farther north, the cold winds bit at Taziar unmercifully. He followed his companions, pulling the door closed behind them.

As Taziar wound through stands of pine, he recalled easier days among innocent Swedish barbarians to whom kindness and honesty came as naturally as breathing. As a thief from one of the most decadent baronies on the continent, Taziar found the barbarians' way of life a comfortable change. Yet, soon he had become bored by its simple perfection. He had no wish to deceive trusting barbarians who were also friends, and his keen mind seemed dulled from disuse. His body craved the rushes of elation inspired by outwitting men and obtaining the impossible. So Taziar had traveled to Norway, seeking Astryd, the woman he loved. She was a sorceress, forced to spend eleven months of each year, without visitors, at the Dragonrank school. Older, more experienced men than Taziar deemed the wizards' training grounds impenetrable. But the immensity of the challenge served only to fuel Taziar's interest. En route to Astryd, Taziar had passed eagerly through Scandinavia's more civilized lands only to find that most of its citizens were only poor farmers. Since his arrival in the town of Kiarrmar, Taziar had uncovered nothing more exciting than a card game called g'mish.

The forest broke to a plain crusted with frost and crisscrossed by boot tracks. Less than ten strides ahead of Taziar and his Viking companions, a rainbow rose like a column from the earth. Its multicolored bands arched across the clearing, their farther ends obscured by distance. Highlights of red, yellow, and blue winked like gems from the delicate lace of ice. Taziar gasped in awe. "Aga'arin's fat priest! I've never seen a rainbow end!" In the past day, he had noticed neither rain nor snow to explain its striking magnificence. It seemed too solidly real, more like a structure than the illusion of light he knew it must be. He crept tentatively toward it. The archway quivered in the breeze, obviously no work of man.

Kolbyr slapped his legs, speaking between low-pitched snickers. "Small man, small brain." He held up a hand and spread his thumb and forefinger slightly.

The Norsemen howled.

Shocked by his companions' levity, Taziar whirled. His face flushed scarlet. A month in a village without cruelty had made him careless. He had forgotten the heated pain of ridicule.

Gradually, the Norsemen's laughter subsided. Bothi gasped for breath. "Little dolt calls the Bifrost Bridge a rainbow.'' This inspired a fresh wave of mirth at Taziar's expense.

Taziar scowled. His gaze followed the perfect sweep of the rainbow bridge. In his youth, he had run with a gang of street orphans. The experience had ingrained the need to preserve self-dignity, to remain collected and in control at all times. To lose face before a group of unforgiving rogues was to become outcast, to lose the shared companionship, food, and plunder, and, perhaps, to lose one's life. Taziar's slightness had made him even more sensitive to humiliation. Now, he struggled to regain his composure and the Vikings' respect. ''Bridge?'' he asked, hoping the brevity of his question would keep him from sacrificing the Norsemen's attention to another round of searing laughter.

Hamar fought a smile. ''The Bifrost links our man world, Midgard, with Asgard, the realm of gods.'' He fidgeted. ''Let's go now. I think we've paused here long enough.''

Taziar chewed his lip, intrigued by Hamar's obvious discomfort. Suddenly, the promise of adventure beckoned, reminding him of past feats which had earned him his pseudonym and his reputation: the boasts of youthful companions which inspired him to climb the highest, slickest walls architects could design; the theft of the greatest artifact of the baron's church which condemned him to Cullinsberg's dungeon, brutal torture, and a sentence of execution; and the lure of the impenetrable Dragonrank school grounds. ''What's it like across the bridge?''

Kolbyr stared incredulously. ''Across it?''

Bothi's voice acquired a patronizing tone. ''You call yourself a climber, Shadow. Why don't you find out?'' He smirked, glancing at his companions for encouragement, but the other Vikings became strangely silent.

Hamar seized Bothi's forearm with a hand as large and furred as a bear's paw. His gray eyes went cold and all amusement left them. ''We're here to spend Shadow's money, not get him killed by gods.'' He addressed Taziar directly. ''You can't cross the Bifrost Bridge. No mortal can.''

Excitement coursed through Taziar. As he had so many

times before, he accepted Kolbyr's dismissal as a challenge. Boldly, he approached the end of the rainbow and laid a hand on the blue-hued upper band. It swayed beneath his touch, but its substance felt real and solid, like a thinly hammered strip of steel. "It seems firm enough."

A lofty shout of indignation suffixed Taziar's assessment. He turned. The Vikings were staring up the colored bands, their pallid faces etched with horror. *What could be terrible enough to frighten battle-mad pirates?* Apprehension prickled the edges of Taziar's consciousness. He followed the direction of his companions' gazes. A huge figure shuffled toward them on the Bifrost Bridge; distance blurred it to a moving mass of whiteness. The rainbow shivered beneath each footfall. "Who?" asked Taziar carefully, his gaze locked on the approaching form.

Kolbyr inched forward and clamped fear-rigid fingers on Taziar's forearm. "Heimdallr," he whispered.

"Heimdallr," Hamar echoed. He took a shuddering backstep.

Even Bothi, who would as soon kill a man as acknowledge his presence, remained frozen, his features twisted in alarm. "The Guardian of the Bifrost."

Taziar had seen a similar expression only once, on the face of an acolyte to Aga'arin before the insane, young priest swore he had looked upon his god. *Superstitious awe.* Taziar snorted. Cullinsberg's temples existed only to wring money from the pious to fill the coffers for their self-indulgent clergy. *What is it about man's nature which forces him to invent gods? And what is it about the gods he invents which makes him panic in their presence?* Taziar had asked himself the question too many times to ponder its significance now. He nudged Kolbyr. "If you fear him, why don't you run now, before he reaches us?"

Kolbyr's fingernails gouged Taziar's flesh. His terror seemed tangible. "No good," he panted. "Heimdallr sees a hundred leagues in front of him and as well by night as day. He knows who we are."

Torben finished the description in the routine monotone of a well-versed holy man. "He can hear grass growing and the wool on sheep and everything that makes more noise.''

Heimdallr's muscled form drew closer.

Painfully, Taziar pulled free of Kolbyr's death grip. He waved his companions silent in the unlikely event they were correct about Heimdallr's acutely developed senses. Taziar had never found a reason to believe in gods, but until he crossed the sea to Scandinavia's strange lands, he had never accepted the existence of sorcerers, pirates, or rainbow bridges either.

Heimdallr's descent seemed to span an eternity. The Vikings stood in quiet awe. And as Heimdallr finally reached the edge of the Bifrost Bridge, Taziar realized the man/god's size had created the illusion of closeness and it explained why his approach appeared to take so long. Heimdallr towered over even the largest Viking. Gold-red curls swarmed his scalp and chin framing angry, gray eyes, a straight nose, and ruddy cheeks. A chain about his neck held an ornately-crafted horn.

Taziar read power and strength in every line of Heimdallr's frame. He stepped forward, aware his atheistic perspective would put him in the best position to bargain.

''What is it you wish?'' As Heimdallr spoke, he flashed teeth of glowing gold.

Doubt suffused Taziar. Surely no normal man would guard a rainbow nor have a mouthful of sculpted metal. Taziar questioned his own concern. *And what difference if he is a god?* He recalled the huge chunks of time priests spent in prayer, glorifying deities with flowery words. *A man who believes himself divine will fall easy victim to praise.* He adopted his most humble expression. ''Lord Heimdallr, forgive me. I am a stranger to this country. Yet tales of your greatness have spread even across the Kattegat to my people. I begged my new friends to bring me to this spot. Ignorant of the consequences, I leaned against the Bifrost. Please accept my sincere apologies and this offering to your magnificence. I assure you I shall not repeat the accident.'' He knelt as if before royalty, pulled the pouch of coins from his belt, and offered it to Heimdallr.

Amusement colored the white god's features. He took

the sack in one beefy hand and, without examining its contents, secured it to his own wide sash. "Thank you, little man, for your dramatic performance and your money." Turning on one booted heel, he tramped back up the Bifrost Bridge.

Heimdallr's easygoing manner left Taziar slack-jawed with astonishment. As the god disappeared into the distance, the Vikings regained their arrogant courage. Bothi opened his mouth, but Taziar waved him silent until Heimdallr had sauntered well beyond the range of his legendary vision and hearing. In the time which passed, all surprise abandoned Taziar, leaving him feeling cheated. The anticipation of matching wits with a god had raised an excitement which could be quenched by nothing less than a noteworthy achievement.

Bothi sputtered. "You stupid little insect! You gave away enough gold to feed a village."

Taziar's blue eyes narrowed. *While you stood like a panicked rabbit, too afraid to move or speak.* He kept this thought to himself, still not crazy enough to do battle with four trained warriors. In his thieving days, the Shadow Climber had donated his stolen proceeds to the needy, the thrill of risking his life and achieving the impossible his only reward. Bothi's concern for a bagful of money seemed illogical to Taziar. "A single battle will earn you all twice as much." An idea came to him suddenly, and he whirled to face the Vikings' glares. "It was *my* money, but if it means so much to you I will happily retrieve it."

"Retrieve it?" Kolbyr shook his head, obviously attributing Taziar's word choice to difficulties with their language. "You mean replace it."

Taziar circled the Bifrost Bridge, studying it from every angle. He recalled, from his touch, that the three-tiered rainbow was unsteady; it quivered in the stronger breezes. Yet his fingers had detected irregularities in its surface. Some lofty architect had constructed it of blocks of an unknown material, chunks of light perhaps. And Taziar knew from experience that anything composed of parts would have cracks between, no matter how careful or divine its crafter. "No," he said slowly. "I will *retrieve* it. I will climb the rainbow and return your gold to the last insignificant chip."

Bothi snickered. "And we'll wait and watch while Heimdallr casually tosses your broken corpse from the bridge."

Hamar explained. "Heimdallr serves as watchman of the gods. It's his job to keep mortals and giants from Asgard. He fathered the races of men, so he can forgive your touch and, perhaps, even a few steps onto the bridge. But I doubt Heimdallr will carry the gold all day. To retrieve it, you will have to sneak past him and into his hall on Asgard. To do that, my friend, you will need to be less than a shadow and more than a climber."

Kolbyr examined Taziar's face, apparently seeking to determine the seriousness of the smaller man's boast. "Heimdallr will see and hear you the instant you stand on his bridge."

Taziar smiled, enjoying the Vikings' attention. "Hear me, perhaps. But I believe your precise description was that Heimdallr sees a hundred leagues *in front of him* and as well by night as day. Is that not so?"

"That's what the legends say."

"Then," said Taziar, crossing around and ducking beneath the rainbow until he could see only the lowest, red band, "I will have to approach from beneath him." He slipped off his boots, sacrificing their warmth for the necessary gripping power and sensory input his bare toes could provide. Soon, exertion would make him forget the cold. With practiced skill, he caught handholds in the all but invisible seams of the structure and swung his feet so his soles rested on the undersurface of the Bifrost Bridge. The band shivered slightly. Knowing the movement would summon Heimdallr, Taziar spoke in a rapid whisper. "Leave now. I'll meet you at the longhouse. For my sake and your own, say nothing to anyone." With that warning, he turned full concentration to the arching band of light above him. Quietly, deliberately, he worked his upside-down way along the bottom edge of the Bifrost Bridge.

An hour passed without sight or sound of Heimdallr. The superficiality of the Bifrost's crevices forced Taziar to concentrate upon them to the exclusion of everything else. His ardor remained, undulled and untainted. By the subtle upward arc of his course, he could tell his journey was still in its infancy, though the ground lay more than a league beneath him. He shook a cramp from his right hand and realized Heimdallr's presence might prove the least of his problems.

Another two hours' climb, and Heimdallr's voice boomed across the rainbow strands. "Is someone here? Identify yourself now, or I shall be forced to kill you."

Taziar slowed his ascent to a crawl. He felt the bridge shudder as the white god shifted position, presumably to block the passage of an invisible foe. Obviously, Heimdallr never even considered the idea that a man might be capable of climbing the underside of the Bifrost. Taziar dragged his aching limbs onward, beginning to understand why.

It took Heimdallr six more hours of angered challenges to dismiss Taziar's breathing and movement as wind. Now, at the peak of the arch, Taziar felt sweat dripping from him like rain despite the frigid gusts. Carefully balancing his grip, he raised his left arm and wiped his forehead. He noticed that blood smeared his fingertips. Aware an assessment of the damage to his hands and feet could only weaken his self-confidence, he forced himself to continue without looking. Searing pain made him curse the inexplicable force which drove him to feats of utter stupidity.

Taziar fell into a climbing rhythm. His limbs continued to draw him upward long after his mind had fogged with exhaustion. The scarlet prints he left with every movement blended into the red expanse of the rainbow band. But the pain never dulled. It remained, sharp and cruel as a knife cut, haunting each movement with accusation.

Nearly there. Nearly there, Taziar promised himself for hours. Finding the irregularities which no less skilled man could locate, let alone scale, became a constant, ceaseless obsession. His head throbbed from his unnatural position. His mind channeled fleeting thoughts only with heroic effort. He struggled against the threat of dark unconsciousness.

Oblivion overtook him on the downward slope. His soles lost the friction of the rainbow, and his body unfolded. He clung, fingers white with strain, suddenly fully awake. For an instant, he imagined himself tumbling, wind-whipped and dizzied, through leagues of open air. Then a deeper portion of his mind kicked in. *You stupid, weak-willed bastard, don't let it beat you!* Self-directed rage filled him. Exhaustion made him uncharacteristically awkward, but he swung his feet back into position. For an instant he hung, contemplating his near demise. And it gave him the strength to draw his aching body a few lengths farther.

A world beyond fatigue closed around him then. His mind bent away from reality, summoning rapidly changing fragments of memory. Taziar thought he caught a glimpse of grass and water beneath him before he collapsed into utter darkness.

Taziar awakened to a blur of black, white, and red, an evil smell in his nostrils, and the dull ache of every muscle and tendon. He felt chilled all over, except for his face which seemed oddly feverish. From habit, he assessed the damage caused by his fall. Blood slicked his hands and feet. Nothing seemed broken, just badly strained. And an unexplained pressure on his rib cage made every breath painful.

Gradually, Taziar's vision unswirled. The colors came together to form the countenance of a narrow-muzzled animal, uncomfortably close. Silver fur covered the underside of its snout and framed eyes like live coals. Black hair capped the upper side of its nose, head, and triangular ears. Rows of teeth as long and sharp as daggers protruded from its open jaw. Its tongue lolled, dripping foul-smelling saliva onto Taziar's face.

Wolf! Taziar gasped in alarm. His eyes followed the contours of the creature. It stood large as a plow horse, and its forepaws were planted firmly on Taziar's chest. Hairs of white and gray were interspersed amid the luxurious thickness of its ebony coat, especially on the legs; they tapered to cream-colored paws. A ribbon, which seemed scarcely strong enough to hold a house cat, enwrapped one of the beast's hind feet. Taziar froze, not daring to move, and hoped a merciful man held the other end of the unusual leash.

As if in answer to Taziar's unspoken question, a malevolent voice broke the silence. "Dessstiny."

Taziar resisted the urge to wipe wolf spittle from his cheeks. "E-excuse me," he stammered carefully.

"Dessstiny." The words were louder, this time accompanied by a burst of the wolf's putrid breath.

Taziar forced a weak smile, and tried to sound matter-of-fact. "Would you mind calling off your dog? It would make it easier to talk."

The wolf's head drifted closer until Taziar could see only its vast forest of teeth. "But he hasn't eaten yet!" The furred muzzle opened and closed with each syllable, punctuated the words with blasts of rank, expelled air.

The same rational portion of Taziar's mind which still did not accept the existence of gods and magic would not allow him to believe in talking animals. Yet he could find no other explanation. *You can speak?* Taziar cut off his incredulous question before he uttered it. Stating the self-evident could only make him sound stupid. *And this is no time to make a mistake.* He met the wolf's fiery gaze as he spoke. "What did you mean by 'destiny'?"

The wolf's jowls twitched. "You've heard of the Fates, little man?"

"Call me Shadow," said Taziar, becoming annoyed with the references to his size. "And yes, I've heard a few things."

The wolf backed off slightly. "Then you know the Fates determine the length of a man's life." Its red eyes sparkled. "Yours has come to an abrupt end. It's your destiny to become my dinner." The beast's jaws stretched wide; it soon became apparent that it could swallow Taziar whole and the world with him.

Taziar flinched to the ground. "Wait!" he called.

The wolf's mouth stopped opening.

Taziar continued quickly. "We could talk more easily if you let me sit up."

There followed a tense and jarring silence.

Then the wolf's muzzle snapped back to its normal

size. "Very well," it said. It backstepped so that its paws no longer held Taziar. "But you had better have something important to say."

Gratefully, Taziar raised his torso.

Immediately, the wolf clamped his paws on Taziar's legs, pinning him into a sitting position. "Speak," it said, and its voice was like thunder.

Taziar wasted a moment freeing his eyes from spit-plastered hair with his hands and a toss of his head. He used the short time this maneuver gained him to evaluate his position. He and the wolf occupied an island surrounded by a narrow ring of crystal waters. The thin coil of string which enwrapped the wolf's hind leg was attached to a staunch chain which encircled a distant crag. Above Taziar, the Bifrost Bridge formed a gentle arch to end in a sun-warmed field of grasses just beyond the unnaturally calm lake. Taziar tried to shift position, but the wolf's padded feet held him with the strength of a giant's vise.

"Well?" the wolf demanded. Its ears swept flat to its head.

Taziar had made a career out of reading intentions and gestures. *It could have eaten me and didn't . . . yet. That can only mean I have something it wants which I can use to barter for my life.* "If you free me, I can supply you with a lot more meat than I have on my body."

The wolf raised its jowls in a snarl. "Don't speak to me as if to some foolish mortal! If I let you go, I'll never see you again."

"You have my word."

The wolf snorted. "Of what value is 'word' to a man who would climb the Bifrost Bridge on a whim? Or was it a dare, *Shadow?* No, thanks for the offer." Its voice went louder with each syllable. "But I think I'll eat you here!"

Taziar's composure broke. "Wait!" he screamed. "There must be something I can do for you. Isn't there anything you need or want? Anything . . ."

The wolf shook its head so hard, its jowls slapped against its teeth. "So long as I remain tied here, I have no needs.'' It lowered its head. Its feet kneaded deeper into Taziar's legs, and its whiskers brushed his nose.

Seeking any opening, Taziar asked the logical question. ''And if you weren't tied?''

The wolf drew back its head. Its expression went soft, and its red-hued eyes held a faraway look.

For an instant, Taziar felt almost sorry for the monster which threatened his life. He read deep sadness in the wolf's demeanor and another emotion, indescribable yet familiar.

''Freed,'' said the wolf, its booming voice softening. ''I would slay a light elf named Allerum and his battle-crazed swordmaster, the ronin, Gaelinar. They killed my father.''

Overwhelmed by memories, Taziar closed his eyes. He recalled the restlessness which had driven him from the day of his own father's death and inspired his insane love for challenges. He recalled how his quest for vengeance had drawn him from his home, everyone and everything he cared about, and eventually forced him to take a man's life. ''I . . . understand.'' Hoping to gain the wolf's good will, he explained further. ''I, too, had occasion to avenge my father's murder. The success was hollow. My father is still dead. But now I have to live with his slayer's blood on my conscience. And I realized this long before I killed him.''

''But you killed him anyway,'' the wolf finished.

''I killed him for other reasons. Ilyrian was a cruel, unscrupulous worm. Left alive, he would have murdered others and broken a score of families . . .''

The wolf loosed a lungful of harsh laughter. ''You ignorant little peon! The crimes this Ilyrian might have perpetrated are of no significance. By killing my father, Allerum and Gaelinar may have destroyed the fabric of the universe.''

Taziar met the wolf's glaring eyes. There was no doubt in his mind that the wolf was telling the truth. ''Explain.''

''Shadow.'' The wolf's tone became conversational. ''Think of our world as a glass rod with a force pulling the two ends in opposite directions. Call one power Law, the other Chaos."

Taziar nodded, looking interested. As long as the wolf talked, he remained alive and able to compose a plan of escape. "Go on."

"Imagine Law and Chaos in a constant struggle to own that bar. So long as they have equal strength, it remains undisturbed. But, if that balance becomes skewed, the glass rod, our world, falls to the ground and shatters. Can you picture it?"

Taziar nodded, though not fully certain of the analogy. He wriggled slightly beneath the wolf's paw and met instant resistance.

The black line of the wolf's mouth twitched upward at the corners, but its tone remained deadly serious. "My father was the strongest proponent on the side of Chaos. When Allerum and Gaelinar took his life, they obliterated him completely, body and soul. He exists on none of our nine worlds: not Asgard, not Hel, not Midgard. The balance has been tipped. The result, Shadow? If not put right soon, our worlds will suffer full annihilation, too. All men, gods, and every manner of creature will die."

A vast silence followed the wolf's revelation. Taziar studied the beast's face for some evidence of deception. But the concern in the wolf's fiery eyes was undeniable. Its intonation and stance conveyed a wickedness beyond that of any man, but it betrayed no signs of falsehood. For all the impossibility of its implications, the wolf was telling what it believed to be the truth. Still, Taziar questioned. "And the solution?"

"Shadowman, it has become your *destiny* to fulfill my vengeance."

It seemed to Taziar that their conversation had come full circle. He studied the wolf's powerful jaws, the evil gleam in its eyes, and the tensely bunched muscles beneath its heavy coat of fur. He knew the beast could cause more than its share of deviltry on Midgard. Gritting his teeth, Taziar gathered his courage. "I don't believe in destiny," he said softly. "And I'd gladly let you eat me before I'd free you to kill innocents, Wolf.'' Taziar cringed, anticipating the beast's wrath.

But the wolf accepted Taziar's proclamation easily. ''*Fenris*wulf,'' it corrected. ''Or Fenrir or the Fenris Wolf.'' It hesitated, as if expecting Taziar to recognize its name. When it received no further reaction, it continued. ''Your words are very brave and also very stupid. The destiny I spoke of has already been fulfilled. If you untie me, I admit I will kill; Gaelinar and Allerum will be the first to die. If I eat you, I remain here. The world is destroyed. All of creation dies, including Gaelinar and Allerum. In either case, you have caused my vengeance to be fulfilled. But which way results in the death of more innocents, Shadow?''

Taziar bit his lower lip, drenched in cold sweat. His eyes followed the slender line of Fenrir's fetter. *Perhaps I'm wrong. Perhaps Fenriswulf is lying.* Taziar's alternatives paraded before him. *If the wolf is telling the truth and I don't free it, the world will end. If it has invented this story and I do allow it to escape, innocent people will die.* Taziar frowned, presented with equally unsatisfying options. He had no odds to play. Despite the seeming impossibility of the wolf's claims, Taziar trusted his own ability to judge expressions. His survival as a con man had depended on it too many times for him to doubt now. *It's being honest, at least partially. And it has promised to kill these men, Allerum and Gaelinar, first. Therefore, while those two live, the remainder of the world is safe from Fenrir. And I will see to it they survive as long as possible!* He spoke aloud. ''These men who killed your father will be your first victims?''

''Man and elf,'' Fenrir amended. ''I swear upon my father's honor. I will kill no one in Midgard before them.'' Its eyes narrowed suddenly. ''Why?''

''No good reason.'' A sensation of pins and needles made Taziar's legs ache. ''I've decided to free you. If I'm going to feel responsible for your wreaking havoc on the world, I just want to make certain the men who caused the trouble will die first. Now what do I have to do? That ribbon hardly seems strong enough to hold a wolf.''

''It's magicked.'' Fenrir stepped off Taziar's legs and

raised a forepaw. "It can't be snapped, but it can be untied. I don't have the necessary hands."

Taziar clambered to his feet and waited while the numbness in his legs faded. He peeled dried blood from the frayed skin and calluses on his fingertips.

Patiently, the Fenris Wolf waited while Taziar prepared.

At length, Taziar stooped by the wolf's ankle and seized the knot. The string lay limp in his hands, constructed of some material he had never seen before. Though smooth as a thread of silk, it felt tough and firm. Dirt coated the knot; it had assumed its present condition through centuries of remaining tied in the same position. It had cinched flush to the wolf's skin, disrupting the fur in a ring. Taziar sighed. In his days with the gang of rogues, one of the tricks he had performed to win food money from passersby consisted of freeing himself from tightly bound ropes. The talent had served him well in later years. But, despite long hours of practice with joints, locks, and links, Taziar knew this knot might defy even his expertise. Resigned, he set his broken fingernails to the fetter.

For a quarter of an hour, Taziar sweated and struggled with the time-stiffened knot amidst Fenrir's growled epithets and insults. He stood, stretched cramps from his legs, and studied his dilemma from a different perspective. *It is a slip knot.* Taziar dropped back to a crouch. Carefully, he worked his little finger behind the wolf's leg and along the edge of the fetter. The string pinched his flesh painfully against the beast's shank. He flexed his finger, and the bonds gave slightly. He tensed again, gaining just enough space to insert another digit. He removed both hands from the ribbon of fabric and pinned the knot to the ground with his foot. "Bring your leg up and forward, slowly now."

Fenrir complied while Taziar readjusted the noose to its optimal position for each of the wolf's movements. The shifting rope scraped fur from Fenrir's toes like a razor. Then the wolf stood free.

Taziar rose, lacking the usual elation his successes inspired. Having chosen to untie Fenrir, he also carried the burden of protecting the world from his decision, beginning with two specific men. *Man and elf,* Taziar corrected himself. *But what, in Karana's darkest hell, is an elf?* He glanced at the shimmering, three-stranded Bifrost Bridge, twice a man's height above him, and marveled for the first time at how lucky he was to have survived the fall without serious injury. He followed the sweep of the rainbow to its end just beyond the waters of the wolf's island. *If I had managed to remain conscious a few more moments, I could have avoided this whole situation.* He turned his attention to the Fenris Wolf.

Fenrir crouched, ready to spring. Its eyes seemed to blaze with real fire. Its mouth parted in a wolfish grin which displayed every tooth. "Thank you, Shadow. And now I eat you."

Taziar took an involuntary backstep. Suddenly, he saw his entire plan crumbling around him. "Y-you made a vow. You promised your father's murderers would die first."

Fenrir hunched lower. "I merely said I would kill no man on Midgard before them. You, my lucky friend, stand in Asgard." It sprang with a snarl.

Taziar dove aside. The wolf's lunge fell short, but its shoulder crashed against Taziar's side. Impact bowled Taziar over. He rolled, then gained his feet from habit. The wolf's huge form sailed toward him again.

Gathering his remaining strength, Taziar leaped. His fingers hooked the edge of the Bifrost Bridge, and he hung there. The wolf loosed a bone-chilling howl of frustration. It rocketed straight upward. Taziar swung his legs. Fenrir's teeth snapped closed where his feet had been. As Taziar flung his body flat to the surface of the Bifrost, Fenrir sprinted for the water and the far end of the bridge.

Taziar jumped to his feet and ran down the quivering form of the rainbow bridge. Too astute to delude himself, he knew the wolf would catch him before he could reach Midgard. Fenrir could cover twenty of his longest strides with every bound.

Suddenly, a figure loomed before Tazier. Not daring to waste his breath in warning, Taziar dodged past. He was jarred backward by a fist wrapped in the folds of his tattered bearskin cloak. He whirled to face Heimdallr. This time, the god's face was dark with anger, his mouth set in a grim line. "You again! How did you get up there?"

Beyond Heimdallr, Fenrir's gigantic, black form filled the horizon. Taziar shrank away. "Behind you!" he screamed. "Wolf!"

Heimdallr's face twisted to a glare of withering disdain. His grip tightened, and he shook Taziar until the little man lost his footing and sank to one knee. "Don't lie to me, weasel! Did you think I'd fall for such an old and stupid trick, that I'd turn around and gave you a chance to escape? You got by me once . . ."

Fenrir sprang.

Taziar cringed away as far as Heimdallr's grip would allow and steeled himself for the inevitable. Wolf and god collided with an explosion of sound. The force sent Taziar sprawling. The bridge rocked and roiled as Fenrir and Heimdallr engaged, hurling thunderous taunts whose meaning Taziar could not fathom. He fought for balance as the whole fabric of the rainbow threatened to collapse beneath him.

The Bifrost bucked like an unbroken stallion. Taziar half-crawled, half-slid toward Midgard, aware that a fall now would spell instant death. But, as he clawed his way farther from the battle, the swaying of the bridge lessened. Gradually, he worked his way to his feet and raced down the rainbow way. Two names swirled through his thoughts: Allerum and Gaelinar. And Taziar knew he would need the help of his Dragonrank girlfriend to locate a man and an elf who could be anywhere on nine worlds.

PART I:

Hel's Mistress

CHAPTER 1:

Hel's Hall

"... Remembrance fallen from heaven,
And madness risen from hell ..."
—Algernon Charles Swinburne
Atalanta in Calydon

For nearly a week, Al Larson and Kensei Gaelinar had journeyed ever deeper into darkness so thick Larson could discern his own arms only as pale blurs. In the last day, Hel's confines had grown colder and damper, but the blackness thinned gradually to a red mist. Larson felt as if he was caught in the bat exhibit at the Bronx Zoo or the pseudo-illumination of a photography developing room. He could see now. Behind him loomed the twenty-foot gate which surrounded Hel's citadel, its upper edges curved inward, as if to keep prisoners within the grounds rather than prevent trespassers from entering. Ahead, the shadowed hulk of Hel's citadel stood, long and flat in the gloom, and no more inviting than its fence.

The unnatural quiet of the underworld crushed in on Larson, as stifling as humid heat. Its continual gloom seeped into his being, intensifying the aching sorrow for his beloved Silme, a grief tainted by guilt. Her own magic had bound her soul to her half brother, Bramin. But it was Larson's sword stroke which claimed Bramin's life ... and Silme's with it.

Gaelinar caught Larson's arm. "Allerum. This way." He started across the waste of packed mud toward Hel's stronghold.

Larson followed Gaelinar without protest. After all, his

own vow, that no world could come between him and Silme, had brought them to Hel's realm of unending night. *My words and Gaelinar's determination.* Larson stared at the Kensei's black-trimmed gold robes and the matched swords which hung through his mentor's sash. *To him, no task is too dangerous to attempt, no cause too small to die for.* Now, an ill-considered oath uttered in a love-blind moment would probably get them both killed.

Despite Larson's somber musings, the task had so far proved easier than he had expected. The foul, animal smell at the entryway to Hel had either faded or become too familiar to notice. The only obstacles to his and Gaelinar's venture had been a bridge roofed with gold and the locked gates around Hel's fortress which they had scaled without difficulty. No being had challenged their descent. After several days of dodging and ducking the shadows which flitted just beyond his vision, Larson had come to accept them as harmless. Even the inevitable hardships, to which he had long ago resigned himself, seemed to have dissolved in the deep oblivion of his sadness. Since Alfheim's god, Freyr, had plucked Larson from his bullet-riddled body in Vietnam, placed him in the guise of an elf, and loosed him in a world which was not quite Old Norway, flashbacks of the war had plagued him unmercifully. Now, even that familiar madness had abandoned him. *I wonder why everyone doesn't come to Hel and reclaim his dead.* Larson suspected he would soon find out.

Gaelinar stopped before the open portal to Hel's citadel and whispered a warning. "Do not address the dead, not even Silme, until we've spoken with Hel."

Beyond his mentor, Larson glimpsed a hallway packed with milling figures. The ruddy haze which enshrouded the scene gave them a ghostly cast. *The dead? Ghostly?* Larson's gut knotted. Suddenly, his mind filled with doubts and questions.

But before Larson could sort through his mental confusion, Gaelinar passed through the doorway and started down a hall of paneled ash. "I'd like to handle this peacefully."

Larson swallowed hard, nodded agreement and trailed Gaelinar closely. He harbored no wish to battle another deity. Although he had slain Loki, he attributed most of his success to the sapphire-rank Dragonmage he had come to rescue and to the silent god, Vidarr, who had been trapped in Larson's sword by Loki's spell.

Lost in thought, Larson nearly collided with a figure which seemed to materialize before him. It was a man, his body green and puckered. Rotted skin hung in strips from a face of yellowed bone. Dull, shriveled eyes turned in their sockets and settled on Larson.

Larson drew a sharp, terrified breath. He shied from the dead man and blundered into a tight pack of walking corpses. Their contact chilled him to the marrow; they seemed to drain the warmth of his very life essence. Their flesh gave like overripe fruit. Shocked and off-balance, Larson clawed through them and fell to one knee. The dead closed around him, staring silently, scowling or leering in murderous agony.

Larson screamed. Memory crowded in on him. But this time, his thoughts lacked the horrifying reality of his flashbacks. He knew who and where he was. Yet he surrendered to the saner world of images to escape the living death his mind could not accept. The dark stillness of Hel became the steamy murk of Vietnam, the muffled swish of Gaelinar's robe a slash of breeze through bamboo jungle. Al Larson stood in a silence of unmatched intensity, the one which can only exist after the mind-shattering explosion of a hidden mine. Blood stained the slender leaves in an arc. In its center, Private John Lewis lay, his face sallow and speckled with gore. His recognizable features ended below his abdomen; his pelvis and legs trailed like tattered streamers. The air hung heavy with the reek of ruptured bowel.

Now Larson flinched, the picture still vivid within him. He remembered how he stood in shocked sorrow. No matter how much death he witnessed, watching the slaughter of another friend never seemed to become easier. But, Lewis' eyes remained open, soulful and seeing. By all anatomical possibility, his hand could no longer function; nevertheless it seized Larson's ankle. Lewis' voice emerged, weak yet frighteningly alive. "I'm hurt bad, huh?"

Larson recalled how his stomach lurched and he dared not speak for fear he might scream or cry, run or puke. He managed a short nod.

"Al." Lewis' fingers tightened spasmodically on Larson's shin then fell away. "I'm going home, right? They're gonna ship me back."

Larson felt the horrified gazes of the entire patrol at his back and wished someone would say something . . . anything. They had all helped injured companions before, but this was different. For all his movement and speech, Lewis was dead. Nothing any doctor could do would change that fact, and the only one who seemed unable to comprehend it was Lewis' own broken, bloodless body.

Larson remembered how he had gathered a courage he'd never believed he had. He knelt at his friend's side, caught the cold, blood-slicked hand, and met glazing brown eyes. "Yeah, buddy." Larson kept his face composed. "You're going home."

Lewis' eyes swept closed. His mouth twitched into a smile which remained until his last drop of life seeped into the jungle floor.

Now, surrounded by corpses in Hel's dank hall, Larson tapped the gentle strength of his memory. The dead studied him with fearless curiosity. Yet they did not reach to touch him nor open their mouths to speak. Unlike the phantoms of the movies, these ghosts appeared to have no designs against the living. Rather it seemed as if they sought to recapture some memory of the upper worlds and the individual existences they once took for granted.

Gaelinar wove through a gap in the crowd. His almond-hued skin and Oriental features seemed oddly out of place amidst the blackly-rotted flesh and wraith's pallor of Hel's dead. The agile movements which belied his advancing age and the brilliant gold of his clothing made him appear a caricature. With an impatient wave of his arm, he summoned Larson to him.

Larson came gladly, noting as he did that the dead separated to open a lane and allow his passage. They had not tried to harm him, he realized. Rather, he had stumbled into them. As warmth filtered back into his being with the painful slowness of thawing frostbite, he harbored no wish to make physical contact with these corpses again.

Gaelinar turned a disapproving glare on Larson. He spoke in a grating whisper. "I told you not to speak to them."

"Speak?" Larson was incredulous. "I didn't speak, I screamed. And it wasn't on purpose."

Gaelinar whirled and strode deeper into the hallway. "Someday, hero, you must learn self-control."

Control! Larson trailed Gaelinar, not bothering to voice his annoyance. *In the past two weeks, I died, was hunted, had my thoughts violated by wizards and warring gods, fell in love with a woman then killed her, assassinated a god, and destroyed the only world I used to know.* There was no longer any doubt in Larson's mind. *When God . . .* He amended. *When* gods *created Gaelinar, they ran out of fear, so they substituted extra intolerance.* He snorted, sending the animated cadavers scuttling from his path.

Farther down the hallway, Hel's citadel opened into a huge, unfurnished room. A chandelier hung crookedly from the ceiling. Thick mist obscured the metalwork so it appeared like a handful of intertwined snakes frozen for eternity. Half of the eight candles had burned out; the others danced in the breeze from the doorway, shedding scarcely enough light to delineate the granite blocks which composed the ceiling. In the entryway, first Gaelinar, then Larson, came upon a throne pushed against one wall, its jeweled magnificence dwarfed by the sad-faced man perched upon it. There was no mold or decay upon this visage. It seemed ageless and timeless, and splendor fairly radiated from it. Beside him sat a woman every bit as well-kept, but her beauty paled in comparison, though she seemed to bear at least as heavy a burden as her companion.

Larson paused, thinking these might be the gods they had come to see. But Gaelinar shook his head and led Larson a little farther into the chamber. The corpses remained huddled and attentive in the portal, but not one crossed into the partially illuminated room. The Kensei stopped and pointed into the cross corridor. "That's her."

Larson squinted as a figure approached through the mist. "Hel?"

Gaelinar nodded. "Queen of the realm she was named for. Choose your words with care, hero."

Larson watched as Hel crept toward them, advancing so slowly, he was uncertain if she moved at all. "Me? I'm going to talk to her?"

"Who else?"

Larson frowned, thinking the answer too obvious for him to bother replying. Nervously, he traced the gold and silver designs on the hilt of the sword he had claimed from Loki's corpse. He gathered breath to protest, but his words were never spoken. In the eon it took Hel to come before them, he realized what Gaelinar had pieced together long ago. *I killed Silme. I won't be able to live with myself unless my own efforts either win her back or lose her forever.* Throughout the trip from Midgard to Hel, grief, guilt, and disbelief had haunted Larson too hard for him to consider the persuasions he might use to charm the goddess who owned Silme's soul.

Hel came before her guests while Larson still brooded. Her face was crinkled and jowly, frozen into an eternal grimace of gloom. She was naked. Above the waist, she looked as normal as any living woman, small breasted, her skin pink and supple as an infant's. But her thighs and legs appeared green-black with decay. Her expression never changed as her eyes flickered over Larson and Gaelinar. She spoke so sluggishly, her words emerged shorter than the pauses between them. "Dead . . . or alive. Neither . . . of you . . . belongs . . . here."

Larson glanced sideways at Gaelinar, seeking some clue to the correct formalities when addressing the queen of the underworld. But Gaelinar remained still, his gaze fixed on Hel, his face impassive. Still uncertain, Larson considered bowing or kneeling, and settled on a simple nod of acknowledgement. "Your majesty, we've come to ask a favor."

Hel shifted her weight, meeting Larson's request with a strained and overlong silence. Then, she replied with the maddening tedium of a dripping faucet. "I . . . make . . . no bargains . . . with . . . the living. Even . . . dead . . . elves . . . do not . . . belong . . ."

Larson found not completing the goddess' sentences an effort in restraint.

". . . here," Hel finished. "Go away." Her stolid features did not betray a hint of the emotion her words implied.

Larson wiped sweating palms on his tunic. His mind conjured images of Silme, long-legged, slim-waisted, her curves as soft yet pronounced as any gilded model of his own era. He could picture each highlight of her honey-colored hair and the gray eyes which betrayed her every mood. Emotionally, she had proven herself as strong as any man. The deep morality Larson had respected and loved led to her downfall, and drove her to sacrifice her own life for the cause of the world. *A world which still sorely needs her.* Larson's longing for Silme inspired the courage to try again. This time, he prefaced his words with a stiffly formal bow. "Queen Hel." The title sounded awkward to Larson's Christian-raised ears. "At least hear me out."

In response, Hel neither moved nor spoke.

At least she didn't turn away. Larson accepted it as a sign of encouragement. He cleared his throat and continued. "Kensei Gaelinar and I came to bring back Silme. She's a sapphire-rank Dragonmage who has done more to protect men and gods then anyone could. Her death was a terrible mistake."

Hel's frown deepened more than Larson thought possible. "Is . . . she . . . dead?"

Surprised by the question, Larson did not phrase his answer carefully. "Well, yeah."

"She . . . was not . . . killed . . . in . . . valorous combat?"

Larson rocked from foot to foot, uncertain where this questioning was leading. "Not in physical combat . . . but . . ."

Hel interrupted, "Then . . . there can be . . . no mistake. She . . . stays. You . . . go. I . . . cannot . . . release . . . the souls . . . which rightfully belong . . . here.''

Larson suddenly realized what common sense had told him all along. *A corpse cannot be made alive again. Gaelinar's determination and my own love allowed me to hope, but I have to accept the fact that Silme is dead.*

Gaelinar's voice held the same inviolate authority as when he berated Larson for inappropriate sword figures. ''You're lying, witch.''

Hel remained, unmoving. She opened her mouth.

But Gaelinar spoke first. ''We are foreigners, but not ignorant. I know the story of the slain god, Baldur. You bargained with the gods, *living* gods for his release.''

''I did,'' Hel admitted. ''With . . . conditions . . . even the gods . . . could not . . . meet. He's . . . still here.'' She inclined her head toward the inhumanly handsome man on the throne. ''Even . . . if I . . . did not oppose . . . Silme's return . . . the Fates would see . . . any provisions I imposed . . . would not be . . . fulfilled.''

Larson followed Hel's gesture. Baldur's dead eyes met his gaze, and the god seemed keenly interested in the conversation.

Gaelinar met Hel's pronouncement with a disinterested shrug. ''Name your price, Lady. Allerum and I will handle the Fates.''

Shocked by Gaelinar's cavalier dismissal of the Fates' power, Larson turned his attention back to the conversation. He recalled his encounter with the three hideous giantesses who controlled the destinies of men and gods. A simple meeting had required the efforts of Silme and Vidarr, an oracle's artifact, and passage through his own flawed mind.

Hel's ghastly face remained locked in its pall of gloom, but a twinkle of amusement softened the gunmetal blue of her eyes. ''No . . . need. I know . . . the . . . means to appease . . . the Fates.''

Hope spiraled through Larson. ''How?''

''I . . . cannot . . . say.'' Hel's tone was maddeningly smug. ''The dead . . . belong . . . to me. I . . . cannot

. . . bow to . . . the whim of . . . every grieving . . . parent. I . . . cannot . . . sacrifice . . . my legions . . . to every . . . man . . . willing to . . . wander . . . through a few . . . short . . . days of . . . darkness . . . to retrieve . . . his lover. I . . . cannot . . ."

Gaelinar's katana hissed from its sheath, a gray blur in a world of shadows. "You cannot speak from a head rolling on the ground."

Surprised by Gaelinar's sudden ferocity, Larson sidestepped.

Hel loosed a noise which sounded like a cough, but Larson recognized it as laughter. "What . . . are you . . . going to do . . . swordmaster? Send . . . me to . . . Hel . . . for eternity? Perhaps . . . you . . . think . . . you can . . . make . . . me . . . uglier?"

Larson caught Gaelinar's arm and drew his teacher aside. He spoke as softly as possible. "She has nothing to lose, and we have everything. You kill her, we'll never be able to bargain for Silme's freedom."

Gaelinar frowned his disapproval, but he sheathed his sword. "She's not going to give in to our demands. Violent persuasion may not help, but it'll make me feel better."

"No." Larson was insistent. "She might take out her anger on Silme's soul." He turned back to Hel and spoke aloud. "Won't you reconsider? Silme's not just my girlfriend. She's got powers I never would have believed in a few weeks ago."

Hel did not seem to take notice of Larson's and Gaelinar's whispered exchange. "All . . . the . . . more . . . reason to . . . keep . . . her here. It . . . is her . . . destiny to . . . remain in . . . Hel. And . . . the world's . . . to live . . . without . . . her."

Larson felt the growing cold of despair. He lowered his head. "At least let me speak with her before I go?"

Hel's reply seemed to span an eternity. "Talk . . . with anyone . . . you wish. Then . . . both of . . . you . . . go."

Larson pivoted, not quite certain what to expect and afraid to pick Silme from among the dead. Discomfort gnawed at him. He steeled himself for the pain of looking upon his lover, her beauty withered and muted into one grimacing corpse among Hel's horde. Yet he knew he had to see her at least one more time.

Hel cried out in sudden surprise. As she struggled to suppress her indiscretion, her dragging speech now appeared to bother her as much as it did Larson. "Where . . . did you . . . get that sword?"

Larson followed her stare to the weapon at his own hip. "That what?" he stammered. It came to him with frightening abruptness. *Hel is Loki's daughter. And the grandeur of his hilt is unmistakable. She knows this is her father's weapon.* He whirled to face the startled goddess, filled with new confidence. "I'll tell you. Immediately after you swear you'll let Silme go and explain how we can get her by the Fates."

Hel hissed, catlike.

Gaelinar remained still. Larson read amusement in a smile cryptic as the Mona Lisa's.

Hel drew up her shriveled form, and another long silence followed.

Larson waited, hiding impatience behind a mask of purpose. He knew he had gained the upper hand. *The ball is in her court. Jesus, I hope I don't blow it.*

Thoughtfulness drew out Hel's pauses even longer. "Agreed . . . but . . ."

Larson fought the urge to hurry Hel.

". . . you . . . must . . . *give* . . . *me* . . . the . . . sword."

Give her . . . Larson struggled against his natural repugnance. In Vietnam, where the emotional closeness necessary for survival meant watching good friends die, Larson recalled many nights huddled in a damp hole haloed by the red streaks of tracers and the glare of illumination rounds. Then, an M-16 and a twisted piece of concertina wire were often the only things between him and the shadowy forms of the NVA. It went against every bit of experience, the rigor of army training, and Gaelinar's unyielding discipline to turn his only weapon over to an enemy. Yet the chance to regain the woman he loved was worth the sacrifice. He pushed aside the heavy-handed instincts ingrained by months of dodging death.

"Okay. It's yours." He unclipped the sheathed sword from his belt and awaited Gaelinar's inevitable reproach. "After you uphold your part of the bargain."

Gaelinar remained silent.

Larson smeared sweat from his palm on his tunic and envied the stoic composure of his mentor.

Hel scratched at her cheek with far more deliberateness than the task required. "Very . . . well. You . . . do not speak . . . or bargain . . . like . . . any elf . . . I've encountered but . . ."

Larson fidgeted. While Hel completed her preliminary comments, he allowed his attention to roam to the milling corpses, dreading the thought of wading through them again. Baldur remained, tense and quiet, on his throne. He met Larson's gaze with uncontained eagerness. It was obvious he wished to talk. A sinuous twist of smoke rose from one of the remaining candles in the chandelier, then it went as dead as Hel's minions.

Hel's halting speech seemed to drag seconds into hours. ". . . I . . . will tell . . . you . . . what . . . you . . . wish . . . to hear. First, I . . . swear . . . upon my oaths . . . to Odin. I . . . will not stand . . . against . . . Silme's . . . return . . . to . . . Midgard . . . so long as . . . you . . . fulfill . . . your . . . part of . . . our . . . bargain."

Larson's heart pounded with eagerness. "And the Fates?" he reminded.

"The . . . Fates." Hel pursed her withered lips and glanced at Gaelinar before answering. "For centuries . . . they have . . . kept . . . our . . . worlds . . . in harmony. No . . . one . . . can know . . . how . . . they decide . . . whose turn . . . it is . . . to die. But . . . it must . . . in part . . . be based on . . . keeping all forces . . . in balance." She turned her gaze to Larson. "The . . . two great . . . powers of our . . . world . . . call them . . . one and two . . . order and randomness . . . good and evil . . . as you will. I know . . . them . . . as . . . law . . . and chaos. Silme . . . died . . . because it . . . was time . . . for a . . . law abiding . . . creature . . . of her strength . . . to die. To . . . bring her back . . .

to Midgard, you . . . would need . . . to open a place . . . for her."

"Open a place for her?" Larson shook his head. "I don't understand."

"I . . . have . . . fulfilled my . . . promise." Hel met Larson's confused stare. "I . . . have . . . told you . . . all . . . you . . . need to know. Give . . . me . . . my . . . sword."

Larson looked to Gaelinar, feeling cheated.

"Hel has proposed we find someone, a person of Silme's means and bent, willing to take her place in Hel. Now, hero, give Hel her sword."

Larson heard nothing after Gaelinar's first sentence. "Replace her? We have to kill a person? Someone as kind as Silme?" He allowed his thoughts to glide backward to a night, a year, and a lifetime ago. He recalled lying, trapped and terrified, at an outside observation post after less than a week in Vietnam. The memory remained heavy and vivid within him: the stab of high grasses, the deadly howl of mortars, and the mixed reek of sulfur and blood. M-16s blattered ceaselessly through the near darkness, punctuated by the louder explosions of grenades hurled at sounds and unidentifiable shadows. Larson remained still, not daring to shoot for fear the muzzle flash would draw enemy, and perhaps even American, fire.

In Larson's memory, a figure materialized from the darkness. For a moment, the man stood motionless, like a department store manikin in the backwash of light. A flare streaked overhead, illuminating the face in olive-red detail. He was a Vietnamese teenager, younger even than Larson. He seemed equally surprised, his dark eyes wide with fear. They stared at one another for several seconds; neither raised a weapon. Larson saw all his own uncertainty, mortality, and horror mirrored perfectly in his enemy's visage. Then, the American beside Larson cursed and swung around a .45 pistol. The last, dying traces of the flare outlined its steel like a blood-colored star. The American fired, the Vietnamese soldier fell dead, and Larson learned an enduring lesson about war, mercy, and the price of life.

Later, in the chilling aftershock of his first firefight,

Larson discovered that the "gook," like himself, carried pictures of his girlfriend and his family. Larson realized, with a vague feeling of dread, that the only difference between his own death and the enemy's was which set of parents would cry.

Now, Larson discarded his remembrances for the misty murk of Hel's citadel, aware he could never take the life of one like Silme, not even to restore the woman he loved. "Gaelinar, I can't . . ."

"Hush!" Gaelinar's voice went harsh with warning. "Hero, give Hel her sword."

Larson bit his lip against welling grief and anger. Gingerly, he offered the sheathed sword to Hel's half-rotted queen.

Hel accepted her father's weapon. "And . . . your explanation?"

"Explanation?" Larson repeated. He had already nearly forgotten his vow to reveal the reason why he carried Loki's sword. He glanced sideways at Gaelinar, not certain how to soften his disclosure.

"May I?" Gaelinar asked sweetly.

Larson nodded, glad to pass the onerous task to his companion.

Gaelinar cleared his throat, his fingers draped casually across the hilt of his katana. "Lady, you have already promised not to stand in the way of Silme's freedom and also that we can see and speak with her before we leave."

"I have," Hel agreed.

Larson swiveled his head and studied the mob of corpses, trying to pick Silme's familiar countenance from the masses. Baldur returned Larson's gaze from his throne.

"That remembered," Gaelinar continued, "I can speak freely."

Larson felt a sudden pang of discomfort.

A mocking smile crept across Gaelinar's features. "We pried Loki's sword from his hand. After we 'helpless mortals' killed him, lady. Good day." He turned to leave.

Hel made a strangled noise of rage.

Larson guessed his mentor's motives for delivering information in such a cruel fashion. *I know of no kind way to tell a woman you've killed her father. To show regret for Loki's slaying would require an insincerity beyond Gaelinar's abilities. And, were I Hel, I wouldn't dare attempt revenge against a warrior with Gaelinar's bold audacity.* Larson cringed, keeping his thoughts to himself.

Hel's expression did not change, but the healthier flesh of her body turned scarlet. She pointed a trembling finger at Gaelinar's back. "Know . . . this well, Kensei. Hel . . . was . . . never . . . designed to . . . keep . . . men . . . *out.*" Her dull eyes gained a hint of amusement as she pirouetted with unhurried grace and shuffled into the gloom.

CHAPTER 2:

Hel's Gate

"It is easy to go down into Hell; night and day, the gates of dark Death stand wide; but to climb back again, to retrace one's steps to the upper air—there's the rub, the task"

—Virgil
Aeneid

Hel's threat hovered in the stagnant air of her citadel long after she disappeared from Larson's sight, but the savagery of her promise withered beneath a more oppressive realization. *I will have to sacrifice an innocent life in exchange for Silme's.* Larson knew the sorceress' death had strengthened his passion for her; his most recent confrontation with mortality reaffirmed the brevity of human life and the value of each minute. Yet Larson felt troubled by an ancient morality instilled by his parents long before a hellish war warped virtue in the name of survival. *Everyone is loved by someone. How can I justify my happiness at the expense of others?* Larson lowered his head.

Even Gaelinar seemed repulsed by their task. Wrinkles etched his sagging cheeks, and his stride lacked its usual confidence. He stepped around Baldur's throne and started back down the long corridor, waving for Larson to follow.

During Gaelinar's and Larson's talk with Hel, her dead minions had assembled, respectfully, at the edge of the conversation. Now they shuffled forward, surrounding man and elf in a hovering, silent mass of decay.

Larson took a few, tentative paces toward his mentor. He knew the ghosts had meant him no harm before, but the memory of their touches and Hel's threat made him shiver. *We can't hope to battle a legion of corpses.* He tried to ignore them, not allowing himself to study them closely enough to glean details of age or sex. They wore an array of costumes, from the faded purple silk of royalty to torn and dirty rags. Some lacked limbs, rotted or hacked away. Others bore slumped and fragile frames; huge, cancerous growths; or bellies swollen with fluid. Larson hurried through the dead as fast as they scampered from his path. In his haste, he brushed against a young female. Coldness spread from her touch, suffused Larson's flesh from shoulder to fingers until his arm felt numb and heavy. Afterward, he moved through the crowd with a respectful caution. *They haven't attacked us yet. Maybe they're not under Hel's command or they lack the strength to intentionally harm the living. Or maybe they just don't care.*

Farther along the grayed corridor, the dead god, Baldur, glided through the masses and stopped before Larson. He stood with legs widely-braced in the center of the hallway, his features white as fresh-fallen snow, a beacon in a grim world of death. Unlike the other cadavers, he did not move aside as Larson came upon him. His sunken, blue eyes glittered with a mixture of sorrow and hope. His lips parted, but no words emerged.

Baldur wore an expression of pure innocence, like a victimized child. Deep sympathy welled up in Larson. Attentively, he waited, but Baldur remained silent, his visage pleading.

Gaelinar's voice shattered the enveloping hush. "Talk to him, hero. By Hel's law, he cannot speak first."

There was an aura about Baldur which unsettled Larson. He had faced gods before. But while Loki had simply seemed an unusually handsome and evil man, Hel a hideously deformed lady, and Vidarr a mere presence in a sword, Baldur conjured images of stained glass windows, cushioned pews, and hymnals. Larson felt intimidated, and his voice revealed his trepidation. "Hello," he said uncomfortably. "Did you want to say something?"

Baldur flashed a candid smile. "Please," he said, his voice high and musical. He extended an arm and opened his fist. A brooch balanced on his palm, an opaque blue gem on which some artist had painted a miniature scene in gold ink. "Take this to my father. Remind him I am still here, and that I have not forgotten him."

Larson stared at the jewel in Baldur's hand, but he made no move to retrieve it. "Your father," Larson repeated. He met Baldur's imploring gaze with puzzlement. "Is he some sort of god?"

Baldur's grin widened, and his face went pink with amusement.

Larson backstepped. "I'm sorry. I have no way to contact gods." He realized how ludicrous he must sound after Gaelinar had announced their slaying of Loki while engaged in conversation with Hel. But he also knew he had spoken honestly.

Baldur inched toward Larson, still offering the gem. His tone became insistent. "Anyone can communicate with gods. They need only pray in the proper temple, consult an oracle, make an appropriate sacrifice." He prodded Larson's forearm with the brooch. "Please, try. I will understand if you cannot deliver my message."

The dead remained still and expectant. Baldur's gleaming presence blocked Larson's retreat from the corridor. Toward the outer doorway, beyond the god, Larson spotted a female figure drifting toward Gaelinar. She moved with the lithe grace of a dancer and the confidence of the living. Golden hair fell in waves to the middle of her back. Larson knew Silme at once; her every detail lay fixed in his memory. Death seemed not to have changed her at all. She carried none of Hel's mold. She remained free of any disfiguring wound or condition. She appeared exactly as Larson had last seen her: slim, pale, everything about her so perfectly formed, he could think of no feature even the gods could improve upon. His desire for her returned in an exhilarating rush. All thought of morality fled him. *I must win back her life . . . and her love.* Suddenly, no task done for her could be too great, no sacrifice too large. He moved toward her and nearly collided with Baldur who still stood in his path.

Frustration tightened Larson's chest. He seized the painted gem from Baldur's hand and jammed it into a pocket of his cloak. "I'll try," he muttered harshly. "Now step aside."

The instant Baldur relaxed his guard, Larson slipped past. Carefully, he threaded through the gathered corpses, avoiding their icy touches. He reached Silme in three running strides and hurled himself into her arms.

Silme shrank away, avoiding his embrace.

Silme's dodge off-balanced Larson. He careened into Gaelinar, then whirled, and stared at her, incredulous. Her rejection seared him like a hot knife. "W-Why?" he stammered.

"Don't," Silme whispered. "It'll only hurt you. My life aura is gone. I have only the blank chill of the dead to offer you now." Her voice quivered with sorrow. "Allerum, you should never have come."

Grief and outrage warred within Larson. Closer, he noticed Silme's fair skin had grown sallow, her fiercely gray eyes hollowed and dull. "But I love you." He fought the urge to cradle her in his arms. "I need you, Silme. We came to bring you back."

Silme rolled her eyes with resignation. She ran a pallid hand through her hair, and a brief smile graced her features. "And I appreciate your effort. If anyone could accomplish such a thing, it would be you." She addressed Larson, but her gaze played over Gaelinar. "But I'm afraid such a thing is impossible. And I'd rather you remembered me as I was than as I am now." She traced her body with her fingertips.

Larson followed Silme's gesture, still certain he faced the most beautiful woman in existence. "We'll free you," he insisted, though not at all certain he could keep his promise. "Hel told us what we need to do." Sudden doubt rushed down upon him, and he paused to consider. "Do you think Hel might have lied to us?"

Silme shook her head. "Probably not. The gods are intolerant of falsehoods, even among themselves. But she would try to mislead you. Consider her words carefully. What did she tell you to do?''

Larson knew Silme would never allow the slaying of an innocent person in exchange for her life. Quickly, he waved Gaelinar silent. ''Never mind.'' Larson changed the subject with an awkward abruptness. ''How long did you know we were here?''

Silme hesitated, shrugged, and followed Larson's tack. ''From the time you arrived. But I avoided you. I didn't want you to see me until you had spoken with Hel and grown accustomed to the appearances of the dead.''

Larson gnawed his lip, gravely aware of the unspoken concern beneath her explanation. The flashbacks had made him unpredictable, emotionally volatile, and, at times, violent. He knew the control he had gained over his memories would please her and hoped she had seen how well he'd handled himself among the walking corpses after his conversation with Hel.

Silme placed her hand into the folds of her baggy, gray cloak and retrieved a fist-sized, rectangular sapphire, cut and shaped like a diamond. She offered it to Larson.

Larson recognized the stone as the one which had nested between the carven claws of Silme's dragonstaff. He accepted the gem, running his fingers across its smoothed facets. ''What should I do with this?''

''Keep it safe,'' came Silme's soft reply. ''It's my rankstone. It symbolized my level of Dragonrank training. But, more importantly, it can store life aura as power.'' She met Larson's stare with pointed intensity, as if to instill in him the knowledge it had taken her years to master. ''Because I had placed energy into the gem before my death, a tiny piece of me remains alive within it. Carry it, and remember me. If, by some miracle, I should be brought to life again, I can track you by it.''

Gaelinar, Silme, and Larson exchanged glances as the gawking ring of corpses closed more tightly around them. Gaelinar cleared his throat. ''We'd best be on our way. If Hel's threats are any indication, our journey is best undertaken well-rested.'' He examined the dead. ''And I don't want to sleep here.''

Larson agreed. *Hel's citadel does not seem the safest*

or most welcome bedroom. "Fine. But I need to know one thing more." He inclined his head toward Silme and scarcely refrained from catching her hands. "We came to Hel for another reason. Have you seen Brendor?" An image of Silme's bumbling, young apprentice formed in Larson's mind. Time had warped the picture. The simple features of the boy he had planned to accept as his son intermingled inseparably with his recollections of his own baby brother, Timmy. "We came to rescue him, too. Where is the little guy?"

Silme winced, shifting uncomfortably. "Allerum, I'm sorry."

Concern made Larson curt. "What do you mean you're sorry? Where's Brendor?"

"Remember Bramin's spell? The one which allowed Brendor to attack you?"

Larson's chest felt pinched. He recalled the madness which had possessed Brendor's lifeless body; the image remained strong within him. He envisioned Brendor's small form punching, gouging, and wrestling with an inhuman power he had never known in life. In vivid detail, he saw the child's glazed features on a frame bloodied and shattered by Silme's magic. "What about Bramin's spell?" he asked in a strangled whisper.

Silme's tone remained reverent and soothing, despite the unpleasantness of her words. "To gain that control, Bramin would have had to destroy Brendor's soul. He's gone, Allerum. There's no means for us to see him again."

Silme's explanation struck Larson dumb. He stood in silence, ensconced in memories of the inept, halfbred child who had proved an aggravating but invaluable companion. He pictured Brendor staring abashedly at his feet while Gaelinar scraped away the beard stubble which had resulted from Brendor's incompetent attempt at a shaving spell. The image made him smile until the pain of realization swept aside his fantasies. Fury bucked against his control; he felt giddy with hatred. Yet Bramin was already dead, and Larson knew his dreams of vengeance could only remain unfulfilled.

Gaelinar stared through the entryway to Hel's barren

fields and the towering gate around them. "We must go now."

Larson remained still, burdened with unresolved sadness. "Wait." He met Silme's gaze, attempting to convey with a wordless glance the support and affection he could only truly express with an embrace. "We may never see Silme again. I need some more time."

"We must go *now.*" Gaelinar's tone left no room for compromise. He strode through the portal.

Gaelinar's tactlessness fueled Larson's anger. He turned his back to the Hel grounds, obstinately willing to sacrifice Gaelinar's company for a few extra minutes with the woman he cherished. "Silme, I love you . . ."

Silme's gaze followed Gaelinar. "I know that, Allerum. I love you, too. But when Gaelinar becomes this insistent about something, he usually has good cause. There's nothing you can do for me here."

Larson plucked idly at his tunic. "Can't you just follow us back?"

Silme's lips framed a slight smile. "I'm dead, Allerum. I exist only in Hel. Even if I could pass the barriers which confine the dead, on Midgard I would still be dead. Go. Quickly now. Good-bye and good luck, hero."

Larson turned, his emotions heavy within him. *After we fulfill the deed which will bring Silme back, not even my mother would call me hero.* He phrased his reply carefully as he walked through the doorway of Hel's citadel into the continuous darkness of her lands. "Farewell, Silme. Until we meet again." He spun toward her one last time, but she had disappeared among the milling corpses in the red gloom of Hel's hall.

"Allerum!" Gaelinar's voice went crisp with impatience.

Larson glimpsed the Kensei near the spidery, silver outline of the gate which surrounded Hel's citadel. He trotted toward it, muttering his annoyance. "Damn gook's always right, and he knows it, too." He shouted, "I'm coming, I'm coming. Keep your . . ." The expression did not translate well. ". . . robes on," he ended lamely.

Gaelinar waited only until Larson reached the base of

the wrought iron gates, then caught the bars and began to climb. As he changed handholds, rust pattered to the dirt beneath him.

Seconds later, Larson seized the crossbars and shinnied after the Kensei, as glad for his childhood antics at the local YMCA as for basic training. The metal seemed no better tended than Hel's minions. Corroded chips and jagged edges bit into his fingers. The closely-spaced posts and cross posts made for adequate hand- and boot-holds, but Hel's threat echoed through Larson's thoughts. His palms went slick with sweat, colored by the abundant rust, and he frequently paused to wipe red-orange streaks across his tunic. His head felt heavy with learned paranoia. His army training made him anxious about his elevated position, easy target for whichever of Hel's horrors might menace them. He climbed faster, catching the pitted metal only long enough to support a grip for his other hand before reaching for the next bar.

Larson's harried ascent brought him past Gaelinar to the top of Hel's gate. There, the bars swept backward over Larson's head, a further reminder of Hel's intention to prevent escapes from her citadel. He slowed and forced himself to think. Seizing a curved pole in each fist, he allowed his body to dangle, and inched his grip backward.

Gaelinar waited, carefully braced, while Larson positioned himself.

At length, Larson felt the down-curled edges beneath his fingers. He tensed, recalling that the elf body in which Freyr had placed him stood slighter and frailer than the strength-trained, human physique he had accepted as his own for the latter part of his twenty years. Gently, testing the power of his elf form, he worked his chest over the curvature, supporting his frame with his arms. He paused, weight evenly distributed across the bars. For an instant, his mind betrayed him. Imagined bullets made his skin prickle, then his thoughts transformed the illusion to a volley of black-fletched arrows. Cursing his overactive imagination he flipped his legs over the grate. Twisting, he caught toeholds, and began his descent. *This world has enough ghosts without me creating my own.* The self-chastisement did nothing to soothe his discomfort. Without waiting for Gaelinar, he continued down the gate. Clambering to within five feet of the ground, he loosed his hold. He struck the ground with bent knees, dropped to a crouch, and remained coiled there until Gaelinar alighted.

Gaelinar studied Larson through the mist. "Well, hero. Is it safe?"

"Very funny." Larson rose, still tensed and troubled. *Enemies could come from anywhere in the darkness.* The realization made him as edgy as a private on his first sniper hunt. He knew from their journey into Hel that the reddish murk would deepen to pitch within a day's travel, and complete blackness would engulf them until they had nearly reached Midgard. "And why were you in such a goddamned hurry that I couldn't spend a little more time with Silme?"

Gaelinar picked rust specks from the brocade of his swords. "Did you notice something different about Silme as compared to the other corpses?"

Equating Silme with the walking mob of death irritated Larson. He crinkled his nose. "Of course. She wasn't . . . disgusting. She was Silme."

"Exactly." Gaelinar continued into the darkness, still speaking. "And what caused the others to decay?"

Larson paced after Gaelinar, wondering if the Kensei wanted a biology lesson on bacteria. "What do you mean 'caused'? Death, I suppose."

"Time," Gaelinar corrected. "The longer Silme remains there, the more she will become like the others. She'll grow rancid, start to forget her life on Midgard, and her mind and body will no longer be worth salvaging."

A sharp chill of foreboding spread through Larson, and he found himself without a reply. *Of course, Gaelinar is right, as always. The faster we act, the better for Silme.* The discovery turned his mood bleak, and the pervasive uneasiness inspired by Hel's threat persisted.

Gaelinar and Larson had no means to judge day and night in Hel's eternal blackness. A few hours from the gate, the Kensei knelt on a flat piece of dusty ground near the banks of the river Gjoll, whose burble would become their guide through the Hel lands and into the cavernous entryway to Midgard. Gaelinar divided a ration of hard bread.

Still anxious, Larson toyed with his food. He broke his share into smaller pieces until nothing remained but crumbs which he dusted into his mouth and washed down with water.

Gaelinar sprawled across the ground.

Larson remained seated, too alert to sleep. "I'll keep watch."

The unremitting night hid Gaelinar's expression. "No need, hero. Our time has grown short, and we both need rest. No living creature could come close enough to harm us without awakening me."

"The corpses," Larson reminded.

"They're trapped within Hel's gate, without the strength or wherewithal to climb it. Those newly dead who might pass us on their way to Hel's inner chambers will be too involved with their own fates to concern themselves with ours."

Larson plucked at Silme's rankstone through the folds of his cloak. He snaked his fingers into his pocket and fondled the smoothed surfaces of Baldur's gem, attempting to define the crafted scene by the raised strokes of gold ink. The figure remained elusive. He pulled the gemstone free and studied it. He could discern only the vague outline of a horse through Hel's crushing darkness. He tossed the stone, caught it, flipped it back into his pocket, and addressed Gaelinar. "Baldur."

Gaelinar's voice wafted sleepily through the gloom. "Mmm. What about him?"

Larson slid to his stomach, his chin propped in his hands. "How come he seems so much more . . ." He struggled for the word. ". . . well, divine than the other gods?"

There was a short silence while Gaelinar pondered Larson's question. "What do you mean by *divine?*"

Larson considered. "I don't exactly know. He didn't

actually do anything, but he seemed so . . . pure . . . and good.'' He thought some more. ''He brought back memories of Christmas masses and Sunday school.'' He laughed at his own words, aware Gaelinar could have no knowledge of the events he had just mentioned.

Gaelinar's reply was confident. ''Hero, you plague yourself with illusions. Just because someone evokes memories of goodness does not mean he embodies them. You live in a different world now than the one you knew. Be careful. Baldur was the most beloved of the gods, but purity and charity are rare in a religion where the greatest ambition is to die in glorious combat while killing as many enemies as possible. Your thoughts have become clouded by what you would like to see. With age, after many years of looking inside yourself, you will gradually see through the delusions which hide reality.''

Larson let his arms slide to the ground and cradled his head on his elbow. He read the wisdom in Gaelinar's words. It had always seemed easy to envision all women with the name Vicky as voluptuous, all Toms as sports heroes, and all Jeffreys as fat and whiny based on his experiences in high school. But Larson still felt it necessary to equate his past and present experiences in many circumstances. At least gravity and physics seemed to function in this world as they did at home, and he had already staked his life on his scant knowledge of both. *How does Gaelinar come up with this stuff so fast?* Larson sighed. ''Do you have an answer for everything?''

Gaelinar replied without hesitation. ''No.''

''No?'' Gaelinar's denial surprised Larson. ''What don't you have an answer for?''

Kensei Gaelinar caught Larson's forearm without groping through the darkness. ''Anything I don't care about, hero.''

Several thoughts converged on Larson. Caught between his awe over Gaelinar's vast knowledge and contempt for the Kensei's smugness, he attempted a carefully considered and well-constructed retort. But, instead, he only managed to blurt, ''You're pretty pompous sometimes.''

Gaelinar loosed Larson's arm. "Perhaps." He rolled to his side, turning his back to Larson. "I told you I'm not a hero."

Not a hero. Larson made no response, and his world went silent as death. He pictured Gaelinar, swathed in cammie, hunched behind an M-79 launcher and flinging grenades like a madman. *No way.* Larson amended his own imaginings. *Gaelinar wouldn't hide behind a gun. He'd be in the front of every combat. He'd volunteer for every special mission. And no one could touch him. In his spare time, he'd rescue children from burning slums and make the New York subway system safe for all humanity.* Larson puckered his lips and caught himself about to whistle "God Bless America." He suppressed a laugh. *And this man has the gall to call* me *hero!*

Larson shook his head at the ridiculousness of his current train of thought. He closed his eyes and tried to sleep. But his exchange with Hel echoed through his mind. *Silme died because it was time for a law-abiding creature of her strength to die. To bring her back to Midgard, you would need to open a place for her.* Larson rolled to his side, but the memory followed him. He heard Gaelinar's explanation, more jarring for its emotionless tone. *Hel has proposed we find someone, a person of Silme's means and bent, willing take her place in Hel.* Larson tried to empty his mind enough to sleep. He forced himself to picture curly-coated sheep jumping a battered fence row. But their whiteness muted to Baldur's gleaming visage, soft and pure and pleading. And Hel's final words returned, unbidden. *Hel was never designed to keep men* out.

Larson twisted to his other side. *Damn you, Larson. You've dozed through worse than this.* But sleep remained elusive and distant. Rolling to his back, he opened his eyes. Hel had no stars to watch; Larson saw only an impenetrable blackness without end. Even the shrill of insects remained conspicuously absent.

The dark, restless night became a dark, restless day. Breakfast sat like a doughy lump in Larson's gut, and he refused lunch and dinner. A steady march brought Gaelinar and Larson deeper into Hel's pitch when they finally stopped to make camp.

Larson consoled himself with realization. *At least we've come one day closer to Midgard. Surely tonight I'll feel tired enough to rest.* But sleep remained just beyond Larson's reach. He tossed from one position to the next, hyperalert and plagued with memory.

Gaelinar tolerated Larson's grumbled curses for several hours. At length, he spoke. "Something troubling you, hero?"

Larson snorted. "I can't sleep."

"You're trying too hard. Let it come to you."

"Yeah, sure." Larson felt too irritable for glib advice or amenities. "Maybe I'll read a book or something."

Gaelinar took no notice of Larson's sarcasm. "As you wish."

"As I wish." Larson stared into the darkness. "You have a flashlight?"

"Close your eyes. Concentrate on something you know well."

Larson rolled to his side. He waited until his annoyance faded, then revived the image of a Bronx sunset. Colored bands of light wafted from behind the jagged row of building silhouettes. Car headlights sheened from the skyscrapers and disappeared, their horns blaring even throughout the night. The familiar scene relaxed Larson enough to fall into a deep and troubled sleep. Within half an hour he was dreaming.

Larson wandered through a graveyard obscured by haze. Moist wisps of fog wound across the weathered, gray tombstones like ghosts, rose and disappeared into the mist. Gravel crunched beneath his boots. Crickets trilled, unseen, between the crypts. Birdsong bounced along the oaks which lined the perimeter, and a dog howled in the distance. Dried and withered flowers sagged across the graves, and the earth lay wet with the spattered tears of a million mourners. In his dream, Larson stopped before a headstone. He cleared slime from the letters with his fingers, and read the words inscribed:

Here lies Al Larson,
Harbinger of Doom,
Slayer of the Human Race.
May he rest in peace,
A luxury he did not afford his followers.

A chill breeze stabbed through Larson's tunic, sending him into a spasm of shivering. "Oh, God. I didn't . . ."

A resonating voice interrupted. "But you did, *Allerum. And you killed my father.*"

In his nightmare, Larson whirled to face a wolf tall as a horse, black above and white beneath. The fur of its spine and hackles bristled. Its eyes flashed red fire. Its presence seemed to fill Larson's mind; the graveyard vanished around them.

"W-what?" Larson stammered.

The wolf exposed a mouthful of sword-sharp, yellowed teeth. "Al Larson, then? So be it. *Allerum Godslayer*, you destroyed my father, but you can't slay the force he represented. Soon you will die beneath my paws. For tonight, you will know only chaos and terror."

"Wait!" Larson started.

The wolf raised a threatening paw. For a moment, Larson glimpsed the carefully woven web of nerves which composed his own thoughts. Then white hot pain crashed through his head. His vision exploded to crimson-black. He stood in frightened awe as a chunk of vine-streaked jungle dissolved into a scorched plain. Smoke slashed the heavens, twining like wraiths through a sky dark with violence. Blindly, the wolf paw jabbed into Larson's thoughts again, jarring the elf like a physical force. He stood before the blackened skeleton of a Huey Cobra. Charred bodies hung, like puppets, from its frame. Shadowy forms low-crawled across Larson's peripheral vision. Mentally, he chased them, and his pursuit flung him into a limitless spiral of illusion.

Desperate and dizzied, Larson cast for some landmark on which to ground his reason. The wolf's muzzle drew into tight focus, slick with slaver. It struck again. A machine gun blasted and howled until its barrel glowed red. Then sudden, sharp pain slammed Larson to consciousness. He sat up with a cry of alarm. The gunfire and the wolf dissolved into Hel's lightless world. Larson's face stung.

Gaelinar clapped a reassuring hand to Larson's shoulder. "Bad dream, hero?"

"Nightmare." Larson rubbed his smarting cheeks, wondering why he still felt physical pain. "Did you hit me?"

Gaelinar's voice went soft with discomfort. "Sorry. You didn't respond to shaking."

"Sorry." Larson felt stupid apologizing, but he could think of nothing better to say. His heart was racing. The visions still seemed vivid. He harbored no wish to return to sleep and more of his dream. He was disappointed in his self-control; it seemed the flashbacks had recurred. And there was still something frighteningly real about his tormentor. "Gaelinar, does Hel have a wolf of some sort?"

"A wolf?" Gaelinar's grip tightened. "Not one I know of."

Larson shook his head, plagued by half-forgotten recollections of the Norse mythology book he had read and quoted in his bunker in Vietnam. "Isn't there some sort of demon wolf or devil dog?" The memory evaded him. "Damn it. I remember reading about a dog with a name like Hel pooch . . . or Hel mutt . . . or something." He laughed at his unintentional pun, dampening the brooding tension inspired by his dream. "It's supposed to guard the entrance to Hel."

"Hel *hound,*" Gaelinar corrected. "Garmr. You're correct. I had forgotten."

"Forgotten!" Larson was incensed. "You recall every mistake I've ever made. When I misplace my feet in a kata, you mention each individual time it happened before, never failing to include the time, the place, and anything else even vaguely related to the practice. You remember every block, stroke, and parry of every fight you've ever seen. But you forgot the Hel hound?"

Gaelinar released Larson's shoulder. "It didn't seem important."

Not for the first time, Gaelinar's logic was lost on Larson. "Not important! A man-eating beast bounding through the darkness to kill us in our sleep didn't seem worth mentioning? Not even casually? Like . . ." Larson simulated Gaelinar's voice in conversation. "So, Allerum. If a wolf the size of a Buick comes by tonight to eat us, you might want to wake me."

Gaelinar remained unruffled. "First, Allerum, Garmr is tied at the entrance to Hel, not running freely. Second, he is a dog, not a wolf. And third . . ." He left a thoughtful pause. "What is a 'Byu Wick'?"

Larson latched on to Gaelinar's second point. "Garmr's a dog?"

"I don't know why you seem so surprised. We passed him in Hel's entryway."

"We did?" Larson blinked, wishing he sounded less careless. "But I didn't see . . ."

"I did," Gaelinar interrupted. "But I could understand how an elf with busy thoughts might miss a mongrel of deepest black lying still in the darkness. Garmr had no interest in us. It is his job to keep the dead from escaping, not entering. He ignored us, so I ignored him."

That explains the animal smell at Hel's entrance. Larson shook his head as the creature from his dream returned to his mind easily. *It wasn't all black. And it didn't look like a mongrel.* "Gaelinar, does Hel also keep a wolf?"

Gaelinar passed Larson a handful of dry cheese. "If you're going to keep me awake, we might as well make this an early morning. As far as I know, Hel has no wolf. Why do you ask?"

"Without sounding stupid," Larson began, well aware he did, "a wolf played a major role in my dream. I think it said I killed its father." Larson bit into a chunk of cheese, awaiting Gaelinar's laughter.

Gaelinar's robes rustled as he rose. "Perhaps it was not a dream."

Food muffled Larson's voice "Don't kid around like that." He swallowed. "Don't be ridiculous. I've never shot a wolf in my life. I've never even hit one with a Byu Wick. I suppose I really went back to Vietnam, too?"

Gaelinar offered an arm and helped Larson to his feet.

"Silme used to talk about how you didn't have any mind . . ."

Larson found it unamusing that Gaelinar chose that particular moment to pause.

". . . barriers, and how anyone with the power and knowledge can enter your thoughts. Loki sired other offspring than Hel, among them a wolf named Fenrir."

Larson choked on a piece of cheese. He coughed until tears rose in his eyes. He recalled how Bramin had plucked the most painful memories from Larson's mind, inciting them into riotous detail. Loki and Vidarr had battled among the coiled and tangled circuitry of his thoughts, and Silme had once used them as a portal. Larson no longer harbored any doubt. Fenrir's mental intrusion seemed every bit as real as Bramin's. "That wolf claimed it would kill me," he said hoarsely.

"Let it try." Gaelinar shrugged with a maddeningly cold courage. "It's too foolish to succeed. Its best weapon was surprise, and it's already given that away."

Larson patted his hip, now more acutely aware of his missing sword. *Will the killing never end?* Over the ceaseless bubbling of the river Gjoll, Larson thought he heard an answering howl.

CHAPTER 3:

Hel's Hound

"It is nought good a slepyng hound to wake."
—Geoffrey Chaucer
Troilus and Criseyde

Another three days passed in Hel's black void, its silence broken only by the ceaseless babble of the river Gjoll, which guided Larson and Gaelinar toward Midgard. Larson saw nothing more of Loki's son; the wolf penetrated neither his life nor his dreams again. Several restful nights restored his flagging spirits. He no longer imagined monsters, ghosts, and snipers huddled in Hel's concealing darkness. Time diluted the ferocity of its mistress' vague warnings and blurred the wolf's threat to ephemeral nightmare.

Oddly, as Larson's anxiety diminished, Gaelinar's caution heightened. He avoided conversation, answering Larson's questions with monosyllables or not at all. He checked points and edges on his knives, swords, and shurikens, though he had used none since his last inspection. He kept his fist on the sheath of his katana with his thumb looped over the crossguard.

Not wishing to become embroiled in another wave of paranoia, Larson ignored Gaelinar's unusual vigilance for several hours. Then the Kensei began repeatedly flicking his hilt a few inches free from its scabbard and sliding it back into place until the gesture became an annoyance. Abruptly, Larson stopped and faced his mentor. "Do you have a problem?"

"Yes." There was unexpected anger in Gaelinar's reply. "Stupid questions." He stepped around Larson and continued walking.

Larson trotted after his mentor, incensed by Gaelinar's chastisement. "What did I do?"

Gaelinar's voice was restrained. "We're half a hundred paces from the single place Hel has most likely stationed her minions. Our one advantage might have been surprise, and you're flapping your tongue like a cock heralding the dawn."

Larson's cheeks felt warm. He knew he would fare best remaining quiet, but Gaelinar's words seemed too important to dismiss without probing further. "Where do you mean?"

"Look to your right, hero."

Larson turned his head. The darkness felt bunched and tangible around him. On more careful inspection, he recognized a diffuse, sallow glow, like the moon on a cloudy night. Thinking back, it had been visible for at least the last two days, but Larson had passed it off as normal. Now, drawn by Gaelinar's concern, Larson recalled the gold-roofed bridge over the Gjoll. Apprehension quickened his pulse. "You think Hel rigged the crossing?"

Gaelinar hesitated. "If you mean she might have made it difficult to pass, yes. Few men and no corpse would have the strength to swim Gjoll's torrent. Anyone attempting escape would need to cross her bridge. Can you think of a better place to stop us? Now, hush. We're almost there."

Larson went silent, head low with shame. *I'm a trained soldier, for Chrissakes. I should have figured this out without Gaelinar's help.* Another worry surfaced with chilling abruptness. *We're about to fight something, and I haven't got a weapon.* Though now only a few yards from the Hel bridge, he dared a whisper. "Gaelinar."

Kensei Gaelinar did not answer.

Shit. Larson groped blindly for his mentor. The air felt cold and empty. "No sword."

Gaelinar seized Larson's arm and jerked.

Larson spun to face his mentor. He could distinguish only the Kensei's outline through the gloom.

"I know," Gaelinar said softly. "That couldn't be helped. We'll have to do the best we can without it."

Larson glanced into the hovering yellow fog. With effort, he could just discern the frame of the crossing, as crudely constructed as a Vietnamese footbridge but thatched with metallic gold. "Do you have a plan?"

Gaelinar released Larson's arm. "A plan?" The Kensei's voice held a tinge of annoyance. "A warrior makes his plans in the instant between sword strokes. You want a plan? Fine, this is my plan. Move toward the bridge. When I signal, you run across as fast as possible. Don't stop until you reach the other side."

"But, I . . ."

Gaelinar cut Larson short. "In this darkness, without a weapon, you can only become an obstacle or a casualty. Do as I say."

Larson scowled, unsatisfied. "What will you do?"

"I don't know yet."

"The signal?" Larson whispered.

Gaelinar's reply sounded distant. "It won't be subtle. Approach, quietly now."

Larson hesitated, his mind filled with the rickety footbridges over Vietnam's chessboard of rivers and swamps. More than once, he had heard the sudden roar of explosives. He had watched flames wash wooden planks while supports shattered, heaving splinters like darts, leaving men, blood-splashed and moaning on the bridges' charred and jutting frames. *But this world has no C-4, no grenades, no M-16s.* Larson's realization brought only scant comfort. He inched uncertainly toward the hovering golden fog, no longer able to discern Gaelinar in the mist.

No sound came from Hel's bridge. Nothing swished, snapped or banged in the windless air. *It's not what you hear, it's what you don't hear that kills you.* Larson chased the thought from his mind, not wishing to cross the fine line between caution and paranoia. He took another careful forward step. His boot touched down on ground slick as glass. His foot shot out from under him. He scrabbled for balance, lost it, and crashed to his buttocks. His toe struck the wooden lip of the bridge with a muffled thunk. Pain shot up his spine, and he fought the urge to curse aloud.

A deep female voice challenged Larson from the bridge. "You cannot cross."

Larson dove to his left and hunkered into Hel's shadows, his mind scrambling for strategy. He understood what had happened. Impervious to cold in his elven form, he had forgotten Hel's chill and slipped on a frozen puddle of river water in the depression before the bridge. He tried to locate the woman who had addressed him, but his vision fought a losing battle with the darkness.

Gaelinar's voice hissed into Larson's ear. "Keep her talking." Then the Kensei disappeared.

Larson cleared his throat and rose to a crouch. "Excuse me?" he said, tensed to roll aside at the twang of a bowstring.

The same voice repeated its warning. "You cannot cross."

Larson asked the obvious questions. "Who are you? And why would you want to keep me from crossing?" He chose the singular pronoun, hoping to keep Gaelinar's presence secret.

The woman replied immediately. "I am Modgudr, guardian of the bridge. It is my job to keep the dead in Hel."

"A noble task." Larson heard nothing to indicate Modgudr had companions. He grew more daring. "But I'm not dead. I'm alive."

Modgudr's voice deepened with contempt. "Undoubtedly. You make more noise than a legion of corpses. But my orders stand. I am to allow no one to pass without Hel's prior command. You cannot cross."

Larson chewed his lip, uncertain where to take the conversation. It appeared no one planned to shoot him down where he stood, and Modgudr seemed reasonably polite. He phrased his next question to glean as much information about Hel's guardian as he could without goading her to attack. "Please forgive my boldness, but you're one woman against a heavily armed man. How do you plan to prevent me from crossing?"

Modgudr's snort echoed beneath the gold-thatched roof

of her bridge. "Do you think me blind? You've no arms but those you were born with. And I believe one Dragonrank sorceress a match for any warrior. Do you still wish to challenge me?"

Modgudr's pronouncement struck Larson dumb. According to Silme, the nine worlds harbored only a handful of Dragonrank, so few the vast majority of men lived a lifetime without having seen or heard of one. In less than a month in Old Scandinavia, Larson had already encountered two: the diamond-rank master, Bramin, and his half sister, Silme. The odds of happening upon another seemed not unlike those of winning the Irish sweepstakes. *Yet,* Larson realized, *a man's chances of entering Hel alive can't be much greater.*

Uncertain whether Modgudr was bluffing, yet not eager to invoke a sorceress' wrath, Larson chose his words with care. "You see pretty well in the dark."

Modgudr's answer was a garbled shriek of syllables. Suddenly, magical light pulsed across the bridge, shattering darkness into streaked shadows. Larson dropped to the ground, shielding aching eyes with his hand. He caught a quick glimpse of a pale female form, arm raised in arched threat, and the golden profile of Gaelinar and his swords. Then the sorceries died, and the air filled with shouted warnings.

Larson hesitated, blinded and weaponless. More than anything, he wanted to aid Gaelinar, but he knew better than to defy his mentor's orders. *The signal?* Crouched, head low and protected beneath his arms, he raced onto the bridge.

Gaelinar and Modgudr yowled like fighting cats. Before Larson, metal rang against metal. He dodged aside. A spear of light slashed Hel's blackness, revealing the two combatants in hazy, red outline. Something wet splashed Larson's cheek, but he was uncertain whether it was water or blood. "Gaelinar!" He paused, fearing for the Kensei's life.

Gaelinar's voice rose above the din. Larson could decipher only one of the Kensei's words, ". . . run!" Obediently, he quickened his pace. Suddenly, a body slammed into him, driving him into a low, wooden rail.

Impact knocked the breath from his lungs and spun him to the ground. He lurched to his feet, cursing the darkness, trying to regain his sense of direction. Again, a bright flare of sorcery clove the darkness and sparked against the rail to Larson's right. The wooden strut sizzled and caught fire. Larson whirled and sprinted for the farther end of the bridge.

Larson's footfalls crashed on the thick lumber of the bridge. Darkness closed over him again. He continued, uncomfortably aware of the tearing clash of magic and metal growing more distant behind him. Then he blundered into the semi-solid magics of an unseen ward. Light flashed. Impact bounced him to the ground, and he rolled to the softer soil beyond the bridge's planks. Sound blared across the Hel lands, shrill and persistent as a fire alarm.

Larson stumbled to his feet. He ached everywhere, as if he had finished a grueling workout in the gym, but he had nothing to blame but the sorceress' ward. Sick and dizzied, he swiveled his head toward the battle on the bridge. The fire had turned the handrail into a spreading inferno which revealed Gaelinar and Modgudr in horrific detail. The Kensei's frenzied strokes kept falling inches from their mark. Though grimacing with fatigue and effort, Modgudr was somehow driving Gaelinar backward, step by step, toward the blaze.

Gaelinar! Hold on. Larson reeled toward Modgudr, the sounds of his progress drowned by the shrieks of her ward. As the flames licked the edges of Gaelinar's robes, the Kensei sheathed his blade and sprang toward Modgudr. He crashed into the same invisible barrier which had impeded his sword. The collision jolted him to one knee, and Modgudr pressed her advantage with desperate glee. Gaelinar slid toward the fire and the rushing river below it.

Larson dove. He caught Modgudr in a flying tackle. His momentum sprawled her to the ground. Woman and elf skidded across the wooden planks, wood slivering through the sorceress' robes. Modgudr howled in pain and anger. Her ward went suddenly quiet. Apparently she had also lost her magical shield because, when Larson glanced up, Gaelinar held his blade pressed to Modgudr's throat. "Don't move."

Larson knew Gaelinar addressed Modgudr, but the malice in the Kensei's voice held him still as well.

"If you make a sound I don't recognize or a single gesture, I'll kill you."

The odor of singed cloth reminded Larson how narrowly his mentor had eluded death. Beneath him, Modgudr was panting. She made no attempt to struggle but loosed a weak snort of disgust. "You cannot slay me. If you did, Hel's dead would escape to Midgard and wreak havoc on mankind."

There followed a moment of careful silence as Gaelinar considered. "That is not my concern, Modgudr. I pledged myself to Silme, not her world. If she remains in Hel, I no longer have cause to live except to train my student to reasonable competence. I am a foreigner. When I die, my soul becomes one with our universe, not caged in a world like Hel. The fate of Midgard's citizens would not interest me any more."

Gaelinar's loyalty touched Larson, but the Kensei's coldness discomforted him. *Surely, he's acting. I once saw him rush down, single-handed, on three bandits raping a young boy. That kind of crazed loyalty to a stranger can only come from the heart, not from dedication to someone else's principles.* But Larson also knew the ancient Japanese culture was one of honor, brutality, and single-minded devotion to lords and their causes. Larson released Modgudr, rising to a cautious crouch. To his left, the flaming rail had dissolved into a charred skeleton. The fire dulled and winked out, plunging them back into Hel's darkness.

Modgudr's tense hiss answered Gaelinar's words.

Gaelinar's reply was patient. "Hel said we could exchange the life of another Dragonrank for Silme. Perhaps you'll do."

Larson could not read Modgudr's expression through the pitch, but she sounded more confused than frightened by Gaelinar's threat. "But I'm not dead."

Gaelinar spoke again. "I can change that."

"Perhaps." Modgudr's voice had withered to a fraction of its former resonance. "But it will do you no good. I don't know what my mistress told you." Though feeble, her tone carried a note of calculation which convinced Larson she knew more than she would tell. "But Silme served Vidarr, a god of Law. Hel is of Chaos. Killing me can only disrupt the balance farther toward Order and make Silme unnecessary."

Modgudr's argument made sense to Larson. *I doubt she would qualify as having a similar "means and bent" to Silme.* He felt uncomfortable leaving a powerful enemy alive at his back; but if Modgudr was the only deterrent to the dead escaping Hel, he could see no other option. Though the corpses had not tried to harm him, they had shown curiosity and an ability to inflict inadvertent pain. Just the sight of mutilated, rotting relatives returning from caskets and graves would surely cause panicked chaos on Midgard. He imagined zombies wandering the New York streets, consuming the strength and warmth of the living, impervious to the weapons of the national guard. *Most basic horror movie plot in existence. And I wouldn't inflict it on America, Norway, or anywhere else.*

Still blinded by Hel's incessant darkness, Larson heard a creak of movement. Modgudr fell silent. Then Gaelinar caught Larson's arm and drew him across the bridge.

Larson waited only until they had withdrawn beyond earshot of Modgudr. "What did you do about her?"

Gaelinar's hand fell away from Larson's sleeve. "I knocked her to sleep."

Larson grumbled, bothered by the thought of an angered and unpredictable sorceress on his heels. "I hope you hit her hard enough to keep her out for a day. If I recall, that's about how long it's going to take us to get out of Hel."

"She'll sleep only a short time. But that's all right. We'll be beyond the range of her spells when she awakens."

"How can you be sure?"

Gaelinar curved toward the left, still following the song of the river. "I can't. But remember, hero. Modgudr is Dragonrank. She draws her power from her own vitality.

Our fight left her weak and winded. Whenever Silme strained her sorcery, a long time would pass before she felt well enough to create magic again. By then, we will have traveled far enough that Modgudr would need to come to us to do battle. That would require her to leave her post on the bridge. In her absence, how many of Hel's corpses might cross? I doubt she would find us worth the risk. Surely pursuing a man and elf with the strength and amorality to kill her, who don't belong in Hel anyway, cannot justify allowing the dead, whom she's pledged to confine, to escape to Midgard."

Gaelinar and Larson continued in thoughtful silence. As they followed the Gjoll, toward the path from Hel, the darkness grew less overwhelming and gradually faded. Larson's spirits soared as his mentor's golden form and the vast spread of Hel's barren lands became more visible. Idly, Larson plucked Silme's gem from his pocket. It gave off a faint glow which seemed cheerful in the thick gray haze which now replaced Hel's blackness. Comforted by its presence, Larson continued to hold it, allowing memories of Silme to replace the oppressive burden of his task. But before he could form a mental image of the woman he loved, a distressing thought filled his mind. "Gaelinar. If this gem holds part of Silme's life aura," he raised the sapphire, "she must have placed it there before she died."

"Correct."

Larson stared at the glimmering facets of the sapphire. "Why would she do that?"

Gaelinar shrugged, looking bored by Larson's questioning. "It was fairly standard. A difficult situation might tax Silme down to her last spell. She always kept enough energy stored in the gem for a transport escape if things became desperate." A light dawned in Gaelinar's eyes. "You're thinking of Modgudr, aren't you?"

Larson nodded. "Did you notice a staff?"

"Amethyst."

"So, Modgudr could have stored power in her rankstone?"

"Certainly."

Larson's fingers tightened around Silme's sapphire.

"Which means she may still have some energy when she awakens. She may claim it immediately, while we're still within spell range. And she may have reserved more than just enough for an escape."

Gaelinar turned, his gaze probing the darkness behind them.

Larson could discern a dull, flapping sound over the rush of the river. *Birds?* He whirled toward Gaelinar as the noise intensified. "What the. . . ?"

"Wyrm!" Gaelinar screamed. Without warning, he dove onto Larson, sprawling him, then rolled free. Hel's hard earth jarred pain through Larson's side. He glanced up as yellow-orange flame gouted before him, hot against his face. Sparks bounced, enmired with smoke. He straggled to his feet, frighteningly aware he would have been burned if Gaelinar had not thrown him. The fumes roiled upward. Larson followed them with his gaze to a lizard-shaped mass, large as a tractor trailer.

"Separate." Gaelinar's voice came from behind Larson. "We can't let it get us both."

Dragon! Holy god, not again. Larson broke into a gallop, still following the river bank. He knew he could never outrun the creature; for all its size, it maneuvered like a hawk. And this time Larson had no cover and no Dragonrank sorceress to aid him.

The pulse of the dragon's wings rose in pitch as it banked for another pass. Larson lowered his head and quickened his pace, following the beast's progress by sound. It swooped, catching him effortlessly. Larson sprang aside. Flame fanned the ground where he had stood. Sparks splattered, sizzling into his tunic. Pinpoints of light rebounded like stars, revealing the grim, gray figure of the dragon. *Weapon. I need a goddamned weapon.* The instant the thought came to mind, he realized he was still clutching Silme's rankstone. He stopped so suddenly, the dragon swished over his head. *I can't throw a stone which contains Silme's last vestiges of life. Can I?* His only answer was the slap of batlike wings. *But I have to try something. Otherwise, I'm dead, and Silme's rankstone will remain in Hel for eternity.*

Before Larson could reposition, the dragon swooped,

turned, and dove for him again. Steam twined from its nostrils, blue-white and visible in the darkness. Larson dodged, lost his footing, and forced himself to roll. This time, the dragon anticipated his movement. A tight bar of fire stabbed the ground an inch from Larson's forearm. Hot cinders splashed across his face and clothing. He gasped in pain, pitching across the ground to suffocate the early flames. The dragon circled for another attack.

Larson clambered to his feet. Smoke burned his lungs. His airways felt raw, and his breath rattled through his throat. *It's only a matter of time before I miss a dodge or grow too fatigued to avoid its strikes.* Cinders which had caught on his clothing fizzled to ash. The smell of burnt linen served as a constant reminder of his near escapes. Larson gripped Silme's rankstone and eased to a crouch, awaiting the dragon's next pass.

To Larson's left, Gaelinar's voice rose above the approaching slap of the dragon's wings. "Hie, beast! Here, you ugly monster. Your father was a toad!" He suffixed the insult with a series of wild howls.

Larson knew the dragon could not understand Gaelinar, but a hunter had once told him predators hated loud noises. Larson recalled a story of a bear attacking a camp because a barking dog drove it mad. Apparently, the dragon held a similar hatred for sound. For an instant, it hovered, listening. Then, roaring in anger, it whirled and whisked toward Gaelinar.

Larson chased the steady flap of the dragon's flight, clasping the gemstone so tightly its facets left squared impressions on his palm. Four running steps brought him within sight of Gaelinar's golden outline. He watched the dragon wheel and dip toward the Kensei, flame billowing from its mouth. Gaelinar danced aside. His arm arched toward the beast. Two shurikens, lit red by the plunging fire, rattled from its facial scales. A third embedded in one glaring, yellow eye.

The dragon loosed a bellow of fury and spiraled to the ground less than thirty yards from Larson. There, it pawed at its face with the frenzy of a dog with a painful burr. Through the fading fires of its attack, Larson watched Gaelinar rush the beast. The Kensei held a sword in one hand, his manrikigusari, a chain with end spikes, in the other. Even as he narrowed the gap, the shuriken dislodged. The dragon raised its head. Its eyes swiveled toward Gaelinar, its wings unfurled, and its jaws splayed open.

Larson shouted. He saw no place for Gaelinar to dodge. This close, there was not time for his mentor to avoid the dragon's flaming breath. "Gaelinar!" Larson cocked his arm and threw. The sapphire slapped the beast's cheek; fierce blue light exploded like a flare. With a snort of surprise, the dragon flinched and whirled to face Larson, crimson sparks spewing from its mouth in a scattered array. The sapphire thumped to the ground.

Desperately, Larson searched the broken grayness with light-slashed vision. The dragon leaped skyward, the chain of Gaelinar's manrikigusari tangled on one of its ankles. The Kensei had wrapped the other end around his own hand, and the beast's abrupt movement jerked him into the air with a wrench which made Larson cringe. *What the hell is that idiot doing?* Larson blotted sweat from his brow with his sleeve, not daring to believe Gaelinar had tethered himself to a flying dragon. The nightmarish flap of wings sounded dangerously close.

Suddenly, the dragon loosed an almost human scream. A sticky liquid rained down on Larson, reeking with the thick, salt odor of fresh blood. The shadow of the dragon grew as it plummeted toward him. He dove free as the beast crashed to the ground, landing on its belly, crowing in rage. Larson watched, horrified, as it rolled from side to side, smashing Gaelinar beneath it.

A huge, red puddle seeped from beneath the dragon. *God! Let it be the* beast's *blood.* Larson raced toward it, wishing he held a weapon, any weapon. He seized Baldur's brooch from his pocket and balled it in his fist to add weight to his punch. The dragon's movements had become more agitated. It seemed to take no notice as Larson positioned himself at its side and raised his arms for a blow.

The dragon lurched heavily first right, then left. Its wings whipped suddenly upward. Larson dodged aside as the leathery limbs unfolded, then he ducked through the opening between a wing and the scaled neck. He cracked his fists down on the back of the beast's head.

The dragon roared. Its head bobbed only slightly. Its neck coiled, and it slashed at Larson, snakelike. He skipped aside; the dragon's uncharacteristic slowness was all that saved his hands. The curved fangs scraped Larson's knuckles as he retreated. The bite burned like fire. Larson swore as the dragon screeched again. It rocked across Gaelinar to its right side. Nursing his hand, Larson watched in horror as a gory hand, clutching a blood-soaked short sword, slid from beneath the dragon's softer underbelly. Gaelinar anchored the shoto's hilt against the dirt as the dragon rolled back. Larson sprang for the weapon too late. The creature swayed to the left, impaling itself on the protruding blade. It shuddered once and lay still.

Larson hesitated only an instant. He ran around the gigantic corpse. Gaelinar sat between the dragon's curled forelegs. Blood still poured from an artery positioned in the pit where the monster's shoulder met its chest, accounting for the scarlet gore which covered Gaelinar from head to toe. The Kensei still clutched the chain of the manrikigusari, wound tight around his hand. His katana lay by his side.

"You're alive." Shocked, Larson could think of nothing more intelligent to say. He replaced Baldur's gem in his pocket.

Gaelinar glanced up, appearing his age for the first time in Larson's memory. "And you have a strange habit of stating the obvious. Do all people where you come from do that?" Carefully, he freed his fingers from the chain. Without awaiting an answer, he continued. "Now come down here and help me get my arm back in place."

Larson stared. Apparently, the impact of the dragon's sudden flight had dislocated Gaelinar's shoulder. His left arm hung lower and farther forward than the right. Larson had seen a similar injury to a friend on his high school wrestling team. The coach had replaced the joint while his friend was still on the mat and all the athletes watched in fascination. "Lie down."

Gaelinar tossed his sword from the path of the dripping

blood and moved away from the dragon. He settled to his back on the ground.

Larson seized Gaelinar's hand.

The Kensei loosed a grunt of pain. "Use the wrist."

Larson readjusted his grip carefully. "Sorry." Gaelinar's flesh had swollen around the indentations of the manrikigusari's chain. Chips and lumps grated beneath his skin. "Gaelinar," he said, alarmed. "I think you've crushed some bones."

"I just fought a creature which should have killed me, and I escaped with only an injured hand and shoulder. A warrior doesn't earn respect through what he learns but from what he survives."

Larson shook his head in disbelief. *Battered, smashed, and hurting, and he still feels obligated to teach me.* He planted his boot in Gaelinar's armpit, tightened his fingers on the Kensei's wrist, and gave a long, steady pull. When he released it, the arm snapped back into place.

Gaelinar accepted the pain without a sound. "Thank you, Lord Allerum."

Larson nodded his acknowledgment of Gaelinar's gratitude, glad the Kensei had not called him "hero." Unarmed and fifty years shy of his mentor's training, Larson's contribution to the dragon's demise seemed paltry.

Exercising his arm and fingers, Gaelinar approached the dark hulk of the dragon. "I need to get my other sword. Then I'm going to the river to clean off. When I get back, I suggest we keep moving. If we press on hard, we may reach Midgard before Modgudr regains her strength."

"And sends another dragon," Larson agreed, but even the battle and Gaelinar's wounds did not allow him to forget that he had thrown Silme's rankstone somewhere in the darkness. "I'll wait for you here. I need to find something." He dropped to his knees, straining his eyes as he pawed the dirt around him.

At length, Gaelinar hacked his short sword free from the dragon's scales and wandered toward the river.

Larson turned. A haggard semicircle illuminated a piece of the bare, black ground. In its center lay Silme's gemstone, appearing expended and spiritless. Its glow sputtered like an old fuse, an eerie reminder of Silme's dwindling time. *What have I done to her?* Larson crawled to it, feeling as feeble as the sapphire appeared. *Did I unleash its powers? Did I cost Silme some of her remaining life force?* He raked the stone into his fist and placed it gingerly in his pocket as though it might break. But, as Larson clambered to his feet, understanding replaced his initial feelings of guilt. His meager knowledge of Dragonrank sorcery made him certain life energy could only be spent by its owner. *I suspect the sapphire flashed because Silme's magic met Modgudr's, nothing more.*

Gaelinar reappeared shortly, his golden robes torn and stained. Water trickled from his gray hair, running in rivulets down his wrinkled face. Early bruises splotched the skin visible through the rents and gaps in his clothing. Yet the sheaths, hilts, and brocade of both swords hung, neat and clean, at his waist. "Let's go."

As Larson and Gaelinar pushed onward, the thinning darkness dwindled to gray mist. Exhaustion hunted Larson, and Gaelinar's silence suggested he, too, was due for sleep. They dragged forward, too tired to speak.

It was well into the tenth hour from Modgudr's bridge when Gaelinar and Larson came upon the cliffs which separated Hel's realm from Midgard. Beyond this natural wall, Larson could hear the roar of Hvergelmir's waterfall, a twisted cascade of eleven rivers which poured ceaselessly into a mile deep hole of death before it once again split into the streams which wound through Hel. It was there, at the top of the falls, where Silme and Bramin had lost their lives. There, too, Larson had hurled Loki into the plunging waters, thereby destroying the god, body and soul, for eternity.

Home. Born and raised in New York City, it seemed odd to Larson to consider the crude world of Midgard his residence now. But light streamed through the gorge which served as Hel's doorway, inviting as a campfire on a cold night. Reflexively, Larson quickened his pace. As he came upon the crack in the mountains which served as Hel's boundary, excitement overtook him. With a wild whoop of joy, he sprang for the opening.

A sudden growl and a shadowed blur of movement cut Larson's leap short. Instinctively, he twisted. A heavy form crashed into his hip, bowling him to the ground. Angry teeth pinched through his breeks and tore flesh. Larson rolled away. He pulled free with a tear of cloth. Blood trickled down his shin, and he stared into the sooty muzzle of a huge dog. It yowled and snarled, straining toward Larson but held in place by a staunch chain.

Larson spun back from the beast, then carefully worked his way to his feet. His injured leg felt numb. He looked at Gaelinar. "H-Hel hound?" he managed at length.

Gaelinar glanced from the frothing, black mongrel to Larson. "No doubt."

Now comfortably beyond range of the Hel hound, Larson examined his wound. It was little more than a deep scratch. He held pressure against it until the bleeding stopped, glad for the quickness of his own reaction despite fatigue. Recalling a dog fight he had witnessed in an alley in Manhattan, he suspected the Hel hound would attack with the ferocity of a pit bull. Had it caught a good hold, it would never have released him.

Gaelinar studied the Hel hound, its iron-link leash, and the entryway to Midgard. "I would have warned you, but you knew it was there. I didn't expect you to feed yourself to the Hel hound."

"I was too damn tired to think." Larson scowled. *If he gives me a lecture about keeping my guard up, there's not a god in this world who could keep me from killing him.* He closed Gaelinar's opening quickly. "How are we going to get past it?"

Gaelinar thumbed the hilts of his shoto and katana, his left hand swollen to twice its normal size. "We have no choice."

Gaelinar's slight, but unmistakable, smile convinced Larson the Kensei would have chosen combat, even if he had another option. Larson watched his mentor tense, becoming annoyed at a teacher with two swords who would let his pupil remain unarmed. "Uh, Gaelinar. Forgive me stating the obvious again, but I don't have a weapon."

Gaelinar turned to Larson. "Not even a knife?"

Larson shook his head. When Freyr had transported him from the Vietnam War to Old Scandinavia, the god had equipped him with only clothing and a sword. The tunic, breeks, and cape had long ago worn through and been exchanged for cleaner attire. He had lost the sword when Loki's death broke the spell which imprisoned the god, Vidarr, within its steel. Larson had misplaced the dagger Gaelinar had given him earlier in their travels, but he kept that information to himself. "Not even a child's slingshot."

The Hel hound crouched at the end of its chain, its growls deep and constant.

Gaelinar reached beneath his cloak and retrieved a pair of matched, ivory-hilted knives, still in their sheaths. "Here, then. Every man should carry a blade, even if he's not fighting dogs."

Though still bothered by Gaelinar's insistence on keeping both his swords, Larson took the daggers and attached them to his belt. His army training returned easily. He had been taught to fight off dogs, though he had never had the opportunity to put the knowledge to use before. *Catch it up under the throat and knife it in the belly.* Larson shook his head, doubting he would want to come so close to the beast while his mentor was flashing swords.

As Larson mentally prepared for battle, another dark shape filled the crevice, blotting out the light from Midgard. A beast twice as large as the Hel hound and thick with fur wound through the crevice and stood, still and proud, before the entryway.

Immediately, Larson recognized the wolf from his dream. "Fenrir," he whispered. Suddenly, the Hel hound no longer concerned him.

Fenrir returned Larson's gaze, its red eyes mocking. Water droplets sparkled at the tip of each hair, silvering the wolf's coat. Its stance was confident and detached, without a hint of fear. "Allerum . . . Kensei." It indicated each with a toss of its narrow muzzle. Its voice darkened, and its ears swept flat against its head. "You're both mine."

Gaelinar's swords whipped free, and the Kensei

adopted a defensive pose. Larson hunched, a knife clenched in each fist. Even the warm rush of adrenaline did little to dispel fatigue. Larson's mind felt heavy and muddled. Gaelinar's stance was devoid of his usual bold confidence.

The Hel hound growled, a low rumble of menace. A ridge of spiked, black hair bristled along its back. It thrust its nose beneath Fenrir's abdomen.

Fenrir's triangular ears flicked forward suddenly. The glimmer of triumph died in its eyes. Its gaze never strayed from Gaelinar and Larson, but it addressed Hel's mongrel. "Get away from me, you stupid mutt."

The Hel hound's snarls deepened. It marched forward, stiff-legged, and stood shoulder to shoulder with the Fenris Wolf. Both animals remained still, frozen like statues.

Gaelinar lowered his swords. His laughter rose over the Hel hound's threats. He assumed his normal posture.

Surprised by his mentor's lapse and finding no humor in the coming battle, Larson hesitated. "Why are you laughing?"

"Can't you see?" Gaelinar broke into another round of mirth. "The hound thinks Fenrir's another dog on his territory. If Fenrir takes a step toward or away, there's going to be a . . . a dog fight." Gaelinar sheathed his swords. Pausing to laugh once more at Fenrir's expense, he stepped around the wolf and into the fissure.

Quickly, Larson followed.

The rush of Hvergelmir's waterfall echoed through the gorge, drowning out the Hel hound's growls. Droplets bounced from Larson's face, a moist, clean change from Hel's stifling darkness. A frenzied howl slashed the air. Slipping through the crevice into Midgard's twilight, Larson caught a glimpse of the Hel hound hurling its solidly-muscled bulk for Fenrir's throat.

Larson turned to watch. The wolf sidestepped easily, then charged the mongrel in a frenzied blur of attack. Fenrir slashed and tore, never in one position longer than a second. Fascinated, Larson stared as each of the Hel hound's mighty lunges fell short.

Gaelinar prodded Larson's shoulder. "Quickly now.

The farther we get before they finish, the better off we are.''

Larson needed no more urging. He whirled and scrambled along the narrow pathway which would take them up the incline from Hvergelmir's pit.

A grating voice rose above the bellowing current of white water. ''I'll find you again. No mere dog will keep me from my vengeance!''

Larson shivered, though whether from the cold sting of water droplets or some deeper discomfort, he did not know. Some trick of the rising sun lit Hvergelmir's falls the color of blood.

PART II:

The Masters of Midgard

CHAPTER 4:

Master Thief

"Who is all-powerful should fear everything."
—Pierre Corneille
Le Cid

Al Larson awakened to utter darkness. He remained immobile in the dirt, not daring to believe he was finally out of Hel. The events of the previous morning: Fenrir's challenge, the dog fight, the rugged climb from Hvergelmir's pit all seemed too vividly real to have been a dream. Filled with bitter disbelief, he stared into the sky. Gradually, he discerned the pinpoint light of stars through interwoven branches, and he realized it was a normal, moonless night in Midgard. The air felt thick with the mingled scents of loam and pine and the comforting, acridly woody smell of a campfire. Larson rolled to his side. "Gaelinar?"

Gaelinar's voice came from Larson's left. "I'm here, hero. Are you ready for practice?"

"Now?" Larson groaned, twisted to face Gaelinar, and swept to a sitting position. "But I still don't have a sword."

Gaelinar perched on a fallen trunk, lit by a weak circle of flame. His golden robes spread about his legs like a crumpled flower, but the black sash around his waist held his katana and shoto, their sheaths and brocade immaculately clean. "That is of no consequence. I train the man, not the sword. The weapon is only a tool, an extension of the spirit. The technique, the intent and motivation of each cut remains regardless of the blade. Come.'' Gaelinar rose and trotted into the woods.

Larson rubbed his eyes, trying to shake the last, heavy vestiges of sleep. *I can't believe this fucking gook's got me up in the middle of the night to swing an imaginary sword.* Grumbling curses in three languages, he followed the Kensei between hardy trunks of birch and aspen to a grove of ancient pines. The lower boughs had withered and broken in the shadow of their younger brothers, leaving a thick blanket of needles as a floor. The higher branches clustered into a tangled roof thirty feet above Larson's head. Huddled trunks stood, as wide as fire hydrants, their limbs forming walls which barred the winds. To Larson, the clearing beneath the pines seemed not unlike an oblong, indoor stadium with the lights turned off.

Gaelinar kicked aside fallen branches to establish practice space. He walked to the center of the grove. ''Sweeps. Begin, hero.''

Larson blinked in the grayness at the edge of the clearing. ''Let me get this straight. You woke me up to practice with a pretend sword? And in the dark for Christ's sake?''

Gaelinar waved Larson to him. ''When I was a *humble* and *lowly* student . . .'' He emphasized the adjectives with malicious glee. ''. . . we sparred blindfolded, standing on ice. When you can't see your opponent's body, you must fight his spirit, and strategy is ultimately a contest of spirits. By training on ice, I was forced to keep my consciousness centered during combat. Until you learn to cut with your spirit as well as your sword, you'll master neither your weapon nor yourself.''

Larson muttered beneath his breath, ''You'd think I'd be used to his nonsense by now.'' Cautiously, he approached Gaelinar. ''Fine, O most exalted swordmaster whom even the gods envy. What do you want me to do?''

Gaelinar ignored Larson's blatant sarcasm. ''Sweeps. As I showed you at your first lesson.''

Larson adjusted his stance. He clenched his hands together, as if to a hilt, and swung in high arcs. He pulled each strike just past his leg.

"Stop," Gaelinar said impatiently. "Is that how you would perform with a sword?"

Larson poised, left foot forward and weight evenly distributed. "Probably not."

"Try it again."

Larson realigned. He envisioned a long sword in his grip and attempted to maneuver once more. The movement felt more comfortable until, unbidden, a thought emerged in his mind. *It's like the old joke about the unarmed soldier who kills his enemies with a fake gun and bayonet while yelling "bangety-bang" or "stickety-stick" until a weaponless adversary tramples him, saying "tankety-tank."* The absurdity of the idea threw off Larson's timing.

Gaelinar shouted. "Allerum, keep your spirit and body in the same realm, please. Start again."

Larson lowered his arms. "I'm sorry, Gaelinar. I just can't take this 'pretend sword' stuff seriously. Maybe if you let me use yours, just for the practice, I . . ."

Gaelinar interrupted, his tone fiercely angry. "After what I just told you, you would dare ask me for my sword? Haven't you been listening at all?" Gaelinar gripped his hilt with such violence Larson took an involuntary backstep. "I've carried this sword longer than you've been alive. Only through years of diligent practice can a weapon become a part of your spirit. Do you expect me to hand over my soul to you because you gave away your sword?" He took a threatening step toward Larson. "Hundreds of years of tradition dictate I could kill you for that question. But it will be forgiven this time and only this time. Handling my sword would be as handling my person. Either would be unwise and at your own peril."

Stunned by Gaelinar's fury, Larson stammered. "I—I'm sorry. I . . . but . . . *you* touch *my* sword!"

Gaelinar relaxed, but his voice retained its deadly sharpness. "This katana was the sole labor of a master smith for five years and the culminating work of his glorious life. He delicately folded joined layers of hard and soft steel, hundreds upon hundreds of times, to create an edge that, in the proper hands and spirit, can cut through armor as if it didn't exist. Your sword . . ." Gaelinar snorted, and his tone softened. "Your sword was beaten on a rock by a fat drunkard barely able to call his life an existence. If such is a fitting receptacle for your soul, so be it."

For a moment, Larson stood in silent confusion. Then, righteous indignation boiled up within him. "I'll have you know, you just called Loki a fat drunkard! We both saw him. He was neither. And I think he would have called his life an existence." When Gaelinar did not interrupt, Larson's self-defense became a tirade. "Look. I come from another world. I don't know all your picky, piss-ant rules. Your society dictates that you kill a man for touching a sword? How the hell am I supposed to know that? What next?" He imitated Gaelinar's gutteral accent. "I'm sorry, hero, but my people behead nose-pickers. Sayanara, Allerum-san. Sukiyaki . . ."

Gaelinar's demeanor returned to normal. "Are you quite finished, hero?"

"I think so."

"Good." Gaelinar again adopted his teaching tone. "Admittedly, we're from different cultures, and we're going to have misunderstandings. Yet you must realize that when I've been taught to take certain things as insults for sixty years, I'm still going to consider them insults. I find insults intolerable. But notice, I didn't kill you."

Larson found it impossible to feel appreciative. "Gee, thanks."

Gaelinar continued. "I expect the same from you. I don't assume you will tolerate things you consider a personal affront from me." He added carefully, "But at least I do not compound my offenses with stupid questions. Now, hero. Change directions in the middle of an overhand strike."

I find nearly everything you say offensive. Americans are just too damn tolerant. Larson kept this thought to himself, believing the conversation had already dragged on too long. "All right." He assumed a fighting stance, his hands before him as if holding a sword. With a short, forward lunge, he raised his arms above his head, then spun on the balls of his feet and executed a strike. His left elbow smacked a pine trunk, shooting agony along his forearm. "Shit!" Larson danced into the clearing as the pain changed to a sensation of pins and needles.

The throb of his injured arm heaped upon the night's frustrations turned Larson's mood completely sour. He tilted his head and regarded Gaelinar through one eye. "Are you sure about this bullshit? Does a sword really work because of the intentions of the man, not the weapon?"

"Yes. It's not the weapon that cuts. It's the focusing of your spirit."

Larson spread his thumb and forefinger and aimed his imaginary gun at Gaelinar's chest. "Bangety-bang!"

Gaelinar's forehead crinkled. "What are you doing?"

"Just trying something." Larson smiled, feeling better for the charade.

"Fine, hero. Now try that strike again. And from now on, whenever you begin a kata, I expect you to finish it."

Larson massaged his aching elbow. "But I hit my funny bone."

Gaelinar caught at his own elbow in imitation and spoke in a perfect mockery of Larson's Bronx accent. "Excuse me, O most worthy opponent. I banged my arm. Please don't decapitate me."

Larson's practice continued deep into the night.

Later, over a breakfast of fresh berries and stale bread, Larson felt invigorated. Gaelinar had insisted on prolonging the sword session until Larson demonstrated some degree of competence. The successful cuts and figures Larson had executed at the conclusion of his practice left him with fonder memories of its last half hour. Now, he basked in the drying tingle of his own sweat and the feeling of accomplishment it represented. "Gaelinar, I know we arrived in Midgard at twilight. But, eventually, we're going to have to reverse our days and nights back to normal."

Gaelinar shrugged. "There are some few advantages to traveling at night."

Larson popped a handful of green, striped berries into his mouth. He recalled shadowy figures, all but invisible in Vietnam's darkness. For all their tanks, jets, and helicopters, the Americans had never conquered the jungle nights. "If you're used to it, I suppose. Otherwise, all the advantages belong to your enemies."

Gaelinar rose and tossed dirt on the fire, plunging them into moonless darkness. "Wolves hunt by sight. In daylight, Fenrir would see us better than we could avoid it. Night disadvantages it more than us."

Larson sighed, sprang to his feet, and helped the Kensei bury the remains of their camp. Wistfully, he wondered if he would ever see sunlight again. "Where are we going, anyway?"

"There's only one place we can find another person with Silme's power." Gaelinar paused, as if uncomfortable with his own revelation. "We're going to the school of Dragonrank magic."

Taziar Medakan kept a loose grip on the pine trunk, his legs braced on the branches beneath him. The tree swayed in the icy autumn breezes, but he felt confident on his carefully chosen perch. Across a stretch of fire-cleared plain stood the wall of the Dragonrank school; the late morning sun gave the granite an eerie red cast.

Taziar had studied the school since dawn, pacing the edges of the forest to define the square of wall which enclosed its grounds. He knew the gate occupied the center of the southern wall. A glance through it had revealed that the Dragonrank mages employed armed sentries in addition to whatever magics they used to protect their fortress. The walls towered to four times Taziar's height, and a climb to the highest secure boughs had gained him only a distant, ill-defined view of rows of buildings, boring in their similarity, and colorful gardens between them.

Suddenly, the gates swung open, and a loose formation of forty Dragonmages emerged. Taziar inched down between the needled branches, curious but fearing discovery. He scanned the disorderly ranks for a leader and singled out four sorcerers, each of whom held one of the trademark staves of the Dragonrank: a rod of polished and stained mahogany tapering to a carven dragon's claw, its black toenails gripping its owner's rankstone. Taziar recognized the gems in their staves as jadestones. Several of their followers carried translucent stones on thongs at their belts. Though faceted, the jewels' scratched and purpled interiors betrayed them as glass. Others fingered rock-sized bulges in their pockets. By their insecurity and quickness to obey their jade-rank masters' commands, these men and women were probably also of glass rank, the most inexperienced of the mages by Astryd's descriptions.

Once outside, the glass-rank sorcerers split into eight groups of four or five. The jade-rank leaders separated, one to each wall, while their students moved to the corners. For most of the morning, Taziar observed the two teams of glass-rank mages working from either corner of the western wall. Facing the granite, their backs to Taziar, they pointed fingers at varying levels of the stonework and muttered garbled, mystic syllables. Weak sparks bounced from the wall stones and fizzled out, leaving no recognizable traces. Then, moving half a step closer to the center of the western wall, the sorcerers would repeat the process.

Taziar had no means of identifying the glass-rank mages' spells, if, indeed, they were using magic, but he suspected their work might make his already rugged climb even more formidable. He was pleased to note that whenever their jade-rank teacher rushed over to reprimand one team, the members of the opposite group would slacken pace. When a flaw in the structure of the wall placed the northernmost crew into a hollow beyond sight of their master, the glass-rank students whispered conspiratorially. They yawned, worked cramps from their hands, and cast only a few spells along the narrow stretch of granite. *Like overtaxed apprentices everywhere,* Taziar noted their laxity with amusement. *But, this time, their negligence may work to my advantage.*

Gradually, dusk turned the sky pewter gray. A crescent moon rose, visible as a pale outline. As the trainee teams approached the center of the western wall, and one another, Taziar clambered from the tree. He crept deeper into the pine forest, stopping well beyond sight and sound of the Dragonrank school grounds. Rummaging through his pockets, he passed over half a dozen gold coins and a gaudy, emerald brooch filched from a gambler during a card game while the shyster smugly cheated Taziar out of a handful of coppers. From beneath the jewel, he retrieved a vial of fish skin glue and a thong. Using the knife at his belt, he shaved slices from the leather strip and blended them with the brown-tinged, transparent paste. A fraction of a drop of the juice of a weed berry gave the mixture the pinkish color Taziar sought.

Satisfied, Taziar used his concoction to craft a claw-shaped mark on the back of his right hand, a copy of the scar which marred Astryd's flesh. His garnet-rank lover had told him the symbol appeared, naturally, on the skin of any person destined to become Dragonrank; it remained as an identifying feature for the remainder of the sorcerer's life. Taziar flexed and extended his fingers while the compound dried, maintaining the freedom of movement he would need to scale the walls. He studied his handiwork with a frown. *Far from adequate, but it should pass a casual inspection in the dark.* He headed back toward the Dragonrank school.

By the time Taziar arrived at the edge of the forest, the sorcerers were gone. He assumed they had returned home to eat dinner and rest after a long day of hurling spells at a wall. *Or perhaps they're tearing through the woods seeking would-be thieves and unwelcome visitors.* Taziar dismissed the thought. *Surely, if they noticed me lurking about, they would have threatened or killed me by now. And the fact that most people believe it impossible to sneak into the school should keep such attempts rare. If I'm lucky, uncommon enough for their security to have become lax.*

Taziar smoothed wrinkles from his shirt and britches. The sun had slid fully below the western horizon, leaving the clearing in darkness. The sliver of moon seemed a welcome friend; Taziar had undertaken nearly all his major conquests in its presence. It hid his black-clothed form better than any phase but the new moon and still left him enough light by which to see. In Cullinsberg, where most citizens had known him as Taziar the junk merchant and a few as a night-stalking thief called the Shadow Climber, Taziar had worn a hood to prevent cross-recognition. Here the extra precaution seemed unnecessary, a form of dress which could only draw attention for its oddity.

Taziar dropped to a crouch, awash in the euphoric mixture of excitement and restlessness which came to him whenever he undertook an impossible task. He savored the accompanying clarity of thought and action which made the remainder of the world seem to move at half speed. Dropping to his chest, he belly-crawled across the cleared ground, tensed for sudden bursts of magic or verbal challenges. He arrived at the base of the wall without incident and examined the massive structure of granite.

Moonlight flashed from chips of pyrite in the stonework, and Taziar's mind registered something out of place. He hesitated, considering. As yet unable to identify this new source of concern, he crept to the depression in the wall where he had seen the glass-rank apprentices grow remiss in their duties. The wall lay flat gray and featureless before him. At the edges of his peripheral vision, the stone still appeared to glitter, lit by the meager glare of the moon and stars. Now, Taziar realized what had bothered him. The reflections formed a pattern of jagged lines not quite random enough to pass for a work of nature. *Magic.* Taziar smiled. *I can see it, so I can avoid it.*

Glad he had taken the time to observe the glass-ranks at work, Taziar found handholds in the stonework of the hollow. Cautiously, he shinnied upward. The granite felt rough and cool against his skin, and the challenge of its ascent seemed, somehow, appropriate. Taziar felt a strange sense of belonging, as if he had been born solely for this climb. He reveled in the sensation until, at a level twice his own height from the ground, he caught a glimpse of silver on the stone upon which he was about the place his fingers. He recoiled, catching his balance on the remainder of his limbs. Hunching closer, he examined a spot on the wall. It appeared dull and benign in the darkness. *Gone?* Too certain of his eyesight to doubt what he had seen, Taziar avoided the site as he continued his climb.

Three quarters of the distance up the wall of the Dragonrank school, Taziar wedged his fingers into an irregular crevice. Sudden pain stabbed through his hand. Instinctively, he jerked away. The movement jarred his toes free. He swung, smashed flat to the granite, clutching desperately to his one remaining handhold. Magic seared his abdomen where it touched the wall. He bit back a scream; it emerged as an anguished whimper. He scrabbled for a toehold, fighting his natural urge to fling himself away from the pain. The sorceries stung his hand and body relentlessly, like the barbs of woodland nettles.

The seconds it took Taziar to secure his position dragged like hours. He squeezed shut his watering eyes, clung to the wall, and nursed his throbbing hand. A breeze swirled around him, cool, gentle, and soothing. He savored its mundaneness as the pain diminished to a steady ache. Visually tracing his path to the summit, he discovered three more of the glowing areas. He winced, wondering why he could see them so clearly now when he had been unable to discern them up close. Without an answer, he memorized the positions of the spells above him. They seemed to disappear as he came upon them, but he avoided their remembered locations and arrived at the top without further incident.

Pressed to the stone, Taziar examined the layout of the Dragonrank school grounds. The night sky turned the scene into a blur of gardens and dormitories. Through a drab curtain of gray and black, Taziar perceived a palatial structure at its middle. It sported at least one crenelated tower, and Taziar could discern globs of oddly-shaped masonry on its roof and walls. One-story buildings, each with its own garden, radiated from it, spiraling outward toward the walls. Nearer the central structure, unidentifiable ivory or metallic figures studded the gardens, and the crops formed straight rows. Nearer the walls, the buildings became squatter and longer, the gardens less ornate.

Taziar shifted on the summit, craning his neck for a better view. *Apparently, the Dragonranks move closer to the center as they advance in skill. It seems likely they use the gardens for practice and training sessions. The outermost quarters could house half a dozen glass-rank mages apiece. The more powerful sorcerers probably live alone.* Taziar counted carefully. *Assuming no more than three actually live in the castle, a maximum of seventy-two sorcerers could reside here at any given time, of which fifty-four would hold a glass or other low rank.* Taziar considered. *Not many, given the necessary maintenance and chores to keep a fortress like this one. That explains why they hire sentries for routine duties such as guarding the gate.*

The area within the walls seemed larger than Taziar's walk around the outer perimeter implied. *Magic. It only makes sense.* The realization turned his thoughts back to his own predicament. *Even with the proper tools, few men could have scaled that wall. Had I not seen them placed and misplaced, the glass-rank sorcerers' spells would likely have killed or, at least, deterred me.* He shook his injured hand. The pain had subsided while he studied the grounds. *Now I'll need to dodge whatever sorcerous defenses lie inside the school as well as the magical and common soldiers which inhabit it. And I still have to find Astryd.* Memories of his lover fueled Taziar's desire, and the enormity of his task only made him more determined. He examined the inner side of the wall for telltale shimmerings of magic but saw none. Quickly, he shinnied down it into the Dragonrank school grounds.

Taziar descended onto the dirt path of a garden enclosed on the north by its accompanying building, by the outer wall to the west, and by whitewashed wooden fences on its other two sides. The walkway led to a gate in the opposite fence. It was crossed at several places by other paths which cut the garden into rectangular beds of soil. Several of the perpendicular routes led to the dormitory. Others dead-ended against the fence. A grotesque-appearing statue stood at the center of the garden, moss-covered and vaguely human in shape. A cluster of bushes graced the central edge of each of a dozen flower and vegetable beds.

Taziar knew he could climb any of the garden's boundaries without difficulty, but a casual stroll through the shadowed edges of the pathways and out through the gate seemed far more inconspicuous. A romp through the soil beds or over a building or gate would surely draw suspicion from anyone who might catch a glimpse of him in the darkness. Otherwise, they might mistake him for a glass-rank mage out for a walk in the night air.

This decided, Taziar started down the trail, prepared to hide at the first indication of unwanted company. He had taken only a couple of steps when something stung his forearm. He slapped at it automatically, cursing silently. A few paces later, a like pain stabbed through his opposite wrist. *Ach!* Taziar clamped his hand to the site. He had known insect stings before, and these felt remarkably similar. *But why should bees fly at night or attack unprovoked?* Taziar took a careful sidestep. The movement earned him another bite in the shoulder accompanied by the jangle of a bell.

The noise startled Taziar. He sprang behind one of the bushes. Moments later, the rhythmic pounding of running footsteps sounded on the path, coming from the direction of the building. An adolescent voice squealed, "My ward! Master Ingharr, did you hear? Someone set off my ward!"

Another voice reprimanded the first in a disdainful baritone. "Learn dignity, Kirbyr. I do not find an improperly placed spell praiseworthy or exciting. This would not be the first time your sloppy wards alarmed without cause."

Taziar flattened to the ground, heart pounding, as the men approached. He considered sprinting for the southern fence but doubted he could make it over without being spotted or setting off more wards. He lay still, hoping the sorcerers would pass by him in the dark.

Closer now, Kirbyr's voice trembled with repressed disappointment and anger. "Master, I-I set them right. I know I did. I swear I did. An intruder . . ."

"Kirbyr." Ingharr spoke with scornful condescension. "Magic incorrectly cast costs life energy, just less. One day, just by chance, you will channel your powers properly, drain your soul force, and you will die. You will die, Kirbyr, of your own laziness."

Taziar judged the Dragonrank mages now stood where he had triggered their ward. He was glad they continued to talk. His own breathing sounded far too loud.

Kirbyr seemed close to tears. "Master, please. I cast them properly."

"Very well." Ingharr adopted a teaching tone. "Let us say we have uncovered an intruder. What do you know about him already?"

Taziar remained immobile, wishing he had risked a run while he had the chance. Ingharr's nonchalance shocked him. No doubt, the sorcerer was in no hurry. He either felt certain of Kirbyr's ineptitude or he knew he was competent to handle anyone who dared to break into the Dragonrank school. So much so, he patiently used it as an opportunity to teach. That degree of arrogance usually arose from multiple successes, though Taziar knew that overconfidence could also become a weakness.

Apparently pleased to abandon the subject of his incompetence, Kirbyr responded to Ingharr's question with enthusiasm. "I know only that he triggered my wards. And, master, he may escape if we don't do something."

"Ah, my young fool. But you know much more." Ingharr shifted to stand on the pathway to the gate. "You know our intruder must be a thief and a foreigner."

The accuracy of Ingharr's guess surprised Taziar. He could now see the gray-robed outline of the elder Dragonrank mage. Ingharr had certainly chosen his position by design. His presence blocked Taziar's escape toward the garden gate. Even in the darkness, the sorcerer surely had a reasonably good view of the flower beds to either side of the pathway. Taziar's only logical means of evasion lay back the way he had come. But once he had climbed partway up the wall, he would become an easily visible target.

Kirbyr seemed stumped by his mentor's logic. "How do you know he's a thief and a foreigner?"

"Easy, Kirbyr." Ingharr's volume increased, and Taziar suspected the mage phrased his explanation as much to scare the potential intruder as to inform his student. "A sorcerer would never have blundered clumsily into a glass-rank apprentice's wards. A swordsman bent on murder would have tried to slay us by now. Theft is the only other rational motive. And only a foreigner could be stupid or ignorant enough to attempt to penetrate our school. The natives know what we did to the last thief we caught.'' He spoke even louder. ''We used him for spell practice: fire, pain, mutilation. We seared out his eyes with lightning strikes. We burned his fingers to shriveled stumps. We tore his body and soul apart, piece by piece. He screamed for two days before he died . . . and three days after.''

Taziar shivered, certain Ingharr was baiting him, yet chilled by his evil tone and description. In choosing to remain still, he had chosen wrongly. Undoubtedly, Ingharr knew he lay within earshot. Taziar would have to slip away, quickly and silently, to retain any chance of surviving this encounter. His one advantage seemed to be Ingharr's insistence on turning this into a learning experience for Kirbyr. Trusting to his black clothing and hair to hide him and the sorcerers' conversation to mask his progress, Taziar inched back toward the outer wall.

Kirbyr seemed discomforted by his master's narrative. He said nothing.

Ingharr returned to his lesson with an abruptness which made his prior threat sound even more menacing. ''Kirbyr, what shall we do with our foreign thief?''

Kirbyr spoke tentatively. ''Spell of slaying?''

Taziar crept faster. As the wall loomed before him, he turned ninety degrees toward the white-washed fence. He hoped it was the type of maneuver Ingharr would not anticipate. If he could slip closer, a mad dash and climb over the southern fence would become Taziar's only chance to find Astryd or escape Kirbyr's garden. A barrage of ''bee stings'' made his journey even more uncomfortable, but luck or Kirbyr's lack of skill kept him from triggering another of the apprentice's audible alarms.

Ingharr went pensive. ''Slaying spell, you say? You're awfully free with my power, aren't you, Kirbyr? And would you have me cast it at random or do you know the precise location of your imaginary thief?''

''Oh.'' Kirbyr hesitated a moment. ''First, a locating triangle.''

Taziar wriggled across the dirt. Moonlight polished the smooth white of the fence, still several body lengths away. Even in the shadow of the next building, Taziar knew his dark dress would work against him clambering, unseen, over the barrier.

"Well thought out plan." The scathing sarcasm in Ingharr's voice was unmistakable. "By the time I'd finished, our thief would have whatever he wanted, and I'd have too little life energy left to cast your slaying spell. Think simple, Kirbyr. How about . . . this!" His voice rose on the last syllable.

Taziar heard a click. A sudden flash shattered his vision. He rolled, stifling a startled scream. Jagged bands of light striped his retinas. He jammed his lids closed, not daring to move until his sight cleared.

Slowly, Taziar opened his eyes. Brilliant, white magic lit a perfect square of the garden like the noonday, summer sun. Around Ingharr's sorceries, the world remained dark as pitch. Taziar noted, with relief, that he lay just beyond the edges of the spell.

"And this!" screamed Ingharr.

Taziar dove behind a bush as light exploded around him, illuminating a second square beside the first. But this one included Taziar, his arms drawn tightly before him. The spells had come too fast, leaving him no time to think. He had chosen this bush because it stood closest. But it was small. A larger man would have found it no protection at all. Even Taziar was uncertain whether it hid him completely from the sorcerers.

Taziar held his breath as a minute crawled mercilessly past. A breeze ruffled the branches, and tiny leaves tickled his face. He knew the end would come fast, and he resented the fact that he would meet it crouched and cringing behind a bush. But he also realized movement of any sort would seal his fate. He had no choice but to wait and hope Ingharr could not see him.

Ingharr's voice boomed through the silence. "Are you satisfied?"

The magical lights winked out, plunging Taziar back into darkness. He paused, allowing his eyes to readjust.

"But, master. I was so certain." Kirbyr sounded sullen. "Maybe he sneaked away while we talked. We waited an awfully long time before . . ."

"Silence!" Anger colored Ingharr's reply. "I can tolerate an apprentice sorcerer who makes mistakes. But an apprentice sorcerer who makes mistakes and refuses to admit them becomes a danger to me and to himself. Admit it, Kirbyr. You misplaced your wards."

There was no response.

Taziar crawled toward the fence which formed the southernmost border of the garden. The mages' voices grew fainter as they walked toward the dormitory building. Taziar smiled in relief.

"Say it, Kirbyr!" Ingharr screamed.

Taziar could not make out the words to Kirbyr's incoherent grumble, but it seemed to satisfy Ingharr. As the Cullinsbergen stood and broke into a hunched run, the elder Dragonrank mage spoke.

"Kirbyr, an inferior enemy should be played. No one 'sneaked away while we talked.' My keen sight and hearing would have detected . . ." His words faded into the distance.

Mardain's mercy, I made it! Taziar grinned in triumph, only three strides from the fence. Suddenly, he struck something unyielding. Light slammed into his eyes, etching red streaks in his vision. His sight of the barrier vanished in a whooshing ball of flame. Fire seared his left arm and set his shirt ablaze. Screaming, Taziar reeled backward. Heat waves shimmered the air before him, bright green and unlike anything he had seen before. He hit the ground with bruising force, and the world plunged into oblivion.

Taziar awoke to pain and darkness. His arm and side still felt on fire. His head ached. By the position of the moon, he realized he had fallen unconscious only a few moments ago. Groggily, his mind registered the sound of approaching footsteps, and he sat up as two gray robed figures came up to him.

"Who are you, boy?" the taller one demanded.

Taziar recognized the voice as Ingharr's. He winced, cradling his injured arm to stall for time. Apparently, the

Dragonrank mage had mistaken Taziar's slightness for immaturity, and Taziar sought a means to capitalize on Ingharr's error. Dizzy with pain, he mimicked the higher-pitched, frightened voice of a child in his best Norwegian accent. "I-I-I. I'm a glass-rank. J-just arrived tonight, master. Please. Don't-don't hurt me any more." He cringed.

"Dragonrank?" Ingharr's voice conveyed bitter disbelief. His eyes crinkled, and he glanced about the garden as if to trace Taziar's route. "Where did you come from?"

Taziar raised his right arm and pointed a shaking finger toward the gate in the eastern fence. The trembling was no act. The burns and his fall had sapped Taziar's strength.

Kirbyr piped up excitedly. "See, master. Someone did trip my ward."

Ingharr waved his apprentice silent. "Did you set off Kirbyr's spell?"

Suspecting it would be safer to lie as little as possible, Taziar nodded, studying his wounds. The fire had melted huge holes in his sleeve and side. The flesh beneath appeared bright red and had already begun to blister.

Ingharr persisted. "Then you heard us talking."

Taziar met Ingharr's stare with widened, blue eyes. "Yes, sir."

"That's 'yes, *master.*' And why didn't you speak up then?"

Taziar let wild anger seep into his voice. "You scared all hell from me, s . . . master. You were going to burn my eyes out and use slaying spells and everything."

Kirbyr added. "And tear his body and soul apart."

"Silence!" Ingharr raised a warning hand toward his apprentice.

Taziar bit back a smile. He seemed to have found an ally. *At worst, Kirbyr's childish exuberance might distract Ingharr.* Night muted the sorcerers' features to blurs, but Kirbyr's blond ringlets and pearly skin were easily visible. Though he held no rankstone in evidence, a telltale lump distended his hip pocket. A sword swung at his opposite side. Ingharr appeared darker. He carried a dragonstaff with a garnet clutched in its claw.

"You don't look or talk like any Northerner I've ever met," Ingharr challenged.

Taziar pursed his lips. He knew Dragonrank mages were a Norwegian phenomenon. South of the Kattegat, only a few seasoned travelers had even heard of sorcerers, and most believed them only as mothers' stories. But Ingharr's swarthy features encouraged Taziar to defend his claim. "I was born and raised in Cullinsberg." He spoke the truth, but saw no way around the lie which followed. "My father was a Viking. A guilty conscience returned him to my mother last year, and he recognized the Dragonmark on me."

Ingharr hesitated. He had to notice Taziar's story, though unlikely, demonstrated knowledge of the Dragonrank school few outsiders could have. "Show me the mark."

Taziar held out his right arm, displaying his doctored scar. When Ingharr reached for a closer look, Taziar clamped his hand to his burn. "I hurt," he pouted.

Kirbyr chimed in helpfully. "You triggered Master Ingharr's ward." He gestured toward his mentor. "A strong one, too."

The immediate danger past, Taziar stumbled to his feet, silently cursing wasted time. He still needed to find Astryd and escape before daylight. "I have to go now. Mistress Astryd may get mad if I'm late."

"Wait." Ingharr stepped between Taziar and the path to the gate. "Your rankstone. I want to see it."

Taziar's chest tightened. Sidestepping the garnet-rank mage, he stalled, adopting a childlike bravado. "No! You threatened me. You called me 'thief' and 'foreigner.' You hurt me, and you made me late for my mistress. I was told to protect my rankstone. Leave me alone."

Ingharr's tone turned menacing. "Show me your rankstone. Now, boy! Or I'll give you a sample of real pain." He signaled Kirbyr with a brisk sweep of his fingers.

Taziar tensed to run, aware he had no further tricks. He considered drawing his sword and rushing the sorcerer, but he doubted his mediocre skill with weapons would serve against a garnet-rank Dragonmage, especially in his weakened state.

Kirbyr caught Taziar's shoulder. The glass-rank mage's sword sheath slapped the Cullinsbergen's thigh. "My master wants to see your rankstone."

Kirbyr's nearness gave Taziar an idea. *And so he shall.* With subtlety gained from years of practice on the streets, he flicked his hand into Kirbyr's hip pocket. Seizing the apprentice's rankstone, he deftly flipped it into a fold of his black britches. The maneuver took less than a second, and Tazier held Ingharr's gaze throughout it. Chin jutting, he displayed Kirbyr's gem-cut glass stone as his own.

Kirbyr's grip loosened. Ingharr took the glass from Taziar and studied it at arm's length, then immediately before his face. He spoke harsh, wordless noises, and the rankstone glowed a brilliant, opaque yellow.

Taziar held his breath, hoping the spell would not reveal the owner of the stone.

Ingharr seemed satisfied. "It's a rankstone. Apparently, you've stored most of your life force in it which explains why I can't see your aura." He offered the stone to Taziar. "What's your name, boy?"

Taziar accepted the glass piece and placed it in his pocket. The first Scandinavian name to come to his mind belonged to a barbarian prince in Sweden. "Manebjorn. Please, master. I have to go. I've obviously wandered into the wrong garden. Where can I find Mistress Astryd?"

"There." Ingharr pointed toward the center of the school grounds. "Leave here through the gate. Follow the road straight. Turn right after the second building, and you'll find the entrance to Astryd's garden on your left."

"Thank you." Taziar trotted down the pathway. The rapid motion jogged pain through his side, but he wanted to leave the garden before Ingharr found more errors in his story.

"Manebjorn, stop!"

Reluctantly, Taziar turned.

Ingharr came up beside him. "Don't move, young fool.

You nearly ran into another of my wards. Didn't the arch-master teach you how to avoid them?''

Taziar shook his head, covering his ignorance as well as he could. ''He said so much, master. I can't recall.''

''Then I will remind you.'' Comfortably, Ingharr slipped back into his teaching role. ''The wards become visible if you don't look at them. What do you see before you?''

Taziar stared. ''A dirt roadway, master,'' he admitted.

''Now.'' Ingharr inclined his head toward the center of the garden. ''Look there.''

''I see a shabby-looking statue.''

''Hey!'' Kirbyr protested the insult to what was, apparently, his magical artwork.

Ingharr loosed a snort which Taziar suspected was a politely suppressed laugh. ''What do you see here?'' He indicated the roadway.

Gaze fixed on the stone figure, Taziar studied the path from the edge of his vision. Just before him, glimmering, narrow bands crossed the walkway in an intertwining pattern. Smaller, less dramatic wards hovered throughout the garden. Taziar recalled the difficulties he had had locating the magics on the wall stones. Now, it all made sense. He knew Ingharr's revelation would serve him well. ''Thank you, Master Ingharr,'' he said with genuine gratitude and left the garden as quickly as possible.

After Taziar's run-in with the Dragonrank mages, dodging spear-toting sentries in the roadways seemed like play. Under normal circumstances, he would have enjoyed the simple challenges eluding guards demanded. But the left half of his body alternated between numbness and excruciating pain, making his usually careful dodges seem unprofessional and clumsy. The pathways outside the gardens contained no magical wards, and Taziar suspected the Dragonmages did not permit the guardsmen in their private gardens. *That would explain why the sorcerers trap their gardens so thoroughly, and yet the sentries can still move freely.*

Four flawless, clean, stone walls enclosed Astryd's residence. Taziar found the gate where Ingharr had told him to look for it. But a complicated ward filled the entryway like a huge, glimmering spider web. It seemed odd to Taziar that anyone would create a gateway, only to render it unusable. As he clambered painfully over the granite wall, he wondered how Astryd entered and left her own garden.

Once inside, Taziar studied the garden from the corners of his eyes and memorized the pattern of Astryd's wards. Skirting them, he followed a winding pathway to Astryd's home. The soil beds on either side sported plump vegetables of varieties Taziar had never seen. He paid them little heed. Born and raised in a crowded city, he knew nothing of the farmer's livelihood. Cullinsberg's food supply came from trade with neighboring towns, hunting, and the bakers' skills with grains from the city's holdings.

At the center of Astryd's courtyard, Taziar paused to examine its single statue. An alabaster horse supported a rider dressed in a simple tunic and breeks. A wine glass in the figure's hand spouted water into a basin on the ground between the animal's dancing forelegs. Taziar could not imagine a carving tool which could have rendered the fountain's surface as smooth as it appeared. But what impressed him most was the rider's features. The face bore a striking likeness to his own. He stared, wondering if this was Astryd's idea of a tribute. *Though, surely, she never expected me to see it.* Flattered, he continued toward Astryd's building.

As Taziar reached the doorway, anticipation filled him with eager excitement. More than a month had passed since he had last seen Astryd, but he recalled her features as if she had departed only yesterday. She stood smaller than him, an asset few women and fewer men shared. She sported the taut, lithe frame of a young swordsman or a dancer. She had a boldness and cunning beyond that of any person Taziar had known since his days with the street gang. Though plain, her face was in its own way attractive; it had become the standard by which he measured beauty.

As Taziar raised his hand to tap on Astryd's door, doubts assailed him. *What if she's forgotten me? What if time has allowed her to realize it was her rankstone, not my charm, which made her fall for me?* He rejected his questions as they arose. *She knows that already, and she claimed it didn't matter. And her fountain would suggest she still cares for me.* He knocked as his fears of rejection turned his thoughts to raving paranoia. *Unless she uses my likeness for target practice.*

Before Taziar could pursue the idea, the door swung open. Astryd stood in the doorway. She wore a faded pink sleeping gown which in no way revealed the gentle curves of her figure. Her blonde hair hung in tangled disarray. As she stared, her eyes lost the glaze of slumber and filled with open astonishment. Her jaw sagged.

Taziar spoke with matter-of-fact politeness. "Good evening, Astryd."

"Shadow," she whispered. Suddenly, she caught him by the arm and jerked him into the hallway.

Caught by surprise, Taziar staggered. He heard the door slam shut behind him as Astryd seized him around the waist and half dragged him past several curtained or open entryways and into a room at the farther end of the hall. Again, he heard a wooden door close. Astryd swept him into a hug.

For some time, they clung in a silent embrace. Astryd's closeness filled Taziar with warm desire. He caught her lips in a passionate kiss, assessing the layout of the room over her shoulder. Behind Astryd, a bed lay, rumpled from sleep. Closed wooden trunks lined the walls on either side, and a shelf at the farther end held a jumble of bric-a-brac, including a transparent pitcher filled with water. Beside it, an oil lamp bathed the room with light. *The bedroom,* Taziar guessed. *How convenient.* He maneuvered Astryd down against the wrinkled sheets and blankets.

Astryd resisted, scrambling out from beneath him to face him from across the bed. "Shadow, stop it! Not now. We need to talk. Why? How?"

Taziar smiled. Here with Astryd, all his pain seemed unimportant. "Could you be more specific?" he asked.

She cocked her head and placed her hands on her hips with mock sternness, studying him in the lamplight.

"How did you get by . . ." She broke off with a gasp. "Shadow, you're hurt."

"Just a scratch," Taziar lied, dropping his left arm into the shadow of his body.

"Take off your shirt."

Not wanting to worry Astryd, Taziar protested. "But I don't need . . ."

"Take it off, Taziar Medakan. Or, I'll rip it off you."

"That sounds like fun." Taziar joked, trying to downplay his injuries. The entire left side of his body throbbed, and the exertion of climbing and running had begun to wear on him. Obediently, he removed his ruined shirt. The linen scratched the blisters on his arm and ribs, reawakening the sharp agony of his burns. Gritting his teeth against the pain, he sat on the edge of the bed.

Astryd took a seat beside him and reached for the raw and swollen areas of his skin.

Taziar flinched away.

"Just a scratch," Astryd mimicked in a wry singsong. "So why did you try to jump off the bed when I looked at it?"

Taziar said nothing. A half blind beggar could see the jagged red burn which ran from his shoulder nearly to his hip, splotched yellow-white with fluid-filled blisters.

"Hold still. I can make it feel better." Gently, Astryd took Taziar's arm, inflicting a fresh wave of pain. She ran her fingers across his shoulder, her touch cold as metal in winter. "I hope this wasn't caused by one of *my* wards. You know, Shadow, if you'd come through the gate, rather than over it, you would have tripped my signal spell. I could have escorted you around my defenses. Why do you always have to do things the hard way?"

That explains the sorceries across her entryway, Taziar mused. Astryd's caress soothed the ache of his wound, and he felt more comfortable as her hand slid along his arm. "It was Ingharr's ward. And while I'm thinking of it, return this to Kirbyr when you get a chance." He retrieved the glass rankstone with his uninjured hand and tossed it to the balled coverlet.

Astryd followed the stone's flight. "A Dragonmage

would sooner give up his eyes than his rankstone. How did you get it?''

Where Astryd had touched Taziar, the blisters disappeared and the flush waned. ''Kirbyr didn't give it up willingly.'' At Astryd's horrified glance, he clarified. ''Don't worry. I didn't hurt him. I stole it.'' While Astryd inched her healing magics across Taziar's puckered skin, he described his experiences infiltrating the school and its protections.

Astryd listened with rapt attention.

Taziar finished as Astryd ran her sorceries along his side. ''. . . But I can't understand why Ingharr lets Kirbyr get away with his annoying, childish whining.''

Astryd smiled knowingly. ''Sometimes we do spoil the glass-ranks.'' Her voice went soft.

Taziar realized Astryd's healing magics had weakened her, and guilt twinged through him. Apparently, the spell was a difficult and taxing one; it had significantly drained her life energy.

''As you know, only one eligible jade-rank can advance to garnet each year.'' Astryd met Taziar's gaze, her fingertips resting against him. ''The others must abandon any further education here. Despite the law forbidding Dragonmages lesser than garnet from killing other Dragonmages, the competition gets evil and fierce.''

Taziar nodded. One such conflict had brought him and Astryd together.

''Once garnet, a Dragonrank mage loses all need to compete, but the rivalry has often become ingrained. So the schoolmaster decided to assign glass-rank apprentices to each garnet.''

Taziar grimaced. ''Sounds lethal for the glass-ranks.''

''Doesn't it?'' Astryd's fingers circled Taziar's ribs. ''You'd be surprised. The time demanded by our training prevents nearly everyone from having a family. The glass-ranks, especially the young ones, become like our own children. We protect them, teach them, and boast about their abilities. It's a proud moment when one's own apprentice becomes a jade-rank graduate. It redirects the competition. Of course, we're not allowed to participate in *their* rivalry in any way.''

Astryd continued. ''Apparently, Kirbyr has become Ingharr's prodigy. Besides, Shadow. There are other reasons to tolerate some glass-rank foolishness. Someday, one of Ingharr's apprentices may become more powerful, and of higher rank, than him. Ingharr wouldn't want his student to recall the time his master punished him for silliness by holding him underwater until he lost consciousness.'' She considered. ''Though I doubt Kirbyr could ever become more powerful than Ingharr.''

Astryd's movements grew sluggish. Her eyelids drooped.

Noting Astryd's somnolence, Taziar redirected the conversation to the school's defenses. He held no illusions that his escape would be much easier than his break-in, even with the knowledge Ingharr had imparted. ''You once told me a Dragonmage's worst enemy is another Dragonmage. But it seems to me an enemy wizard could find a way over the walls, if he didn't already live here. And he would surely know how to avoid the wards.'' Nothing remained of Taziar's burn but a faded pink scar and an occasional flattened blister. Not wishing to weaken Astryd further, he reached for his shirt before she could continue her healing.

''The school's actually far better protected against sorcerers than thieves. We have a law against Dragonmages at the school killing one another, and the schoolmaster has ways of finding and dealing with criminals. Not very pretty, I'm afraid. Magic, by its nature, functions best against creations or users of magic. The ward which harmed you might have killed Kirbyr. And most of our spells work only when used for or against sorcerers. For example, an invisible barrier lines our outer walls and forms a ceiling over the school. Any attempt to pass through by magical means would result in the sorcerer's death. It's a powerful spell, the result of years of high rank cooperation. No one has managed to create anything similar to use against nonmagical creatures; if possible at all, such a spell would prove far more challenging to invent or to cast.''

Carefully, Taziar pulled on his shirt.

"For a sorcerer, the only safe entrance is our front gate. And we have protections there, too. You, however, blundered unscathed through wards which would have killed the most powerful diamond-rank master."

Taziar mulled over Astryd's explanation. Though confident of his own abilities, he was not arrogant enough to believe no other thief could have sneaked into the Dragonrank school. Still, the mundane and magical defenses would have thwarted all but a handful of men and women. Of those capable of penetrating the training grounds, few or none would have good cause. *By Astryd's descriptions, any mage above glass-rank could defeat all but the most skilled and cunning warrior. It seems strange that I could survive magics which would kill a sorcerer.* Yet, somehow, it seemed appropriate, part of the natural scheme of the gods to assure mankind's survival. Most societies had some moratorium against soldiers killing civilians; and, aside from the odd plague, fatal diseases were always rarer than those the body could overcome.

Astryd stretched, arching her arms overhead.

Taziar watched her, awed as always by her beauty. Fatigue had slowed her words and movements, but it diminished none of her natural grace and charm. Staring, he fell in love with her again. Jealousy of the Dragonrank school which held her as student and prisoner stirred within him. He scooted closer to her, aware they had whiled away precious time deliberating matters of no importance. He also knew why they had kept their conversation to trivia. The Dragonrank school's defenses, the wards in Astryd's courtyard, the relationship between Ingharr and Kirbyr, all kept Astryd and Taziar from addressing the single issue they needed to discuss: themselves. Now, Taziar stared at his feet, fighting the wellspring of emotion Astryd's closeness inspired. In his life, he had made her only two vows. He had already fulfilled the first; he had found a way to enter the forbidden school grounds to see her again. He had also sworn never to interfere with her Dragonrank training. At the time, he meant both with equal assurance. He knew he could no more deny her the right to her power and schooling than she could deny him the reckless thefts and escapades which kept his life interesting. Yet here in her presence, his good intentions seemed to crumble. "I have to go soon," he mumbled, afraid of what he might say. "I'll see you next week?"

"No." Astryd's voice went firm, but her expression betrayed a hint of grief. "By morning, Ingharr will know we have no new glass-rank named 'Manebjorn.' He'll change security. If you're caught, they'll kill you . . . and perhaps me, as well. Shadow, I love you. But you mustn't ever return. When vacation time comes, I'll find you."

Taziar met Astryd's moist, blue eyes, and she looked away quickly. Her welling tears hurt him worse than her rejection. He caught her hand and thoughtlessly mouthed the words he had promised himself never to say to her. "Astryd, marry me." Even as he spoke, he knew he should not have forced her into such a decision.

Her grip tightened about his. She turned back to him, her face now composed. "You know I can't."

"I'm sorry." Taziar hid disappointment behind humor. "I went wildly insane, but I think I have it under control now."

Astryd's forehead crinkled thoughtfully. "Unless . . ." She dismissed the idea with a grin. "My turn to go insane."

Taziar leaped on the opening. "Unless?"

"Unless nothing. I made a mistake."

"Unless," Taziar repeated relentlessly. "I distinctly heard you say 'unless.' "

"All right." Astryd went defensive. I said 'unless.' I made a mistake. I had a thought, but I realized it would be impossib . . ." Astryd broke off suddenly, her expression pained; apparently she knew Taziar too well.

Excitement suffused Taziar. Despite the trials of his break-in and a day and a night without sleep, he felt suddenly wide awake. The lure of a task deemed impossible inspired him every bit as much as the chance to marry Astryd. "Explain. Let me decide if it's impossible."

Astryd sighed resignedly. "Very well. But only because I know you won't leave until I do. If you stay here much longer, we'll get caught and killed.'' She squeezed his fingers affectionately, which softened the reprimand. ''In order for me to gain rank, I have to remain at the school. But the attainment of power and ability requires only practice, initiative, and guidance. I could leave the school and still reach my potential if a high ranking Dragonmage would accept me as an apprentice.''

Taziar tapped his thumb on his knee as he considered. ''You'd always be garnet-rank?''

''True. But that doesn't matter. The rank itself is only a symbol. A king without a crown is still a king. The color of the gem in my staff doesn't matter if I've gained the knowledge of a master.''

It sounded too simple to Taziar. ''So all I'd need to do is find a Dragonrank outside the school willing to train you? That doesn't sound impossible.''

Astryd drifted to her back and stared at the ceiling. ''It would have to be a sorcerer of ultimate advancement, a diamond-rank master or a sapphire-rank, at least. I know of only one of each, siblings locked in a bitter war who would have better things to do than concern themselves with a Dragonmage of comparatively insignificant experience. Bramin, the diamond-rank, would gleefully torture you to death for no cause. Silme might listen, but her powers and attention are stretched far enough trying to protect the world from Bramin's evil. Her assistant takes a dim view of anyone he considers incompetent.''

''Assistant?'' Taziar lay down beside Astryd. ''If Silme can handle one assistant, why not another?''

Astryd snickered at a private joke. ''He's not that type of assistant. Gaelinar's a ronin samurai and quite capable of taking care of himself.''

Taziar shot bolt upright. ''Gaelinar?'' He whirled toward Astryd, catching her arm in an anxious grip. ''Did you say Gaelinar?''

''Yes. Why? Do you know him?''

''Not yet.'' Astryd's words reminded Taziar of the real purpose of his visit. The challenges of his entrance and his love for Astryd had allowed him to forget. ''I need to locate this Gaelinar as quickly as possible. This may sound ridiculous, but many lives depend on it. Can you do some sort of . . . 'Gaelinar-finding' spell?''

Astryd laughed, but stopped abruptly when she met Taziar's solemn gaze. ''You're not joking.''

Taziar shook his head.

''The location triangle is not in my regular repertoire. I haven't enough practice to try it with my life aura partially spent. I've drained it far too low healing you.''

Taziar cursed himself ruthlessly. His delay in raising the most critical issue might have jeopardized matters far more crucial than his relationship with Astryd. ''Save your strength. I'll be back, Astryd. I'll just have to handle whatever additional protections Ingharr takes. We have no choice.'' Before Astryd could protest, Taziar rose, retraced his steps to the outer doorway, and disappeared into the twilight.

CHAPTER 5:

Schoolmaster

"Example is the school of mankind, and they will learn at no other."

—Edmund Burke
Letters on a Regicide Peace

Al Larson and Kensei Gaelinar emerged from the twilit depths of the pine forest to stand before the forbidding walls which enclosed the Dragonrank school. The first stray sun rays illuminated circles of quartz set in the stonework, making it appear to shimmer with magics. Larson stared at the twenty feet of cold granite which barred his entry into a world of secrecy and sorcery where, he knew, Silme had spent eleven months of every year for a decade and a half until she abandoned her training to protect innocents from Bramin's wrath. "Want to make camp?"

Gaelinar said nothing. His yellow-brown eyes probed the dawn.

"Gaelinar?"

The Kensei made a sharp, cutting motion with his hand.

Taking Gaelinar's gesture as a plea for silence, Larson stopped speaking. He tried to discern the cause of Gaelinar's concern but found only the ceaseless trill of insects and a blank stretch of wall.

Gaelinar crept forward, his movements calculated and quiet. His fingers rested on the brocade of his katana.

Larson's breathing went soft and rapid with anticipation. Cautiously, he followed Gaelinar. As his mentor's stalk became more directed, Larson glimpsed a blurred movement. His eyes traced the outline of a figure, soundlessly descending the wall stones. It was small, dressed from hood to boots in black. *A woman or child,* Larson guessed. The stranger moved with graceful ease. Each shaded stone seemed to conform itself to his or her position. The fading fragment of moon was not bright enough to reveal the climber as more than a shifting shadow.

Gaelinar waited, nearly touching the wall. Before Larson could think to stop the Kensei, his katana leaped from its sheath and cut a silver arc through the grayness. The unsharpened side of its blade impacted the climber's knuckles with a painful slap. The black-cloaked form plummeted, twisted like a cat in midair, and struck the ground with bent knees. Larson caught a brief glimpse of a pale face, etched with surprise and horror.

The point of Gaelinar's katana poised, dangerously near the stranger's throat. "Prepare to die, worm."

The climber crouched, tensed to dodge. His voice was a masculine tenor. "What did I do?" His harsh, German accent mangled the thick melody of the Norwegian tongue.

Gaelinar remained alert and unmoving. "Your people have plagued me since I can remember. You're not a man. You're a disease." He raised his sword for a killing stroke.

Alarmed, Larson caught the Kensei's shoulder. "What the hell?"

Menaced from behind, Gaelinar spun, redirecting his strike. For an instant, the sword hovered threateningly above Larson's head. Then, sputtering curses in Japanese, Gaelinar whirled back to the stranger.

But the man was gone.

Gaelinar slammed his sword into its sheath and rounded on Larson, his olive-skinned face flushed pink with rage. "You had no right to interfere."

"No right to interfere!" Larson's features turned as dark as his mentor's. "You don't even know that man. You were going to kill him for no reason."

Gaelinar scanned the wall, apparently seeking the black-suited stranger. "Just because you don't see a reason, doesn't mean it doesn't exist. You've been hunted by that wolf for a couple of days, and I'm certain you wish it dead. I've been hunted for ten years."

Larson still found no logic to Gaelinar's motives. "You've been hunted by a German midget less than a third your age and maybe a hundred pounds soaking wet? That man can't be more than twenty years old. How could he have stalked you ten of them? And what were you going to do? Sentence him to death for climbing a wall?"

Gaelinar's hands balled to angry fists. "Quiet! I've had enough of your insolence. You won't earn the right to speak to me again until you've learned the proper respect for your superior and your teacher."

Larson clenched his teeth, scarcely able to contain his indignation. "How dare . . ."

Quick as a cobra, Gaelinar caught Larson's sword arm with his left hand. His right pinched Larson's throat closed. His voice was a menacing rasp. "Don't you dare." As suddenly, he released his grip.

Silently, Larson backed toward the forest, quivering with raw fury at Gaelinar's attack. Driven beyond sane reasoning, he drew his daggers, angling their tips between himself and Gaelinar. "Damn you. I have something to say, and I'm going to talk." He hesitated, watching the Kensei's hands for any sign of movement. "You're not the world's sole repository of wisdom. You almost killed a stranger out of hand. How can someone who's lived as long as you have so little respect for human life?"

To Larson's surprise, Gaelinar's lips formed a grim smile. "Put the knives away. You know they won't do you any good."

Larson remained crouched, not daring to allow the Kensei too close.

With a snort of amusement, Gaelinar continued. "You're not the brightest student I've ever taught. You're neither the fastest nor the most capable. But you've got more nerve than any three of them together. It's precisely because I have lived so long that I've lost respect for human life. People are content to toil their lives away for mere survival. They give no consideration to honor or glory. If they place no value on their lives, why should I?''

Larson's anger faded slightly, and he sheathed his daggers. ''You've got the audacity to judge the value of other people's lives?''

Gaelinar shrugged. ''The value of a life is the same as the value of anything else. If a man's not strong enough to keep it, he doesn't deserve to have it.''

''How can you say that!'' Larson had grown sick of a mentality he had come to consider adolescent. ''Life isn't property. Life is sacred.''

''Flaws like that are why you're the hero.'' Gaelinar's expression went as solemn as his words. ''The belief that human life is special is dangerous and expensive. Remember what it did to Silme.''

Larson considered, finding a disturbing truth in Gaelinar's explanation. He knew his own unshakable faith in the sanctity of human life was the cause of his deep-set feelings of guilt and, ultimately, of the flashbacks, hallucinations, and nightmares which had plagued him since leaving the war in Vietnam. But it was a morality instilled since childhood, by caring parents, a free society, and The United Church of Christ. He doubted he could escape it, nor did he want to. ''Gaelinar,'' he said. ''This is one of those times when our cultures and upbringings clash. If I see you trying to kill someone without a good reason, I will try to stop you.''

Gaelinar's eyes went hard as diamonds. ''Very well. But if you come between me and our enemies, you will hamper our chances for survival. And if I feel I must slay someone, neither you nor any man on Midgard could keep me from it.''

Larson hesitated. Nearly all his anger had dispersed, leaving him feeling uncertain and somewhat repentant for having challenged his teacher. ''I understand,'' he said at length. ''But I hope it never comes to that.'' He turned and headed deeper into the woods. ''Come on, Gaelinar. I'm sick to death of arguing. Let's make camp and get some rest.''

Al Larson and Kensei Gaelinar slept through the remainder of the morning and well into the day. After a sword practice far more satisfying than the one of the previous night, and a breakfast scavenged from the forest, Larson felt ready to face the Dragonrank school and its master. "So what's it like inside?" He imagined stony-faced youths in neat rows transforming one another into newts and toads. The vision made him smile.

Gaelinar paced to the tree line and studied the granite wall which confined the sorcerer's school. "I don't know."

"What do you mean? Didn't Silme give you the grand tour?"

Gaelinar followed the eastern wall southward. A breeze fanned his robes into a golden flower. "I only know the outside. Silme had business here once, but I waited for her in the woods." He flicked his fingers to indicate the forest of birch and evergreen in which they had made camp. "The Dragonrank don't welcome outsiders, and they allow their trainees no visitors."

Larson trailed Gaelinar around a sharp corner, continuing westward. Ahead, halfway along the southern wall, he saw the black silhouette of a gate; the angle of their approach hid the school grounds beyond it. Larson noticed no activity outside the walls. But as he and Gaelinar came up to the gate, he found two soldiers guarding the entrance just inside the iron framework. Both wore shirts of riveted links which fell to their knees and were belted at the waist. Iron helmets with decorative bubbles and swirls and long, curled horns perched on their heads. They stood, rigid and motionless, with their spears crossed. Each carried a sheathed broadsword with a jutting, crudely bulbous hilt within easy reach. Larson wondered whether the guards had seen him and Gaelinar approaching or simply spent their entire watch at complete attention.

Larson took advantage of the sentries' silence to study the gate. Some artisan had crafted it from strips of blackened iron, carefully shaped into straight, even bars. In its center, the double doors of the gateway came together to form a dragon, an exact likeness of the one which had attacked them in Hel, its head cocked back in preparation for a blast of fiery breath. Beyond the sharp featured guardsmen, Larson saw rows of squat, one- and two-story buildings. Between them, gardens of late blooming flowers and crops added color to an otherwise grave looking schoolyard.

Gaelinar lowered and raised his head respectfully. "I am Kensei Gaelinar, and my companion is Lord Allerum. We need to see the schoolmaster."

The sentries uncrossed their spears. As one, they jabbed the wooden butts to the ground at their feet. The leftmost one replied. "Karrold isn't seeing anyone."

Larson met the sentry's gaze. The man stood as tall as himself, about six feet. But the guard's linebacker frame gave him nearly a hundred pounds on Larson's fragile elf form. The second guardsman, slightly smaller than his companion, remained still.

Gaelinar nodded again, this time curtly. "Karrold will see us."

The larger guard repeated his warning. "Karrold isn't seeing anyone."

Gaelinar's fist curled around the sheath of his katana. The thumb he looped over his crossguard blanched. "You can take us to the schoolmaster now, or I can climb this gate and take your heads to him."

As one, the sentries back-stepped and lowered their spears. "Try it, old man," the larger one said. "We'll run you through before you reach the ground."

Gaelinar tensed.

Larson held his breath. For an instant, he feared the Kensei might accept the guardsman's challenge. Then an idea came to him suddenly, and he strode around his mentor. "What my . . . um . . . irritable friend forgot to mention . . ." He heard the rustle of Gaelinar's robes behind him but resisted the urge to turn. "A Dragonrank mage sent us." He plucked Silme's rankstone from his pocket and displayed it for the guards.

The spear tips sagged. The sentries came together for a whispered exchange. The smaller one turned and trotted toward an elegant building at the center of the compound. The remaining guardsman watched Gaelinar, his eyes squinting with suspicion.

Larson rocked back and forth, annoyed by the formality. Silme's mind and body were withering each moment he spent arguing with insolent guardsmen. *As if we haven't already wasted enough time chasing cat burglars and swinging an imaginary sword.*

Several minutes passed in uncomfortable silence before the sentry returned. "Karrold asked me to bring him the sapphire."

Larson cradled the gem in both hands. "Tell Karrold we're a package. The sapphire does not leave my possession." His own bold words reawakened his guilt over having hurled Silme's rankstone at the dragon in Hel. He winced.

The larger guard glanced at his companion. "Who's our supervisor today?"

"Ketel."

"Ketel?"

"Ruby-rank."

"Call him."

Again the smaller guard trotted off into the school grounds.

Gaelinar muttered something incomprehensible about "delays" and "incompetence." He exchanged glares with the remaining sentry through the wrought iron gate.

Larson began to pace.

Soon the guardsman returned with a shorter, slighter man in tow. The newcomer wore royal blue silk trimmed with golden thread. Silver streaked his yellow hair at the temples. He carried a wooden staff, darkly-stained, which tapered to a four-toed, black-nailed claw clutching a faceted ruby. His lined face appeared friendly. He confronted Larson and Gaelinar with raised brows, and his narrow features framed a tight-lipped smile. "The guard tells me you've brought a rankstone."

Larson uncovered the sapphire.

Ketel spoke a heavy, unrecognizable syllable. In response, Silme's rankstone darkened to black. Ketel raised his palm, his eyes fixed on the gemstone in Larson's hand. Gradually, it took on a weak, purplish glow. Larson looped his fingers about the stone, uncertain whether he should allow the sorcerer to manipulate Silme's life aura. Before he could whisk it back into his pocket, Ketel dropped his hand, and the light winked out as if choked.

"It's a rankstone," Ketel confirmed. "Sapphire-rank." He seemed impressed. "Who sent you?"

Larson returned the gemstone to his pocket. "Lady Silme." He did not bother to clarify the term "sent."

"We've come to speak with Karrold," Gaelinar added impatiently.

Ignoring the sentries on either side, Ketel nodded agreement. "And indeed you shall." He ended the sentence with a low-pitched sound, and the wrought iron gates swung outward, as if of their own accord. The guards stepped aside, grips rigid on their spears. The smaller one shifted nervously from one booted foot to the other.

Gaelinar and Larson walked through the entryway, and the gates inched closed behind them.

Ketel leaned on his staff, eyeing Larson's knives and the swords, shurikens, and less familiar weapons which girded Gaelinar's waist. "Before we go on, as a show of good will, I must ask you to leave your weapons here."

Larson hesitated, the memory of Gaelinar's threat in the pine clearing still strong within him. *If he would kill a friend for merely touching his sword* . . . He did not dare to finish the thought. Even as it came to his mind, he saw the larger guard reaching for Gaelinar's katana with reckless boldness.

Larson cringed away from the inevitable combat.

Gaelinar's features remained placid. He waited, motionless, until the sentry's hand nearly touched his sash. Then, fast as a ferret, he slapped the guard's wrist away and dodged aside. He glared at the younger man, his voice deadly calm. "In my country, the value of a katana is judged on its ability to cleanly decapitate a man in one stroke. Touch it, and you'll receive a demonstration."

The sentries raised their spears, the sharp, steel points leveled at Gaelinar. The three men stood in a silent triangle of threat. No one seemed willing to make the first strike.

"We've come in peace. No need for violence." Larson sidled beyond spear range and glanced at the sorcerer for aid.

Ketel did not disappoint him. "At ease. These men carry a sapphire rankstone. That means either a powerful Dragonmage holds them in her complete trust or they killed her. In either case, I don't think the two of you can stand against them."

Obediently, the sentries backed away and lowered their weapons.

Ketel faced Gaelinar and spoke soothingly, as if to a frightened child. "We'll return your weapons after your audience with Karrold, I promise. It's just a show of good will."

Gaelinar remained crouched, his gaze still fixed on the bigger guard. "And how will you show your good will? I suppose Karrold's guards and sorcerers will leave their spears and staves outside the school grounds? I've tired of nonsense. Either we see Karrold as we are, or we take the rankstone elsewhere and our business into our own hands."

Larson chewed his lip, aware he, alone, understood the consequences of Gaelinar's words. *In order to find and slay a sapphire-rank Dragonmage to replace Silme, we would need free run of the school grounds. That would require us to kill every guard or sorcerer who tried to stop us.* The thought reawakened the doubts he had quelled in Hel. *It makes no sense. How can killing another magician restore Silme's life?* Larson addressed his own question with another. *Why do I find that any stranger than Ketel's opening and closing a gate with a thought, a talking wolf who can haunt my dreams, or a god trapped within a sword?*

Ketel turned his gaze upon Larson, then the spearmen, and back to Gaelinar. "Very well. You may carry whatever you have to Karrold." He added, as if in apology, "But we cannot grant a private audience as long as you insist on bringing swords."

Larson spoke before Gaelinar could open his mouth. "That's fine. The more Dragonrank who know Silme's dilemma, the more likely one will come forward to help her."

Gaelinar relaxed.

Ketel gave a slow, sad nod. "So Silme is in trouble?"

Larson found the question a gross understatement. "As bad as it comes."

"We must see the schoolmaster," Gaelinar said for what seemed like his hundredth repetition.

This time, Ketel responded to Gaelinar's insistence. "Follow me carefully, and, for your sake, don't stray from my path. I, for one, want to hear what you have to say to Karrold." He trotted toward one of the gardens and the palatial structure at the center of the compound. "Silme is a talented sorceress and an avid teacher. I credit her with my promotion from semi-precious. There aren't many things I wouldn't do for her."

Would you die for her? Larson wondered as he and Gaelinar followed Ketel, the spearmen in single file at their backs. As they passed through a garden artistically decorated with fountains and beds of soil in animal shapes, Larson felt smothered beneath a sudden avalanche of uncertainty. *Could Ketel substitute his life for Silme, or must we find another sapphire-rank? Does it matter that one is male, the other female? Exactly what does this exchange require?* Larson scarcely noticed the withering vegetation of the Dragonrank garden. He recalled Hel's words, indelibly burned into his memory. *"To bring her back to Midgard, you would need to open a place for her . . . I have told you all you need to know."*

They passed a patch of dirt sculpted into the form of a bear. Emaciated, brown stalks stood in a line, each bowed to the ground by a single, plump, orange fruit. But the significance of the magical harvest was lost on Larson. *Open a place for her. What does that mean? Gaelinar believes we have to find a person of "Silme's means and bent willing to take her place in Hel." But just how like Silme must her alternate be?*

Oblivious to Larson's concerns, Ketel led his visitors through a stone archway. The view beyond jolted Larson from his thoughts. A two-story building lay before them, stately as an ancient castle. Cut blocks of white granite formed each wall. A portico set off the arched doorway.

A single, crenelated tower rose from the center of the ceiling. A sculpted dragon, lifelike in its clarity, curled about the base of the tower. Fangs jutted from its open mouth. Its tail hung over the building to merge with the stonework of the colonnade.

Larson stared in slack-mouthed awe. Since his arrival in Old Scandinavia, he had seen no architecture more complicated than an ivy-covered, decaying temple and the granite wall around the Dragonrank grounds. Yet this structure appeared flawless. Though smaller, it stood as grand as any palace in his own school textbooks. A pair of sentries, dressed like the spearmen at Larson's back, stood motionless as carvings before the wooden door.

Ketel brought Larson and Gaelinar directly to the portal. Without a word, one of the guardsmen opened the panel, and the three passed through into a hallway more splendid than the outside of the building. Shelves lined every wall, garishly covered with figurines of glass or pewter interrupted by stretches of leather-covered books. Between the shelves stood mute sentries, each with a spear and sword and a matched twin against the opposite wall. Lush, crimson carpet lined the parquet floor, and gold filigree wound like veins through the polished walls.

Gaelinar snorted and tossed a whispered comment to Larson. "Karrold's gaudy toys would make those spears unusable. Every guard's strike or dodge would cost fortunes of gold in trinkets."

Larson made no reply, too struck with the splendor to concern himself with a violence which would surely never occur. Only a fool would challenge a Dragonrank master on his own territory.

Ketel wandered through a maze of gilded hallways then stopped before a double set of doors emblazoned with the claw symbol of the Dragonrank mages. He tapped the rightmost panel with the bronze-rimmed base of his staff.

The door opened silently on oiled hinges. The room beyond contained so many books, Larson felt uncertain whether there were walls behind the shelves. The lower spine of each volume sported a tiny, white square of paper. For an instant, Larson thought he read an Arabic numerical figure on every tag. Then, distance blurred them to obscurity, and larger concerns drew his attention. A half dozen guardsmen stood, evenly spaced, around the room. They wore black tabards over their mail, emblazoned with the claw symbol stitched in crimson. Six pairs of blue eyes settled on Gaelinar and Larson, each man appearing grimly capable.

Beyond the soldiers, another man studied a tome opened on a table of pine and ivory. He appeared gaunt with age. The paper-thin skin of his hands revealed a network of veins. Folds of wrinkled flesh peeked from beneath a collar of scarlet brocade. White hair spilled to his neck, and long sideburns joined a stiff, silver beard. A dragonstaff leaned against one bookshelf; a diamond glimmered between its claws.

The sentry closest to the doorway rattled titles in a practiced monotone. "Introduce yourselves before Lord High Karrold, archmaster of the Dragonrank school, summoner of dragons, commander of the winds, controller of fire, sovereign over all magics of the earth, highest of all Dragonmages and most feared of the nine worlds' two diamond-rank sorcerers."

Tough act to follow. Larson watched Gaelinar for clues to the proper etiquette.

Without so much as a respectful nod, Gaelinar strode toward the schoolmaster. The guards' hands swept to their sword hilts. They closed on the Kensei, but he seemed oblivious. "Lord Karrold, I think you might wish to amend your title."

The elder glanced up from his book, his angular features lost beneath a mass of aged creases. His countenance echoed none of his guards' concern. "And why is that?"

"Was the other diamond-rank mage an evil-tempered, half-human creature called Bramin?"

Karrold's wrinkles deepened. "Some might describe him that way."

"He's dead now. I suppose that makes you the most feared of the nine worlds' *only* diamond-rank sorcerers."

Larson winced, afraid Gaelinar might add some comment like "hardly a distinctive title anymore." He swiveled his attention from the eager guardsmen to the book shelves. Though still unreadable, the ink strokes on the spine tags seemed unsettlingly akin to Library of Congress call numbers.

"Ah." Karrold considered. "I suspected as much. That would explain why my tracking spells failed. I couldn't be sure. A Master can find ways around any magic, and Bramin often eluded me when engaged in his cruelest deeds." Briskly, he returned to the matter at hand. "Who are you, soldier?"

"I am Kensei Gaelinar, and Lord Allerum is my student."

Karrold's gaze swept casually across the strangers. He squinted his watery, pale eyes and regarded Larson more carefully. "You're an elf."

And Gaelinar berates me for speaking the self-evident. Larson saw no reason to reply. But the schoolmaster seemed to expect a response, and Larson did not wish to antagonize him. "Yes," he said simply.

The schoolmaster fingered his beard, studying Larson for several seconds. Reluctantly, he returned his attention to Gaelinar. "And how do you know of Bramin's death?"

"We killed him."

Karrold's eyes shot wide open. He recovered his composure instantly, but a quaver in his ancient voice betrayed the discomfort he otherwise hid. "How did you accomplish such a thing?"

"Purer spirit and a more focused intent," Gaelinar explained blandly.

Larson wondered how much of the Kensei's reply had been spoken for his benefit.

Gaelinar continued. "We didn't come to speak of Bramin. He's not worthy of our time or effort. But Silme linked her soul to Bramin's and lost her life with his."

Sudden grief formed a knot in Larson's throat. He fought off remembrance of the battle before Hvergelmir's falls, but Silme's dying scream pierced his memory like a knife. His hands trembled. He lowered his head and clenched a clammy fist to his forehead. Dizziness enfolded his consciousness, driving him with the mystical force of the flashbacks he had thought conquered. Fearing for his sanity, he fixed his gaze on one of the guards with fanatical intensity. Reality sharpened into focus, and the roar of the waterfall became the fragile voice of the Dragonrank schoolmaster.

"... miracles even I cannot perform. I have no enchantments to raise the dead."

Gaelinar addressed Karrold, but his golden eyes probed Larson's questioningly. "We don't need your magic. We need only a mage who serves law. One of similar rank to Silme and willing to give his life for hers."

Karrold's face went as grim as his soldiers'. "You're asking my permission to kill one of my students? Are you mad?"

Gaelinar's rejoinder was an open challenge. "If we wished to slay one by force, we would have done so already."

Larson broke in, still feeling ill. "Can't you ask? Silme gave her life to rescue Midgard from utter destruction. Perhaps someone might be willing to sacrifice their life for her. I know I would if it was within my power." Now, standing before the Dragonrank schoolmaster, the suggestion seemed ludicrous. *But we have to try.*

Karrold knotted his gnarled fingers on the desktop. "Last I heard, there was only one diamond-rank, two sapphire, three emerald, and five jacinth. Of those, less than half still attend the school. Some serve gods or kings, some law, some chaos. But most serve only their own interests. I'm sorry. I cannot help you." He turned his attention back to his book, apparently considering the conversation finished.

Gaelinar did not change position, yet his attitude suddenly became deadly alert. "So be it, schoolmaster. We came peacefully, seeking a willing replacement for Silme. You have denied us the simple courtesy of asking, but we will not be stayed. You leave us no choice but to *slay every high ranking sorcerer we can find until we discover Silme's equal.*"

The guardsmen's spears dropped to a rigid circle. Karrold's fist crashed against the table. "Fool! You'll never leave this room alive!"

Larson's nerves drew tight as bowstrings. He coiled up, prepared to dive beneath the readied spears.

Aside from a finger which tapped the katana's sheath, Gaelinar seemed unimpressed with the sentries' display. He met the sorcerer's query with sullen silence.

From the doorway, Ketel's voice broke the ensuing hush. "Master Karrold, may I speak now?"

The schoolmaster sat with hands tensely bridged. His gaze remained on Gaelinar, and he nodded his head curtly.

Ketel coughed nervously and continued. "I owe my life and my ruby to Silme. If I thought my rank high enough, I might give my life for her. Others may be equally grateful. If you would grant the Kensei and his student time within the grounds to speak with my peers, I will take full responsibility for their actions."

Larson held his breath.

Anxious murmurs broke out among the sentries, swiftly silenced by Karrold's glare. "Very well." The schoolmaster addressed Ketel, but his words were obviously intended for Gaelinar. "But if they take a single, unwilling life, they will have to deal with me and the entire school. And I want them gone by nightfall."

As one, the spear butts slapped to the tiled floor.

Gaelinar whirled and followed Ketel back into the hallway.

Karrold called after them. "Ketel?"

The ruby-rank sorcerer turned.

"Don't let me regret my decision."

Ketel mumbled. "Yes, master." He shuffled down the gaudy corridor.

Larson felt obligated to say something. "Good day." He used a friendly tone; but after the tension which had nearly turned to violence, his words sounded like a mockery. He trotted behind Ketel and Gaelinar, relaxing only after they stepped out the main door and into the afternoon sunlight.

As they threaded through the gardens outside Karrold's holding, Larson caught Ketel's arm. "Thank you."

Ketel shook free of Larson's grip. "Please. I didn't do it for you. I did it for Silme." He cocked his head toward Larson as he walked. "After years of competition, most of our higher rank mages become reclusive or actively hostile. Some dedicate their lives to destroying other Dragonrank." He added as an afterthought, "Outside the school, of course."

Ketel led Larson and Gaelinar around a bed of multi-hued flowers. "Silme wasn't like that. She was unexcelled as a teacher, always willing to give lower rank mages the benefits of her labors and mistakes. It comes as no surprise she died for Midgard's innocents. She left the school expecting such a fate."

Larson changed the subject, avoiding his aching memories of Silme's death. "Where are you taking us?"

Ketel marched around a line of fountains. "There is a sapphire-rank sorceress who owes Silme more than any other."

Hope spiraled through Larson. "Who is she?"

"Her name is Bengta. Her dragonmark appeared when she was in her mid twenties. When ten-year-old Silme arrived a decade later, Bengta had made garnet-rank." Ketel waved to a pair of men on a stone bench as they passed. "Shy and timid, Bengta caused a stir among the higher ranking mages. Here, promotion is achieved by boldness; a sorcerer reckless enough to practice spells until his life aura is nearly drained either dies or advances quickly. Only one sorcerer can advance to garnet each year, and there was concern that Bengta had been chosen over jade-ranks more committed and deserving."

Ketel paused to unlatch a gate. He, Larson, and Gaelinar filed through it, onto a dirt and gravel street between the dwellings. "As gossip and contempt ran rampant, Bengta became despondent. She spent less time working spells and more time mumbling about leaving. Then came her apprentice, Silme." A strange smile curled Ketel's lips. "Silme and her brother advanced through the ranks as if magic had been created for them. At first, we blamed youthful exuberance. We thought they were too ignorant of death to fear it; surely they would both die as children. But as they climbed the mountain of success, leaving most of us behind, there was no doubt they had an unusually fine grasp of their own limits."

Ketel stopped to lean against a blocked archway into another garden. "Silme's enthusiasm inspired Bengta.

They became as close as mother and daughter. Though, sometimes, it was difficult to tell who was which. Bengta had age and maturity, Silme knowledge and ability. They shared freely with each other. Bengta owes her rank to Silme. And I have yet to meet a mother unwilling to sacrifice her life for her only child."

Excitement thrilled through Larson, but a vague queasiness accompanied it. Something felt wrong.

Gaelinar worked a cramp from his hand. "Where can we find her?"

Ketel waggled his finger toward the arched entryway then stepped through it. Suddenly, a loud crack echoed between the walls. Light flared, bathing the garden an eerie blue. Instinctively, Larson backpedaled behind the wall and dropped to his stomach.

Several seconds passed in silence.

"Lord Allerum?" Ketel sounded more curious than concerned.

Larson rose to a crouch, hugged the wall stones, and peeked through the archway. Around Gaelinar and Ketel's legs, he saw symmetrical beds of flowers, each giant petal a deep, natural indigo. At the farthest end, seated on a wooden bench, an elderly woman regarded them quizzically. She clasped a sapphire dragonstaff between her knees.

Feeling foolish, Larson sidled up to his companions. "What was that?" He tried to sound casual.

"Warding spell." Ketel raised a hand in welcome to the woman. "Bengta's way of announcing company."

Bengta returned Ketel's greeting.

Larson grumbled. "Sort of a magical doorbell."

Ketel's brow furrowed. "Magical what?" He looked askance at Gaelinar.

More accustomed to Larson's unrecognizable English phrases, Gaelinar shrugged it off. "I don't understand half of what he says." He added scornfully, "In return, he doesn't listen to half of what I say."

Larson rattled off a vulgar American phrase accompanied by a gesture he was glad Gaelinar could not recognize. "Let's get this over with."

Ketel motioned to Larson and Gaelinar to remain, then trotted off to converse with Bengta.

Larson paced like an expectant father. He pictured Silme as she had appeared at their first meeting: her smile mischievous in a face pale as new-fallen snow, her slender curves accentuated by her gray cloak, and gold-white hair glowing in a halo of magics. All the desire he had felt reemerged, strengthened by the love he had come to know over time. *But Silme is dead.* Somehow, Larson's mind which had come to accept a Scandinavia centuries prior to his birth, magic, swords, and gods could not concede rebirth from death. The concept had reawakened the once conquered madness which had nearly overtaken him in Karrold's palace. Larson harbored no desire to surrender to the conscience-searing flashbacks again.

Ketel returned, his expression somber. "Come with me." He led Larson and Gaelinar to Bengta.

The woman rose as they approached. Despite a rotund figure, she moved with regal grace. Her neatly-coiffed hair was an odd mixture of brown, gold, and gray which shaded sorrowful blue eyes and a grimly-lined visage. She leaned her dragonstaff against the bench and spoke in a resigned soprano. "Ketel has explained your need. I'll do it."

Gaelinar regarded Ketel with arched brows, as if to confirm Bengta's willingness.

Ketel gave a slow nod. "When you leave, make certain you follow the same path. I'll be waiting to escort you from the school grounds." Without explaining further, he turned and shuffled from the garden.

Larson pinched his lips between his fingers. He knew he should feel ecstatic. *Silme will live again.* But the realization brought only a racking wave of nausea. He tried to read emotion in Bengta's eyes. "Do you understand what you agreed to do?"

The sapphire-rank sorceress avoided Larson's gaze. "I've traded an elderly life for one younger. I've traced Silme's passage since she left the Dragonrank school. She and the Kensei rescued the world, though the world may never realize it. And you helped, too, lord elf. I would give my life and more for her."

The woman's words seemed heartfelt, yet Larson felt plagued by restlessness. "You're certain?"

"My life is yours, Kensei. Just let me . . ."

Her pause seemed unnatural to Larson.

". . . go . . . in my world." Bengta made a sweeping gesture to indicate the garden.

Bengta's use of a euphemism fueled Larson's discomfort. *People who have accepted death, as she claims she has, speak freely of it.*

Gaelinar's katana skimmed silently from its sheath.

For an instant, Bengta's glance met Larson's. Her eyes went wide with a sheer terror which crashed against Larson's conscience, hurling him violently into the past. He stood in a night gone strangely dark and silent. Wind ruffled the trees, their swish forming a muffled chorus with the creak of concertina wire from the Fire Support Base at his back. His orders echoed like song through his mind. "Anything enters the perimeter, shoot it." Larson let the M-16 in his right hand sag to his side. He dug through a pocket with his left, searching for a cigarette.

A crackling of brush froze him in position. As the sound grew louder and more persistent, Larson eased to a crouch. Quietly, he freed his hand, raised the gun, and switched it to automatic. A lone figure emerged from the brush. Carefully, Larson aimed. Even as his finger tightened on the trigger, a distant flare slashed the darkness. Larson caught a glimpse of a heavily-wrinkled female face.

She had seen him, too. The panic in her eyes was permanently inscribed into Larson's memory. A thousand years of guilt tore through him before his own bullets ripped through her chest and left her, dead and bleeding, on the dirt.

Larson had waited in the sudden, jarring silence, then crept toward the corpse cautiously. Yellow-white, bloodless skin felt thin as ash beneath his fingers. Desperately, he sought a weapon tucked in some fold of flesh or clothing. But he found nothing to justify the woman's death. *She was a peasant searching for something: an herb to cure an ill relative, a wandering grandchild.* Larson cursed her with every vile word he knew, not realizing in his rage that he was really damning himself.

The scene rushed through Larson's mind in the fraction of a second it took Gaelinar to strike. "No!" Larson sprang. His shoulder smashed into Bengta's gut, tumbling her. Larson landed heavily on top of her. The point of Gaelinar's katana shaved a line of skin from Larson's back before the Kensei could pull his cut.

Larson whirled to face his mentor, still shielding Bengta with his body. "Don't do it."

Gaelinar swore. "Allerum, you idiot! Out of my way. I vow to any god listening, I'll run you both through if I must."

"No." Larson shook his head, still disoriented and uncertain what force or thought had driven him to defy Gaelinar and deny Silme the life he wanted so much to return to her. He attempted a reply. "It's wrong, Gaelinar." The explanation sounded lame, even to Larson.

The muscles in Gaelinar's cheeks twitched. He glared down at Larson, his expression dark with a bitter anger which bordered on hatred. "At least you won't have far to fall when I behead you."

Frozen by the realization he had slain Silme for the second time, Larson felt little concern for his own welfare. "You wouldn't kill me. We're friends . . ."

Gaelinar crouched, sword still poised to strike. "Hero, you really don't understand. I pledged myself to Silme and her cause. Lives, even of friends, are nothing compared with honor. If I have to kill twenty thousand people to fulfill my pledge to Silme, I will." He tensed. "I would regret killing you. But if I'm willing to spend my life on a cause, why wouldn't I spend yours?"

Larson met Gaelinar's stare with an insolent scowl. He knew his defiance had lost him everything: his sanity, Silme's life, Gaelinar's companionship. The threat of his own death lost all meaning in comparison. He wrapped an arm more tightly about the woman beneath him. "You're a liar!" he screamed. "You may have served Silme once. Now you work against her."

Gaelinar's reply was a sudden snap of his foot to Larson's face.

Pain jarred a whimper from Larson and drove his world into a deeper haze. "You bastard." His voice was hoarse. "I loved Silme more than anyone. I know her mind, Gaelinar. Deep down, I think you do, too. Were she here, Silme would never let us sacrifice an innocent life for hers. If we brought her back by killing Bengta, Silme would never forgive either of us and neither could I." Tears stung Larson's eyes. "If you want to kill us both, Gaelinar, go ahead. But, don't delude yourself into thinking you did it for Silme. Don't mistake your own cause for hers."

Larson felt Bengta shudder beneath him. Then her body shook rhythmically as she wept.

Crouched behind a trellis swarming with fleshy, purple wine grapes, Taziar Medakan observed the scene in Bengta's garden, moved by Larson's sensitivity. At first, sneaking into the Dragonrank school grounds in broad daylight had seemed like folly. But Gaelinar's ravings had held the attention of guards and sorcerers while Taziar slipped boldly through the front gate. Not quite foolish enough to brave the archmaster's palace, Taziar had waited outside while Gaelinar and Larson conversed with Karrold. Then, catching sight of his quarries as they emerged from between the columns of the portico, Taziar trailed them to Bengta's garden where he easily dodged her wards.

It surprised and impressed Taziar that Gaelinar and Larson had discovered a cause so unthinkable even he had never considered attempting it. If Ketel's assessment was correct, the Kensei and his partner were working to restore life to a corpse. Furthermore, the sorcerers seemed to believe it possible. *I want a hand in this.* From habit, Taziar ignored the cramp of muscles held too long in one position. *And Silme could hardly refuse to accept Astryd as an apprentice after I assisted in her resurrection.*

Taziar studied Larson, recalling Fenrir had called Gaelinar's companion an "elf." In the dawn light, Larson had appeared the same as any man. But now Taziar could discern subtle differences. Unnaturally lean for his height, Larson sported sharply-defined, angular features. His ears tapered to delicate points. Larson's gestures and some of his speech were unlike any Taziar had ever encountered, and the elf's accent was unfamiliar. Larson's morality pleased Taziar. It had saved not only Bengta's life but, earlier, his own as well.

Reluctantly, Taziar turned his attention to Gaelinar. The Kensei watched Larson and Bengta with grim impassivity. There was no doubt in Taziar's mind. *If we meet again, he'll kill me without giving me a chance to speak. But I have no choice. I freed Fenrir; the wolf is my responsibility. And I'll have to gain Gaelinar's trust if I want a role in rescuing Silme.* Taziar had always prided himself on accurately reading intentions. Yet Gaelinar's mentality confused him. He had met men inclined to sacrifice friends, usually to further their own power. He had known patriots who gave their lives for their friends or countries. But never before had Taziar seen someone willing to forfeit the lives of his friends and himself for a cause. *Somehow I have to make Gaelinar listen. I have to prove myself his equal.* As Taziar considered his withdrawal from Bengta's garden, he realized persuading Gaelinar would require every bit of cunning he could muster. And it pleased him.

CHAPTER 6:

Master of Illusion

"Morality is a private and costly luxury."
—Henry Brooks Adams
The Education of Henry Adams

Al Larson sat in a tavern whose sign he had not read, in a town he had not bothered to identify, sipping a bitter liquid which tasted vaguely like beer. A dozen other patrons chatted and laughed over food and drinks, but in Larson's mind he was alone. Four days' travel through nameless woods had brought him and Gaelinar to a nameless bar in a nameless city, their only communication the Kensei's barked commands during brutal sword practices. But the grief which haunted Larson was not nameless.

Silme. Larson took another long pull at his mug. *They say every beer kills a hundred brain cells. If I could only hit the right ones.* He downed the remaining beer and gestured at the waitress for a fourth. *There's not enough liquor in Scandinavia to make me forget I killed Silme again; I destroyed her in the name of her own cause. The good must die to make the world safe for the simple. God bless America.* He amended. *Gods bless Norway.*

A skinny, young woman in a tattered dress refilled Larson's mug from a dented, bronze tankard. She rushed away to fill another order.

"Allerum?" Gaelinar's voice stirred lazily through Larson's thoughts. "Allerum, there's a blacksmith just a few cottages from here. Remember Fenrir. You'll need a sword."

Protectively, Larson looped a hand around his drink. "Maybe later."

Gaelinar's voice grated with the ire which seemed to taint all of his words and actions since the incident at the Dragonrank school. "The tavern will not run out of beer in your absence."

Larson downed half the contents of his mug without pausing for breath. "Get it yourself." Immediately, guilt gnawed at his conscience. "Please," he added, attempting to soften the demand to a request. When that proved unsuccessful, he explained. "I'm sorry, Gaelinar. I didn't mean that. I just need some time alone. I wouldn't know what to look for in a sword, anyway."

Gaelinar made no reply, but the hand he clamped on Larson's forearm felt sympathetic. He turned in a swirl of golden robes and walked from the bar.

Larson stared into the amber depths of his beer, not bothering to watch his companion leave.

When Gaelinar returned, Larson was nursing his eleventh drink. He watched his mentor through a pleasant mental haze as the Kensei shuffled between tables and sprawled into the chair across from Larson. "I got your weapon." He slid a sheathed long sword across the tabletop. "It may interest you to know the blacksmith's girth was large, his breath reeked of wine, and his workmanship was only fair."

Larson smiled crookedly but made no move to examine Gaelinar's purchase. "You're saying it was beaten on a rock by a fat drunkard." Larson's words emerged unexpectedly slurred. *I'm smaller now. And who knows how well elves metabolize alcohol.*

Gaelinar frowned his displeasure at Larson's condition. "This sword will have to do until we can get somewhere civilized where men respect their weapons and artisans take pride in their craft."

Larson traced the rim of his mug with a finger. *Japan perhaps? Why not. Where else do we have to go now?* He took another gulp of beer, not at all certain he could stand to return to a world of Oriental faces or even bear Gaelinar's sullen company much longer.

Gaelinar placed a heavy palm over the hand Larson kept wrapped around his drink. Though the gesture was obviously intended as a plea for moderation, the Kensei spoke with quiet understanding. ''Allerum, we need to talk. I . . .'' He broke off with a strangled gasp. His eyes focused on something beyond Larson.

Giddy with alcohol, Larson did not ponder Gaelinar's strange behavior. He twisted in his chair, seeking the target of his mentor's attention. A lone man occupied the table behind Larson. He appeared small; the hand which gripped his wine glass was no bigger than a child's. Despite this, the patron was so well-proportioned, Larson could not guess his height and breadth through beer blurred vision. Jet-black hair fringed finely-sculpted features. A single curl seemed determined to slip into eyes the color of Silme's rankstone. The stranger chewed thoughtfully and returned Larson's stare with friendly interest.

Larson turned back to Gaelinar. ''Who's that?''

The Kensei locked his gaze on the stranger, as silent and still as the calm before a storm. ''It's him. The climber at the school.''

Larson did not ponder a situation which, if sober, he would have found a nearly impossible coincidence. He swiveled his head back toward the stranger just in time to see the little man rise, brush crumbs from his linen britches, and swagger toward them. Concern whittled at the edges of Larson's alcohol-inspired peace of mind.

The climber marched directly to Larson's and Gaelinar's table. Selecting a chair between them, he spun it until the backrest faced Gaelinar. The black-haired man straddled the seat. He leaned across the wooden rail and regarded Gaelinar with sharp accusation. ''I believe you owe me an explanation.''

Gaelinar's jaw clenched. ''I believe not.''

The climber rested his fingers on the chair back, his voice unexpectedly calm. ''I harmed no one at the school, least of all you. But you tried to kill me for no reason. I deserve an explanation.''

Larson watched an angry line of crimson spread from Gaelinar's head to his neck. Certain that violence would follow, Larson fought the mind-dimming curtain of the beer. He felt flushed.

"Go away or I'll slay you where you sit! Leave and you'll gain the time it takes me to hunt you down like the animal you are." Gaelinar's answer carried a hostility which went beyond logic. No doubt, he would happily, even eagerly, vent the frustrations of the last few days on this stranger.

"Kensei Gaelinar." The climber's words carried the reprimanding tone of a sergeant, and his German accent reminded Larson of a cheap World War II movie. "We're in a crowded tavern. Barbaric as the tiny Northern towns may seem to foreigners like us, they still follow rules. We all know if you kill me in a public place, you'll have the law to deal with. Your friend there stopped you from doing something stupid once. I think he's smart enough to do so again. Besides . . ." He smiled arrogantly. "You have both knees beneath the table. To draw a sword, you would have to shift your chair. By that time, I'd be half-way to Cullinsberg."

The next thing Larson knew, Gaelinar had a death grip on the stranger's hand with his thumb on the smallest knuckle. The Kensei drew the other man partway up from his chair.

Surprise flashed in the climber's blue eyes, replaced by a mixture of pain, fear, and an emotion Larson could not identify.

Gaelinar lowered his head until his face nearly touched the stranger's. "I could break your arm with a movement so subtle, no one in the tavern would hold me responsible. We'll meet again, I promise. And I will kill you. But you'll see me coming. Unlike you, I have honor. I wouldn't cut a man in the back." He shoved the smaller man away with an angry violence.

The chair toppled to the floor, but the climber caught his balance with a simple grace. He sidestepped beyond Gaelinar's reach. "I've never stabbed anyone in the back, and I don't plan to start now. My name's Taziar, but I'm called Shadow. We need to talk, desperately. When you decide to start acting civilized, we'll finish this." Taziar whirled. He acknowledged Larson with a stiff nod, then returned to his table.

To Larson, the tavern seemed to be spinning. The incident had occurred so quickly and quietly, only the nearest handful of patrons watched Gaelinar curiously. With an odd detachment, Larson realized Taziar stood no more than an inch above five feet, but he found himself unable to process the information.

Gaelinar leaped up and stormed toward the barkeep. "We're leaving. Now!" he called to Larson over his shoulder.

Larson straggled awkwardly after the Kensei. He watched without comprehension while his mentor rummaged through his pockets for his pouch of coins to pay Larson's beer tab.

On the opposite side of the counter, the barkeep waited with his hand outstretched. As Gaelinar's search became frantic, annoyance chased patience from the barkeep's features. He tapped his fingers on the polished wood, regarding the Kensei with unconcealed suspicion.

When Larson strode up, Gaelinar nudged him with an elbow. "Do you have money?"

Larson seized the countertop unsteadily. "No. Why would I . . ."

"I'll take care of it." Taziar's sudden appearance beside Gaelinar made even the Kensei stiffen with surprise.

Taziar scattered coins to the countertop.

The barkeep gathered them with a glare at Gaelinar. Briskly, he trotted off to tend his other customers.

Taziar tossed a battered, leather pouch tied with a cord of red and blue to the counter in front of Gaelinar. Immediately, Larson identified the offering as Gaelinar's missing purse. As the Kensei stared in disbelief, Taziar tossed a shuriken to the bar, followed by a second, third and fourth. Each struck the bar with a tinny ring.

Unconsciously, Gaelinar's fingers massaged his empty arm sheath.

Larson watched in slack-mouthed awe as the last shuriken hit the countertop. *My god! The little thief must have stolen them while Gaelinar was twisting his arm.* Light-headedness transformed the tavern to a blur. *But who the hell could rob Gaelinar blind that fast and without his knowledge?*

The same realization must have stunned Gaelinar. For Taziar found the time to sprint for the door before the Kensei's vengeful howl chased him from the tavern.

Al Larson trotted through the twilit streets of the town, seeking respite from the thoughts and emotions which plagued him. He had left Gaelinar, still blustering, at a camp at the perimeter. The pleasurable fuzziness from the beer had faded, leaving Larson battling a residual, frustratingly lingering mental fog. *Church. I need a church.* Larson had never seriously practiced a religion. But he found himself longing for the warmth of a New York City spring raked by cool, Easter breezes. He missed the surreptitious pinches and finger flicks exchanged with his sister, Pam, and his little brother's whispered prattle about the jelly beans and other goodies that awaited them at home. He had spent his last Easter in a foxhole with seven men who reeked of sweat and fear, pinned beneath the crossfire of the enemy and his own troops. Now, hammered by guilt and uncertainty, he sought familiarity in a world of strangeness. *I need to talk with Vidarr. Perhaps he can help me find Baldur's father.*

Larson fumbled through his pocket for the stone Baldur had so insistently given him in Hel. Nearly forgotten for other concerns, the gem lay nestled deep in the folds of Larson's tunic. He pulled it free and studied it in the waning light. Gold ink striped the indigo surface. Larson identified the painted scene as a man astride a muscular horse. But the craftsman seemed to have erred; he had doubled each of the beast's legs and the rider had a single eye. *A one-eyed Viking on an eight-legged horse.* Memory groped through Larson's beer-muddled senses. He recalled his readings of Norse mythology. *Odin. The leader of the pantheon. A god whose idea of fun was to stir up war among mortals and watch them die, whose desired sacrifices were enemies hung or butchered in his name. Odin the AllFather. All father?* Larson frowned. *Guess that explains his relationship to Baldur.* He flipped the stone back into his pocket and considered turning back. *Odin's cruel enough to have incited wars like the one in Vietnam. Do I really want to have dealings with him?* Larson hesitated, suddenly faced with the truths inspired by his contemplation. *But it wasn't Odin who started Vietnam, was it? It was my own ever-merciful, turn-the-other-cheek, Christian God.* Larson shook aside his current train of thought. *I need to speak with Vidarr.*

A man hurried past Larson, huddled in a coat worn thin with use.

Larson called after the stranger. "Excuse me, sir."

The man turned. He studied Larson's pointed ears and the wind-whipped, white-blond hair which danced around his angular features. The peasant hunched deeper into his coat.

"Please." Larson approached, and the man took a wary step back. "Where can I find a church?"

The stranger shook his head and risked a glance over his shoulder.

Larson pursed his lips. *Nobody seemed to notice my strangeness at the tavern. I guess an odd-looking, beer-drinking traveler seems less of a threat than a "demon" on a dark, deserted street.* "A temple," he clarified. "A place to worship gods."

"The shrine." The man pointed down a side street. "A few steps and to your right. You'll see a cleared area and a big stone." He pivoted and trotted off down the roadway without waiting for Larson's thanks.

With a shrug of resignation, Larson hummed "What Do You Do With a Drunken Sailor" as he followed the peasant's directions. Soon he came upon a rock the size of a coffin off to the side of the road. . . . *Ear-lye in the morning* . . . Leaning against the lump of granite, he tangled with a new problem. *Now, how do I contact Vidarr?* Idly, he ran his hand along the rough surface of stone. His touch met something sticky, and he jerked away reflexively. The substance colored his fingers red-brown.

Blood. Larson sprang away from the stone and wiped his hand on the surrounding weeds. *Human offerings to Odin?* A more logical explanation sifted through the beer haze. *Animals. Damn this paranoia, even my God used to take goats and sheep in sacrifice.* He approached the stone again. But this time, he thought it wiser not to slouch against the shrine. "Vidarr?" he called tentatively.

No answer.

"Vidarr."

Still nothing.

Larson considered. *What was it Baldur said? Anyone can communicate with gods. They need only pray in the proper temple . . . make the appropriate sacrifice.* Larson brushed hair from his face. "Oh, no. I'm not going to steal and kill some farmer's pig just to talk to a dead god's father." He slid both hands into his pockets and rubbed the smoothed facets of Silme's sapphire and the rounded curves of Baldur's gem. He pictured the collection plate in the church in New York. *Maybe they'll take money.* He pulled free the painted stone and pitched it to the shrine. It clicked against the granite, bounced once, and skidded to a stop. "Yo, Vidarr!"

Larson felt a pressure in his mind. Attributing it to the beer, he shook his head to clear it. But the sensation sharpened and grew more persistent. Larson froze. "Vidarr?"

The presence in Larson's mind became stronger, then waned again.

"Vidarr?" Larson tried again.

Once more, the pressure heightened and dulled.

"Vidarr! Cut the crap. We need to talk."

Sullenness trickled through Larson's thoughts. It felt as if his entire mind was pouting.

Familiar with Vidarr's designation as the silent god and the deity's use of emotion and imagery as a form of communication, Larson sighed. "Look. I'm half-drunk, frustrated, and tired. I saved your life once. You owe me the courtesy of speaking in words."

There was a long pause. Resignation flowed through Larson's thoughts. *Very well, Allerum. A reasonable request. But first, tell me where you got that gem.*

"From a dead god in Hel. Baldur said to remember him to his father."

Remorse washed across Larson, as heavy as his grief for Silme. *Use your mind, Allerum.*

Annoyed by what seemed like an undeserved reprimand, Larson countered. "What did I say that was so stupid?"

No, the god amended. *I meant you don't have to speak aloud. Just think what you want to say. Remember?*

Right. Sorry. It seemed like an eternity since Larson had carried on a conversation in this manner. Now it felt as uncomfortable as the first time Vidarr had contacted him.

Vidarr radiated pensiveness. *Allerum, wait here. I'm going to leave you for a moment. I have to discuss this with someone. I'll be right back.* Before Larson could protest, Vidarr was gone.

I don't believe this. Larson fumed. *A thousand years before the invention of the telephone, and Vidarr just put me on "hold!"* He paced an anxious circle around the stone.

Allerum!

Vidarr's sudden reappearance in Larson's mind caused him to jump in fright. *Don't do that.*

Now it was Vidarr's turn to apologize. *Sorry. I've got a task you need to do for me.*

Vidarr's casual assumption that Larson would perform the deed roused the American's ire. In annoyance, he spoke aloud. "I *need* to do a task for you? First, the least you could do is ask me. I've been out of the army too long to take commands. Second, the last favor I did for you resulted in Silme's death, not to mention pitting me against a god and a dark elf sorcerer/swordsman who tortured me, like a cat does a mouse, before I killed him." He paused for breath. "And third, *I* called *you*. Where I come from, that means I get to tell you *my* demands first."

Very well. Vidarr seemed appropriately repentant. *What do you desire?*

Silme.

Impatience weaved through Larson's mind. *I already told you at the falls. I have no power to raise her.*

I know. But I do. His claim to have more influence

than a god offered a smug satisfaction which Larson tried to keep back from his readable thoughts. *Hel told us a way to bring Silme back. So far, we've failed. But I'm not quite ready to give up yet.*

Vidarr's reply came in a rush of incredulity. *Show me, Allerum. Concentrate on what has happened since I saw you. That'll highlight those instances so I can move to the appropriate portion of your thoughts.*

Larson hesitated. In the past, he had found these mind intrusions extremely discomforting. The manipulation of his thoughts seemed dangerous and obscene. *All right. But only for Silme. And don't you go wandering off anywhere else.* Cautiously, he plucked the incidents in Hel from his memory. The eager crash of Vidarr through his consciousness made Larson cringe. He felt like a scaled fish, naked, deboned, his very being flayed open for the world to see. When he calculated that the god had spent enough time examining his conversation with Hel, he switched to the near slaying of Bengta at the Dragonrank School.

Vidarr scanned quietly for some time before he withdrew. *It is good you didn't let Gaelinar kill the sorceress.*

Good for my conscience. Not so good for Silme.

Not really, Allerum. Taking Bengta's life would not have restored Silme's.

No? Larson felt as if a great burden had lifted from his chest. *But she was a sapphire-rank and a woman who served law. How much more like Silme could a person get? Does Hel expect us to find Silme an identical twin?*

Hel expects you to fail. Vidarr cloaked his emotions with practiced thoroughness. *She was deliberately vague, hoping you'd make the precise mistake you did make. You see, Allerum, our Fates control the balance of our world. You could have slain Bengta only if there was a gap. That is, only if it was time for a law-abiding creature of her strength to die. . . .*

Well, of course, but . . . Larson hesitated, wishing he had never drunk the first beer. *This makes no sense, Vidarr. How else can I "open a place" for Silme?* Larson clenched his hands until his knuckles blanched. *Don't tell me. It's a "catch-22."*

Vidarr hesitated, enwrapped in an aura of confusion. *Explain.*

Hel had no intention of letting Silme go free. In order to kill Bengta, we needed to "open a place" in Hel by raising Silme. But to raise Silme, we need to "open a place" on Midgard by killing Bengta. It can't be done.

On the contrary, Allerum. It can be done and in such a way neither you nor Silme would morally object to the method.

Excitement swept through Larson. He found himself unable to speak or even compose a coherent thought.

Vidarr waited patiently.

How? Larson managed at last.

I'm sorry, Allerum. I can't tell you.

What do you mean you can't tell me! With effort, he restrained his anger until Vidarr had a chance to elaborate.

I can't tell you until you complete my task.

Your task. Larson felt feverish. *Your task! To hell with your task. You know how to save Silme. Tell me. Now!*

Vidarr was mercilessly repetitive. *I can't tell you until you complete my task.*

Larson blustered in wordless rage. If Vidarr had stood before him, he would have attacked without thinking. As it was, his fist pounded the shrine stone with enough force to cause physical pain. Larson contented himself with a visual image of his own hands throttling Vidarr. He made no effort to shield the picture from his surface thoughts.

Very nice, Allerum. Bland indulgence colored Vidarr's reply. *But I think it's a sacrilege. An impiety at the very least.*

Larson dropped the concept. *I don't care if you are a god. You're a bastard. Silme served you faithfully. She gave her life for your cause.*

She gave her life for all mankind. Vidarr's tolerance waned. *My father has several illegitimate children, not the least among them Thor. I, however, am not one. And neither was my brother, Baldur.* His reprimand softened. *I want Silme back as much as you do. Listen, Allerum . . .*

Larson broke in. *No, you listen. If you wanted her back*

as much as me, no task in the world would come before her. For god's sake, Vidarr. Larson winced, wishing he could rephrase his argument. *I rescued you from Loki's spell. You owe me.*

Vidarr's anger echoed Larson's. *And I repaid you.*

How? Larson challenged.

Didn't you even notice? Allerum, I took away your madness.

Larson screamed in frustration. "Well, put it back!" The absurdity of his own suggestion jarred him to realization. *Wait a minute. You're lying. I had a flashback at the Dragonrank school.*

I fixed what was there. I cut the odd connections and loops of thought. But I didn't change who and what you are, Allerum. Apparently, you have a tendency to develop this particular madness in certain situations.

And you keep putting me into those situations.

Don't blame me. You went to Hel on your own.

Stalemate. Larson worked the conversation to a different tack. *What's so important about this task that you're willing to put it before rescuing Silme?*

Vidarr's emotions slid through a spectrum from relief to discomfort. *I can't tell you.*

This is bullshit! You're not going to tell me why I'm risking my life, and Silme's? Forget it, Vidarr. I'm not doing it.

Wait. Vidarr went utterly still in Larson's mind. Just as Larson thought the god had abandoned him, Vidarr continued. *This isn't easy for me. You know I'm not used to phrasing points. I usually communicate only with emotions.*

Larson folded his arms across his chest unsympathetically. *Go on.*

I'm sending you to retrieve the rod of the first Dragonrank mage, Geirmagnus. He hesitated in what felt to Larson like uncertainty. But when Larson showed no recognition, Vidarr's confidence returned. *Your success would bring Baldur back from Hel.*

Outrage scrambled Larson's thoughts.

Patiently, Vidarr waited while Larson formed a reply.

So, you want me to raise Baldur from death while Silme rots in Hel! I'd rather die.

No. No. Vidarr waded through Larson's thoughts in agitation. *I never said that. Baldur is my brother. I love him dearly. And yes, I want him back. But not in exchange for Silme, in addition to her. She won't become irretrievable in the few days it takes to obtain Geirmagnus' rod.*

Repeatedly, Larson clenched and opened his fists, wishing he had something to hit. *Silme first. Baldur second. And hold still. You're making me dizzy.*

Vidarr ceased pacing. *I'm sorry, Allerum. Baldur must come first. I cannot compromise.*

Why not?

Because the method you would need to use to raise Silme would make the quest for Geirmagnus' rod far more difficult, if not impossible. Vidarr winced. *Allerum, stop pushing me. Don't make me lie to you. I could tell you retrieving the rod would bring Silme back. Then you'd run off and get it. Nothing could stand in your way. But I wouldn't do that to you.*

Larson said nothing as he let Vidarr's revelations sink in.

Vidarr continued. *Do you know who my father is, Allerum?*

I can guess.

He is called by many names, including Smiter, Destroyer, and The Terrible One. He is Odin. And he made me swear I would do nothing else before raising Baldur, the most beloved of the gods, from Hel. For your sake and my own, Odin should never be crossed. Besides, I was telling the truth when I said the method of raising Silme would make the quest far more difficult.

Larson struggled to salvage his argument. *Silme could help us get the rod. You know she'd do anything for you.*

Larson's attempt to stir Vidarr's guilt and loyalty failed. *Silme's abilities would not outweigh the dangers of raising her. Allerum, it would be best for us both if you saw the retrieval of Geirmagnus' rod as a means to restore Silme. Dedicate yourself to Baldur as you would to Silme. In truth, their fates are wholly entwined.*

It's not fair! Larson blustered. *Why don't you make someone else go after this sorcerer's rod? If you love your brother so damned much, why don't you get it yourself?*

Deep sadness assaulted Larson's consciousness. *I would do anything for Baldur. I would die for him, if necessary. But you are the only one I know who could successfully complete the task.*

Me? Larson shook his head. *How can that be? I'm a stranger here; an elf not by choice; and, at best, a mediocre swordsman.*

Vidarr went uncharacteristically sullen. *I don't have to explain everything to you. You'll have to take some things on faith. Good-bye, Allerum.* Vidarr's presence faded.

Wait! Larson thought desperately. *At least tell me where to find this rod.*

Vidarr pressed back into position. *Gaelinar will know. Enlist his aid if you still can.* He added dryly, *You'll need it. And you may want to bring the little foreigner with you too.*

That Shadow fellow? He can help us? Larson's natural curiosity died before a gathering wave of anger. *Hey, wait a minute, Vidarr. How did you know about Shadow?*

Your thoughts . . .

My thoughts! Larson hissed in revulsion. "You immortal bastard! Is nothing sacred? I asked you to stay the hell out of my memories. It's bad enough you manipulate my mind at will. How dare you . . ." Larson raged on long after Vidarr had quietly withdrawn from his consciousness.

CHAPTER 7:

Swordmaster

> "The business of the Samurai consists in reflecting on his own station in life, in discharging loyal service to his master if he has one, in deepening his fidelity in associations with friends and, with due consideration of his own position, in devoting himself to duty above all."
>
> —Yamaga Soko
> *The Way of the Samurai*

The autumn sun hovered, a diffuse halo of light just above the eastern horizon; its meager glow sifted through the forest of evergreens. Beside Gaelinar, Al Larson watched Taziar weave a trail between the shadow-splotched boughs and trunks, a full ten paces before them. The needled branches slid easily from the tough, black linen of the climber's clothing. Jabbed and scraped through his thinner tunic and cloak, Larson felt a pang of envy.

"Why would Vidarr suggest we drag along a foul, filthy bandit?" Gaelinar spoke loudly, oblivious or indifferent to the fact that Taziar could not help but overhear him.

Larson sighed. *Only fifteen minutes from town and already Gaelinar's trying to goad Shadow to attack him.* "I don't know." Annoyed with the prospect of having to deal with feuding companions and still bitter about Vidarr's secrecy and intrusion, Larson did not care if Taziar or Gaelinar found his tone insulting. "That's only one of a zillion questions I wish I'd asked Vidarr while I had the chance. Maybe this rod thing's hidden in a place too small for us to reach. Maybe we have to steal it." He dismissed the subject with a flick of his hand. "You're the one who knows about the rod. You promised you'd tell me what you could. So what is it we have to do?"

Gaelinar stared after Taziar, ignoring Larson's query. "There's a saying where I come from: 'Meet a man once, it's a chance. Meet twice and it's coincidence. The third time, you must embrace him or slay him.' To happen upon Shadow in the tavern seems unlikely enough. But to discover him snooping around our camp just when we're planning our journey? The dishonorable rodent owes us an explanation."

Taziar froze in his tracks. "The 'dishonorable rodent' would appreciate it if you would stop speaking to him in the third person." He turned to Gaelinar. "And I wasn't snooping. I was taking a walk."

"In the dark?" Gaelinar snorted. "And you just stumbled upon our camp by accident?"

Taziar shrugged. "However it happened, you and Allerum invited me along. If you want me to leave, say so. I'll gladly trail you unseen."

Larson kicked a dead branch at his feet, wishing his companions would stop bickering and continue walking. *Time is of the essence.* The delay turned his mood cruel. *Maybe I should just have let Gaelinar kill Shadow at the Dragonrank school.*

Gaelinar's tone carried a hint of threat. "You may find tracking us more difficult than you think."

Taziar met Gaelinar's glare with a triumphant grin. "I didn't have any trouble following you from the school. Shall I stay or leave? I'll abide by your decision."

Gaelinar's nostrils flared. Otherwise, his bland features betrayed no surprise or anger. "Stay. An enemy within sword range is safer than one concealed. But I warn you. If you try to kill Allerum or me, you will find us stronger than you can handle. If you take anything belonging to us, if you betray us at any time, you will die in the most horrible fashion I can design."

Taziar's blue eyes narrowed in offense. "In my life, I have killed only twice. Both times, my hand was forced; and never, before or since, have I had to do anything so vile.'' His fingers curled at his sides. ''I'm not an enemy. What is in your best interests is in mine as well. And if I wanted something you carried, I would have it already.'' He spun on the balls of his feet and returned to his path, shoving branches aside with a new violence.

Relieved to continue their quest, Larson trotted after Taziar. He suppressed the urge to question the thief's motives for tailing them, not wanting to incite another argument. Instead, he attempted to distract Gaelinar. ''It's time, now. Tell me about Geirmagnus' rod.''

Gaelinar walked beside Larson, his attention still fixed on Taziar. ''Geirmagnus was the first and most powerful Dragonrank Master. His estate still stands, a day's travel south of the city of Rajarkmar. Some say removing his rod from its resting place will restore life to the dead god, Baldur.''

Larson creased his forehead. ''That's common knowledge?''

''For almost a century.''

Confusion rode Larson. ''But if Baldur is as well loved as Vidarr tells me, why hasn't anyone retrieved the rod yet?''

''Many have tried. None have succeeded.''

Larson brushed dried needles from his hair, concerned by the multitude of potential barriers to completing Vidarr's task and obtaining the knowledge he needed to rescue Silme. ''Why has no one succeeded?''

Gaelinar turned his gaze to Larson. ''To tell you would doom you to failure, too.''

Curiosity piqued, Larson pressed further. ''How could that be?''

Larson's insistence strained Gaelinar's patience. ''To answer your second question, Allerum, I would obviously need to address the first. As I said, that would assure your failure.''

It makes no sense. How can knowledge doom me to failure? I would think ignorance would prove far more dangerous. Larson kept the comment to himself, not wishing to further antagonize Gaelinar. ''But exactly what is . . .'' He adopted the melodramatic tone of a bad Shakespearean actor. ''. . . the rod of Geirmagnus?''

"No one knows." Gaelinar spoke with casual indifference as they traced Taziar's path through the densely-clustered branches. "No one has gotten into Geirmagnus' estate."

"And I suppose you can't tell me why."

An impatient frown formed on Gaelinar's lips. "I could. For Silme's sake, though, I've chosen not to."

Wonderful. Larson folded his arms across his chest. "You know, Gaelinar. If there's some sort of monster guarding this place, I believe I have a right to know."

The crow's feet at the corners of Gaelinar's eyes deepened with cynical amusement. "Trust me, Allerum."

Larson pictured the Hel hound howling and slavering at the entrance to Midgard and found the Kensei's reassurance less than comforting.

Ignoring Larson's worry, Gaelinar cleared his throat and returned the conversation to the matter which concerned him. "Now tell me, Allerum. Why would Vidarr suggest we drag along an arrogant, little thief?"

Gaelinar's question was still unresolved when evening descended upon the pine forest. The world dulled to silver haze, broken by the towering, skeletal forms of the trees. Aggravated by Gaelinar's and Taziar's exchanged slurs and plagued by events beyond his control, Larson felt restless. "I'll take first watch."

To Larson's relief, neither of his companions argued. After a supper of jerked meat and tasteless bread, each chose a piece of cleared ground, some distance apart, and dropped into sleep.

Surrounded by the soft rhythms of his companions' breathing, Larson brooded. *I'm a goddamned pawn. As far as the gods are concerned, they saved my life and now they own it.* He leaped to his feet.

Gaelinar and Taziar stirred briefly at the movement, then returned to their dreams.

Carefully, Larson paced between them. *What's going to happen if I do retrieve Geirmagnus' rod? I'll get Silme back . . . maybe. Then Vidarr or Freyr or Odin will find some new form of blackmail.* He slammed his fist into his palm. *Well, forget it. I've paid my dues. From now on, if Vidarr wants a favor, he can ask like anyone else.*

Larson retook his seat on the needle-blanketed woodland floor. Frustration settled over him, suffocatingly heavy in the silence. *I've got to stop thinking like this. The gods can read my every treasonous thought as if I shouted it from the highest mountaintop.* The realization further fueled his ire. *And that, too, makes damn little sense. Vidarr claimed Freyr chose me for the initial quest because I have no "mind barriers." Silme believed this defect was very rare, perhaps unique. Whatever these "mind barriers" are, having none seems to mean certain beings—dream-readers, sorcerers, gods, and giant wolves—have access to my thoughts and memories. AND I DON'T LIKE IT!*

Larson scowled, allowing his mind to run freely with the topic until fatigue grew strong enough to overpower anger. By the position of the moon and the color of the night sky, he could tell several hours had passed. Yawning, he scrutinized his companions and chose Taziar as the least comfortable of the pair. Larson approached the climber, caught a thin forearm, and shook.

Taziar opened his eyes.

"Your turn on watch." Feeling spiteful, Larson added, "Though I can't say I'll sleep all that well with a thief guarding me."

Taziar sat up, suddenly fully alert. "I'd appreciate it if the two of you would stop calling me a thief."

Larson stretched out on his side and leaned on one elbow, prepared to vent this irritation on his newest companion. "Why?" he asked gruffly.

"Why?" Taziar's voice rose with incredulity, then went gruff with annoyance. From a larger man, his tone might have sounded menacing. "First, it's insulting. Second, it makes me and anyone who hears you uneasy. And third, it's not true."

Larson blinked twice in succession. "But you steal. You take other people's things. Where I come from, that makes you a thief."

"Allerum. Have you ever killed?"

"Yes," Larson confessed.

Taziar hugged his knees to his chest. "Then you won't mind if I call you 'murderer.' "

Taziar's words infuriated Larson. Guilt slammed against his conscience, and the old, Vietnamese woman near the fire base filled his memory. "Don't you dare! There's a difference between killing and murder, you know."

Taziar quirked one eyebrow. "Taking things and stealing aren't the same either."

"Taking things against a person's will after he earned them is stealing."

"Oh." Taziar rocked from his heels to his buttocks. "You mean like taxes."

"No!" Larson heaved an exasperated sigh. "You're playing games with me, and I don't like it."

"I'm just defending myself from undeserved abuse. Mardain knows, I've taken my share today."

Larson rolled to his stomach and propped his chin in his hands. "Give it up, Shadow. I may learn to tolerate you, but I'm not going to approve of pickpocketing. I don't think much of people who steal from working men because they're too lazy to get jobs of their own."

Taziar scooted toward Larson and thrust a palm near the elf's face. The fingers appeared badly scarred and yellow-gray with calluses. "Does this look the hand of an idle man?"

"No," Larson admitted.

"Then quit judging me on a single incident and Gaelinar's prejudice."

"Look." Larson swept to a sitting position, legs crossed before him. "I wish Gaelinar would ease up on you, too. But he does have a point. I don't like traveling with men I don't trust any more than he does. Dishonesty is not an admirable trait in a companion."

Taziar laid a hand on the sheathed sword by his knee, but his maneuver seemed more of a gesture than a threat. "Dishonesty? You had best be speaking of Gaelinar. I assure you, my integrity is genuine and intact."

"A man who would steal wouldn't hesitate to lie."

Taziar leaned forward. "That's nonsense, Allerum. The one has nothing to do with the other. And when have I ever taken anything from you?"

"Never." Larson yawned. "At least, I don't believe you have. But you stole from Gaelinar."

"Aga'arin's fat, metallic ass, Allerum. I gave everything back to him. Does that sound like stealing to you?"

"No. But you robbed Gaelinar too easily for me to believe you haven't had practice. A *lot* of practice."

"Sure, I've taken things before."

"Ah ha!" Larson crowed his triumph. "So you do lie. And you are a thief."

"No." Taziar clamped a hand to his face in disgust. "I never said I didn't take things. I said I wasn't a thief."

It seemed to Larson the conversation had returned to its original premise without moving an inch nearer to resolution. "What's the difference between taking and stealing?"

"The same as that between killing and murder. Intent. Have you ever lived in a big city, Allerum?"

Larson smiled. "You could say that."

"How large?"

"When I left it, New York City had a population of about eight million people."

Taziar snorted. "That's not funny. I'm serious."

"So am I."

"Eight million of the two million people in the world live in this city 'New York'. And I've never even heard of it?" Taziar hesitated. "Is this an elven city?"

Larson sighed, wishing he had not answered Taziar's population question truthfully. "Not exactly. It's too hard to explain. Just go on with your point."

"Fine." Taziar rose to his knees, raked his sword to his hand, and fastened it to his belt. "Then you must have noticed beggars and street orphans and lunatics living in the roadways."

"Sure."

"How do you think they eat?"

Larson smiled. "Food stamps?"

Taziar crinkled his face, perplexed. "I've only recently learned your language. I've never heard those words used that way. Explain."

Larson shrugged off Taziar's confusion. "It's an inside

joke and not a very good one. I imagine they beg or find jobs."

Taziar climbed to his feet. He seemed intent and agitated, as if the conversation had become too familiar. "Find jobs? Allerum, these people are children, elderly, ill, crippled, blind, or crazy. They steal, Allerum. They steal whatever they can from whoever they can. They steal, or they starve. Believe me, I know. I was orphaned at twelve. And, yes, I stole, too. When I got good enough at it to feed myself and my friends, I chose my victims more carefully. I targeted men and institutions who could afford to nourish the hungry. And it didn't stop there. You see, Allerum, the more I took, the more empty bellies I could fill."

Now Larson snorted. "Right. Sure. Sort of a . . . miniature, German Robin Hood. I always pictured Errol Flynn taller."

Taziar cocked his head. His eyes widened with confusion. "What language are you speaking?"

"Never mind." Larson cajoled Taziar, his voice heavy with mockery. "Go on. Tell me more about your . . ." He chose his words with care, ". . . astounding altruism."

Taziar's shoulders rose and fell; apparently Larson's sarcasm went unrecognized. "There's not much left to tell. For years, my father loyally led the baron's troops through a senseless war. When my father died, the baron's politics condemned me to the streets. The baron owed a chance at life to the orphans and cripples his stupid battles created, and I simply took it for them. I'd be there still if I hadn't been betrayed and nearly executed. Perhaps, in a few years, I'll go back."

Larson smiled, amused. Though he doubted every word of Taziar's story, the simple, amiable exchange of conversation had dispelled his aggravation. "That was a pretty good yarn. I'm impressed." He tipped his head to meet Taziar's face which wore a look of solemn innocence. "I'm still going to keep my wallet in my jock strap, but I am impressed." He considered. Taziar reminded him of a certain high school senior who was a great asset at a fight or any athletic event but who could never be trusted near a sister or girlfriend. The climber had a smooth, friendly confidence which made him likable though not reliable. "And you know something, Shadow? Even though you just spent half an hour spouting bald-faced lies . . ."

Taziar opened his mouth to protest, but Larson waved him silent.

"Even though you just wasted half an hour of my sleeping time with fiction," Larson nodded repeatedly to emphasize his point, "I think you're all right."

Taziar chewed his lip in contemplation. " 'All right,' huh?" He knelt, imitating Larson's head bobbing. "That, my friend, is what I've been trying to tell you."

"Wolf!"

Larson was asleep only a few minutes when Taziar's shout jarred him awake. Instinctively, he leaped to his feet, clawing at his belt for a weapon. The instant he rose, Fenrir slammed into him with express train force. Impact sprawled him. Something gashed his scalp, and he heard the snap of teeth as the wolf's bite fell short.

Fenrir! Larson struggled for breath. The pain which plowed through his body lost meaning in the battle for air. Through vision blurred by darkness and anguish, he glimpsed the giant form of the wolf towering over him. Jaws wide, Fenrir loosed a harsh bellow of contempt. Its neck went taut, and it lunged again.

Larson tensed; his sinews shrieked in complaint. Chest heaving with effort, he forced himself to roll. Fenrir's canines slashed his collar like a razor. The cloth tore away, revealing a grim line of scarlet. He tried to scream for help, but his air-starved lungs resisted.

Gaelinar! God, Gaelinar, where are you? Larson's breaths came in tortured moans he could not suppress. He threw up his arms to guard his throat. It was a feeble gesture at best; he knew the wolf's next attack would claim his life.

Again, Fenrir's gaping mouth plunged toward Larson. He winced, gathering his failing strength to twist away. Rows of sword-sharp teeth the color of old ivory filled his vision. Then, from the corner of his eye, he saw a dark figure dive at the wolf's face. Fenrir yowled and staggered back, Taziar clinging to the beast's great neck. Moonlight glinted from the dagger in his fist, and it struck through Fenrir's fur again and again.

The Fenris wolf bellowed in rage. It reared, forelegs pawing for Taziar, tossing its head in chaotic circles. Blood splashed Larson. The knife tore from Taziar's fist and flew between the huddled pines. The thief clung, ashen-faced, arms wrapped around the wolf's neck until a final buck dislodged him. Taziar soared in an ungainly arc, struck a tree trunk, and crumpled in an awkward, motionless heap.

Larson cringed in sympathy, breathing more easily now. He wallowed through agony to his sword hilt. The blade rattled free with maddening slowness.

Fenrir whirled back to Larson. Blood speckled the dark fur between its ears. It wore a broad grimace of triumph; malice darkened its eyes.

"My turn, wolf." Beyond Fenrir, Gaelinar adopted a perfect fighting stance. Still and coiled, he appeared like a statue carved in gold. His swords remained in their sheaths.

Fenrir spun toward Gaelinar. A ridge of hair rose along its spine. Its plumed tail went low with threat. "Your turn, Kensei? Your turn *to die!*" It charged Gaelinar with the same wild rush which had toppled Larson.

Larson straggled to a sitting position, ignoring the warning ache of his hip.

In a single motion, Gaelinar dodged, drew, and cut. The wolf swerved with him; its movement dulled the impact of their clash. Gaelinar bounced to the ground, but his strike opened Fenrir's shoulder. With a snarl of pain, the wolf overran Gaelinar, then whirled to face the Kensei again.

Fenrir staggered slightly. Its bloodied head swung from Taziar's broken form; to Larson, clumsily attempting to stand; to Gaelinar braced for another attack. The wolf's tongue lolled. "One dead. Two left. Next time, you won't hear me coming." With that warning, Fenrir turned and bounded into the forest.

With some satisfaction, Larson noted Fenrir was limping. *At least we hurt it, too.* He accepted Gaelinar's extended hand and stood. Trying to hide his own lameness, he tottered unsteadily to a nearby pine and leaned against its trunk. The pain localized to his left arm and hip. His vision swirled.

Gently, Gaelinar knelt over Taziar and pressed two fingers to the smaller man's throat.

"Is he?" Larson asked, fairly certain Fenrir's assessment was correct. Taziar seemed too still to be breathing, and dark blood trickled from one ear.

"He's alive, but he needs our help." Gaelinar twisted to face Larson as he sat beside the fallen man. "I suppose he's earned it." He looked pensive. "Allerum, I'm not often wrong, but this time I may have judged too quickly. He's . . ."

"All right," Larson finished hoarsely. "I know." Dizzy and aching, he fought a wave of nausea. "That's what he kept trying to tell us."

A careful assessment revealed Larson's wounds less severe than they might have been. From the sharp pains he suffered with every breath, he knew he had strained the cartilage between his ribs and sternum. Irregular, tender patches of red on his hip, chest, and forearm warned of coming bruises. Though the gash from Fenrir's teeth ached, he doubted it would cause a problem as long as it did not become infected.

Larson found Taziar's injuries more difficult to evaluate. A brief inspection confirmed all the damage Taziar had taken was internal. And Larson knew from experience there was nothing less predictable or more dangerous than a blow to the head.

Gaelinar hefted Taziar's limp form. "Let's find some other place to finish our sleep. I don't think Fenrir will return tonight. But if it does, I'd rather it had to hunt for us."

Larson nodded, feeling battered and exhausted. "Let's go."

Gaelinar and Larson wandered to a sheltered grove a short distance farther into the woods. The Kensei placed Taziar on a soft pile of shed needles, and the two conscious men cleared ground for their own beds. Provisions and weapons within easy reach, Larson listened to the purr of insects and strained his hearing for the crackle of wolf paws through brush.

Before Larson or Gaelinar found sleep, Taziar sat up. His gaze swept the clearing in confusion then focused on Gaelinar. He spoke as if awakening from a simple nap. "Kensei . . ." His voice went tremulous and faint. "You still owe me an explanation."

Larson crouched, glad Taziar had awakened but afraid the climber believed they were still in the tavern. "What did you say?"

Taziar's pale eyes remained fixed on Gaelinar. "Allerum, your friend still has not told me why he attacked me at the Dragonrank school. I think I earned the right to know."

Larson bit his lip to keep from smiling.

Gaelinar laughed aloud. "Agreed. But does it have to be now? We're all hurt and tired."

Taziar's face tensed into a solemn mask. "It can't wait. I'm not stupid. We all know I may not survive the night."

Larson thought he could discern a note of sadness beneath Taziar's matter-of-fact tone. He winced. Taziar was no older than his war companions in Vietnam. And, for some reason he could not fathom, this bothered Larson.

Gaelinar tucked his legs beneath him and lowered his buttocks to his heels. "Very well. But the story begins long before we met. It may take some time."

Shakily, Taziar lay flat on the ground. "I'm not going anywhere soon."

Larson scooted backward and hunched against a pine tree. He suspected Gaelinar's tale would address some of the issues which plagued him as well. He listened with closed eyes, allowing Gaelinar's descriptions to fill his mind with imagery.

"My country is one of rugged peaks and low, silken valleys enclosed and protected by the clear blue waters of its ocean. Aside from the crafted stone castles of the emperors, we lived in wooden cottages with sliding doors and shutters. It is a land where every man must have a skill to sell. The farmers toil, raising rice to feed the lords and their own families. The artisans master tools and plans. The merchants live to profit from the others. But the samurai must sell his very soul, his way with weapons and strategy. He must adhere to a rigid code of honor, loyalty, courage, and the resolute acceptance of death at all times.'' Gaelinar's eyes held a distant look.

Larson and Taziar waited in respectful silence until Gaelinar continued. ''My training as a warrior began almost before I could walk. The weapons skills and the use of my spirit in combat came as naturally as breathing. I was pledged to the emperor before I reached manhood, but my *musha shugyo,* my spiritual path to enlightenment through combat, did not begin until many years later, when Silme came to Edo.''

Interest replaced Larson's fatigue. Gaelinar's relationship to Silme had always engrossed and, sometimes, troubled him.

Gaelinar leaned forward and braced his hands on his thighs. ''Before Silme arrived, I had served my lord, and later his son, for more than forty years. I had never strayed from the code of *bushido.* Because of my skill and dedication . . .''

Larson smiled at Gaelinar's confidence which approached pomposity. It had become too familiar to bother him any longer.

''. . . I had risen in the emperor's service until I became his personal bodyguard. Then, one day, a young, yellow-haired woman named Silme arrived from the west. She asked to speak with my lord, in private, and he granted her request.'' Gaelinar closed his eyes. His chin sank to his chest.

For a moment, Larson thought the Kensei had drifted off to sleep.

But Gaelinar raised his head and continued. ''While Silme and my lord conversed alone, illness claimed my master. Since it was my duty to protect him, and I was not present when he perished, I had failed. Honor bound me to die with him. In fact, I was preparing to commit *seppuku,* when Silme convinced me otherwise. She argued that death is a normal part of life. Since my master was not slain by an enemy, I would have shirked my duty had I saved his life and prevented him from fulfilling his destiny. Then Silme told me of the larger world beyond my experience. She described the powers I had not yet tested my skills against and the glory I could win by proving myself the greatest swordmaster, not of an isolated chain of islands, but of the entire world.'' Gaelinar's muddy eyes glimmered with elation and determination. A cruel smile twitched across his features.

Something uncharacteristically evil about Gaelinar's demeanor made Larson shiver.

Gaelinar continued, oblivious. ''Despite this new challenge, I still felt the need of some personal sacrifice to sever the final bonds between me and my master. In order to face the challenges of the world, my body remained alive, but my birthname died. The moment I left the white sand beach of Honshu, Fujiwara Hida No Kami Shokan ceased to exist; and Silme renamed me Gaelinar.''

Larson suppressed the urge to ask Gaelinar how he ever remembered his full title. ''Why 'Gaelinar'? It doesn't sound Japanese or Norwegian.''

Gaelinar shrugged. ''I don't know. It took me a year to learn to pronounce it, and I still have no idea what it means. But Silme insisted, and one foreign name seemed the same as another to me.''

Larson grinned, recalling how a spell of inept stuttering had earned him the strange sounding monicker of Allerum. *And Shadow doesn't use his real name either.* ''But you still haven't explained why you tried to kill Shadow.''

Taziar nodded in agreement, then winced in pain.

''Patience is a rare and wonderful thing.'' Gaelinar spoke soberly but ruined the effect by adding, ''I wish I had some.''

Larson laughed.

Taziar smiled weakly.

''One of my lord's advisers had always been jealous of my favor with the emperor. In order to avenge himself on me, he claimed I had shamed my master by refusing to commit *seppuku.* For years afterward, assassins followed me. They always wore black. They hid in the shadows, attacking, unseen, from behind every corner and tree. Instead of learning the way of the sword, overcoming men for honor and glory, these would-be killers were students of treachery, deceit, and cowardice.

"Many times, they tried to catch me unaware and slay me in sleep." Gaelinar's bitterness returned. "And many times, they failed. Finally, the attempts ceased. Whether I was forgotten or had merely killed all the assassins who knew where to find me, I cannot know. But I have not seen one for three years." He looked directly at Taziar. "Until I found you clinging to the walls of the Dragonrank school. After seven years during which my survival depended on striking first, when I saw you, I had no need to question. In my mind, it was my life or yours."

Gaelinar raised and lowered his head in an abbreviated gesture of respect. "In ten years, Shadow, you're the first one who escaped me."

Taziar lay in quiet contemplation. At length, he spoke, his voice subdued. "I find it difficult to consider my luck an honor. And I still don't understand. Surely you could tell me from an assassin of your people."

Gaelinar ran the edges of his hands along his face. "Ten years of habit are hard to break. And others besides the Japanese will kill for money."

Taziar's features crinkled with concern. "But now, I hope, you realize I'm not one of those 'others.' "

Gaelinar dropped his hands. "I don't know, Shadow. You've followed us, at least since the Dragonrank school. You've put a lot of effort into gaining my attention. And, by the way, you're lucky I didn't kill you for that incident in the tavern. You agreed to join us with little or no knowledge of our quest. And you haven't offered a plausible explanation for any of that."

Taziar's face bunched tighter. "So you still believe I've come to kill you?"

Gaelinar shrugged. "You've given me no reason to think otherwise."

The words surprised Larson. *He nearly died for me and still may. That's enough proof for me.* He opened his mouth to voice his thought, but Taziar's feeble voice broke the encroaching stillness first.

"Fair enough. My motives are honorable, if somewhat odd. You see Kensei . . . Allerum . . ." He rolled his eyes to each of his companions in turn. ". . . I am possessed by love."

Larson suppressed a laugh. *That's the corniest line I've ever heard.* It occurred to him suddenly that traveling to Hel, battling dragons, and beseeching gods and sorcerers to restore life to a dead lover might fall well within Taziar's description. *Corny or not, I guess I can identify with that.* Larson found a comfortable position, certain he would find Taziar's story intriguing if not particularly accurate.

Taziar let his lids drift closed. The overhanging boughs draped his sallow face in shadow. With careful yet flowery words, he detailed his love for Astryd, his visit to the Dragonrank school, and the information gained there. "It seemed to me the best way to make Silme receptive to taking Astryd on as apprentice would be for me to assist her return from death. You know the rest."

Gaelinar's voice sounded unusually loud after Taziar's soft-spoken defense. "Why did you not tell us this before?"

"You never gave me a chance."

Apparently satisfied, Gaelinar rolled to his side.

Larson hesitated, listening to the owlish, whirring barks of foxes. A distant wolf howl sent a chill along his spine. *There's still something he's not telling us. His story doesn't explain why he was he so willing to die for me.* Larson replayed Fenrir's attack in his mind. Taziar's dive for the great wolf's neck had been an act of fanatical and reckless courage. *Why? No one could be that self-sacrificing.* He recalled how Silme had dedicated her life to neutralizing her half brother's atrocities. Another scene filled his mind, a trench in Vietnam filled with American soldiers and a single, live grenade. Before anyone else could act, an eighteen-year-old private leaped upon it, shielding his buddies from the blast. It exploded, spraying the others with shrapnel and blood. Chest and abdomen torn open, the hero had suppressed his moans of pain until death claimed him.

Larson shuddered, chasing the memory from his thoughts. He studied Taziar in the dappled light of early morning. The climber lay, limp and silent, breaths deep but uneven. ''Do you think he'll make it?''

Gaelinar said nothing as he pondered Larson's euphemism. When he did reply, it was with a fatalistic detachment. ''We'll know by evening.''

CHAPTER 8:

Masters of the Mind

"What is life? A madness. What is life? An illusion, a shadow, a story. And the greatest good is little enough: for all life is a dream, and dreams themselves are only dreams."

—Pedro Calderon de la Barca
Life is a Dream

Larson rolled over in his sleep. Immediately, darkness enfolded his consciousness. He found himself in blackness as thick, heavy, and tangible as pitch. All memory escaped him. He stood, blind and disoriented, heart pounding with apprehension. He tensed to a crouch, felt the searing presence of enemy eyes watching, unseen, from the impenetrable night. Somehow they could see him, he had no doubt.

Suddenly, a wolf howled behind him, a wordless, exultant song of evil. Larson whirled. Pain hammered his body; his chest spasmed, making every breath painful. A second howl sounded, louder, contemptuous, and directly across from the first. He spun again. Before he could react to the dull chorus of aches, another howl rent the air to his right, closer now. Larson twisted toward it. He backstepped, clawing the air behind him for a barrier against which to press his back. His fingers met empty space, and another howl shattered the silence directly behind him.

Larson leaped in surprise. His foot came down on a root. His ankle rocked sideways, and he tumbled to the ground. He floundered through darkness to his hands and knees, tensed to rise, and found himself gazing into blazing crimson eyes. He screamed, staggered back, and again tripped over the root, now behind him. He fell, hard, on his spine and stared up at a row of saliva-slicked, yellowed teeth, each as long and sharp as a saber.

Larson threw back his head and bellowed with fright. He lurched away from the creature, sparking a fresh wave of agony through his chest and hip. Foul breath struck his face, and he saw that the beast, and all its teeth, had swerved with him. *Pain.* Larson panted. *Damn this pain. If this is a dream, why do I feel so much goddamned pain?* The thought electrified him. All fear drained away. His sense of self returned, hot and strong within him, and he recognized the pain as the bruises from his battle with Fenrir. He clambered to his feet, oblivious to the wolf which threatened him with jaws widely-hinged. "You've lost, Fenrir! This time, you're not real. You're nothing but an intruder in my dreams tonight, and I know you cannot hurt me." Larson's words echoed through the vast cavern of his mind.

The darkness fell away, revealing the heavily-muscled form of the Fenris wolf. Clotted blood darkened one shoulder, but its red eyes glowed with life. It growled, deep in its throat. "Allerum. Even in your own thoughts, I am stronger than you!" As it spoke the last syllable, it sprang toward Larson's dream-form, lashing at the twisted coils of thought.

Despite his bold words, Larson dodged aside instinctively. The wolf struck a glancing blow which knocked him to the ground. The fall stole his breath and his courage. Realization of dream slipped from his grasp. Fear and confusion regained their hold, leaving Larson with a bad taste in his mouth and the knowledge that something seemed out of place. He struggled for the lost concept. Great peals of mocking laughter rocked the wolf as it slid the recognition of dream further from Larson's conscious understanding.

Abruptly, another being appeared in Larson's mind. The wolf dropped its attack; a spark of insight roused Larson. *Dream. It's a . . .* Then both intruders' emotions crashed against him, knocking his consciousness askew.

He felt suffocated by wolf-inspired panic followed by Fenrir's own shock and surprise, alien but powerful as the tide. The other presence radiated determination.

Larson groped for some semblance of sanity on which to anchor his shattered reason. The world exploded, hurling him into nothingness. He fell, spinning and tumbling through leagues of empty air, shot through with terror and the certainty of death. Desperately, his fingers cleaved the darkness. Another clash rocked his being, tossing him as carelessly as flotsam. His foot touched something solid. Arching, he flung his body sideways and clung to the only reality he could find.

A rocket screeched. Directly overhead, it splintered with a roar, splattering multihued pinpoints across the summer sky. Larson clapped, surrounded by gasps of awe and childish squeals of appreciation. He scooted back against the windshield of his father's Dart and glanced at his brother. Suddenly, the scene dissolved around him, and he realized he was alone. Fear struck like madness. Larson groped through the moonless darkness which ensued between one barrage and the next. The car was gone. The crowd had disappeared, replaced by muffled sounds of movement. Larson froze.

Mortars slashed red trails through the heavens; thickening clouds kept their light alive long after the explosion of sound. Man-shadows and distantly familiar faces replaced the cheering mob. And Larson seized a tenuous grasp on reality. *Incoming. Incoming! And I'm sitting here impressed, like I'm watching some stupid Fourth of July fireworks.* He leaped to his feet. Whirling, he ran toward the bunker.

Larson had taken only three steps when he crashed into an unyielding mass of fur and muscle. Pain descended on him. He staggered sideways. The darkness fled and the firebase faded into memory, replaced by a stretch of frozen ground as barren as a tank-cleared plain. Fenrir spun with a startled curse. Old blood still matted its shoulder. No other marks marred its dark hide, but it panted as if from great exertion. Beyond the wolf, Vidarr crouched, sword angled defensively before him. Sweat sheened on his pale limbs. Flaps of clothing dangled, woven through with silver threads. Anger darkened his fair features.

Fenrir advanced toward Larson, ears laid flat to its head, crimson eyes gleaming. Larson dove aside. Gaelinar's words hissed in his ear, foreign and uninterpretable, their inflection wholly alien. Some force outside Larson's mind racked his body, reawakening the ache of his injuries. Fenrir sprang. Larson ducked. The beast sailed over Larson's head and vanished through a yawning gap into the infinity of world beyond his mind. The wolf's voice echoed in threat. ''Next time, Allerum, I come for real. No god can save you then.''

Larson staggered, feeling weak and spent. Anchored in his own mind, he heard Gaelinar only as distant noise. He glanced at the gold and silver figure of Vidarr. *Where? How?*

Larson did not expect an answer, so Vidarr's reply startled him. *Fenrir invaded your mind. I came to aid you.*

Larson studied his surroundings in bleary detachment. Vidarr stood among loops of mental circuitry, a chaotic array of wires which Larson knew must represent his own brain. Light flickered and slashed along the pathways as the scene registered and he contemplated its significance. *Fenrir,* he repeated, dazed. *In my dream.* Larson's voice seemed to issue from a tangled coil a short distance before the exit; he held no material form in his own mind. With that discovery, he felt himself drawing back into his physical body. He resisted, strengthened by the early stirrings of resentment. *Vidarr, I was fighting Fenrir off until you came.*

Derisive laughter rang through Larson's thoughts. *Until I came, Fenrir was playing you like a mouse.*

No!

Vidarr radiated an aura of contempt. *Yes, Allerum. I've told you before, you lack the natural mental barriers people of this era possess. Your mind is like a book. Any force with enough knowledge and power can penetrate and manipulate it, writing and rewriting as it pleases.*

Wrong, Vidarr! Growing rage lent power to Larson's rebuttal. *Fenrir can wake old memories. It can inspire thoughts and torture me with images. But, while inside my mind, Fenrir can cause me no physical harm.*

Vidarr's anger echoed Larson's. *Of what consequence is physical harm! Your strongest enemies can control your beliefs. They can turn you away from your important goals.*

Ah ha!

Vidarr hesitated. *Ah ha?*

This is what it all comes down to, isn't it, Vidarr? You're scared Fenrir might convince me not to fetch Geirmagnus' rod.

Vidarr was accustomed to communicating with emotions; his self-righteousness came through every bit as clearly as his words. *Whatever happened to gratitude, Allerum? I just faced the strongest chaos force in existence for you. Fenrir may not be able to hurt you in your mind, but it could have killed me. And you seem to have forgotten that Freyr rescued you from death to bring you here, at no small risk to his own life.*

Larson snorted. The sound filled every crevice of his mind. *Freyr brought me here because he needed someone from my age. He needed a person without mind barriers to communicate with you by wielding the sword in which Loki had trapped you. He summoned me to slay a god. I accomplished that. In doing so, I destroyed my own world. My debt is paid. I'm free now. I don't owe you or Freyr any favors. I didn't ask him to bring me here, and I didn't ask you for help against Fenrir. In fact, I politely requested you to STAY OUT OF MY PERSONAL MEMORIES!*

Vidarr dismissed Larson's tirade, his annoyance hot and tangible through the cramped corners of Larson's mind. *Listen, Allerum. I'm tired of your disrespect. I don't know what gods are like in your world, but here, we seldom deign to speak with humble mortals. When we do, it's considered the greatest honor.*

Spare me the speech . . . and the honor, Vidarr. Freyr chose me because I yelled his name in my last moment of life. Freyr doesn't exist in my world. Calling on him was a sacrilege. If I don't respect the God I was taught to worship since childhood, how can you expect me to respect you?

Vidarr's eyes followed the shifting lights which betrayed Larson's current abstraction.

Larson seized the god's silence to continue. *I'm sick of everyone expecting me to kowtow and cast aside my own ideals for theirs. Protected or not, my mind is my own. Your presence is as much a violation of my privacy as Fenrir's.* Recalling Vidarr was an ally, Larson tried to soften his words. *Damn it, Vidarr. I feel like I'm being raped. I have to learn to handle this handicap on my own. Don't worry about my thoughts. I know myself well enough to recognize and ignore a concept which goes against my nature.*

Vidarr remained haughty and relentless. *Bramin once convinced you I was an unholy being and your mission was to destroy me.*

That was before either of us knew he could influence my dreams.

Regardless, Allerum. It's my job to keep you on task. Freyr pulled you from a hellish war . . .

. . . To place me into another hellish war. Into Hel itself even! I'm supposed to feel grateful that Freyr ripped me from a world of technological miracles and dumped me into the body of a ninety-eight pound weakling?

Vidarr persisted. *Technological miracles or not. You were dead.*

Dead or not, I was free. I'm no slave. You tell me "get Geirmagnus' rod," but you won't describe what guardians I'll have to face. You know how to raise Silme, but you won't tell me. Instead, you used the information to blackmail me. I say enough! If I am to serve gods, I shall do so willingly or not at all. Otherwise, you can kill me right now.

Allerum! Vidarr's presence shook with impatience. *Stop this nonsense.*

Driven nearly to violence, Larson pressed onward. *These are the ground rules, Vidarr. From now on, if you need a favor, you ask. Second, any uninvited intrusion into my mind will be considered an act of war.*

An act of what! Exasperation beat through Larson's mind. *My battle with Fenrir has addled you.*

Not addled! Larson screamed. *Enlightened. It was you who triggered my memories, not Fenrir. The wolf merely came to threaten me.*

Irritation sifted through Vidarr's reply. *This is crazy. You've gone crazy. I'll return when you've recovered your senses.* He took a step toward the gap through which Fenrir had exited Larson's mind.

No! If you return without settling this, I'll consider it an attack.

Vidarr paused. *Good-bye, Allerum.*

No! Larson realized he could not allow Vidarr to leave yet. It would take all meaning from future promises and threats. Desperate, he gathered every fiber of mental energy and channeled it into the image of a restraining wall, hard and high as the one which enclosed the Dragonrank school. To Larson's surprise, a broad shape shimmered to life before Vidarr, hazy and indistinct.

The god hesitated. *Allerum? What are you doing, Allerum?*

Larson said nothing. He gritted his teeth, tensing every muscle. Pain ground through him. He ignored it, mind and body drawn together in effort. Sweat rolled from his forehead. Unbeknownst to him, his physical body contorted to a knot of concentration. Gradually, the wall came into focus, neatly blocking Vidarr's escape.

Larson could barely perceive Vidarr's mix of shock and sudden fear. *Allerum! What?*

Larson replied carefully. Every syllable seemed to weaken him. *Tell . . . how . . . to . . . rescue . . . Silme.* The wall behind Vidarr collapsed. Larson fell silent. A fresh wave of frustrated anger gave him the strength to reconstruct it, brick by mental brick. He hoped the barricade would also keep Vidarr from seeing the self-doubt which filled the remainder of his consciousness. He knew he had to get Vidarr's answer quickly. If the god stalled long enough, Larson would lose the strength to hold him.

Apparently, Vidarr did not recognize the tenuousness of Larson's trap. Discomfort shot through his reply, and he seemed on the edge of panic. *Allerum. Calm down. We can discuss . . .*

Spasms racked Larson's material form, and he feared he might be having a convulsion. The momentary redirection of his thoughts blurred the mental walls. Rage warred with the threat of defeat.

Allerum?

Quickly, Larson refocused his mind. The walls wavered, then grew more visible. Anger speared through him. *Now!* He shouted with such directed fury, fire splattered the ground at Vidarr's feet.

Vidarr lurched backward with a startled cry. *All right. Stop! I'll tell you.*

Now. Larson managed to insist. The effort of that single word nearly drove him to unconsciousness.

Vidarr hesitated only a second, but it dragged like hours. *Now,* the god agreed reluctantly. *But you're making a mistake.*

Larson's concentration snapped. The wall dissolved. Pain crushed down on him, well beyond the bruises Fenrir had inflicted, and it sapped his remaining strength. Voices wafted to him, drowned by a harsh ringing in his ears. He opened his eyes. His bleary gaze registered little. He lay on the ground. Gaelinar knelt at his side, speaking softly and incomprehensibly. "A minute," he forced himself to say. His tongue felt twisted and heavy.

Gaelinar fell silent.

Larson concentrated on a thought. *Vidarr?*

I'm still here. The god amended, *Actually, I'm no longer inside your mind. I'm communicating through a probe.*

Larson was careful not to reveal any information about his mental trap; it would not do to reveal the difficulty of its construction nor the frailty of his barrier. *Explain.*

Explain what?

Larson felt weak as a rag. *What the hell is a "probe?" And how do I free Silme?* Even as he asked, Larson wished he had reversed the order.

When we communicate telepathically or I just need to read some surface thought or a memory you've highlighted for me, I use a magical, mental link to do it.

Vidarr paused, as if waiting for some indication Larson understood the concept. When he got none, he continued. *In order to manipulate your thoughts, spark old memories, or fight Fenrir, I have to actually enter your mind. That's why I could have taken physical damage from the wolf. Do you understand?*

Yes. Larson lied. His mind felt fuzzy, and he needed to consider Vidarr's descriptions at a more opportune time. *And Silme?*

Vidarr hesitated.

Larson could raise no more than a faint spark of anger. *The truth, Vidarr, or I swear Baldur will rot in Hel.*

In his weakness, Larson could not read Vidarr's intentions. *Allerum, you promised.*

So did you, Vidarr.

Only under duress.

Oh! Larson tried to work sarcasm into his reply. *And my vow was obtained in good faith? Quit stalling and tell me how to free Silme.*

Very well. Vidarr's mental words grew so soft, Larson had to strain to discern them. *To bring Silme back to Midgard, you need to open a place for her. You must keep Chaos and Law in balance.*

Larson struggled against unconsciousness. He felt drained, body and soul. *Tell me something I don't know.*

Allerum, think. Annoyance increased Vidarr's volume. *The Fates will allow you to kill a man only if his time has come to die. You can't "open a place for Silme" by slaying a servant of Law. You have to balance her resurrection with the resurrection of a tool of Chaos . . .*

. . . of similar strength to Silme. The revelation lent Larson a second wind. *So, I have to find a Chaos-serving, sapphire-rank Dragonmage who died some time in the past.*

Again Vidarr hesitated, apparently grappling with a decision. *Allerum, for some reason, you're not thinking clearly. Eventually, you're going to figure this out, so I might as well take credit for telling you. Do you recall the dead in Hel?*

Larson nodded, not wasting the effort of retrieving the memory.

Vidarr continued. *Then you know that the longer they remain in Hel, the less human they become. Gradually, they lose all sense of self. The sorcerer you raise with Silme cannot have died too long before her.*

Despair filled Larson. *I have to find a sapphire-rank mage who died about the same time as Silme? Is there one?*

Vidarr radiated exasperation with such intensity, Larson acknowledged it even through his failing perceptions. *Your slaying of the god, Loki, tipped the world's balance toward Law. Hel is of Chaos. Therefore, she must be willing to compensate Silme's freedom with a Chaos-serving sorcerer somewhat more powerful than Silme.*

Suddenly, everything came together. *Bramin! God, Vidarr! You're talking about Bramin.* An image came, unbidden. Again, Larson saw Bramin's features, sharply defined and slender with a deadly, sinuous grace. He stared into eyes as red as Fenrir's but flashing with an evil which defied the ages. Bramin's dark elf father had stolen the virginity from Silme's mother by rape. The cruelty of townsfolk and Bramin's demon breeding had trained him to hate, and the Dragonrank teachings gave him the power to turn his bitterness into violence. Worse, in addition to having mastered Dragonrank sorcery to its highest level, Bramin was also a swordsman of superior talent.

Vidarr's manner became soothing. *So you understand now why I couldn't tell you how to free Silme earlier. Bramin would stand against your quest. He might prove powerful enough to prevent you from retrieving Geirmagnus' rod. Surely, you understand why you must revive Baldur first, while you're still unopposed. Then you can raise Silme and Bramin.* Vidarr's words came faster, and Larson thought he detected a note of nervousness. *Do it in that order, the only logical way, and I'll aid you against Bramin as much as the laws which govern gods allow.* He waited.

A red curtain of fatigue blinded Larson. His thoughts stumbled through mist, and it took every last vestige of energy to form a coherent answer. *Vidarr, I'm going to*

Hel. Darkness descended on Larson, and a long time passed before he knew anything more.

Larson awoke to the gray haze of evening. He rolled to his back, braced for a barrage of pain. But he felt only the dull ache of his injured ribs and hip. Sleep had healed the fog of his mental battle, and, though it taxed him in mind and sinew, it seemed to have left no physical aftereffects.

Gaelinar took a seat next to Larson and set a handkerchief full of berries in the elf's lap. "Are you well now, hero?"

Larson stretched, though the maneuver sent berries tumbling onto his breeches. "I feel great." He considered his conversation with Vidarr. *Was it all a dream?* "Gaelinar, I think I know how to get Silme back."

Gaelinar studied Larson curiously. "Are you certain?"

Larson popped a handful of berries into his mouth, their taste an equal mixture of sweet and sour. "I believe so. We have to return to Hel and ask its queen to release Silme and Bramin together."

Gaelinar went still. For a full minute, he did not move so much as a finger or an eyelid.

Larson fidgeted. He had expected almost any reaction but none at all, and Gaelinar's silence unnerved him. "I said . . ."

"I heard you."

"And?" Larson prompted.

Gaelinar leaped to his feet. "Let's go."

Larson crammed berries into his cheeks, dumped the remainder to the ground as he stood, and returned Gaelinar's handkerchief. He hoped it was his own imagination which made the Kensei's movements seem less fluid than usual. Then another concern usurped his attention. "Where's Shadow?" In his moments of lucidity, Larson had noticed only Gaelinar. *When I last saw Shadow, we didn't know if he'd make it till evening.*

"He's washing up." Gaelinar jerked a thumb toward the ring of pine which surrounded the grove. Wrinkling his nose, he added, "You might do well to join him."

Larson smiled, too glad at the news to take offense. "He's all right, then?"

Gaelinar nodded. "A lot better than you looked today. What happened? Nightmares again?"

"Sort of." Larson knelt, scooped up a few stray berries, and ate them. He ignored the dirt which grated beneath his teeth. "Vidarr and I had a disagreement."

Gaelinar met Larson's gaze. His eyes gained a glint of satisfaction, and his lips gradually bent into a smile. "Just another god, after all."

"Just another god," Larson agreed, though without Gaelinar's wry pleasure. "Now, where'd you say that water is?"

Gaelinar pointed.

Larson turned in the direction of the Kensei's gesture. He twisted his head back toward his mentor. "Is it frozen over?"

"It's a hot spring," Gaelinar explained.

"Oh." Larson brushed through the needled branches. He paced a straight course in the indicated direction and, shortly, came upon a natural, oblong pool. Wisps of steam curled from its surface, merging into the shadowing branches of the pine. A stream exited the northern bank. In the center of the spring, Taziar floated on his back, scrubbing his abdomen with a handful of grit. He acknowledged Larson with a brief nod. His linens lay, neatly folded, at the American's feet.

Larson stripped down and dropped his clothes into a pile beside Taziar's black climbing outfit. Measuring the distance with a careful glance, he took a shallow dive. The water parted before him, then closed around him. It felt near body temperature, warm, wet, and comfortable in the autumn chill. From experience, Larson knew cold would not bother him in his elf form, but he imagined Taziar would wish to dawdle in the tepid waters as long as possible.

Larson came up for air within five feet of Taziar who was now washing his crotch. Larson chuckled and called conversationally. "Don't you hate jock itch?"

Taziar spent some time in deep contemplation, as if

Larson had said something particularly profound. At length, he asked carefully, "What's 'jock itch?' "

"That." Larson pointed. "What you've got."

Taziar traced Larson's gesture to its logical conclusion. "Hmmm. Well, Allerum. You may call yours Jock, but I call mine . . . Thor."

Larson laughed, the humor tempered by the fact that Taziar had chosen the name of one of the few gods who might actually hear and take offense. "You're all right."

Taziar nodded agreement and turned his attention to his legs.

Larson flipped and dove. He scooped up a handful of pebbles and, treading water, scoured his own anatomy. "I'm glad. You're all right, I mean. You looked pretty hurt."

Taziar raked plastered hair from his eyes. "You, too. Gaelinar'll probably get mad I told you, but he worried about you."

"Really?" Larson smiled. He found it hard to imagine Gaelinar concerned about anything.

"Yes." Taziar bathed his other leg. "I think he feared he'd have to travel with me alone."

"Horrors!" Larson mocked. "A fate worse than death."

Taziar considered Larson's word choice. Even literally, it would be difficult to take the expression as anything but an insult. "Very nice. Thank you."

"Just a little joke."

Taziar splashed a wave of spring water over Larson, his tone colored with feigned offense. "So now you're be*littling* my size."

Larson grinned broadly. "An accident. But it was *small* of me," he quipped.

"Watch it. I'll start telling elf jokes." Taziar rolled and swam back to the shore, deliberately kicking water onto Larson.

Larson finished washing quickly and followed the Cullinsbergen to the banks. He enjoyed the exchange. Locker room gibes had been one of the few pleasures which made Vietnam tolerable, though fast friendships had a way of becoming fast deaths and faster grief. Since coming to

Old Scandinavia, Larson's only companion near his own age was Silme. But trading digs and caustic cracks with the woman of his dreams did not appeal to him.

Larson and Taziar dressed in silence. Larson was fastening his sword belt when Taziar questioned. "Did Gaelinar tell you about our new wolf weapon?"

"No." Larson patted the buckle in place. "I hope it's a tank."

Brow furrowed, Taziar took a step toward Larson. "A what?"

"Never mind." Larson waved Taziar off. "Just one of those stupid things I like to say to amuse myself. What's the new toy?"

"This." Taziar pulled a folded square of linen from his pocket. He rummaged through his clothing for some time, then raised his hand to flick hair from his face before producing a handkerchief. "Gaelinar put together a powder. He says it burns if thrown in the eyes." Taziar knelt, unwrapped the parcel to reveal a pile of gray-white dust, and spread the second scrap of cloth beside it. Using a stick, he divided its contents in half and prepared to scrape powder from one to the other.

Noticing the difficulty Taziar had had producing the second handkerchief, Larson dug through his pocket for one of his own. "Here. Use mine."

Taziar did not look up from his work. "This is yours."

Larson's fingers groped an empty pocket. "What?"

"Sorry. Habit." Taziar stood, a neatly tied bundle in each hand. He passed one to Larson and turned the elf a wicked smile.

"You . . ." Before Larson could think of a suitably vile insult, a cry of pained rage rent the woodland peace followed by an animal growl of determination. *Gaelinar!* Larson sprinted toward the grove, Taziar on his heels.

The pines parted easily before Larson. Following the direction of the sound, he clawed through jumbles of needled branches, leaped over a deadfall, and emerged in a star-shaped clearing near the grove. At the farther edge stood Fenrir, its bristled fur brushing the higher branches. Fresh blood trickled from a gash in its flank. Gaelinar dangled from its jaws; the wolf's teeth closed over a thick crease on the back of the Kensei's robes. Gaelinar's swords formed a perfect cross, locking the wolf's neck between them.

"Come on, wolf! Shake me!" Gaelinar's voice rang with challenge. "You may kill me, but you'll slash your own throat as well. I'm ready. Do you fear death, puppy?"

Fenrir growled.

Larson froze, taking a moment to assess the situation. There was truth to Gaelinar's words, but it seemed a perfect stalemate. For the Kensei to strike, he would need to draw back for momentum, removing any deterrent to Fenrir shaking the life from him. But Fenrir could not bite unless it loosed the hold it already had, granting Gaelinar a chance at escape.

In his moment of hesitation, Larson heard Taziar's sword rasp free. He drew his own and charged the wolf.

Fenrir raised its eyes. Suddenly, it dropped Gaelinar. The Kensei tumbled to the ground with a gasp of jarred breath and tensed to rise. But, before he could move, Fenrir planted a lion-sized paw squarely on his chest.

Larson quickened his pace.

Using Gaelinar as its launching site, Fenrir sprang to meet Larson. The elf sidled. The wolf's shoulder struck a glancing blow which staggered Larson. He caught a brief glimpse of Gaelinar, limp and still, before his own defense absorbed his full attention. He twisted, catching his balance, and found himself staring into Fenrir's lowered face. The wolf's lips curled into a cruel parody of a human smile, revealing a sharp row of canines. "Let's see how well you fare without your swordmaster."

Larson raised his sword. Fenrir back-stepped and circled clockwise, ears flat back, tail low and full. Larson rotated, keeping his sword arm toward Fenrir. From the periphery of his vision, he watched Taziar follow the wolf. Fenrir slowed, just beyond Larson's reach, allowing Taziar to close the gap between them.

Larson lunged. Fenrir sprang aside, then dove for Larson. Its teeth slashed his tunic, missing flesh. Taziar rushed Fenrir, sword high. The wolf spun, redirecting its attack for Taziar's unprotected side. The Cullinsbergen recoiled midstrike, and Fenrir reversed his stalk, keeping to Taziar's left.

Larson wove around behind Taziar, trying to approach from Fenrir's opposite side. But the wolf spun, herding Taziar so that, once again, it had both enemies before it.

Larson howled in frustration. "You want to fight or dance?"

Fenrir plunged toward Larson. Larson raised his sword to meet the attack. At the last moment, Fenrir pulled his feint and leaped for Taziar. The Cullinsbergen dodged hard left, but the wolf's canines closed on his arm. The force of the bite drove the sword from his fingers, and it spun into the darkness at the edge of the clearing. Larson thrust for Fenrir's throat, his free hand groping for bundled powder. His fingers closed over the cloth as he completed the strike.

With a toss of his head, Fenrir flung Taziar at Larson. Taziar stumbled toward the blade. With sudden terror, Larson realized his own sword would impale his companion. He dropped the hilt; there was time for nothing else. The sword toppled as man and elf crashed to the dirt. Larson's handkerchief tore open, scattering powder harmlessly across the clearing.

Fangs bared, Fenrir leaped for Larson and Taziar. Both rolled aside. The wolf landed, claws chewing through frozen ground, the sword lying at its feet. Sweat blurred Larson's vision, turning the glint of moonlight on its steel into a dull glaze. He dove for the crossguard. His reach fell short; he felt the cool metal of its sharpened edge beneath his grip. Then Fenrir's paw slammed down on his knuckles, pinning his hand against the blade. Larson twisted his neck to find himself staring into Fenrir's wide, red jaws. "You can't win, insect! So long as the balance remains tipped toward Law, no one can slay me!" Its open mouth dipped toward Larson.

There was no time for grace. Larson wrenched backward with a force which strained every muscle in his forearm. The blade slashed his palm as he pulled free, and he tumbled into the center of the clearing. Fenrir tensed. Larson gathered breath, willing his spent muscles to draw him away from the beast's next attack.

Suddenly, Taziar leaped in front of Fenrir. Weaponless and dwarfed by the bulk of the great wolf, the Cullinsberg man had little chance of deterring Fenrir for more than a few seconds. Larson struggled to weak legs as the wolf raised a paw to dash Taziar aside. Then, Larson noticed the parcel in his companion's hand. Taziar ripped and threw. The bundle struck home, splashing powder across Fenrir's muzzle.

Fenrir reared backward with a bellow of pain. It bounded through the circle of pines which surrounded the clearing and disappeared between the huddled branches of the trees. Too tired to give chase, Larson listened to the sounds of its stumbling progress until they faded to silence.

Taziar handed Larson his sword and helped the elf to his feet. Blood showed through the shallow bite on Taziar's arm; apparently, Fenrir had gripped with only his foreteeth. Larson knew the wolf's molars would have crushed the climber's bones to splinters. The gash across Larson's fingers was also superficial.

Taziar trotted toward the border of the clearing. "I need to find my sword. You better tend Gaelinar." He inclined his head toward the swordmaster.

Larson cringed, bracing himself to face the newest victim of Fenrir's violence. It had become too familiar. Since Larson's arrival in Scandinavia, one battle had followed another. No longer could he crouch behind a gun and fire at distant shadows and enemies. He had moved beyond counting piles of dead soldiers to confronting gods face to face, sword to sword, sword to tooth. And after every skirmish, there was more death and more wounds. He realized Fenrir was weakening them all, in increments.

Larson turned his gaze to Gaelinar. To his relief, the old man was sitting, methodically cleaning his swords with a torn scrap from his golden robe. There was a strange awkwardness to Gaelinar's movements which drew Larson's attention to the Kensei's hands. The right appeared supple and freckled, lacking the depressions between the tendons which marked the atrophy of aging skin and muscle. But the left had swollen to twice its normal size. A ring of purple-black marred the palm, and the protruding fingers appeared thin and yellowed by comparison.

Larson winced. *It's from his run-in with the dragon in Hel. How could I have forgotten?* Larson berated himself, though he felt certain Gaelinar had made an effort to hide the injury. He walked to the Kensei's side and flopped to the ground beside him. Peering into the wrinkled countenance, he noticed something even more alarming. Gaelinar's dark eyes had gone dull. His features sagged, blank with defeat. Larson caught his mentor's shoulder. "Are you all right?"

Gaelinar went still. His voice emerged flat and toneless. "I'm fine. Just fine for an old man."

Gaelinar's docile manner struck terror through Larson. He felt as if he conversed with a stranger. "What do you mean 'fine'? You're beat to hell." He waved a hand over the tattered, filthy robes and the greenish-brown bruises revealed through the holes. "You look like you swallowed a porcupine. How can you feel fine after fighting a wolf the size of a Clydesdale? And what do you mean old?"

Gaelinar did not look up from his swords, but his tone became angry and color returned to his features. "If I was strong, no mere animal could best me. My spirit has grown old and tired."

"Are you stupid?" Larson tightened his grip. "The damn wolf's a god."

"Just another god." Gaelinar let his sword fall into his lap and looked directly at Larson. "I lost not because of Fenrir's strength but because of my weakness. If I was still strong, you would see a dead wolf here. I failed you. I failed Silme. And I failed myself." He shook free of Larson's hand. "I failed myself, Allerum. That, I can't tolerate."

Words did not come easily to Larson. He sputtered. "But you heard Fenrir. Right now, no one could kill him."

"There are no excuses."

Larson slapped his palms over his face, unable to understand the events which had suddenly turned his arrogant swordmaster into this self-deprecating ''old'' man. Disgusted, he stood.

Before Larson could walk away, Gaelinar caught his hand. ''I'm mad at myself, hero, not you. You and the small one bested Fenrir while I lay here like an old lady.''

''Damn it, Gaelinar. I . . .''

The Kensei waved his student silent. The glimmer of determination returned to his eyes. ''My life and everything I believed in has stood on a table supported by three legs. One leg is duty, one spirit, and the last strength. I've seen beauty and horror beyond most men's imaginings. I also saw my own mortality when Fenrir bested me the second time.''

Larson felt duty-bound to interrupt. ''Fenrir didn't best you the first time. He ran away.''

Gaelinar shrugged. ''He lived to come back this time. And his return made my life a table with only two legs. My body can no longer do what my spirit demands.'' He flexed the fingers of his injured hand. ''As a two-legged table must fall, I cannot accept less than perfection. But I can accept my own death. And you, hero, must carry on my teachings.''

''Carry on . . .'' Suddenly, Gaelinar's meaning seemed all too clear. ''Oh, no. You can't kill yourself. I haven't learned anything.''

Gaelinar smiled, and all his confident power seemed to return. ''I can't kill myself now. I promised to bring Silme back, and I will see that through.''

Larson dropped to a crouch. ''But you have more reasons to live. You want me to carry on your way. I've only been with you a few weeks. Surely you have more to teach than that.''

Gaelinar sheathed his short sword. ''I've taught you all that one man can teach another. I've trained you to have a bold spirit, a sense of honor, and that death need not be feared. Anything beyond that, hero, you must teach yourself.''

Frustration made Larson angry. ''Gaelinar! Cut it out. There's no time for this nonsense. You've been old for a long time. There's a difference between being old and giving up. You talk about bold spirits, but you're afraid to face old age."

"It's the only time for this 'nonsense.' " Gaelinar rose, catlike. To Larson's relief, he seemed his familiar self again. "Every day, I have grown slower and weaker than the day before. My death may come soon or years from now. But it approaches. I'm not afraid of getting old. I'm not afraid of dying." He slid his katana into its scabbard. "Now, hero. Let's go kill a wolf."

Gaelinar's talk of death and defeat unnerved Larson. When Taziar approached, sword recovered and sheathed, Larson was glad to abandon his previous conversation. "Shadow. Found it, I see."

Taziar nodded, but his attention seemed fixed on Gaelinar. He stopped, well beyond sword range, within a step of the darkening periphery of the pine trees. His eyes darted from the bunched figure of the Kensei to the seemingly endless stretch of forest. "I have an idea which may stop the Fenris Wolf."

Larson's spirit soared. He passed a reassuring glance to Gaelinar.

"But," Taziar continued, "it would require a few day's journey to the Bifrost Bridge."

"Bifrost Bridge," Larson repeated. It sounded familiar from his readings of Norse mythology in the Vietnam bunker. He shrugged, wondering why Taziar seemed so nervous. "Why not? We know how to free Silme now. After we go to Hel, we can veer toward this bridge thing."

At the mention of Silme's rescue, Taziar shuffled a step forward. He pursed his lips in consideration then shook his head with resignation. "No, Allerum. I doubt that powder will deter Fenrir long. You two get Silme." He smiled. "Tell her the essential role I had in her resurrection, and convince her she needs a garnet-rank apprentice. I'll take care of Fenrir."

Larson was beginning to believe he was the only sane man left in existence. "You'll take care of Fenrir, huh? When you're traveling alone and the wolf attacks, I suppose you'll just grab it by the tail and swing it till it cries 'uncle.' "

Taziar gave Larson a curious look. "Don't worry about me. Once we've separated, Fenrir will go after you, not me." He spoke with a bold certainty which intrigued Larson but changed the subject before the elf could ask the obvious question. "One way or the other, my business won't take as long as yours. I'll meet you near the great falls outside Hel. If I'm not there, don't wait."

Gaelinar returned the conversation to its earlier tack. "How can you be so certain Fenrir will come after us?"

Taziar swallowed hard. He shifted from foot to foot, each movement inching him closer to the tree line. His face screwed into a mask of discomfort and guilt, but his tone sounded apologetic. "Forgive me, my friends. I can't hold this secret from you any longer. Two weeks ago, I freed Fenrir from centuries of bondage and allowed him to hunt down his father's slayers."

The news shocked Larson. He recalled Taziar's reckless courage against the wolf, and, suddenly, it all came together. Larson gathered breath to question further.

But in the instant it took Larson's mind to register the meaning of the words, Taziar had faded into the shadows of the woodlands and quietly disappeared.

CHAPTER 9:

Master of Fate

"Yet they, believe me, who await
No gifts from Chance, have conquered Fate."
—Matthew Arnold
Resignation

After the evening sword lesson, the first night of Larson's and Gaelinar's journey progressed in tense silence. Never one to speak unless he had something important to say, Gaelinar left Larson alone with his thoughts. And, as they retraced their earlier route through the pine forest, Larson found his own contemplations disquieting. He considered his mental struggle with Fenrir, the battle between the wolf and Vidarr which had ignited random memories, and his own careful and taxing trap which walled Vidarr into a corner of his mind. None of it seemed possible, yet the gods' manipulations had become too familiar to deny or condemn with simple logic.

The world faded to an endless blur of shadows as Larson continued to look inside himself. Apparently, he lacked the natural, anatomical barriers which protected people of this era from gods and sorcerers who would manipulate their thoughts. Until the previous morning, he had believed that defect left him helpless against such attacks. Now he had discovered a weapon, albeit weak and untrained. He could not help but wonder whether practice might strengthen his skills. If so, his mind and memories could become his own again.

As he walked, Larson rehearsed imagining walls. He pictured brick, stone, wire, and mortar without difficulty, but they had no relation or corresponding location in his mind. Each was just a barrier floating in his thoughts like any other conjured fantasy. They lacked the reality of time and place Larson had imparted to the wall he'd used against Vidarr while the god and he were standing within his mind. Larson considered. *Perhaps that's it. I need to be inside myself to erect a solid barrier.* The proposition intrigued him. He tried to place himself into his thoughts. But although he could picture himself among the circuitry which represented his brain, he could not actually work himself into his own mind. Apparently, that procedure required an outside force or being to trip his memories.

Larson relaxed, trying to view the puzzle from the other side. *Maybe I can build the walls while outside my mind, but I have to be inside to set them in place.* It seemed as likely as any other conclusion; anything seemed possible when dealing with a situation as absurd as treating thoughts and memories as physical entities. *If so, practice might hone my abilities.* He returned to mentally drawing walls. He imagined barbed wire fences, prison barricades, and great castle bastions. He tried to consider each invented partition as a step toward mental freedom, but he only managed to make himself feel foolish. *I'm probably wasting my time. Even if I'm on the right track, I can't be certain I'm crafting the walls correctly. And, as Gaelinar has often said, "Practicing a maneuver incompetently is worse than not practicing at all."*

Larson abandoned his psychic enterprise, and turned his attention elsewhere. Tree branches and dark wisps of cloud striped the full moon, dappling the forest with shadows. Gaelinar slipped quietly between the needled branches, his posture alert, prepared for Fenrir's next attack. The realization turned Larson's thoughts to the wolf. *Fenrir claimed no one could kill it, yet it refused Gaelinar's challenge in our last fight.* Larson recalled Fenrir clutching Gaelinar by the back of his robes, the wolf bunched and angered by the swords at its throat. *If Fenrir truly could not be slain, why didn't it shake Gaelinar? Why did it run from us when Shadow's powder blinded it? Why bide time between attacks?*

Larson closed the widening gap between himself and

Gaelinar, intending to bring his questions to his mentor. But the Kensei's solemn expression convinced him otherwise. *Why do I expect Gaelinar to know the answers any more than I do? Apparently, part of being unslayable is knowing when to retreat. Or, more likely, Fenrir lied. The certainty of defeat could damage our morale, making us easier to conquer. Besides, even the will of the Fates can be overthrown. According to Vidarr, it was Loki's destiny to survive and lead an assault against the gods of Law. No Norse mythology book I ever read mentioned a dead American soldier from 'Nam.*

The night dragged on. Heavy cloud cover obscured the gradual lightening of the sky toward dawn. Freezing drizzle pattered against the tight umbrella of overhanging branches, and very little penetrated to the travelers beneath it. A hearty dinner whittled their supplies dangerously low but brought sleep easily to exhausted men with full bellies.

Early in the cycle of slumber, Larson felt a pressure in his mind. Doubts prickled through his thoughts, strangely alien. He lay in half repose, dimly aware of the intrusion. It seemed to him like the moments before sleep, when reality fades to dream and the implausible mingles with the concerns of the previous day. This odd sense of uncertainty winked out with unnatural suddenness, as if suppressed. A wavering image filled Larson's awareness. Gradually, it solidified, forming into the contours of a face, its skin and hair dark as the depths of Hel. It was not a racial, human blackness but rather the solid, gunmetal hue of a panther. High, arched cheekbones formed hollows for eyes the color of fresh blood. A sharp chin and gaunt, cadaverous features gave an impression of points and angles.

Bramin! Larson struggled to awaken. Foreign frustration rattled through his mind, choked off with the same abruptness as the uncertainty. Larson jarred awake. He stared into a chaotic jumble of branches and a broken array of muted sunlight. The clicking of insects formed a strange duet with the ceaseless rattle of the rain. Carefully, Larson reoriented. He held sleep at bay long enough to convince himself of the reality of the forest and to recognize Bramin's image as fleeting fantasy. Then he closed his eyes and allowed himself to drift off again.

Sleep returned almost immediately, and with it the same entity which had conjured Bramin's features. Some portion of Larson's unconscious acknowledged the being and mistakenly dismissed it. This time, the dream weaver made certain not to reveal its own emotions as it fashioned Larson's thoughts. The picture of Bramin again sharpened into existence. The half man's eyes seemed to flay Larson. Thin lips twisted into a malicious sneer, and Bramin's voice wound through Larson's consciousness. ". . . To save you from my sorceries, Silme linked her life aura to mine. . . . Her fate and mine have become one. . . . If you kill me, you kill Silme, too!"

Despair rushed down on Larson. *No!* He struggled against the memory and momentarily caught another glimpse of waking reality. The intruder's emotions pulsed against him, a mixture of guilt and sudden desperation, then it pummeled Larson with a collage of memory: Bramin demanding the sword which held Vidarr prisoner; Bramin sweeping his blade with dazzling speed; Bramin pounding his fist repeatedly into Larson's face, his knuckles striped red with blood. The images relentlessly howled through Larson's mind bringing with them remembered tortures, guilt, grief, and violent pain. Each new angle struck Larson like a physical blow. He spun, ran, blundered into another memory carefully placed by the intruder. Bramin's laughter pulsed through Larson's mind, heavy with hatred. Sparks splashed across Larson's vision, then the dark elf stood before him again, hand raised in threat.

Larson cringed away as Bramin's spell ripped into him. Agony stabbed and spiraled, stealing strength from body and soul. Larson heard his own screams as distant echoes. Then, abruptly, the assault stopped. The visions of Bramin disappeared. The pain subsided. Larson found himself standing in a clearing in the pine forest, panting from mental exertion. He was gripping his drawn sword as if fighting some unseen enemy. When he sheathed it, he discovered the knurling on the hilt had left a ring of diamond-shaped impressions across his palm.

Gaelinar knelt at the edge of the clearing, watching Larson curiously. "Dream?"

Larson considered. He could vaguely recall a presence in his mind before the sequence had started, and it lacked the cold courage of Bramin, Loki, or the Fenris Wolf. Those three had sparked painful memories with malicious pleasure while the entity who conjured the facets of Bramin seemed almost apologetic. "No," he replied carefully. "Not a dream. Excuse me for a moment, please. I need to discuss this with someone."

Gaelinar shrugged, too accustomed to Larson's oddities to comment further.

Larson sat on a dry circle of fallen needles. He gathered as much accusation and resentment as he could, then focused all his concentration on a single word. *Vidarr!*

There followed a lengthy silence.

Anger and impatience joined Larson's chosen sentiments. *VIDARR!*

No emotion accompanied Vidarr's reply. *You bellowed for me, Allerum?*

I did. Though I can't imagine why it took you so long to respond. I know you were already here.

Perfect confusion radiated from Vidarr. *I don't understand.*

I don't understand, Larson mimicked, his rage magnified by Vidarr's denial. *Vidarr, I'm not stupid. Quit playing dumb or I'll consider your cruelty an intentional attack rather than an ignorant gesture.*

Vidarr did not answer; he held his feelings thoroughly masked.

Well? Larson demanded.

Vidarr's voice emerged as a barely perceptible mumble. *All right. I did it.*

Larson snorted, hoping his thoughts made it obvious he harbored no doubts about Vidarr's guilt. *That was never in question.* He supposed the god had searched his thoughts. Otherwise, Larson suspected Vidarr would not have confessed so quickly. *Now tell me why. What's the matter? Fenrir hasn't destroyed my sleep to your satisfaction? Did you feel I hadn't suffered enough?*

I wasn't trying to hurt you.

Liar! You had to know reviving memories of Bramin would cause pain.

Vidarr persisted. *I just wanted to remind you how dangerous Bramin is. Before you plead with Hel to raise Bramin from the dead, I needed you to remember his evil.*

Larson stared at his hands in frantic disbelief. *Did you think I could forget?*

Regardless . . .

Don't regardless me! Furious, Larson interrupted. *I saved your life. I thought we were friends. But in the last few days you've done worse to me than any enemy I ever had. You demand favors. You intrude on my private thoughts. Now, you've attacked me.*

Annoyance sifted through Vidarr's defenses. *I saved your life, too. I neutralized Loki's magic, turning your conflict into a battle of swords. And, without my assistance with parries and strikes, you would have lost that contest.* Vidarr hesitated. Then, apparently afraid Larson would break in, he continued quickly. *And I didn't "attack" you. You just don't understand, do you?*

I understand you assaulted my mind with memories which caused me emotional anguish and physical pain.

Baldur is my brother.

Larson remained unmoved. Loki's final words before his death at Hvergelmir's falls returned, unbidden: "If you slay me, no one will contest Odin. The Norse pantheon will endure, supreme through eternity. Christianity can never reign. Al Larson, if you kill me, your world, your family, and the people you loved will never exist!"

Larson spat. *I had a brother, too, Vidarr. Rescuing you doomed him for eternity.*

Vidarr paused. He made no attempt to hide his surprise. *Are you still bitter about that?*

Did you think I'd just forget I destroyed my world and everyone in it?

No, Vidarr admitted. *But I did think you'd realize you had no choice. Loki determined that the day he trapped my soul in the piece of steel the other gods shaped into your sword. Without me, the gods of Chaos would surely have won the final battle, the "Ragnarok." Loki would have destroyed all humanity; your world and ours would no longer have existed. Killing Loki was the only way to free me, and that, as you know, also prevented the arrival of the White Christ and the coming of your people.*

Larson pondered Vidarr's words, words that appeased some of the guilt he had felt since the day Bramin, Silme, and Loki had died near the entrance to Hel. But something still seemed amiss. . . . *Thereby defying the Fates who determined Ragnarok WOULD occur, the White Christ WOULD come, and my era WOULD exist.*

Apparently.

The Fates can be resisted. Destiny can be changed.

Apparently. Vidarr's presence seemed more relaxed as Larson's attention shifted from the assault upon his memory.

Larson licked his lips thoughtfully. *Explain something to me, Vidarr. How long ago did Baldur die?*

Vidarr became evasive. *I don't remember exactly.*

Vidarr's caution made Larson suspicious. *Approximately.*

A century.

Stunned, Larson found it temporarily impossible to form a coherent thought.

Maybe two or three.

Baldur's been dead longer than a hundred years? So why, all of a sudden, has his resurrection become my emergency?

Vidarr's presence squirmed. *It was Baldur's destiny to rise from the dead after Ragnarok and to rule the era of peace which would follow our father's reign of war. We could tolerate Baldur's absence knowing he would, one day, live again. By preventing Ragnarok, you banished Baldur to Hel. We want him back, and retrieving Geirmagnus' rod is the only way we know to achieve his return.*

Larson's jaw sagged, and all anger drained from him. He recalled the odd feeling of divinity Baldur had radiated. It all came together now, a coincidence too strong to deny. *Resurrection. A god of peace who is the son of a god of war. Divinity.* His thoughts swirled. Not everything fit, but the parallel was frightening. *And if Baldur is, in fact, Jesus, will raising him restore the future?*

Larson suppressed the idea, wishing to evaluate the possibilities at a time when Vidarr could not read his thoughts. It would not do to set the entire Norse pantheon against him. *Certainly, my meddling will have changed the later ages. Perhaps this altered future won't have a Vietnam War. Already, my presence appears to have changed history. I don't recall sorcerers or elves in any textbook.*

Vidarr seemed confused by Larson's jagged leaps of logic. *What are you thinking about?* he demanded.

Larson kept his reply friendly, hoping to discourage Vidarr from penetrating the deeper portions of his mind for answers. *I'm thinking I certainly will retrieve Geirmagnus' rod.*

Joy suffused Larson's mind.

Larson added, *After I rescue Silme.*

Loki's children, Vidarr swore. *I thought you were coming to your senses.*

I am. And, Vidarr, if you keep interrupting my sleep, it'll take twice as long to finish my bargaining with Hel. It'll take twice as long to retrieve the rod, and it'll give Fenrir twice as long to eat me before I free Baldur. This is my last warning. If you penetrate my mind again, other than to talk, I'll shoot first and ask questions later.

Vidarr seemed unsure. *Allerum?*

Please, Vidarr. We're supposed to be allies. The last thing I need is more enemies.

Vidarr said nothing. Larson could feel the heated stirrings of the god's rising anger.

Good day, Vidarr. Larson finished firmly.

Good day. Vidarr responded curtly. His presence disappeared from Larson's mind.

Yawning, Larson stretched out on the ground. Thoughts of gods and churches filled his last waking moments then seeped softly into dream.

Taziar Medakan straddled a pine seedling at the edge of the clearing outside the northern town of Kiarrmar. A fresh carpet of snow covered the straight stretch of open plain, though no clouds marred the sky. The autumn sun shimmered from the distant arch of the Bifrost Bridge, scattering highlights of red, yellow, and blue across the ice. To the southeast, smoke from the town curled into the heavens. In every other direction, Taziar saw nothing but trees.

Now, four days after his last encounter with Fenrir's snapping jaws and howled threats, Taziar's errand seemed madness. It would require him to slip past Heimdallr a second time, a feat he did not relish despite its challenge. He doubted the same ploy would work twice or that Heimdallr would show any mercy if he caught Taziar defying his orders again.

Taziar sidestepped around the seedling and dropped to a crouch. He did have another option, though it seemed equally foolish. He could summon Heimdallr, and, if the god did not kill him on the spot, convince him of the importance of his cause. Either course of action would sabotage the other. Once caught attempting to gain access to the realm of the gods, Taziar doubted Heimdallr would be interested in his reasons. And, if talking to Heimdallr failed, the god would be watching for Taziar to try to climb the Bifrost.

Talking to Heimdallr will waste less time. Having come to a decision, Taziar marched openly across the snow. His feet crunched through the frozen crust into a thin layer of powder. His toes felt chilled despite the leather of his boots. A wind gust hurled icy particles against his cheeks, reddening the skin. *And this is only autumn. I don't think I want to experience a winter in Norway.* He hunched deeper into his cloak.

Suddenly, light exploded before Taziar. Half-blinded, he staggered backward with a startled cry. He blinked through an etched web of shadow and found himself facing another man. The stranger was tall; Taziar's head scarcely reached his waist. A tunic and breeks of the most expensive leather hugged a heavily-muscled frame. Silver thread shimmered through his cloak. His left foot sported a crafted sandal, the right a boot cobbled from mismatched scraps. The entire effect inspired awe. Taziar stared, struck speechless.

The giant glared down at Taziar. Blond braids swung

around grimly handsome features. "Come here, Shadow."

Taziar recovered quickly. He inched a half step closer. *He knows my name . . . or my alias, at least.* "You seem to have me at a disadvantage." He added carefully, "Sir."

"That is as it should be." Apparently, the giant misunderstood Taziar's intention, for his next words answered Taziar's question thereby spoiling the effect of his own arrogance. "I am Vidarr. You must perform a task for me."

Vidarr? Allerum's god? Taziar studied Vidarr and found the god's disposition suspiciously easy to read. Anger and confidence seemed to radiate from him. Taziar doubted he could be the cause of Vidarr's rage, though he knew the wrong words might earn him the brunt of it. He considered his reply carefully. "Lord Vidarr. I am honored." He lowered his head and worked humility into his voice, hoping it would not sound feigned. "What service can this humble mortal perform?"

To Taziar's relief, Vidarr's anger faded slightly. "You will return to Allerum."

Taziar played along. Vidarr's request matched his plans. "I shall."

"And you will see to it he never discovers that the recovery of Geirmagnus' rod is impossible."

"What?" Taziar's question was startled from him. For the first time, "impossible" conjured bewilderment rather than interest. "You sent Allerum on an impossible quest? Why?" Fighting to keep accusation from his tone, Taziar dropped his pretense of modesty.

Vidarr's huge brows beetled. "Because, Little One, I have waited centuries to find a capable mortal ignorant enough of the impossible to achieve it."

Taziar regained his composure. "Forgive my questioning, lord. I'm not certain I understand."

Vidarr kneaded his fists with the casual power of a war machine. "Many have tried, men and gods, all with the knowledge their goal was impossible. None even made it past the entrance."

"Because of some guardian?"

"Geirmagnus' estate has no guardian," Vidarr roared. "I believe their own doubts defeated them."

Taziar hesitated, intrigued. "And realizing that, could you retrieve the rod? Apparently, you believe the task possible. Otherwise, you would not have sent Allerum after it."

Sadness entered Vidarr's aura. "I cannot. For all my self-convincing, deep within myself, I do believe the task cannot be done. I harbor enough doubts to prevent success."

Taziar considered. "Lord Vidarr, I will do my best to keep the knowledge from Allerum. By the conversations I have overheard, I believe Gaelinar is already aware of the impossibility of the quest and is protecting Allerum from the information." He tried to hold judgment from his next comment. "I'm afraid, Lord Vidarr, your revelation may have served only to doom me from completing the task if Allerum fails."

Fresh anger flared. "What do you mean?"

Taziar bowed respectfully, wishing he could erase his last statement. "My lord, I am a foreigner. I had no idea the task could not be done. Should Allerum die or surrender midway through it, I might have been able to complete it for him." He glanced up into a face gone pink with annoyance. "I thought, perhaps, that was the reason you told Allerum to bring me along."

The god snapped, "I suggested he take you because he seemed so awed by your sleight of hand, no other reason. Your act pulled him from depression. I had hoped you might keep his spirits up."

Taziar licked his lips several times. "And have I?"

Vidarr shrugged. "Adequately." He waved Taziar off with an exaggerated gesture. "I've become bored by you. Begone." He spun on his booted heel.

"My lord, wait."

Vidarr froze. He turned slowly, regarding Taziar as if he were a bothersome insect. "This had better be important."

Taziar had tired of mincing words and feeding Vidarr's ego. He stood his ground. "It is, sir. I need the magical rope which used to bind Fenrir, and I don't think Heimdallr would allow me across the Bifrost. Would you be willing to get it for me?''

Vidarr's sharp blue eyes passed over Taziar from head to foot before meeting his gaze directly. The silver threads in his cloak glimmered and sparked as he drew breath. ''No. Men serve gods, not the other way. Be glad I didn't kill you for asking.''

Taziar bit off an expletive. ''Please, lord, I'm not requesting you serve us but rather your own cause. I doubt Allerum could survive another of Fenrir's attacks. The elf is of no use to you dead.''

Vidarr's visage turned from red to purple, and Taziar felt certain he had struck the cause of the god's fury. Vidarr's tangible emotion blazed from anger to murderous fury. Abruptly, he lunged. Taziar dodged aside, but the god instantly corrected for the movement. Hands the size of boulders clamped onto Taziar's neck, lifting him effortlessly from the ground.

Taziar caught wrists wider than his fingers could circle. Bracing against them, he struggled to free himself from a grip as unyielding as a vice. Vidarr brought Taziar's face to the level of his own. He continued speaking; Taziar's weight and exertion seemed no more troubling to him than the dying breeze. ''Allerum is the chosen of the gods. He's going to die on this quest, but he's going to die for my brother. I don't like his insolence, but I can accept it in exchange for his life and service. You, I can crush like a weed.'' His fingers twined deeper into Taziar's throat.

Taziar gathered words to bargain. ''V-'' he sputtered. He could manage nothing further; each labored breath rattled. He turned incredulous eyes toward Vidarr, realizing he was about to die for something Larson had said.

Gradually, Vidarr's anger withered. His grip loosened, and he lowered Taziar to the ground.

The moment his feet met the snow, Taziar scuttled beyond the god's reach. He took great gulps of breath. The cold air stung his lungs but soothed his aching throat.

Vidarr masked his intentions, but his face betrayed remorse. His voice, though soft, commanded obedience.

"Stay here, Shadow. Don't move." With that warning, Vidarr disappeared.

Taziar rubbed at his neck while his vision blurred and spun. He stared at the snow until dizziness passed, then glanced up to the towering arch of the Bifrost Bridge. A distant figure stood on the rainbow strands. *Heimdallr, probably. Hope he enjoyed the show.* Taziar considered running but thought better of it. *Vidarr did seem genuinely sorry, and the last thing I need to do is anger him again.*

Taziar's wait did not last long. Within moments, a faint light shimmered before him. He threw up an arm to shield his eyes as the glow shattered and Vidarr returned, clutching the filthy, delicate cord which Taziar had slipped from the leg of the Fenris Wolf.

Taziar said nothing. He met Vidarr's blue stare expectantly.

Vidarr set the rope across his palms. It dangled limply to the ground. "This is Gleipnir, a prize of unequaled value. It was forged by one of the dark elves back in the times when they held all the most powerful magics of the world. Many of the things you and I believe not to exist were simply in the dark elves' keeping, among them Gleipnir's six ingredients: the noise of a cat's footfall, the beard of a woman, the roots of a mountain, the nerves of a bear, a fish's breath, and the spittle of a bird." He tossed the string at Taziar's feet.

Taziar retrieved Gleipnir, rolled it into a ball, and tucked it into his pocket. It felt flimsy and unlike any of its claimed components. But Taziar had already seen it hold the Fenris Wolf in place.

Vidarr continued. "We had Gleipnir fashioned after Fenrir snapped fetters of iron and adamantine, and a god lost his hand so that we might fasten Gleipnir. Fenrir will not willingly allow himself to be tied again."

Taziar nodded. He did not expect capturing the Fenris Wolf to become an easy task just because he now possessed the rope. *But if we can't slay him, at least we might bind him.*

"If you lose Gleipnir, we will hunt you down and kill

you.'' Vidarr used a matter-of-fact tone, as if it were the most natural statement in the world.

If I lose Gleipnir, it'll be because Fenrir killed me. You won't need to hunt me down. Taziar kept this thought to himself. He tensed to turn, but concern for Larson gave him the courage to question further. ''I mean no disrespect, Lord Vidarr. Please forgive my gall. As one of Allerum's companions, am I not doomed to death as well? If the task is impossible and we're all attempting it together, Gaelinar, Allerum, and I are all going to die for Baldur.''

Vidarr's manner softened. ''Likely, you'll all die. But even Allerum's fate is uncertain. Although I believe he'll be killed, the outcome is not mine to decide.''

Taziar considered, emboldened by Vidarr's cooperation. ''I can't let Allerum take this risk without knowing. I have no choice but to tell him.'' He inched beyond Vidarr's reach.

Vidarr's expression went somber. He made no move toward Taziar. ''Telling Allerum can only doom him to failure or convince him not to retrieve Geirmagnus' rod. Refusal to perform the quest would be the only certain death he would face. His fate if he seeks to perform the task is still a question. If he angers Odin, his fate and mine become certain. We'll die at my father's hand. Allerum might be able to thwart the Fates, but even the gods know there's no way to best Odin.''

Taziar lowered his head. Without a word, he turned.

A weight dropped to Taziar's shoulder. He whirled back in surprise to face Vidarr again, the god's hand gentle on his arm. This time, the emotion Vidarr shared was comradely, his voice soothing. ''Good luck.''

Taziar fingered his collar and the bruises beneath it, feeling awkward and confused. ''Thank you,'' he replied.

Al Larson peered through the rocky crevice which formed the entrance to Hel. Behind him, eleven rivers, braided into one, raged down from the cliffs of Midgard to batter the ground before Hel's entryway. The torrent flung icy droplets which bounced from his skin and stung like tiny wasps. The lake surrounding the waterfall occupied most of the circular valley which enclosed it, leaving a shelf of packed and cold-hardened silt through which the combined rivers flowed into Hel.

Gaelinar descended from the narrow pathway which threaded into the valley. "Go on." He gestured at the tunnel.

Larson stared. He could see nothing but the black infinity of Hel. "The Hel hound." Recalling how he had blundered blindly into the beast and nearly paid with his leg, Larson felt unwilling to make the same mistake twice. "We'll have to get past it."

"No difficulty to that." Gaelinar walked to Larson's side. "As Hel said, her realm was never designed to keep men *out*. The hound is trained to prevent escapes, not entrances. If Fenrir didn't kill the Hel hound, you won't even see it."

Larson edged forward. He had known the answer before he spoke the question; he had asked more to stall and to reassure himself than from actual concern. Despite the thrill of freeing Silme, he was still not eager to enter Hel's lightless, lifeless realm nor to encounter its guardians again. And Vidarr's cruel awakening of memory had forced Larson to realize he would also raise an enemy as cunning and powerful as a god and far more dangerous than Fenrir.

Larson stepped into Hel's entryway. A putrid, animal smell hung in the air around him. He crinkled his nose against the odor of the Hel hound and its droppings until time accustomed him to it and, later, distance obscured it. Once beyond the remembered length of the Hel hounds' chain, he breathed a heavy sigh of relief.

Several hours deeper into the Hel lands, Larson and Gaelinar made camp. A visit to the village in which Gaelinar had purchased Larson's sword had given them the chance to buy provisions and fresh clothing, and they ate well that night. Exhaustion invited sleep, despite the discomfort of Hel. Larson awakened, refreshed. He shouldered his share of the food and drink, refastened his weapons, and prepared to travel.

Gaelinar's voice sounded startlingly loud in the looming silence. "From here on, not a single word or sound. If you have any stupid questions, ask now."

Larson lowered his pack to the ground. *How does Gaelinar always make his simplest statements seem insulting?* "Why this sudden need for quiet? I thought nothing in Hel would oppose us."

"Nothing in Hel will oppose us, but we can oppose them."

Larson shook his head in bewilderment.

Gaelinar said nothing further.

Realizing Gaelinar had not seen his gesture in the dark, Larson voiced his confusion. "Could you run that by me again?"

A brief pause followed. "You want me to explain it?"

"Please."

"Quite simply, if we want Silme back, we're going to need a bargaining tool."

Larson placed a foot on his pack to keep track of it. "We have a bargaining tool. Bramin holds more power than Silme. Raising them both will give advantage to Chaos."

Gaelinar dissented with maddening certainty. "Hel will not agree to the exchange."

Annoyed by Gaelinar's bold assurance, Larson insisted. "Vidarr said she would."

"Vidarr is mistaken."

"Vidarr is a god," Larson reminded his haughty companion.

"The two are not exclusive, Allerum. Loki would still live if he hadn't underestimated you. The fact is, we need a bargaining tool against Hel. If she wanted us to raise Silme and Bramin together, she would have told us the first time we came here. She wouldn't have sent us off with misconceptions to kill powerful servants of Law."

Larson considered. "Why not? Our killing powerful servants of Law is in her interests, after all. And she must of figured we would eventually realize the right way to raise Silme. This way she gets the best of both worlds."

"Perhaps." Gaelinar seemed unconvinced. "But as angry as she was with us last time, I doubt she'll cooperate. A bargaining tool won't hurt."

Larson found Gaelinar's logic inarguable. "And that tool is . . . ?"

"Modgudr."

Understanding chilled Larson to his core. "The sorceress who sent a dragon at us? How can she become a bargaining tool?"

"That," Gaelinar said in the wickedly wry voice he reserved for insulting gods and describing reckless feats, "is why we must continue in silence." His tone returned to normal. "Come on."

Larson hefted his pack. "Wait. One thing more, Gaelinar. When I crossed the bridge last time, I ran into some magical wall-type thing."

"Modgudr would have no cause to set wards to prevent people from entering Hel. Hero, I traveled with Silme for years. I know how to avoid Dragonrank wards. Don't worry about me. As for you, I want you out of my way. When I signal, stay still and don't move until I tell you. Now, come on. Our delays only weaken Silme."

Unable to see his companion, Larson followed the music of the river, Gjoll, knowing Gaelinar would do the same. Despite Hel's emptiness, its blackness was vibrant with a menace which set Larson's nerves tingling with the premonition of imminent peril. Apprehension kept Larson crouched and hyperalert. But finally the terrors of this world had come to overshadow those of Vietnam. His mind conjured images of gnashing teeth and magic long before he considered and easily discarded the possibility of snipers. He doubted Fenrir would follow them into Hel; Baldur's continued presence suggested that the same defenses which kept ghosts and men from escaping would also discourage a god. More likely, the wolf would bide its time, waiting for Larson and Gaelinar to emerge from the Hel lands, perhaps weakened by another fight.

As Larson walked, the glow of Modgudr's gold-thatched bridge appeared, brightened, and sharpened. Well before Larson's eyes could discern the distant outline of the crossing, Gaelinar pressed a hand to his chest. Larson gathered breath to whisper a question, but Gaelinar's fingers pinched his flesh in warning. Larson went obediently still, watching Gaelinar's yellow robes disappear into the darkness before him.

Several minutes passed. Larson fondled his sword hilt, prepared to rush down on Modgudr in defense of his mentor at the first flash of magic or cry of pain. Gaelinar's depression after Fenrir's last attack remained alarmingly vivid in Larson's memory. Although the Kensei's manner seemed no different after the incident than before it, Larson was concerned that, single-handed and without his normal boundless confidence, Gaelinar was taking on a powerful enemy.

Gaelinar's voice echoed from the confines of the bridge. "Come, hero."

Larson trotted forward obediently. "Modgudr?"

"Unconscious."

Larson climbed onto the wooden bridge, groping through the darkness so as not to collide with Gaelinar. "How?"

"I hit her."

Larson turned to his left, following the direction of Gaelinar's voice. "You sapped her?"

"No, I . . ." Gaelinar broke off, leaving the foreign term undefined. "I caught her off her guard, hit her with the flat of my sword, and knocked her unconscious. Now, hero. I'll wait here. You go talk with Hel."

Larson recoiled in dismay. He reached tentatively until his fingers brushed Gaelinar's head. The Kensei was kneeling. "Me? Alone? You're not coming with me."

"Someone has to stay with Modgudr. Otherwise, I just wasted my time and gave her a headache for nothing. When you discuss terms with Hel, mention my shoto at Modgudr's throat."

Larson let his hand swing free, as much appalled by the thought of leaving his sword master with a sorcerer as by the idea of wading through corpses and facing a god alone. At their last encounter with Modgudr, Gaelinar had underestimated the sorceress' remaining strength. That mistake had cost the Kensei the bones of his hand and nearly his life as well. "Do you think Hel will bargain? Maybe she'll let us kill Modgudr and just replace her with another guardian."

"Not likely. There are few enough Dragonrank mages to make it difficult to find one willing to spend his years alone in darkness herding corpses. Apparently, Modgudr found that to her liking."

"Apparently." Larson twisted Silme's sapphire through the cloth of his pocket. "Can't we take Modgudr with us? It would make a more graphic display for Hel."

"And let the corpses escape Hel? Someone has to stay and guard the bridge."

"Let the Hel hound take care of the ghosts."

"Believe me, hero. If the Hel hound could keep all the corpses off Midgard, Modgudr would not be here. Now on with you. The sooner you return, the sooner I finish babysitting."

Larson stared off into the seemingly endless sea of darkness beyond the bridge. Once again, it had fallen to him to bargain with Hel, to reverse the damage his sword stroke had inflicted on Silme. But, difficult as it had seemed with Gaelinar at his side, alone the task became like a lead weight upon him. He tried to remind himself that Gaelinar's intolerance of small talk and delay had also raised Hel's hatred against them; surely he could perform better without the Kensei. But Larson could not shake a feeling of betrayal as strong as that he still harbored against his father, who had died and left Larson's family penniless.

"Well?" Gaelinar's voice startled Larson from his thoughts.

"I'm going," Larson replied defensively. He trotted across the bridge planks and into the darkness beyond it.

The miles passed swiftly. In an attempt to keep his mind free of distressing concerns, Larson traveled until exhaustion overtook him, ate and drank from his pack of rations, slept, awoke, ate, and again marched until he collapsed. While he walked, he sang pop tunes remembered from the half semester he had managed at college before the financial burdens of his family forced him to enlist in the army. Many of the lyrics escaped him. He found himself longing for a radio to fill in the missing rhymes and verses, and was suddenly reminded of his mother's strange affliction. She knew the melody to every popular song ever written since well before her birth, but she only remembered a handful of the lyrics. She substituted the remainder of the words with whistles, humming, or la-la's.

By the third day, Larson's strategy failed. The constant, ominous threat of Hel's blackness pushed in, spurring the neatly hidden portion of his mind which held his apprehensions. He wondered about Taziar's plan and whether the little foreigner would reach the Bifrost Bridge to accomplish whatever purpose he had there. He worried about Gaelinar, keeping watch over a crafty, unpredictable enemy night after day. He considered Baldur and what relation, if any, this single peaceful god in a warrior pantheon had to his own Christ. And, already, Larson felt responsible for the cruelty and chaos Bramin would inflict upon Midgard.

Soon the fence which hemmed Hel's citadel became visible as the darkness thinned to the red mist which defined this corner of the land of the dead. Larson set to the task of climbing, shifting his concentration to his handholds and footholds. Through the gaps between the bars, he could see the squat, flat shadow of Hel's fortress. A few ghostly figures flitted through the courtyard, stained oily red by the haze.

Sharp flakes of rust embedded in Larson's palms as he pulled himself higher up the barrier. Shortly, he reached the top, maneuvered around the upper poles which arched toward the stronghold, and scrambled down the inner side. He dropped the last five feet to the ground, turned, and found himself staring into gaunt but familiar features. *Gilbyr?* Horrified, Larson remembered the bandit who had tried to steal his Vidarr-sword for Bramin. The corpse's face was locked in a permanent expression of terror. A stiff beard encased his chin, the effect of Silme's young apprentice incompetently casting his shaving spells. Larson had taken advantage of the child's ineptitude by convincing Gilbyr the boy would turn him into a wolfman. A bloody hole marred Gilbyr's chest where he had run, panicked, onto a companions' sword. Earlier, one of Silme's wards had burned Gilbyr's hand; it had rotted off leaving a blackened stump.

With a gasp, Larson flinched back against the fence. The corpse turned hollow eyes on him. A glimmer of recognition passed through them. Shock and anger twisted the masklike features. Gilbyr's remaining hand latched onto his sword hilt, and he took a menacing step forward.

Rammed against the fence in a startled wonder, Larson clasped his own haft. Corroded crossbars bored into his back. His gaze locked on Gilbyr's fist, awaiting the first aggressive move.

Gradually, Gilbyr's fingers fell away from his hilt. Larson looked up to find the corpse's eyes had gone as dead as their owner. Gilbyr peered at Larson with mild curiosity then stumbled off into the strange, red glow of Hel's courtyard.

Larson watched Gilbyr's huddled form disappear into the gloom. He released his own hilt and stepped away from the fence. The thwarted encounter filled him not with relief but with alarm. *Gilbyr's already nearly forgotten me. And Silme died only about two weeks after him.* The realization sparked urgency. *If I want Silme back intact, I'm going to have to barter quickly.* Larson ran to Hel's squat citadel.

A layer of mold coated the open door to Hel's fortress, its dead plant odor mingling with the rot of the corpses which filled the corridor. Larson paused in the portal, ill with the recollection of the searing cold touches of the ghosts. The smell of death raised memories of cadavers decaying in the heat more vividly than any visual image could. But purpose gave him the courage to pick his way among the corpses until the stench became lost in the now familiar background of Hel's brooding promises of pain and despair.

Larson dodged through the crowd, glad the effort kept him focused on his pathway rather than the milling cadavers which defined it. Soon he reached the paired thrones at the portal to Hel's meeting room; Baldur and his wife perched upon them in morose silence. The god raised a hand in greeting. Light from the lopsided chandelier in the chamber fell upon multihued jewels embedded in the stone of Baldur's chair. Their reflection formed halos of color which Larson had not seen since entering the limitless blacks and grays of Hel. Again, Larson felt the aura of divinity radiating from the dead god. More familiar images of slim white candles, stained glass windows, and temple arches replaced the looming tension inspired by Hel's imprisoned minions.

Larson studied Baldur in the blood-colored gloom of the hallway and the guttering candlelight which escaped from the room beyond them. He found little resemblance between this hardy, blond god of peace and the emaciated, dark-haired Jesus artists painted upon the cross. *Yet I can't know how much the paradox of my own existence and the slaying of a god have changed the course of history.* Larson glanced beyond Baldur and noticed Hel gliding toward the room at her snail's pace. A faint breeze from the doorway eddied candle smoke around her like a robe.

Larson turned his attention back to Baldur, aware it would take Hel some time to creep into the meeting room. Recalling that the dead could not speak first, Larson addressed Baldur in the softest voice he could manage. "You can have this back." He offered the painted stone Baldur had given him at their last encounter.

Baldur made no move to retrieve it, but his visage sank into sadness. "You could not find my father?"

"I gave your message to Vidarr."

A hopeful glimmer returned to Baldur's eyes, like sunlight fractured on a sea of darkest blue. "And?"

Larson glanced toward Hel. The goddess seemed to have moved no closer, though her toes inched toward the chamber. "And Vidarr made me give up my own task to work at rescuing you." Resentment flared. "If I had known your intention, I would never have accepted this." Larson tossed the gem in his hand, then dropped it into Baldur's lap. Despite his words, he felt all his anger channeled against Vidarr rather than Baldur.

The god looked stricken. His eyes glazed with moisture, and his fingers gripped the arms of his throne with desperate self-sacrifice. "Forgive me, please. You must believe I did not know. Vidarr is good, and he surely meant you no harm. Love for a woman, a sister, a brother can make even a god do things against his nature. And my mother's hope for retrieving her youngest child might have spurred my father to pressure Vidarr. Odin is the one even the gods do not dare to cross.'' He plucked the painted stone from his thigh. ''I have no means to communicate with my family. Otherwise, I would insist they not demand from you. The kindness you performed for me was appreciated. Were it within my power, I would make them realize I would rather remain here for eternity than allow them to torture you.''

Aware Vidarr could read his every thought, Larson smiled. ''You don't realize it, but you may have just told them. I'm not mad at you. Once I've returned to Midgard, I will do everything in my power to free you from Hel.'' Larson was surprised by his own sincerity.

Repeatedly, Baldur turned the gemstone between his fingers. ''Because of my brother?''

''No,'' Larson insisted. ''Because I want to.''

Baldur reached out, stone pinched between his thumb and first finger. ''You keep this. My mother left it on my pyre. It's worth a rich man's share of gold, but it's scant payment for the favor you've done me.''

Larson accepted the stone, realizing as he did that Hel had reached the center of her chamber. He eyed the sword at Baldur's hip. ''One more thing. Can you keep the corpses from the room and the doorway while I talk with Hel?''

Baldur nodded. ''They won't enter the chamber while Hel is in conference. I can't do much, but I'll help as I can.''

Larson settled for the vague promise, then trotted into the room to meet with the half dead queen of Hel.

She watched Larson approach through narrowed eyes. Tangled blonde hair framed features sharp with angry accusation. ''So . . . you have . . . returned . . . *murderer.*''

The statement required no reply, but Larson spoke before Hel could continue in her maddeningly halting style. ''I am no murderer, lady. I killed your father in self-defense. I understand your grief, but it wasn't my fault.'' Hel's mouth quivered, but Larson continued before she could respond. ''I have returned to ask you to free Silme with Bramin to balance the trade.''

Hel shifted from one rotted leg to the other. ''No.''

''No?'' Larson allowed surprise to color his tone. Hel's refusal annoyed him every bit as much as learning that Gaelinar had been correct, as always. ''You can't refuse. You promised on your oaths to Odin you would not oppose Silme's return to Midgard.''

''And . . . I . . . will . . . keep . . . my . . . word.'' Hel stared at Larson directly and with dignity. ''But . . . I . . . made . . . no similar . . . promise . . . for . . . Bramin. He . . . stays. Without him as . . . counterbalance . . . the Fates . . . will . . . prevent . . . Silme's escape.''

Each tedious syllable further enraged Larson. ''Why? Why would you do that? Bramin is more powerful than Silme. The trade can only strengthen your cause.''

Hel's expression never changed. ''My . . . legion . . . is . . . my strength. The . . . dead . . . are my . . . subjects. Releasing . . . even one . . . weakens . . . me. And . . . you . . . are . . . requesting . . . two of my . . . most mighty . . .''

Impatient, Larson interrupted. ''Without life force, neither can cast spells. And, with time, they will lose all memory and become no more valuable than any other.''

''Eventually. Until . . . then . . . they . . . strengthen . . . my power. Besides . . . if I . . . free . . . Bramin and . . . Silme . . . every man .. on Midgard . . . would . . . come . . . seeking . . . his dead. To . . . give in . . . to even . . . one . . . would . . . take all . . . permanence and . . . all . . . glory from . . . death.''

Hel's words spun through Larson's mind like fragments of dream. He saw truth in them and understood, but the cause of Silme's life still seemed more important than any rule of nature. ''I had hoped to bargain peacefully, but you leave me no choice. My companion holds Modgudr prisoner. If I do not come back or I return unsuccessful, he will kill her.''

Hel's face remained locked in its gloomy pall, but her eyes flashed in the candlelight. ''I . . . don't . . . believe you.''

"That is your prerogative."

Larson waited in a silence which jarred every nerve while Hel considered. He kept his face expressionless.

"Prove . . . it."

"How?"

Another long pause.

Larson bided his time with admirable patience. He recalled the uncertainty which characterized his previous actions. No doubt, Gaelinar's example and his own arguments with Vidarr had fueled his confidence. When Hel did not speak after a full minute, Larson took control of the conversation. "Surely you know we got past Modgudr, her dragon, and the Hel hound on our last visit. Do you doubt Gaelinar's ability to capture Modgudr?"

"Fool!" Hel shook her head, and a snarl of golden hair obscured her face. "If . . . you . . . moved Modgudr . . . from . . . her post . . . the dead . . . will . . . escape . . . Hel. The . . . havoc . . . they wreak . . . will seem . . . minor . . . compared with . . . the wrath . . . Odin . . . will . . . bring . . . down . . . upon me . . . you . . . and your . . . stupid . . . companion. Odin . . . has . . . no . . . room . . . in his heart . . . for mercy. Men . . . and . . . gods . . . live . . . only . . . to furnish . . . him . . . sport . . ."

The description sent a chill through Larson, but his love for Silme remained, reducing fear to an obscuring fog. Purpose drove him to speak with Gaelinar's reckless courage. "Lady, if Silme remains in Hel, there is nothing Odin can do to make my life more miserable. I do not fear him. It is your stubbornness which will bring his wrath upon us. If you agree to my demands, we will free Modgudr unharmed."

The grim-eyed goddess quivered with anger. "You . . . would . . . let . . . your selfish . . . love . . . for a . . . woman result . . . in hordes . . . of the dead . . . running . . . free . . . to torture . . . the . . . living?"

"Yes," Larson said. He hid the lie behind his best poker face and hoped his eyes would not betray him. "You made it clear that if we killed you, it would only result in your staying here." He tossed a casual gesture over one shoulder. "Judging by Baldur, I would guess death would not change you. But, lady, *there are worse things a man can do with a sword than kill.*'' The room echoed with the sudden sound of Larson's sword clearing its sheath.

Hel did not flinch. ''You'll . . . never . . . leave . . . my hall . . . alive. I will . . . turn . . . my hordes . . . against . . . you!''

Larson hesitated. His Gaelinar-like maneuver had achieved much the same results as the Kensei's threats in the Dragonrank school, and Larson liked them even less now that he stood alone. Still, it was too late to change his approach. ''Hmmm. You keep Silme and Bramin and kill me. I get the satisfaction of torturing you before Odin gets to you and of knowing Modgudr dies with me.'' He stood in mock contemplation, then shrugged. ''Sounds fair.'' He took a menacing step toward Hel, trusting Baldur to hold the corpses at bay.

''Wait.'' Hel spoke with uncharacteristic speed. ''We can . . . find . . . an agreeable . . . compromise.''

Larson's fear was forgotten in a moment of fierce triumph. ''No compromises. You free Silme and Bramin. Then you allow Gaelinar and me to leave your lands completely unmolested. In exchange, we won't harm you or Modgudr. We won't allow any ghosts to escape while Modgudr is captive, and we won't tell anyone who doesn't already know that we raised Silme from the dead.''

Hel gathered her shattered composure. Ignoring Larson's naked sword, she leaned toward him conspiratorially. ''Accepted. With . . . one . . . further condition.'' She stared beyond Larson.

Larson resisted the urge to follow her gaze and watched the goddess distrustfully. ''Which is?''

''That . . . you . . . send . . . five . . . souls to . . . replace . . . each of . . . them. Their . . . identities . . . and . . . philosophies . . . do not concern me. They . . . can . . . be your . . . enemies . . . or strangers. Adults . . . or . . . children. But . . . they . . . must . . . come to me . . . not . . . Odin's . . . Valhalla. You . . . must . . . not kill . . . them in fair . . . combat.''

Desperation forced Larson to consider Hel's offer, but

his morality would not allow him to accept it. ''The deal is as I said. I will not compromise.''

''Neither . . . will . . . I.''

Larson accepted Hel's decision with dour fatalism. He doubted he could fight his way past Hel's minions. Yet, he could condone his own death more easily than he could take the lives of more innocents. Trusting that Gaelinar would release Modgudr and not allow the corpses free run of Midgard, Larson sealed his own fate. ''Then you leave me no choice.'' He raised his sword. Smoke from the candles swirled like ghosts around the blade.

''Wait.''

Larson thought he detected fear in Hel's voice. He froze in position.

''All . . . right. I . . . accept . . . your bargain . . . as offered. But . . . you . . . must . . . swear . . . never to . . . return . . . here.''

Larson lowered his sword and suddenly realized he was shaking. He bit his lip to keep from smiling. ''I swear it,'' he said.

CHAPTER 10:

Mastering War

"The art of war is simple enough. Find out where your enemy is. Get at him as soon as you can. Strike at him as hard as you can and as often as you can, and keep moving on."

—Ulysses S. Grant

Gradually, the elation inspired by Larson's successful negotiation with Hel faded into the cold, dark infinity of her realm. As promised, Larson and Gaelinar escaped through the entryway to Midgard without interference from the released Modgudr or the Hel hound. But even the magnificence of the waterfall, streaked through with silver sunlight, brought no joy to Larson. Air scoured clean by recent snows might as well have been the putrid aura of Hel's corpses for all the interest he paid it.

Taziar met Larson and Gaelinar on the cliffs above the falls. Two weeks had passed since the Cullinsbergen had set off to amend the mistake he had made by freeing the Fenris Wolf. Yet Larson managed only a weak smile of welcome. Something he could not name lay like lead upon his soul.

The days passed in wooden silence. Though mostly through evergreen forests devoid of underbrush, the route seemed vaguely familiar. Each of Larson's daily sword lessons began with distracted incompetence until Gaelinar's reprimands spurred his student to angered sweeps and counter thrusts. Taziar made sincere attempts at conversation. But after Larson's third inappropriately harsh rebuke, Gaelinar and Taziar left their companion to his own sullen company.

Late afternoon of their third day in Midgard, they reached the town where Larson had consulted Vidarr at the open shrine. Taziar glanced longingly down the main pathway. "Anyone object to a night on the tavern floor? I've slept on enough pine needles to satisfy me for a lifetime."

Gaelinar shrugged. "Fenrir's less likely to attack with the extra swords of the villagers against him."

Larson raised no objections. He hoped a couple of tankards of beer might soothe the evil mood he seemed unable to shake. "Lead on."

They shuffled down the narrow, snow-covered roadway in silence. For the first time, Larson noticed just how little there was to the village. Crooked, spindly roads wound between thatch-roofed cottages. The clang of the blacksmith's hammer reverberated through the threadlike lanes. Only a few sets of footprints marred the crust of ice which glazed the roads; the recent snows appeared to have inhibited some of the trade which kept the town alive.

Larson, Gaelinar, and Taziar headed directly for the sod-chinked structure of the tavern at the center of the village. As they passed, a middle-aged woman pointed from the doorway of her cottage, her form a plump shadow backlit by candles in the room beyond. Three children peered at the travelers from around their mother's skirt. Otherwise, the village seemed deserted.

Gaelinar caught the brass ring of the tavern door and wrenched it open. Wind gusted into the stale, windowless interior. Fed by fresh air, the hearth fire blazed, drafting smoke up the stone chimney. Its flare revealed nine square tables with wooden chairs and benches worn to polished smoothness by use. A portly man sprawled across three stools on the business side of the bar. Sleepy-eyed, he glanced over three greasy-haired Norsemen seated near the doorway and waved the newcomers inside.

Larson followed his companions to a table near the fireplace, allowing the door to slam closed behind him. The flames shriveled to their previous height. Woodsweetened smoke leaked back into the common room. As Larson slid his chair to the table, two teen-age girls descended upon them. One seized the remaining seat and positioned herself at the table. The other paused at Gaelinar's elbow. "What can we get you?"

Larson folded his arms and let his head sink to the hollow between them, not bothering with a response.

"Food," Gaelinar said. "Whatever you have."

"And plenty of beer," Larson added, his voice muffled by the sleeve of his cloak.

The serving girl trotted off toward the bar. The remaining woman threw back hip-length blonde hair and regarded Taziar, her blue eyes wide and interested. "From which direction did you come?"

"North," Taziar replied.

"What news do you bring from the North?"

Larson watched Taziar with one eye.

The Shadow Climber shrugged apologetically. "None, I'm afraid. Our business has kept us in the forests and away from farmers and towns."

The girl lowered her head in genuine disappointment, and the fire struck bronze highlights through her hair. "Very well." She spoke naturally, but betrayal sifted through her tone. Apparently, the tavern served as a place to exchange information as well as to provide food and shelter and direct trade.

The woman lost interest. Her eyes strayed beyond the table to the patrons near the door, and a gesture caught her attention. Gracefully, she rose and walked toward the other customers, just as her sister returned with three full mugs of beer and set them before Larson, Gaelinar, and Taziar. "Another moment for the food."

Larson raised his head long enough to guzzle down his drink without even tasting it. He waited while his companions nodded acknowledgement of the service, then shoved his mug into the woman's hand. "More." He added as an afterthought, "Please."

Ignoring Taziar's curious stare, Larson lowered his head back to his arms. His companions' conversation about a magical rope and a wolf-god flowed past him, mostly unheard. The words seemed distant, another place, another era, some other man's concern.

Larson accepted his fourth mug of beer while his companions still nursed their second. The alcohol shifted his mood from somber to heated. He felt restless. No longer content to sit with his head on the table, he fidgeted, eyes probing the half-lighted, smoky haze of the common room. The conversations of the filthy, war-stained men near the door wafted to him in crude snatches intermingled with boisterous laughter which prodded at the edges of Larson's temper. He watched the waitress, tankard in hand, approach a large patron with a wild snarl of red hair and beard.

The woman leaned forward and poured ale from the tankard into the mug. The Norseman ran his tongue over his grimy teeth and stared into the cleavage of her patched and faded bodice. He waited only until she finished filling his drink, then caught her around the waist and pulled her to his lap. He thrust his other hand down the front of her dress.

The woman squealed in surprise and fear. She twisted away. Linen tore, leaving a scrap of fabric in the man's fingers. She struggled free as the Norsemen laughed, and the red-haired patron dragged her back onto his knee.

Larson's control snapped, driving him into a rage beyond any he had known before. He leaped to his feet and charged to the other table. Not until he arrived did he realize he still clutched his drink. Slamming the mug to a nearby table, he glared at the Norseman over the girl's ragged shoulder. "Let her go."

The Norseman rose, dumping the girl from his lap. She landed in a heap at his feet, rolled to her hands and knees, and skittered toward the bar. Larson found himself glaring up into steely eyes and a face ugly with anger. "By what right do you pretend to command me?" the Norseman demanded.

Larson dropped his gaze to the Norseman's hands which rested on the hilt of a broadsword. Each finger seemed thick as Larson's wrist. Blood and dirt framed the edges of the nails. "By the same right that men have always commanded swine,'' Larson returned. Rage pushed him far beyond fear.

The Norseman followed Larson's stare. He leaned forward, his arm extended. ''It's good you've noticed these hands.'' The muscles bunched into a fist. ''In a moment, they'll crush your head like a leaf.''

Larson remained unmoving. ''I'm not worried about those hands. Size and competence are two different things. Otherwise, you'd be able to get women by other means than force.''

The Norseman gathered breath.

Before he could speak, the bartender shouted to the Norseman's blond companions. ''You'd best hobble your friend or the three of you will no longer be welcome here.''

One of the other Norsemen responded instantly. ''Sit down, Alsvithr. You've been thrown out of enough taverns. We won't be able to get a drink between here and Forste-Mar.''

Oblivious, Alsvithr lunged.

Larson tensed to meet the attack.

But before Alsvithr could reach the elf, his companions caught him by either arm and dragged him back to the table. Howling, Alsvithr struggled against his friends. ''Cowards, let me go. What's one bar?''

The bartender tossed aside a cleaning rag and stepped around the counter. ''One bar's important when it's the only one that'll take your business.'' He fixed his gaze on Larson. ''And you, stranger. Sit down, or I'll let Alsvithr kill you. The girls expect this sort of thing. It comes with the job.'' He turned back to his work, muttering, ''All women are whores.''

The bartender's words stung Larson. *Silme's no whore!* The Norsemen ceased to bother him. He took a menacing step toward the bartender.

The bartender whirled to face him.

Gaelinar's voice cut over the hiss of the fire. ''Allerum. Sit down right now!''

For a rebellious moment, Larson refused to move. His attention jumped from the bartender, whose fingers crept toward some weapon behind the counter, to the red-faced

Norseman, to the Kensei. The look on Gaelinar's features warned that he would brook no disobedience. Larson retrieved his drink and spun back toward his companions.

Alsvithr's mumbled threat barely penetrated the silence. "His mother must have been a whore for him to take this so seriously. I'd have smashed the bony bastard."

Larson's self-restraint shattered. He whirled. A snap of his wrist splashed beer over Alsvithr.

Surprise crossed Alsvithr's sodden features, immediately replaced by an anger which echoed Larson's own. He ripped free of his companions' hold.

The bartender raised a club and rushed down on Larson. Before he had taken two steps, a shuriken embedded into the wood a finger's breadth from his hand. Gaelinar's warning followed. "Get back!" Shocked, the man obeyed.

Fists clenched, Alsvithr charged Larson. His blond companions advanced behind him.

Larson fought back the red curtain of anger which clouded his mind. Mug still in his hand, he threw a punch which caught Alsvithr across the jaw. Metal folded in Larson's fingers. The larger man staggered. Larson pressed his advantage. He tensed for another blow just as Gaelinar's fingers tightened around his shoulder. The Kensei lodged a foot behind Larson's heel and spun the elf into the table behind him.

Larson's chest struck the edge with enough force to drive the air from his lungs. He blundered into a chair and crashed, with it, to the ground. Rising to a crouch, he watched Gaelinar face off with Alsvithr. The Kensei spoke softly, but his tone carried the confidence of a man used to mastery. "This fight is over."

Blood trickled from Alsvithr's nose. "Step aside, old man!" he screamed. "Your stupid friend dumped beer on me. He hit me in the face. No one does that to Alsvithr and lives!"

Gaelinar held his ground, his manner deadly calm. "This fight is over. Sit down."

Alsvithr aimed a wide punch for Gaelinar. The Kensei's expression never changed. He caught the Norseman's meaty wrist and effortlessly spun him into his companions. One's back struck the table, lifting the side several inches. Half full mugs tipped and rolled; they hit the floor with a ringing clangor, splattering beer across the planks. Alsvithr regained his balance quickly. His sword leaped from its sheath, and he rushed down on Gaelinar.

Larson surged to his feet, hand clamped to his hilt. He had barely begun to draw the blade when Gaelinar's katana whisked silently through the air. It sliced through Alsvithr's sword as if through a twig. Two feet of worked iron fell to the ground at Alsvithr's boots while he stared, incredulous, at the stump of his mangled sword.

Gaelinar resheathed his katana in the same motion. "This fight *is* over. Sit down, or next time I take your wrists."

"Sit down," repeated one of Alsvithr's companions urgently. He gathered up the dented mugs.

Alsvithr grumbled something unintelligible, but took his seat. He slammed the broken haft to the tabletop so hard a crack wound along the wood grain.

Gaelinar turned and threw Larson a look of outrage more severe than any reprimand. "Move." He caught Larson's arm, spun him, and herded him toward the table where Taziar sat, watching. Larson knew he would pay for the incident with strained muscles and bruises at his next sword lesson. But, oddly, he did not care. He marched toward the table in quiet resentment and dropped into the chair across from Taziar.

Gaelinar glanced over at the bartender, washing the damaged mugs with unexpectedly calm detachment. "I imagine we'll have to leave?"

Taziar took a gulp of his drink. "We're staying the night. Where I come from, an incident like that would have earned you all a few nights in the dungeons. But here I've noticed people get forgiving when you give them enough money."

Larson slouched, arms folded across his chest and eyes locked on a spidery beer stain on the table before him. He knew he had earned every bit of derision his companions could voice. But the same unreasoning anger which had compelled him to incite the fight also made him unwilling to listen.

Gaelinar spoke without emotion, but Larson sensed the subtle threat beneath the Kensei's outward serenity. "You've shamed your honor, and mine as well. This is not the way you use the skills I've taught you."

Larson remained sullenly silent. The fire danced as the Norsemen opened the door and made their exit from the tavern.

Gaelinar's hands twitched, like the warning rattle of a snake. Before he could speak, Taziar interrupted. "What in darkest hell is the matter with you, Allerum? You respect life. It's not like you to start a fight which could get people killed."

Remorse poked through Larson's fury long enough to make him realize he had inappropriately translated frustration into violence. His anger had nothing to do with Alsvithr or his companions or the tavern. "She lied to me, damn it!" His vision glazed, and he fought away tears with an effort which reawakened hostility.

"Who lied to you?" Taziar pressed.

"Hel." Larson raised his voice and met Gaelinar's stare for the first time in days. "It's been more than a week since she promised to free Silme. Where is she? Damn it, where is she?" His fist crashed to the tabletop, scaring away the serving girl who had arrived with the food.

"Calm yourself." Gaelinar's words were a command. "Have patience. Give Silme time to find us."

"Time? Time!" Larson screamed. He raked dirt-streaked fingers through his hair, and a twig fell into his palm. "I've got her rankstone, remember? She knows where we are. She would be with us if she could. For God's sake, Gaelinar. She's Dragonrank. She travels instantly."

Taziar added helpfully, "I've never known anyone to return from the dead before. Maybe it takes time. Maybe she has to regain strength or reorient herself."

Larson shook his head. He could not say why his companions were mistaken, he just knew something had gone wrong. "I've killed. I've shared thoughts I can hardly bear myself. I've gone to Hel twice. I've defied and fought and threatened gods for her. I'm not giving up Silme now. Promise or not, I'm going back to Hel. If she doesn't deliver Silme right into my hands, I'm going to rip Hel apart fragment by rotting fragment.'' He shredded the stick in example.

Timidly, the serving girl sidled to the table and placed steaming rolls and bowls of stew in front of them. She refilled the mugs, spilling little despite her shaking hands, and left as quickly as courtesy allowed.

Gaelinar's voice held an edge as sharp as his katana. ''I want Silme back every bit as much as you do. But I won't tolerate your going against the tenets of my teaching. I'll kill you before I let you unleash underserved anger against me, Shadow, or innocents again.''

Pressed beneath a tangle of conflicting emotions, Larson accepted Gaelinar's rebuke. ''Punish as you will. I have it coming.'' As the burning ardor of his ire died, Larson understood his motivations more clearly. ''I can't remember wanting anything as much as Silme. I was willing to . . .'' He paused in consideration.

''. . . spend your life and others for her cause.'' Gaelinar finished neatly.

Larson stared at his mentor, open-mouthed but unable to speak. Gaelinar had finished the sentence far differently than Larson intended. Yet there was a truth to the Kensei's words which jolted Larson to the depths of his conscience.

A log collapsed in the hearth. Sparks sprayed. As the flames chewed into pockets of sap, there followed a series of pops like distant gunfire.

Larson tensed at the sound then relaxed back into his chair. ''My own life, maybe, but no one else's. I won't give up my morals for any cause.''

Gaelinar skillfully guided Larson away from the source of his anger. ''Apparently, these morals don't preclude your instigating fights.''

Larson shrugged. ''I'm sorry. I made a mistake.'' He formed a mischievous grin. ''You're the one who tells me heroes have flaws.''

Taziar tore a piece from his roll. ''Heroes have heroic

flaws. Flaws which earn us more enemies, we don't need. Control your temper, please, Allerum. Crazed challenges against large Vikings get little bystanders like me killed.''

Larson suspected the street-raised city thief had seen enough fist fights to know how to avoid the consequences. He winked, holding a hand to the level of Taziar's head. ''How hard can it be to duck when you're only this tall?''

Blankets of wool and furs softened the floor before the tavern hearth, but quilts and pillows of satin would not have brought sleep to Larson's troubled soul. The recognition of the cause of his anger forced him to channel it more appropriately. It freed him to treat Gaelinar with the respect he deserved and to exchange gibes with Taziar. But Larson's hatred for the decaying queen of the underworld heightened and spread like a cancer. He lay, staring at the wall, resisting the urge to roll from side to side. He knew the movement would bring him no comfort; it would only deny Taziar and Gaelinar the sleep they had earned.

The fire burned low, chasing flickering shadows across the beamed ceiling. Larson gathered his legs beneath him, with slow, fluent movements so as not to awaken his companions. The shifting curtain of light revealed Gaelinar's chiseled features beneath white hair hacked functionally short. A fold of blanket hid Taziar's face, but his chest rose and fell in the steady rhythm of sleep.

Larson retrieved his sword belt from the floor and buckled it about his rumpled cloak. He rose and crept to the door. Not a single plank creaked beneath his footfalls. The portal opened on silent, well-oiled hinges. The breeze from the doorway did not affect the dying flames other than to slightly shift the speckled pattern of their light. Carefully, Larson pulled the panel closed behind him.

Ice-grained air bit down from the north, whipping snowflakes up from the ground into a whirling dance. Larson paused in the roadway. He was uncertain what force had driven him to abandon his companions and the tavern's comforting warmth, but he suspected it was the same irrational anger which had defined his mood over the past week. One thing seemed unquestionable. Hel had cheated him, and she would pay a heavy price for her deceit. There was no time to waste. Already, Silme's identity might have withered to bits of memory. Despite Gaelinar's insistence on patience, Larson knew delay would doom Silme. *If Gaelinar and Shadow can't realize it, I have no choice but to go alone.*

Larson knew his footprints left an easily followed trail in the snow, and he secretly hoped his companions would track him once they noticed his absence. He had no wish to be wholly free of their company nor to face the Fenris Wolf without their aid. He just wanted a way to turn their route back toward Hel before either of his friends could convince him otherwise.

Larson rounded a crook in the roadway. Ahead, a depression the size of a horse and ringed by boot tracks disrupted the blanket of snow. Larson approached and stared in curiosity. Furrows gouged to the stoney roadway and ridges of higher snow gave the impression of a struggle. A red-brown puddle near its center and similar smaller, stains splashed around it completed the picture. A blood trail and deeper human prints led off toward the border. It appeared to Larson as if some hunter had shot an animal here, perhaps a deer, then hefted and carried it from the town. *But why would a deer leave the forest to enter a village? And why would a hunter carry his dinner back into the woods?*

Larson's self-questioning raised doubts and concerns. He considered turning back, but a fresh wave of anger against Hel caused him to discard the idea. *Gaelinar will only try to talk me into giving Hel more time.* He pushed onward, following the red droplets with newly aroused caution.

The trail took him to the boundary of the village and the edge of the evergreen forest. Snow sagged the needled branches, enhancing the reflected light of the half-moon. A round, dark shape perched upon the weather-beaten sign which identified the village. Unable to read it, Larson crept closer and wished he had thought to bring a lantern from the tavern.

Larson hunched before the sign and focused on the letters. Winding paths of red marred the neatly painted name. Something warm dripped on Larson's head. He froze in position. His eyes went wide with apprehension. By inches, he straightened. His gaze roved up the battered wood to the undefined thing perched atop it, and he found himself staring into Alsvithr's severed head.

Larson recoiled with a sharp intake of breath. He had seen a similar sign before; his troop had once passed through a village to find the V.C. had left every citizen's head speared on a pole. But the horror etched on Alsvithr's dead features went beyond any natural human expression.

"Consider it a gift." The sibilant voice made Larson's skin prickle.

Larson edged away from the sign and dropped into a crouch, seeking the location of the voice. He thought he heard the sound of leather whisking across snow and spun toward the town.

But a moment later, the same voice hissed from behind Larson. "He would have waylaid you when you left the tavern. But I wanted you for myself. You're a one-man job, Allerum."

The voice was unmistakably Bramin's. Larson whirled back to the forest as the dark elf/man emerged from the tree line. Moonlight traced features black as the night. Red eyes glowed like embers. Larson felt helpless and exposed before evil more primitive than murder. Hatred burned like acid, and realization swept nausea through him. *Bramin played me. Some magic or mind game enhanced my anger, driving me to start a bar fight and abandon my companions. And he did it with such subtle mastery, I never noticed his meddling.* Larson's hand dropped to his sword hilt as his rage shifted from Hel and channeled against the creature before him.

Bramin advanced, his stance loose and casual. His left arm held a plain wooden shield without adornment or metal bracing. His right hand dangled well away from the broadsword at his hip. "No sorceress. No magic weapon. No swordmaster. Can you fight so badly crippled? Or will you fall to your knees and beg mercy?"

Larson retreated, tensed for violence. Bramin's taunts fueled his already excessive anger. His fist tightened around his haft, but he made no reply.

Bramin went still. "You want my sister, Futurespawn? You want to bed her? Well, perhaps I'll have her first!"

Larson's self-control shattered, plunging him into a darkness deeper than Hel. He drew his sword and charged.

Bramin met the attack with a lunge. His shield crashed into Larson's chest and face. Pain exploded in ribs scarcely healed from Larson's battle with Fenrir, and Bramin's superior weight and strength sprawled Larson. He struck the ground with a force which jarred the breath from his lungs. It took him desperate seconds to regain enough balance to move. He cringed as he rolled, certain Bramin's sword would take him. But as Larson gained his feet, he realized Bramin had not pressed his advantage. The dark elf had taken only enough time to draw his broadsword and then waited for Larson to recover.

Bramin's laughter rang between the pines, mocking and filled with ancient evil. "Trained by the most capable swordmaster in existence, and you have learned nothing."

Inflamed, Larson sprang. He feigned a straight cut, then spun backward and delivered a strike to Bramin's opposite side. His sword thunked against the shield. He back-stepped as Bramin's riposte slashed a line through his cloak.

Larson bore in, blood lust hot within him. Repeatedly, he hammered his long sword at Bramin's head. Each time, his strokes slammed against the shield. On the fourth attempt, Bramin tipped his shield. Larson's sword bit into the wooden edge and stuck fast. Bramin flung his shield arm outward drawing Larson's sword and arm with it and opening Larson's defense. Realizing his mistake, Larson ducked as he leaped backward. His sword wrenched free. Bramin's blade whistled inches above his head.

Larson retreated, fighting off the fury which had made him careless. He forced himself to concentrate on Gaelinar's words. *Anyone who attacks an equal opponent in anger is doomed to failure. You must willingly commit everything to your goal. When you can calmly accept your own death as a means to your end, you become unbeatable.* The familiarity of a sword lesson settled over him, and he raised his sword with a new and deadly peace.

"You bore me," Bramin baited. "I'm tired of playing with such a child. This time, I think I'll kill you."

Larson adopted a defensive pose, allowing Bramin's words to flow past, unheard. He let the dark elf make the first move.

Bramin approached, taut as a stalking cat. They attacked simultaneously. Larson's sword rattled from the shield. He spun off the wood as Bramin's sword stabbed through the air where he had stood. Larson jabbed his heel behind Bramin's leg and rammed his shoulder into the shield. The dark elf tumbled to the ground and rolled. Larson pursued. Bramin rose to a crouch as Larson's sword slashed down upon him. Bramin met the strike with his shield and gained just enough time to shift his weight before he was forced to block Larson's side cut. Again, Bramin sacrificed his opportunity to strike to improve his footing.

Larson undercut. A quick descent of the shield saved Bramin's abdomen but opened his upper defenses. Larson drove his hand into the dark elf's face. Bramin fell again, then rolled. Larson chopped for Bramin's head in silent fury. Bramin twisted. He raised a hand, as if to block the killing stroke with his bare fingers.

Larson howled, drawing all his strength into the final cut. Inches from Bramin, his sword struck something solid. Light flared and splintered with the sound of breaking glass. Orange sparks streaked Larson's vision. Power surged through him, hurling him into a tangled copse of brambles. Branches jabbed painfully into his back, and his own scream rang in his ears. He ripped himself free, tearing his hands on thorns, and pulled his sword from the brush with a force which scattered sticks across the battleground.

Bramin stood, still and straight, awaiting Larson's next attack. Darkness hid the half man's features, but Larson knew the angular face held a smile of cruel triumph. He also knew his only chance to survive was to engage Bramin in swordplay so rapid the dark elf would not have the chance or energy to work his magic. Dizziness wrapped Larson in a fog of whirling spots, and the moon transformed the forest into a blur of trunks. His legs felt as unsteady as rubber. He stumbled forward. Gathering strength and determination, he raised his sword and rushed down upon Bramin.

Bramin held a stance of casual indifference. He let the edge of his shield rest on the ground, leaning the remainder against his leg. He gripped his sword in a lax hand, its point scraping the dirt. When Larson narrowed the distance between them, Bramin raised his arm to reveal a sunbright ball of sorceries blazing beneath his dark fingers.

Too late to rework his strike, Larson made an urgent dive for Bramin. Magics sheeted through the air. White light burned Larson's eyes, and a shimmering web entangled him. He crashed to the ground. His limbs felt detached, as if they belonged to someone else. He could not gather enough strength to lift his head. Through aching eyes, he watched Bramin's booted feet shuffle toward him.

Larson struggled against the spell which held him immobile and helpless. He managed only to roll his gaze to Bramin's face, as cold and evil as death. Red eyes flashed through the gloom, alive with blood sickness and savage joy. Sudden fear swept a chill through Larson, but he felt only the numbing power of the magics which held him. *If Bramin delays his killing stroke until his spell wears off enough for me to notice pain, I may yet have a chance.*

Bramin granted Larson no quarter. He stood and raised his sword above Larson's neck.

Larson fought to flinch away. He attempted speech, but the spell did not allow even these simple movements. He caught a glimpse of motion beyond Bramin, a shadow moving silently through darkness. He blinked uncertainly.

All malice left Bramin's voice. "It is over. This time,

the better man won." His hand tightened on his sword hilt.

Larson resisted the urge to close his eyes against the coming blow. He watched in fascination as a small, pink hand snaked around Bramin's shoulder and closed on the dark elf's chin. Moonlight flashed off the steel of a drawn sword.

From the woods, light flickered at the corner of Larson's vision. The tree line seemed to dance with the white flame of Bramin's hidden staff and rankstone. Abruptly, Bramin disappeared.

Taziar staggered out of the darkness, stamping on Larson's hand before regaining his equilibrium. "Sorry," the Cullinsbergen mumbled.

I can't feel it. Larson discovered he still could not speak. *And don't apologize for saving my life.*

Taziar sat beside Larson and rested a reassuring hand on the elf's shoulder. "Too bad Gaelinar wasn't the one who followed you from the tavern. A better swordsman than me might have killed that creature before he could escape. Bramin, I assume?"

Larson nodded habitually and noted his head moved slightly. Pain fuzzed through his body, like the pins and needles sensation of blood flow returning to a limb. *If Bramin had caught even a glimpse of Shadow, he would have killed him and me before departing.*

Taziar studied Larson. "Feeling better?"

Larson nodded again, more successfully this time. Grass prickled his arms and legs. His ribs and fingers throbbed. Taziar's grip felt warm through his cloak. As slowly as Hel's queen, Larson worked to a sitting position.

Taziar watched Larson's clumsiness without comment. "You shouldn't have left the tavern alone. Many lives depend on you, and your enemies are too strong to face alone."

Larson met Taziar's gaze but did not attempt speech.

"You have many more enemies than you know. You have to trust someone. Despite his unusual ethics, Gaelinar has your best interests in mind." Taziar's face held a solemnity which suggested a deeper awareness.

But Larson felt too ill to question further. The fiery anger which had driven him for the last several hours had died, and he felt as spent as a used match.

Taziar would not let his point rest. He rose and helped Larson to shaky legs. Still clutching the elf's arms, Taziar met his gaze. "My full name is Taziar Medakan. I'm from a city across the Kattegat Sea called Cullinsberg. Under the alias 'Shadow Climber,' I have a price on my head which could make you rich for the rest of your life. I tell you this because I trust you not to turn me in. And I need you to trust me." Taziar's eyes probed Larson's with sincere urgency. "I can't explain why, but your life depends on trusting Gaelinar and me *and no one else.*"

Larson pulled free of Taziar's grip. He tried to reassure. "Of course I trust you, you little idiot. You just saved my life. What choice do I have?"

Taziar smiled, but he still looked tense.

Larson continued. "I don't believe leaving you and Gaelinar was my own decision. I think Bramin influenced me with magic. Thanks for your help. We'd better get back to Gaelinar before Bramin returns." Larson started slowly toward town. "I don't feel much like killing Hel anymore."

Taziar walked at Larson's side. "If Bramin's loose, so is Silme. You say she can find us. We may as well continue Vidarr's quest and let her come to us."

Fatigued by lack of sleep and his battle with Bramin, Larson yawned. He patted his pocket, reassured by the faceted presence of Silme's rankstone. "Shadow, you've done enough to convince me to talk Silme into taking on Astryd as her apprentice. You have no interest in Geirmagnus' rod, and my enemies want nothing from you. Why are you still helping us?"

"Allerum," Taziar replied carefully, "trust me."

Bramin's laughter haunted Larson's weary trip back to the tavern and pierced his dreams as if from habit. A rumble as mournful as surf echoed through his mind. With fatalistic acceptance, Larson's unconscious acknowledged Bramin's domination of his nightmare. The intrusions had become too familiar to resist, and Larson had learned never to trust his dreams. Too tired to fight, he accepted the scenes Bramin wound through his mind with indifference.

Again, Larson faced Bramin. But this time, Bramin's assault was a wild blur of attack. His sword thrust and parried like a live thing. Larson defended with harried slashes. Repeatedly, steel rang against steel, and Bramin's superior size and skill drove Larson backward.

Suddenly, Larson's foot fell on empty air. He stumbled forward to avoid the new danger behind him, impaling himself on Bramin's sword. The blade sank deep. Pain tore through his chest, and blood ran like spilled wine. Jarred backward, he fell through leagues of blackness, his body tumbling and wind-slashed. Bramin's challenge chased him down the chasm. "Allerum, you are only the first. I have a debt to pay against mankind. They will suffer as I did, and the gods will die with them!"

The scene shattered to evening light. Still in directed dream, Larson watched a village on the eastern coast of Norway. Fishermen in patched homespun carried split cod on poles, their stocky boats angled on the shore. From out of the darkness beyond the town, Bramin rushed down upon the populace. His face was a mask of menace, his skin black as ink. He howled with the pure joy of slaughter as his sword slashed and rent through the crowd. The fishermen grabbed up axes and staves, but their weapons did nothing to slow the half man. Bramin moved with the speed and grace of a whirlwind, leaving piles of red corpses in his wake.

"Stop!" Larson charged Bramin, grimly aware of his own blood, brown and sticky, on his hands. The world upended. The village vanished in a roaring ball of fire. A wave of heat buffeted Larson, and he dove from the path of the inferno. Flames ate men and women, huts and single-sailed boats indiscriminately, then danced like red demons into the forest. Cries of anguish rose above the sour note of the wind. Bramin's savage laughter formed melody to the background of human despair.

Larson gathered his spirit to defend himself from Bramin's threat. He plucked a picture of reality from the exploited wreckage of his thoughts: a village tavern, faithful companions, and a hearth. Bramin's fire withered, trailing smoke. Blackened, uprooted stumps softened to brown, and the green needles of pine replaced skeletal branches. Then the image of the common room filled his mind's eye. Even as Larson basked in his success, Bramin lashed out against Larson's conjured image. Gaelinar's sleeping form turned corpse-pale; blood welled from the mangled ruin of his throat. Taziar's scalp lay flayed open to the bone, and splintered, white skull poked from beneath the wound.

No! Larson wrenched against Bramin's hold on his mind. The vision strengthened, wavered. Abruptly, another entity crashed into Larson's mind. Bramin's scene dissolved with unnatural suddenness. The half man loosed a startled cry followed by an angry hiss.

Larson clung to consciousness with the desperation of a wounded soldier on enemy ground. The effort flung him into the tangled tapestry of his own mind. The figures of Vidarr and Bramin circled, more vivid than his grasp on reality. Bramin lunged, slicing white-hot agony through Larson's mind. Vidarr dodged, inadvertently tripping a memory of the New York skyline. Larson's anger flared against the dark elf who filled his life and mind with terror and the god who had, again, violated his thoughts. Though dizzied by Bramin's and Vidarr's battle, Larson gathered resolve and struck back.

A wall took shape, a solid bastion of brick and mortar, neatly trapping Vidarr and Bramin in a corner of Larson's mind. Surprise broke the battle. The combatants stood in shocked silence, their contest forgotten in the face of this new menace. Larson channeled his spirit against them, clinging to the image of the wall. It was easier the second time, but he did not trust himself to explore the intruders' emotions or allow his thoughts to wander from his invented vision.

Although Vidarr was more familiar with Larson's trap, Bramin recovered his senses first. He smirked, his voice echoing in the confines created by the wall. "Very pretty, Allerum. Sturdy, too. Perhaps the king might hire you as mason."

Larson gritted his teeth, mentally following Bramin's

pacing. The outer edges of wall crumbled. Quickly, he turned his attention back to the structure, allowing the dark elf to wander as he would.

Vidarr remained silent, but Larson suspected the aura of hatred which tainted his thoughts came as much from the god as from the half man.

Bramin seemed more amused than thwarted. "You made a fatal mistake, Futurespawn. You trapped me here with lots of playthings."

Larson resisted the urge to track Bramin's path. He knew he had enclosed coils of recollection with Vidarr and Bramin, and the realization chilled him.

"Hmmm." Bramin spoke with exaggerated attentiveness. "Where shall I start. Which memory will make you suffer most?"

Larson ignored the threat. He kept hold of his creation, not daring to speak or consider anything else. He needed time to think, but the concentration his trap required would not spare him.

Vidarr's voice boomed in warning. "Touch at your own peril, Bramin, and earn the wrath of a god."

Larson felt someone lurch within the realm of his trap. The scent of rain-washed evergreens filled his nostrils, summer sun glinting from droplets perched between the needles. Fifteen years old, Larson pressed his back to the trunk, his rifle clutched to his chest. Wind ruffled the treetops, showering him with stored water. The memory of a deer hunt in New Hampshire threw Larson off-balance. The bricks of his mental wall toppled to dust, and Bramin sprang for the opening.

Larson hovered on the brink of sanity. He clawed for the remnants of his previous control, just as Vidarr dove for Bramin's retreating form. The collision scattered Larson's reason. Bramin and Vidarr skidded through his mind, crashed, and tangled with Larson's memories.

Larson walked through a steamy murk of underbrush in a jungle of palm, teak, and rubber trees so dense he could not guess the time of day. Ahead, he could hear the hushed whispers of the point men. The six soldiers around him reeked of sweat and mud. Beside him, the staff sergeant, Buck Curto, seemed uncharacteristically nervous. It was Larson's second sniper hunt, Curto's twenty-fifth. Curto was a Texas farm boy, a muscled giant who had grown up branding cattle and had spent some time on the rodeo circuit. Larson knew Curto as a hero, afraid of nothing, seven times decorated in the first six months of his shift. This time, though, Curto had a premonition. "I don't know what," he confided to Larson, his drawl apparent even at a mumble. "Something ain't right."

Nothing felt right to Larson, not the suffocating sauna of brush, not his own quiet lack of response, not even the reality of his presence in Vietnam. The scene was a blur not wholly attributable to the crushing darkness of the jungle or the fuzz of rising heat. Pressed by a feeling of alienation and fear he dared not express, he shifted a half step closer to Curto.

Suddenly, a burst of gunfire from the trees ripped open one of the point men from neck to belly. Larson found himself sprawled on the dirt, not certain how he had gotten there. An answering round sounded from one of his buddies, then AK-47s opened up on them from both sides. "Cross fire," Curto yelled. "Run!" The soldier directly in front of Larson fell, the top of his head torn away. Another started to bolt, and bullets in his back dropped him to the brush.

Larson sprinted for heavy cover, M-16 raised for a parting shot. Curto followed, pausing just long enough to pull the pin from a grenade. His arm struck Larson's gun on the backsweep, knocking Larson's aim wild. The grenade bounced from the foliage. Before Curto could react, it shattered, taking his hand and most of his abdomen. Blood splashed Larson. A fragment of shrapnel ricocheted from his M-16, driving the gun into his stomach. Screams cut in over the gunshots. Larson caught a brief glimpse of flesh chewed to hamburger and a seeping puddle of blood before panic descended upon him and he raced into a deeper part of the jungle.

Larson ran until he stumbled, panting, to the ground. He sat for several moments, listening to the spattering of birdsong and the dull croak of lizards. The world seemed unreal, as if someone had replaced the trees with plastic imitations. He felt out of place and time, marked by a heavy sense of not belonging which went beyond parrying death in a foreign country. His fear seemed as watered down as his last beer. He pulled the M-16 into his lap. Grenade fragments had dented the mechanism. He pressed the button to remove the magazine, then pulled the bolt with two fingers. It resisted him, refusing to eject the round.

The gun was dead weight. Larson tossed it to the ground, fighting the swirling chaos of emotion which battered against his reason. This was no time to think, only to survive. He waited until his heart settled to its normal rate, then slipped back through the jungle, alone.

Larson chose his direction at random, moving always downhill, seeking an opening in the double-canopy where a helicopter pilot might spot him. As he walked, his identity strayed. The trees muted to the hickory, birch, and ferns of the New Hampshire autumns then gradually shifted to the mixed evergreens of a distant world and era. The ambush seemed both minutes and centuries past; dead friends and strangers mingled inseparably. His thoughts were not wholly his own.

Larson pressed through a knotted copse of brush. A lull in the buzz of flies and shrills of monkeys brought hissed words to his ears. A branch snapped with frightening clarity. He peeked through a hole in the undergrowth to see three Oriental men in loose-fitting clothing carrying battered, bolt action rifles. *V.C.* Larson felt his pulse quicken. Quietly, he fell back into the brush, prepared to slip away. Then, madness descended upon him.

The scene blasted to orange-red light than faded to darkness the moon could not graze. Nightmare visions rose to smother Larson's will. Before he could focus on his new surroundings, they shifted again to a tavern in an unknown city. Faces flashed through memory, too fast and blurred to identify. Recollections flurried like sparks from a campfire: people, places, things splashed across his consciousness in an endless array of color and movement. Dizzied and disoriented, Larson clung to the rough bark of a palm tree. A momentary lapse in the unseen battle in his mind allowed the reality of the Viet Cong to slip back into awareness. He saw the V.C. coming toward him through an echoing tunnel of darkness. Recognizing the need to have all his wits about him, he grasped the tree trunk so tightly its bark dug furrows into his palms. His thoughts stumbled through a fog of memory and emotion as he used the tree to ground his reason with desperate ferocity.

The sudden jolt of thought brought the jungle to vivid detail. Ripped from the battle in Larson's mind which had triggered his erratic jumps of memory, Vidarr and Bramin crouched with swords poised, inches apart. Faced by a new and inexplicable menace, they disengaged. Bramin stared at the broad-boned, muscular human form which had replaced the slight elf he knew as Allerum. Before the half man could react, the Viet Cong crashed through the brush and trained their guns on Vidarr's eight-foot figure.

For one freeze-framed moment, nothing happened. The Viet Cong seemed as shocked at coming upon a giant and an elf wielding broadswords as Vidarr and Bramin were at finding themselves hurled into a future war. More familiar with the situation, Larson responded first. "Run!" He lunged for Vidarr. His hands struck flesh immobile as rock. The force jarred Larson to the ground. Vidarr staggered a step forward as three rifles roared at point-blank range. A bullet tore through Vidarr's arm, one whined over Larson's head, and the third was lost in the undergrowth.

Bolt actions snapped as the Viet Cong prepared for another round. Pain seemed to enrage Vidarr. As the enemy finished reloading, he sprang. He caught one man by the throat. A flick of his wrist snapped the man's neck. The gun spun away into a circle of ferns and orchids, and Larson dove after it. He rolled to his feet, gun in hand, as Vidarr tossed the corpse into a companion. The soldier collapsed beneath the weight of his dead ally. Larson trained his rifle on the third.

The scene registered dimly in Larson's mind. He saw the remaining V.C., finger tensed on the trigger of a rifle aimed at Bramin's chest. Ignorant of its firepower, Bramin was rushing the soldier with his sword. Larson acted without thinking. He shot first. A tiny hole appeared in the soldier's chest, and his answering bullet flew wild. He tottered, hand fumbling over the mechanism. Bramin hesitated. Larson slammed his own bolt home and fired again. The slug split the Viet Cong's nose, driving his head backward. He crumpled to the ground.

Mechanically, Larson chambered another round. Vidarr had killed the last of the V.C. *There's only one enemy left.* He turned the sights on Bramin. Immediately, a presence brushed the edge of Larson's mind. He fought against it, slapping a concrete wall across the remembered location of the entrance to his thoughts.

Bramin recoiled with a hiss. Seconds later, Vidarr's mental probe met the same barrier. The god exclaimed in surprise. "Allerum, what are you doing?"

Larson held the rifle in place, aware that every moment of delay would give Bramin a chance to weave his sorceries. "No one leaves until I get some answers." His own words sparked understanding. *I need Bramin alive to tell me what happened to Silme.* Reluctantly, he lowered the gun.

Bramin's confidence returned. He baited Larson. "Fine, Allerum. Leave me here. Your people have no mind defenses. I'll rule them as I please. I've read your thoughts and seen your family. The tortures I'll bring down upon them go beyond your imagination."

Larson forced himself to think. Of them all, he was the most eager to depart. But he knew he might never have the chance to trap Bramin and Vidarr again. "We have a magic called 'technology' which makes your sorceries look like a stage magician's tricks. You wouldn't survive a day here." From his memories of his original encounter with this sector of the jungle, Larson recalled a nearby V.C. encampment. The radio man from his own patrol had also escaped the ambush and, wandering in the same direction as Larson, had called a fire strike down upon the enemy. "In fact, none of us is going to survive the next few minutes if we don't move quickly. Those gunshots'll bring more V.C., and, this time, they'll bring automatic weapons instead of toys. Come on.'' Still clutching the rifle, he sprinted into the jungle.

Carefully, Bramin and Vidarr followed.

Larson chose his course with quiet deliberation. He wanted to put some distance between himself and the battle yet remain within sight of the napalm. There was no longer any reason to find a helicopter. The pilot would as likely shoot as save the monstrous trio, and Larson knew escape back to Norway lay only through his own mind. Unable to hold his mental barrier more than a few seconds at a time, he remained alert to Bramin's or Vidarr's further attempts to enter a deeper layer of his thoughts.

At length, Larson stopped and dropped to a crouch, bracing the rifle against his knee. ''Now, Bramin, talk.''

Bramin kept a respectable distance between Vidarr, Larson, and himself. ''I'll kill you.''

''Go ahead,'' Larson challenged. ''But brazen as you are, I believe you're wise enough to realize my death would trap you here forever.''

Bramin shrugged, eyes blazing red hatred. ''No matter. It's men I despise. I can take my vengeance against your people as easily as mine.''

Larson sought words to convince the dark elf of the folly of his decision. Vidarr's hand kneaded the hilt of his sword, but Larson felt uncertain whether even a god could stand before Bramin's magic, or whether the sorcerer could stand against a gun. Before Larson could settle on a reply, he heard the distant roar of jets banking for an approach. A smile twitched across his features. ''Suit yourself,'' he said softly.

The noise of the jets disappeared, then returned as a high-pitched whine. Bramin hesitated as the phantoms screamed overhead, visible only as paired red lights through the leaves. Five hundred yards away, a section of jungle burst into flame. Fire leaped toward the heavens, wound through with smoke and the gasoline reek of napalm. Even as the trailing rumble of the jets faded, a second round approached with the same earsplitting shrill of sound.

After weeks in a world without planes, the grandeur of

the scene struck even Larson by surprise. Vidarr's and Bramin's bolt for his mind caught him off guard. It was all he could do to snap closed the entrance with a suddenness which caused Vidarr to cry out in physical pain. The blaze glared higher, encompassing another circle of jungle.

Dead silence followed. Gradually, the monkeys resumed their chatter. A macaw shrieked its mournful song of death, and the birds twittered in a more minor key. Bramin abandoned his attempt to enter Larson's mind, and the barrier melted away. Larson took advantage of the dark elf's confusion. "Where's Silme?"

"What?" Bramin seemed genuinely startled by the question.

Vidarr broke in. "Just before you brought us here, I consulted the Fates. Bramin threw some sort of spell over Silme. I don't understand the workings of sorcery, but he bound her destiny to the balance of Chaos. Allerum, *Silme will not go free until Geirmagnus' rod has been retrieved.*"

"He lies!" Bramin screamed. "I've not seen Silme since you killed her at the falls. And everyone knows the quest for Geirmagnus' rod is . . ."

Vidarr broke in with incongruous fury. His sword rattled free. "Stop now, Dark One, or I swear you'll never leave this world alive."

Larson swore. "Quiet, both of you, or none of us will leave this world alive. He turned his gaze to Bramin, uncertain of who to believe. Vidarr had always been honest with him, but the god's love for Baldur had driven him beyond honor. Binding Silme's fate to that of a doomed god seemed precisely the sort of scheme Bramin would use, but Larson could see no advantage to the Dragonrank sorcerer in using such a strategy. And, in the past, Bramin had always maliciously delighted in revealing his treacheries.

Now, the dark elf's face lay impassive. He said nothing in his defense, but a bright web of light glowed to life between his fingers.

Larson sprang to his feet and trained the rifle on Bramin. Instantly, a memory flashed through his thoughts.

Once before, Larson's flawed sanity had pulled Vidarr and Silme into the war in Vietnam. Then, Vidarr had assessed his visit with a single sentence: *The men of your world removed all the glory from war and left only the killing.* On the heels of the memory came Gaelinar's words: *The goal of combat is spiritual enlightenment. This can only come through willingly pitting your life and skill against your enemies in fair combat. Anything less is merely murder, in which nothing is gained and courage is surrendered.* ''Hang honor,'' Larson mumbled, but his die was already cast. He let the gun sag in his arms. ''No one's going to be killed here. We're all going back. But I need a promise from both of you.''

Vidarr sheathed his weapon.

Bramin's spell died in his hands, and he seemed relieved. Larson suspected the battle at the town border and the run-in with Vidarr had taxed Bramin down to his last spell.

Larson confronted Vidarr. ''From you, I need a vow that you will not harm Bramin unless he kills me or directly affronts the gods. Our rivalry is our own. If I can't handle it, I deserve to die.''

Vidarr regarded Bramin with distaste, but nodded his agreement.

''And you.'' Larson turned on Bramin. ''You will not hamper or hurt me or my companions, mentally or physically, until we either retrieve Geirmagnus' rod or fail in the attempt.''

Bramin watched the flames wither into black wraiths of smoke. He glanced at Vidarr. ''Agreed, if you and your companions will not attempt to harm me either. And afterward . . .'' The sounds of the jungle filled Bramin's long-drawn pause. ''. . . you and I will fight alone. To the death, Allerum.''

Sweat beaded Larson's brow, and the rifle seemed unusually heavy in his hand. ''By skill. Without magic,'' he added.

''Very well.'' Bramin glared viciously. Though a prisoner in Larson's war and era, there was no doubt he was in control. ''Clever of you to bring a god to witness our oaths. Most would settle for reciting their vows at a shrine." He grinned at Vidarr. "Regardless of your bias, it is your obligation to see that both sides of this bargain are kept."

Vidarr nodded grudging acceptance. "Don't patronize me, elf, or I'll consider it a direct affront to the gods."

Larson caught the rifle bolt, pulled it free, and hurled it into the foliage. He dropped the useless rifle to the ground. "Let's go home."

CHAPTER 11:

Master Plan

"I know death hath ten thousand several doors
For men to take their exits."

—John Webster
Duchess of Malfi

Al Larson, Kensei Gaelinar, and Taziar Medakan shared a breakfast of rolls and stew left over from dinner the previous evening. Larson's gaze traced the beamed ceiling of the tavern. Lack of sleep made his mind feel hazy and distant; even simple thoughts taxed him. While Taziar described the conflict with Bramin at the town border, Larson ate in methodical silence, glad his small friend omitted details which would reveal Larson's initial angry incompetence.

The food tasted like ash in Larson's mouth, and fatigue gave it the consistency of rubber. He shook his head to clear it, but his perceptions still felt thick and sluggish. "I fought another battle last night."

Gaelinar dipped a piece of roll into his stew. "We know."

Taziar added, "You kicked and twitched and cried out enough to keep everyone from sleep. I tried, but I couldn't wake you. What happened?"

Larson shook his head again with the same unsatisfactory results. He harbored no wish to spend hours explaining Vietnam to his otherworld companions; instead, he replied simply. "I trapped Vidarr and Bramin in my mind. I asked each about Silme. Bramin pleaded ignorance. Vidarr claimed Silme's destiny is tied in with this

Law and Chaos balancing act. He says we have to get Geirmagnus' rod to free her. And . . ." Larson trailed off in frustration.

"And?" Gaelinar prompted.

Larson struggled for clarity of thought, and the effort made him irritable. "And I don't fully believe either of them. Hel must have kept her end of the bargain. Bramin's free. She had to compensate his release with someone else. Who but Silme would be recently dead and have anywhere near Bramin's power? So, right now, Hel is the only one I trust." He appended hastily, "And the two of you, of course." He paused as memory stumbled through the mists of his sleeplessness. *Just last night, Taziar said something about trusting only him and Gaelinar.* He glanced at Taziar who hid a smile behind a mouthful of stew. "How did you know . . . ?"

"Lucky guess." The irony in Taziar's voice was unmistakable.

Larson suspected Taziar had learned some revealing piece of information on his journey to the Bifrost Bridge. But before he could question further, Gaelinar interrupted. "So we're back to the same task. And our bargaining with Hel only gained us another powerful enemy."

Larson fidgeted in his chair, the food forgotten. "Uh, not exactly."

His companions waited for an explanation.

Choosing his words with care, Larson detailed the promises exchanged with Bramin in Vietnam.

In response, Gaelinar chewed thoughtfully. "Very honorable, hero. But I suggest you pay as much heed to Bramin's words as to his intentions. I doubt he would directly break a vow, but he might find ways around it."

Larson nodded. That had already occurred to him, and he had tried to phrase his requests to Bramin appropriately. "What do we do now? Do we go after the rod? Or do we try to find some oracle or sorcerer to locate Silme?"

Gaelinar and Taziar exchanged knowing glances. "May I?" the Cullinsbergen asked.

Gaelinar lowered his head in assent.

Taziar pushed aside his empty bowl. "Do you have cause to trust Bramin?"

Larson picked at his roll. "Well, no, but . . ."

Taziar continued. "Has Vidarr ever lied to you before?"

"I don't think so, but . . ."

Taziar broke in again. "Will you agree most people find being called a liar offensive?"

Unable to get a word in, Larson stuffed the remainder of his bread into his mouth and nodded acceptance.

"You already have a deal with Bramin; you can offend him with impunity. But insulting a god might have . . . um . . . certain consequences."

Larson recalled the words of a war buddy in Vietnam: *Sure I believe in God. If He doesn't exist, it don't make no difference, and if He does, I'm covered.* Taziar's statement held the same inarguable logic. *Whether or not Vidarr is lying now, I want him on my side when I go after Silme. She's out of Hel; we don't have to worry about time anymore. Once we've retrieved Geirmagnus' rod, Vidarr will owe us a favor. Even if he doesn't feel obligated to help us save Silme, Baldur certainly will.*

"Besides . . ." Gaelinar said.

Larson was startled. It took him a moment to realize Gaelinar was addressing the question about consulting an oracle rather than Larson's thoughts.

". . . you told Bramin you would fight him after you attempted to retrieve Geirmagnus' rod. It would dishonor you to make such a vow, then go wandering off to do other things."

Larson swallowed, gazing from Gaelinar to Taziar and back. "Neither of you has a stake in this rod thing. Why are you both suddenly eager to complete the quest?"

Again, Larson's companions exchanged glances. Taziar replied. "The Kensei and I had a talk while you thrashed last night. Baldur has other relatives. Most are not as patient or nice as Vidarr. If we delay too long, we may earn the wrath of gods. I enjoy a good challenge, but being crushed by Odin doesn't sound like fun to me." He changed the subject abruptly, as if he had received some nonverbal signal, perhaps a kick or poke from Gaelinar beneath the table. "We decided one other thing, too."

Taziar paused for so long, Larson felt obligated to ask. "And that is?"

Taziar stared at his hands. "I'm not going with you."

Larson looked sharply at Gaelinar who shrugged his innocence.

Taziar noted the exchange. "Allerum, it was my decision. You already agreed to convince Silme to take Astryd on as apprentice. There's no reason for all of us to die on your quest."

Larson fought down rising aggravation. *After all, I told him the same thing yesterday. He's twice saved my life. I think that makes up for loosing Fenrir.* "How will we find you and Astryd?"

Taziar rose from the table. "I'll meet you here. When you get back, I'll buy you a drink. You'll need it." He trotted to the hearth fire and shouldered the gray linen pack which held his supplies. "I'll head back to the Dragonrank school and see if I can find out anything about Silme while you're gone. When I last left Astryd, I told her I would return the following day. She probably thinks I'm dead, a misconception I would eagerly correct." He trotted for the door.

"Shadow, wait!" Larson stood.

Hand on the pull ring of the door, Taziar turned.

Larson crossed the room. He retrieved Baldur's stone from his pocket and pressed it into Taziar's hand. "Take this. It's worth a small fortune and ought to keep you out of trouble for a while."

Taziar studied the gem in his palm, then turned a smile on Larson. "I learned something years ago. No man or woman and no amount of money could keep me out of trouble." He flipped the stone back to Larson, opened the door, and slipped out into the morning light.

Larson caught the trinket and kneaded it between his fingers while he watched Taziar go. "I'll miss the little jerk," he mumbled in English.

A few hours' journey through the pine forest brought Gaelinar and Larson to the base of a mountain range.

Beyond the trees, gray peaks stretched skyward. Choosing a different route toward Geirmagnus' estate, Gaelinar trudged up the hillside until he passed the timberline. Larson followed without comment. Snow capped the summits, whitened the scrub at the edge of the forest, and coated the meadows and ridges beyond it.

They followed the tree line. It seemed odd to Larson that Gaelinar chose to lead him along thickets, boulder covered fields, and gorges when a few steps would take them into the forest. *Perhaps Gaelinar has grown as tired of the endless trees and underbrush as Shadow, and he thinks the mountainous terrain might provide a welcome change.* It also placed them in the open, but Fenrir had already shown he could locate his quarry easily even in the cover of forest.

Snow-slicked rocks among the crushed, brown foliage of the meadows kept Larson's attention on his footing. By midday, he had found his second wind. Then, too, a vague, unnameable discomfort settled over him. His steps grew more cautious. The sudden rattle of falling stones from behind startled him. Larson jumped, nearly sliding from a precariously situated ledge. "Gaelinar, are we being followed?"

"Yes," Gaelinar replied in a matter-of-fact manner.

"Fenrir?"

"Bramin."

"Oh." Larson mulled over this bit of news. "Why would Bramin follow us?"

"I don't know." Gaelinar stepped around a large, ungrounded rock. "Whatever his reason, he wants us to know he's there. He can move silently as wind if he chooses. I'd guess he's trying to unnerve you. Of course, we could turn around and ask him."

"Never mind." Larson pushed onward, reminded of Gaelinar's words when Taziar had joined them. "A wise man once said 'An enemy within sword range is safer than one concealed.' "

Gaelinar smiled. "And it might do you well to listen to that wise man now and again."

They continued on into the day, always traveling parallel to the dwarf pines, aspens, and poplars which defined the timberline. Well before dark, Gaelinar began taking an inordinate interest in the many caves which dotted the hillside.

After a time, Larson tired of waiting alone while Gaelinar explored crevices and caverns. A day of travel after a sleepless night made him curt. "Are you looking for something?"

"Yes," Gaelinar said. "When I'm ready, I'll explain what."

Larson sighed. He knew better than to provoke Gaelinar with questions. Exhaustion had settled over him again, and it seemed like too much effort to press his luck.

At length, Gaelinar found a cave which seemed to satisfy him. Its huge, misshapen mouth seemed particularly unwelcoming. A boulder field covered the ground before it, the loose, piled stone riddled with holes and clefts which seemed to drop off into nowhere.

Gaelinar tossed his pack to a flat stone wedged between the cliff face and several boulders. "Camp."

Larson studied the gray infinity of rock in the dim light of evening. The anchoring lichens surely lay dead beneath the blanket of snow, but the bulk of the boulders would hold them in place. The hard, jagged surfaces of rock looked uninviting. If Larson rolled in his sleep, he might fall through the chinks between boulders, quite possibly to his death. "Here? On the rocks?"

"Yes. You set up camp, and I'll be back shortly." Gaelinar wandered into the forest. Grumbling epithets against the Kensei's sanity, Larson brushed snow from the smoothest rocks, laid blankets, and selected cheese and bread from the sack of rations.

Within minutes, Gaelinar returned with a stout, green branch. Perched atop a stacked throne of boulders, he whittled one end of his stick to a point. He poked at the barb with a fingertip, rose, and trotted into the cave. Shortly, he joined Larson again.

Larson watched Gaelinar's antics without comment. Curiosity gnawed at him, but he knew his mentor would appreciate patience. *He may even be testing me.* Larson dismissed the thought; when Gaelinar was ready, he would discuss his plans.

Gaelinar's secretiveness extended through a sword practice tempered by fatigue and through a meal eaten nearly in silence. It was not until they lay between thick blankets, nestled around the craggy protrusions of the rocks, that Gaelinar chose to reveal his scheme. "I couched the spear at the level of Fenrir's chest. If at any time the wolf chases you, run into the cave. Be careful of the point. It sits about here." Using his finger, the Kensei traced a depiction of the cave on Larson's arm. He emphasized a location which corresponded to three-quarters of the distance from entrance to end. "Run straight. Ignore any branches. I picked a cavern with an exit in the back, so we have an escape if the trap fails." He added in a reluctant tone which discouraged inquiries, "Any questions?"

Larson yawned. Already, he could feel sleep huddled at the edge of his consciousness. "What if Fenrir doesn't attack tonight?"

Gaelinar removed his hand from Larson's arm. "No matter. There are plenty of caves in these mountains. We'll set the same trap every night until we reach Geirmagnus' estate."

A sudden gust showered snow down upon Larson and Gaelinar. Larson huddled deeper beneath the blankets, more from habit than need. He had long ago learned cold did not faze him in the elf form Freyr had given him.

Wind and gathering darkness swallowed Gaelinar's words. They came to Larson muffled. "I think the wolf will attack tonight. We haven't seen it for weeks. It's biding its time, studying us, waiting until we're most vulnerable. Tonight, we're far from civilization and short a companion. I don't know how that mental combat of yours works, but a drunken beggar can see how lack of sleep has impaired your coordination and your judgment. And I'm not at my best either."

Gaelinar trailed off, and Larson turned his head to see whether his mentor had paused or simply dropped his voice too low to hear over the hiss of wind through crevices.

Gaelinar's features appeared twisted in thought. "Speaking of your faulty mind barriers, I suggest you do whatever you can to keep our plan hidden from the wolf. If it's delayed this long, it'll surely read what thoughts of yours it can. Given its preparation and ours, one way or the other, this will be our last fight. Right now, the wolf has all the advantages, except one. If you reveal our plan, we lose surprise, too."

Larson clenched his jaws. He knew Gaelinar was aware he would not divulge the trap on purpose, but Larson could not evade a feeling of resentment. *What was it Vidarr said about probes?* He racked his memory of the night when Fenrir invaded his dreams and Vidarr came to his rescue. *Vidarr said he needed to actually enter my mind to manipulate it, but to communicate or read "surface" thoughts, he used a mental probe. I'm always aware of intruders in my mind. The probes seem to pass unnoticed.* Larson followed his thoughts to the natural conclusion. *Gaelinar's right. Fenrir has access to anything I'm concentrating on. Therefore, I'll have to stop thinking about the trap.*

Careful not to slip between cracks, Larson shifted to his side. Immediately, he pictured the cave in the mountainside. He smothered the image, turning his thoughts toward his uncle's farm in Kansas. His mind followed tight miles of corn rows, tassels swaying in the breezes of early summer. Landscape as flat as the Coney Island beaches filled his mind's eye. Sleep replaced the memory, flooding Larson's dreams with caves, carved spears, and giant wolves. A lighter phase in the cycle of sleep brought him close enough to awareness to attempt to redirect his thoughts. He began to roll again, and Gaelinar's warning touch drew him fully awake.

Larson went still. His ears sifted out the harmony of wind, owls, and foxes which had lulled him to sleep. Beneath these familiar noises, he heard the click of tumbling pebbles. Now, the wisdom of Gaelinar's decision to sleep in a boulder field seemed clear. Something was moving toward the Kensei, slowly and stealthily. Head turned the wrong way to see the creature, Larson inched his hand to his sword hilt and loosened the blade in its scabbard.

Gaelinar's fingers locked on Larson's wrist, restraining him. The patter of dislodged rocks disappeared.

Larson held his breath, seeking a misstep which would reveal the stalker. He hoped Gaelinar was following the intruder's progress by something other than sound.

Gaelinar released Larson with an urgent snap. In the same motion, the Kensei leaped to his feet, drew his katana, and slashed. Larson followed, but a pebble rocked beneath his foot. He stumbled and caught his balance at a crouch, barely managing to keep hold of his sword. Fenrir jumped backward to avoid Gaelinar's strike, its dark form blocking Larson's view of the woods. Moonlight silvered bristled fur.

Fenrir circled, keeping Gaelinar between itself and Larson. Abruptly, it sprang for the Kensei. The boulder from which it launched toppled down the mountainside, crushing young alders and dwarf pines. The unexpected shift of Fenrir's foundation threw off its sense of distance. Its attack fell short. Gaelinar's blade plunged toward the wolf's neck. Fenrir swerved but not quite far enough. The katana drew a long cut in its side before Fenrir grounded its footing.

Giant boulders which seemed immobile to Larson pitched beneath Fenrir's tremendous bulk. The wolf went on the defensive. It crouched, taunting with arrogant challenges, its breath pale smoke in the autumn air. "Come on, *murderers!* You know I cannot be killed. If you insist on trying, I will joyfully tear you both apart." Dark blood parted a trail through the fur over Fenrir's ribs, but it seemed unaffected by the wound.

Gaelinar worked his way around the wolf, leaving Larson at the front. Larson took a halfhearted thrust at Fenrir in an attempt to buy time for the Kensei to position himself. Fenrir dodged easily, then spun and lunged for Gaelinar. The Kensei sidled. His sword darted up to meet the wolf. The beast twisted in midair. Gaelinar's blade carved harmlessly across fur, and Fenrir's shoulder jarred the Kensei's forearm. Unable to keep up with Fenrir's tremendous leaps, Larson rushed to his mentor's aid.

Gaelinar backstepped for stability. A rock turned beneath his foot and he lost his balance, tumbling awkwardly to the boulder field. Fenrir snapped for Gaelinar's head. The Kensei scrambled desperately aside. In his blind haste, he misplaced a knee and toppled through one of the crevices between the boulders. A shower of pebbles followed Gaelinar through the crack. A single pained cry echoed up from below, mournful and final as a rabbit's death squeal. The sound froze Larson in mid-charge.

Fenrir swung its head up, as surprised as Larson. Slitted, red eyes measured the hundred feet of treacherous ground between them. Its jaws hinged open to a gaping smile, revealing teeth yellowed as old bone. Shaken by Gaelinar's certain death, Larson whirled and ran toward the cave. Howling in triumph, the wolf pursued.

A patch of marble-sized stones rolled beneath Larson's foot. He fell headlong. His nose struck rock, drawing blood, and he clambered to his feet without looking back. Another sprint for the cave mouth brought him crashing to the stone, gravel abrading his open hand and the fist which clutched his sword. As he rose, he risked a glance over one shoulder. Fenrir's paws were also slipping on the rocky ground, but it was narrowing the gap at a slow, steady trot.

Larson forced himself to slacken his own gait, timing each step to a heartbeat. He gained the entrance to the cave, and quickened his pace on the smoother surface of its floor. Moonlight slanted into the shaft, defining the outcroppings of wall and shallow puddles in the uneven surface of ground. He saw no stalagmites or holes, and the discovery encouraged him to break into a run. *If the trap has any chance of success, Fenrir will have to be moving fast when he hits it.* Sword clasped in his right hand, his left scraping the wall for orientation, Larson sprinted beyond the spear of moonlight into the darkness deeper in the cave.

Behind Larson, Fenrir's huge paws splashed through the stagnant water, revealing its ever-changing location like an alarm. The stable floor of the cave allowed Fenrir the traction it required. Each of its leaps covered the same distance as five of Larson's running steps.

Larson's fingers brushed empty air as he passed a cross corridor then met stone wall again. Moonlight glimmered ahead. Directly beside Larson, the rodlike shadow of the spear became visible in the center of the cave, then disappeared behind him. Larson darted for the back exit. He had just emerged into the pooled light of the opening, when he heard the crash of impact behind him. Wood clattered across stone. Fenrir loosed a shrill whimper, then all went still.

The exit was little more than a crack. Larson hunched to pass through, straining his hearing for some sound from Fenrir. He had seen men endure too much to believe a single spear could kill Fenrir instantly. Yet the quiet seemed to indicate otherwise. *Maybe it caught the wolf just right, in the spinal cord or the heart.* Curious, he turned and crept back into the black depths of the cave.

Larson was met by silence. He edged deeper into the cavern, groping for wall with his free hand. The broken end of the spear rolled beneath his foot. Larson stumbled, the sudden movement all that saved him from death. Fenrir's jaws, aimed to gouge open Larson's abdomen, glanced instead from his hip. The force thrust Larson completely off balance. Tossed sideways, he crashed to the cave floor. The back of his head and one shoulder blade struck the wall. His sword jarred from his grip and fell, ringing, to the stone.

Larson's awareness blurred and spun. The wolf's hot breath stirred his collar. He made a frantic effort to rise, and a lion-sized paw clamped on his abdomen.

"Dare to move, elf, and I'll tear out your throat!" Fenrir's challenge echoed through the confines of the cave.

Larson sank back to the ground. The darkness seemed crushing, and his wits floundered through a haze as dense as water.

"Did you really believe I would fall for an ill-conceived toy of a trap designed for mortal wolves?"

"I'd hoped so." Larson talked to keep Fenrir occupied while his eyes adjusted to the gloom. His sword lay beyond his reach, its hilt submerged in a puddle. Gradually, sense seeped back into his numbed mind, and he berated himself with profanity. *Fenrir set me up, and I walked into its trap like an ignorant "fucking new guy."*

Fenrir's eyes appeared flat and black beneath fur-hooded sockets. Its lowered muzzle hovered at Larson's neck. He could smell the foul odor of exhaled air as it spoke. "Then you're as stupid as your scheme. Did you forget I can read your thoughts? You might just as well have included me in its planning."

Larson said nothing. He slid his hand to a pocket of his britches, counting on the darkness to hide the movement from Fenrir. *Keep talking, you hairy moron. This isn't over yet.*

"The Kensei's dead. Compared to you, he's lucky."

Larson's fingers inched toward Silme's rankstone, and he did not allow himself to dwell too long on Fenrir's words. *The wolf's been wrong before. I won't believe in Gaelinar's death until I see the corpse.*

Fenrir's toenails jabbed the skin over Larson's stomach. "You'll pay for my father's murder. I'm going to eat you, piece by bloody piece, and let you watch yourself bleed to death."

Larson's hand closed over the sapphire. Despite his predicament, he found himself considering Fenrir's threat. *Bleeding is not the worst way to die; I've heard it's relatively painless. Though I doubt the same applies to being eaten alive.*

"I think I'll start with a leg." Fenrir tensed to strike.

Deprived of the precious minutes he needed for strategy, Larson wrenched the sapphire. Cloth tore, and the linen of the pocket flapped open, spilling Baldur's trinket to the ground. The sudden violent movement caused Fenrir to pause for the moment it took Larson to slam the rankstone into its face.

Fierce blue light blazed at the impact. Fenrir reared backward in astonishment, and Larson claimed the seconds surprise gained him. Clutching the sapphire in a bloodless fist, he lurched free of Fenrir's loosened paw and ran for the exit. The aftereffects of the flash superimposed stars and streaks of color across the darkness. He made a grab for his sword as he passed. His fingertips jammed against rock, stabbing pain into his knuckles.

His palm curled through water. The wet leather of the hilt touched calluses. Ignoring the throb of his injured hand, he delayed to grip the sword before continuing his mad rush for the patch of moonlight ahead.

Fenrir's teeth seized the back of Larson's cloak. A quick jerk nearly pulled him off his feet. Larson reeled backward, regained equilibrium, and dove for the opening. For an instant, he hovered in air. Then the cloak tore, and Larson jolted forward. He sailed through the crack, skidding across the surface of rock, arms clamped protectively over his head, hands tightened to death grips about the sword and sapphire. Stones caught on his tunic, jerking him to a halt.

For a long moment, he lay there, staring at the cliffs before him and listening to Fenrir snuffling at the exit. The crack was too small for the wolf-god to slip through, a provision Larson suspected Gaelinar had purposefully arranged when he chose the cave. *Gaelinar! He may be alive and in need of my help.* The thought mobilized Larson. He leaped to his feet. The Kensei's scream had sounded convincingly terminal, almost animal. But, before he could abandon his companion, Larson had to be sure. Tucking the sapphire into another pocket, he ran toward the boulder field.

Larson had passed only halfway around the outer side of the ledge which held the cave when Taziar's familiar voice sounded from up ahead. "Stupid as your murdered father, you overfed cur. Forgot about me, didn't you?"

Shadow? Larson broke into a gallop, soaked with sweat despite the cold. The many mad dashes had grown taxing; his chest heaved with each labored breath. He rounded the corner just in time to see Taziar hopping across precariously grounded stones with the agile grace of an acrobat. A moment later, Fenrir burst through the ill-shaped mouth of the cave. Its chest struck rope thin as a thread, and its momentum dislodged the meticulously placed notched sticks which held the snare in place. A coil of magical cord encircled Fenrir's neck like a hangman's noose. The wolf's charge snapped the line taut; the abrupt impact knocked it, choking, from its feet. Larson followed the glint of moonlight off the string to a peak above the cave. Under ordinary circumstances, he suspected Fenrir could shatter the restraining formation to pebbles. Now, the slightest motion would only serve to cinch the snare deeper into the wolf's throat.

Larson stared, unable to make sense of what he saw. Fenrir writhed, pawing madly at a string which seemed too slight to hold anything larger than a house cat. Taziar perched on Larson's sleeping blanket, watching the wolf with unbridled amusement. Larson prepared to question the Shadow Climber, but the sight of Gaelinar emerging, grimy and tattered, from the scrub struck Larson mute with astonishment.

Fenrir howled crude oaths, but the pressure of the magical rope kept its words too hoarse to decipher. Understanding came to Larson in a rush. He pointed an accusing finger at Taziar. "You lied to me." Sheathing his sword, he jabbed another digit at Gaelinar. "You set me up with Fenrir. You bastards used me for wolf bait."

Gaelinar shrugged. "We had no choice."

Larson would not let his mentor off that easily. "I almost got killed in that cave. What the hell were you thinking?"

Taziar accepted the burden of an explanation. "After Fenrir told us it couldn't be killed, it occurred to me there are other ways to be rid of enemies. I fetched the only rope I knew was capable of holding it, the magical cord the gods used for centuries. Then, while you played mind wars with Bramin, we plotted."

Fenrir ceased thrashing, listening with the same intent curiosity as Larson.

Taziar rose. "We couldn't tell you the plan. We might just as well have stood on the city walls of Cullinsberg and shouted it to Fenrir. I pretended to go in the other direction which gave me the chance to trail you unseen and set up the snare while you and Gaelinar slept." He trotted to Larson's side. "I was a little disappointed you accepted my leaving so easily."

Larson smiled, breathing without difficulty now. Drying sweat prickled his skin to gooseflesh. "I was tired. And that line about Astryd was a good touch." He turned to Gaelinar. "So it was Shadow following, not Bramin."

Gaelinar shook his head. "No, I told the truth about Bramin. In fact, I spoke to him in the woods. Not a pleasant conversation. He'll stalk us all the way to Geirmagnus' estate, awaiting his first opportunity to kill you. Your arrangement means we can't do anything about him." Gaelinar's stance went suddenly angry. "In the future, Allerum, I don't want you making any vows for me. He verbally abused me in a fashion which would have earned any other man the thrill of having his head detached from his body."

Taziar confirmed Gaelinar's assessment. "I figured you knew Bramin was there. He seized every chance to make you aware of his presence. It made my job that much simpler."

Larson needed to know one thing more from Gaelinar. "And your fall through the crevice?"

"Real." Gaelinar rubbed an abraded elbow with a hand which was no longer swollen. "But I faked the death scream and then lay still. With you at Fenrir's back, I didn't think the wolf would have time to make certain. I needed him to chase you into the cave, but I doubted he would do so if he knew I was alive and waiting for him outside. Of course, the spear was a ploy to give you reason to lead Fenrir into that particular cave. I wanted the wolf to know the same plan I fed you. That way, it entered the cave believing it held the advantage." He grinned wickedly. "There's no surer way to get a man thinking about something than to tell him not to."

"Very clever." Despite the success, Larson felt irritated that his companions had used his handicap to their advantage. "But tell me this. Now that we've leashed the puppy-dog, what do we do with it? If we leave it, someone will let it go. Most probably Bramin. I doubt Fenrir will have the decency to heel." He considered. "I guess we can always keep our distance and stone it. We'll know for sure whether or not it can die."

Gaelinar tossed his head. Wind caught white hair, fanning it like a horse's mane. "Possible or not, killing Fenrir can only further disrupt Midgard's balance."

Taziar added, "If we can drag Fenrir to the Bifrost Bridge, I'll bet the gods would help us."

Larson pulled his frayed cloak across his shoulders. "Fenrir's an evil, ugly monster. What makes you think the gods will take it back?"

The gods will take it back.

"The gods will take it back," Taziar echoed.

It took Larson several seconds to realize someone other than his companions spoke the initial statement. *Vidarr?* Larson tried hopefully.

A friendly aura filled Larson's mind. *It's me, Allerum. Fenrir was never intended to become a burden to mankind, only to the gods.*

Taziar gave a simultaneous explanation which Larson never heard. He held up a finger to silence his companion, then returned to the conversation in his mind. *So why wouldn't any of the gods help us catch the brute? We all could have gotten killed.*

There are laws which govern hostilities between gods. Fenrir isn't actually a god, but it is the son of one. Quite frankly, the fact that we never killed Fenrir before is the only reason the balance hasn't become skewed beyond salvaging. Fenrir has taken Loki's place as a strong Chaos-force.

Larson studied the great form of the wolf. *Sort of a god substitute, eh? So we need to get it to the Bifrost Bridge?*

By Thor's beard, no. Vidarr seemed taken aback by Larson's suggestion. *The gods will take care of Fenriswulf. I wouldn't allow your quest to be delayed another several days.*

Afraid to lose Fenrir after the tremendous effort and pain of catching it, Larson warned Vidarr. *Bramin's here, somewhere. He may try to free Fenrir before you can lead it away.*

Amusement colored Vidarr's reply. *Believe me, Allerum. If Bramin interferes, we will consider it a direct affront to the gods. Nothing would please me more than to have Bramin break his vow so I could pound him back to Hel. Anything more you wish to know?*

Curiosity goaded Larson. *One thing. How did you manage to show up just when I wanted to speak with you?*

A strained pause followed. Larson sensed reluctance

before Vidarr answered warily. *You have twice abandoned your quest. Yesterday, you transported me to a fiery forest with trees which looked like a child's drawing. There, some puny, mortal archer without a bow shot an unshafted, unfletched arrowhead through my arm.* Vidarr grumbled as if to himself, *Still damn well hurts, too.* He continued in his normal pattern. *I promise I'll avoid your memories. But until you retrieve the rod, I have no choice but to keep a close watch over you. Can you live with that?*

Larson yawned, stretching muscles bruised from his battle with Fenrir. The excitement finished, the fatigue of two sleepless nights settled over him. *I can live with that, but I can't live without rest. If it's all right with you and all the gods in the heavens, I'm going to lie here for a week.* Larson picked his way to the rumpled pile of blankets. Offering no explanation to his companions, he collapsed upon the padded rock and fell instantly asleep.

PART III:

The Dragonrank Master

CHAPTER 12:

Geirmagnus

'Our fathers and ourselves sowed dragon's teeth.
Our children know and suffer the armed men.'
—Stephen Vincent Benet
Litany for Dictatorships

The next week of travel passed in unaccustomed peace. Bramin trailed closely, making no attempt to hide his presence. Whenever Larson or Gaelinar or Taziar wandered into the woods alone, to wash up or relieve himself, the dark elf would hurl insults and threats. Still, Bramin kept his vow not to harm them; his taunts and invasions of privacy soon became familiar. Larson suspected the half man was as interested in the result of the quest for Geirmagnus' rod as he was in his coming battle with Larson.

Life seemed simpler without the Fenris Wolf. Sleep came easily to Larson, no longer interrupted by divine or magical intruders. Only Silme's continued absence and the oaths exchanged with Bramin remained to haunt him. Now, in the quiet serenity of the pine forest, Larson's agreement to fight the dark elf to the death seemed foolish bravado. Bramin was one of the most skilled warriors in the realm, while Larson had never seen a sword outside a museum until less than three months ago. Gaelinar's intensive training would help even the odds, and Larson hoped death might have weakened Bramin. Even so, Larson harbored little hope he could win a fair fight. *But what choice did I have? At least this way, Bramin won't interfere with our efforts to rescue Baldur and Silme.*

Gradually, the towering evergreens gave way to spindly aspens and alders and stocky dwarf pines which admitted the glow of the sun. Larson and his companions pressed through thinning forest toward the timber edge. Gaelinar stopped. He pointed through a gap between the trunks. "There it is."

Eagerly, Larson pushed forward and stared over Gaelinar's shoulder. A blanket of snow lay over the dead and dying perennials which defined a short line of clearing. Beyond it, a wall of molded concrete rose above the younger trees to twice Larson's height. Vines with curled brown leaves swarmed over its surface. Coiled wire perched atop, its steel glinting in the sunlight despite centuries of exposure to the elements. *Stainless? How?* Stunned by the enormity of this anachronism, Larson stared in silent wonderment. *This can't be Old Norway. My God, what kind of game are they playing with me?* He searched his memories of his time in Midgard. Ever since his arrival, he had noticed differences between this world and his scanty knowledge of Norway's history, geography, and weather, inconsistencies which went beyond the simple reality of mythical and fabled creatures. The uncertainty shocked him. "What the hell is this thing? How did it get here? Where are we?"

Gaelinar met Larson's verbal volley with a quizzical look. "It's Geirmagnus' estate. He built it, and we walked here." The Kensei's tone went patronizingly gentle. "Are you well, hero?"

The familiarity of Gaelinar's voice made Larson reconsider. *I have to be in Old Norway. Too much has happened for this to be a joke.* "I'm fine, just surprised. The estate looks like something out of my own world." *Imagine the power this Geirmagnus must have commanded to build a steel and concrete fortress without factories or supplies.* Fascinated, Larson approached the wall and scraped a finger along its surface. Dirt lined pits and cracks, but the recent snows had scoured the main surface clear. It felt cold and coarse beneath his touch, like twentieth century cement.

Gaelinar and Taziar joined Larson. Together, they circled the clearing. The inspection took nearly an hour; each wall spanned a quarter mile. Scattered at the bases, a few bleached bones poked from beneath the snow. A gate interrupted the southeastern wall, a tombstone-shaped entryway of stainless steel bars reinforced with metal triangles and set flush with the concrete. Nicks and dents in the surface indicated failed attempts to hack through it with weapons of iron, copper, or wood.

Taziar assessed his findings. "It would be difficult, but I could climb it."

The casual claim horrified Larson. He caught Taziar's arm to prevent the Cullinsbergen from carrying out his plan. "You see that shiny stuff at the top?" He pointed. "That's razor wire. It'll saw off your fingers as fast as you can touch it. I'm willing to bet the bones lying about are from people who tried to break in."

Taziar gazed at the corkscrew of steel, his expression appropriately impressed. "How do you know?"

This time, it was Larson's turn to respond with, "Trust me."

Gaelinar chipped ice and dirt from an inscription on a square of wall several feet from the gate. "What's this? It's not in any language I know."

Bramin's answer wafted from the forest edge, his tone flat as a remembered chant. "My rod holds the key to unlimited power. Once freed, the future will be changed and nothing will be impossible." He stepped into the clearing, twisting the bottom rim of his dragonstaff into the snow. "And it's signed 'Geirmagnus, Dragonrank Master.' "

Gaelinar and Taziar whirled to face the half man.

Larson came up behind Gaelinar and studied the message. Someone had carved it into the concrete using an impact drill, a power chisel, or some other instrument well beyond the technology of the Vikings. Larson blinked, unable to believe his eyes. The message was inscribed in English. Aside from the substitution of the name 'Gary Mannix' for 'Geirmagnus,' it read exactly as Bramin had translated. *This doesn't make any sense. It can't be.* Larson tapped the resilience of spirit which had seen him through months of combat in Vietnam. *I can't afford these distractions. I'm in a situation where I have to fight for my life. If I live, I'll have time to figure this out later. If not, it doesn't matter.* Too surprised by Bramin's knowledge to concern himself with rivalry, Larson questioned. "How did you know what it said?"

Bramin wore an expression of haughty amusement. "Every glass-rank Dragonmage has learned the words since the second master broke Geirmagnus' code with magic. The gods believe the final sentence refers to bringing Baldur back from the dead."

"And does it?" Taziar asked.

Bramin arched narrow shoulders. "How would I know?"

Larson turned his attention to the gate, leaving Gaelinar to keep watch over Bramin. The straight, central edges of the metal doors matched perfectly, leaving no crack between them. Larson found no keyholes nor even a chain for a padlock. Tentatively, he laid a hand against the bars and pushed. The panels did not yield.

Gaelinar spoke. "They say no one has ever penetrated Geirmagnus' estate. The sharpened wire explains why no man's gone over the walls, but what's to stop people from digging under it? Why haven't gods or sorcerers flown over?"

Larson turned his attention to the space of wall beside the gates as Taziar addressed Gaelinar's questions. "Invisible, lethal spells protect the Dragonrank school. According to—" Taziar caught himself, apparently not wishing to reveal his source in Bramin's presence. —"someone, they're harmful only to sorcerers and magically-created creatures. I'd guess the original Dragonrank Master might have similar defenses. Either that, or no sorcerer's been brave enough to try."

Larson realized Taziar had addressed his last statement to Bramin, because the half man responded. "I have no interest in freeing Baldur."

Taziar continued. "As for digging under, there must be some barrier. It's possible no one's succeeded for the same reason no trees have yet grown close enough to provide branches to climb safely over the wire. I've never seen soil so sandy."

"Sandy?" Larson lowered his head. But before Taziar could scoop aside enough snow to demonstrate, Larson caught sight of a battered and twisted clasp jutting from the wall near the gates. He reached for it. The metal fell free in his hands; it had not weathered the elements and trespassers as well as the rest of the fortress. Closer, Larson recognized a panel set into the concrete. He pushed. The steel resisted. He caught his fingernails under the irregularity left by the broken clasp and pulled. The metal did not budge. Larson exerted sideways pressure, and the panel slid haltingly into runner slits in the concrete, uncovering a recess.

Buttons of black plastic confronted Larson in four rows of three. Arabic numerals from one through nine were engraved on the keys of the first three rows, one digit on each. The last row contained a zero on the central button while the ones on either side read "close." Beneath the configuration, an etched plaque held the English instructions: "To open, dial information."

Dial? How? Larson stared in confusion. The setup appeared unlike any telephone he could recall from his last days in America in the late 1960s. He tapped his fingers on the concrete. *And who the hell am I supposed to call?* The idea seemed so ludicrous, he could not suppress the mental scenario. *Hello, police? This is Al Larson. I'm calling from eleventh century Norway. You see, officer, I'm standing here with a German pickpocket, a samurai, and a demon sorcerer. Pause. That's right, sir, a demon sorcerer. And did I happen to mention I'm an elf? Click. Hello? Hello?*

Larson redirected his thoughts to appropriately serious matters. Bramin had not moved from the timberline; the dark elf was returning Gaelinar's unflinching scrutiny with icy detachment. Larson saw no immediate threat. *Dial information. Press it, perhaps?* Feeling foolish, he raised a finger and tapped out 555-1212 on the keys. He heard a muffled, metallic snap followed by a hydraulic whine. The gates inched open, plowing snow into drifts.

Larson thought he should try to talk to whomever this

odd telephone might have connected him with, but realization made the words stick in his throat. Suddenly, an idea which had seemed crazed became a stroke of genius. *Geirmagnus, or rather, Gary Mannix apparently wanted to be sure that only someone with knowledge of twentieth century American technology could enter his estate. But why?* Again he shook the thought aside, but there was no longer any doubt. *Vidarr claimed I was the only person the gods ever transported in time, and my transfer cost too much for them to attempt it again. But to gain the knowledge to build a fortress like this and with a name like Gary Mannix, the first Dragonrank sorcerer had to be a time traveler!* The theme from *Twilight Zone* flashed through Larson's mind and could not be fully banished.

Taziar stared incredulously at the opened entryway. "How did you do that?"

"Magic," Larson replied offhandedly. A full explanation would have taken too much time, and he had not yet decided how much he wanted Bramin to know. "Let's go." He walked through the portal.

Two buildings rose from a snow-covered courtyard, the smaller and closer an unadorned square of concrete, the other a homey, two-story with windows. A metal panel lay inset into the wall by the gateway, a duplicate of the one on the outside which housed the buttons, except with the clasp unmolested. Larson opened the box as Taziar and Gaelinar filed through the entry behind him.

Bramin trailed after them.

Gaelinar whirled to face the half man, hand light on his sword hilt. "You're not coming in."

Bramin slammed down the base of his staff, kicking up a spray of snow which settled across the hem of his cloak. "You can't deny me, Kensei. My presence causes you no harm."

Larson hated to agree with Bramin, but he knew the dark elf could read his mind. The instant Bramin explored Larson's thoughts, the button code could no longer remain secret. Bramin could come and go as he pleased, sharing the method of entry with anyone he chose. Larson addressed Gaelinar, phrasing his words so as not to encourage Bramin to probe. "Recall what that wise man said about the vicinity of enemies."

Gaelinar hesitated while the deeper meaning of Larson's words became clear. He made no reply, but he did step aside and allow Bramin to enter.

Larson waited until everyone had cleared the area around the gate before punching the "close" key. The high-pitched sound recurred as the gates wound shut. Larson secured the panel and hooked the clasp. He turned, staring over the expanse of snow. Excitement swept him. The thrill of his discovery went far beyond the chance to find a rod or even to raise a god who might become the chosen of his own people. Whatever his original time or place, Gary Mannix had known and emulated twentieth century America. Larson considered further. *The gate mechanism was unlike anything I've ever seen. Maybe it's twenty-first or twenty-second century knowledge. Maybe it's not even American.* The possibilities seemed endless, but Larson knew the answers lay beyond the walls of the buildings. He approached the nearer structure.

It seemed odd to Larson that Taziar, Gaelinar, and Bramin accepted Geirmagnus' estate and its protections without question. Larson imagined their nonchalance came as a result of viewing constructions so far beyond their understanding that they attributed it all to magic. *And they're probably right. Every bit of technology for the next eight hundred years won't allow men to build a place like this.*

The steel door of the smaller building opened easily to Larson's touch, revealing a single room packed with metal gadgets. A water tank the size of a family car filled one corner. Thick, steel tubing came out of one side, passed through a pump, and disappeared into the earth of the floor. A short distance away, the pipe resurfaced into a cylinder, humming like an insect and connected by another pipe to a turbine. A pair of naked wires passed out of holes into a cable of heavy plastic which plunged into the sand. *A generator of some kind. And by the sound, it's functioning.* Larson backstepped, pulling the door closed. "We won't find what we're looking for here."

Though not at all certain of his statement, Larson wanted the chance to explore the main house. It was far more likely to furnish answers to the many questions which plagued him.

To Larson's relief, neither of his companions challenged him. Apparently, they realized he had more knowledge of the first Dragonrank Master's estate than seemed reasonably possible. In silence, they followed him to the house. Larson circled the building, trampling a lane of snow to the pale sands beneath it. Two casement windows set in the lower level were half buried in a drift. Time and wind-borne sand had worn the glass to polished convexity. The upper story held three windows, all intact and similarly timeworn. Concrete steps led up to a gray door into the second level. Larson climbed to the portal. The paint was apparently some sort of bonded epoxy; aside from some chipped flakes in the corners, it had weathered the centuries well.

Larson grasped the aluminum doorknob. For several seconds, he stood without moving. Something seemed fundamentally wrong with dragging his companions into the world beyond the door; he had no idea what the collision of past and future might yield. And Gary Mannix might have set magical or technological traps to protect his estate. Larson suspected a device in this dwelling converted the electricity harnessed from the smaller building into usable household current. The possibilities were endless and more than possibly lethal. *Still*, Larson reasoned, *if Mannix didn't want people in his estate, he wouldn't have revealed the gate opening sequence. Even a person familiar with such a device would have required years of trial to crack a seven digit code.* Comforted by this thought, Larson twisted the knob and pushed the door open.

A blast of hot, stale air struck Larson. The panel swung a full ninety degrees. Sunlight flooded in, revealing a rectangular room which ended in a window. Office furniture lined the longer walls, choked with dust. Directly to the left of the entryway, a set of stairs led to the lower level. A short distance farther, on the same side, a doorway opened into another room.

Larson took in the scene at a glance. The furnishings consisted of three filing cabinets, a laboratory desk with a scattering of journals, bookshelves built into the wall and crammed full of texts, and an unidentifiable assembly of gauges and dials in the far corner. A human skeleton was draped awkwardly across a chair of wood and vinyl before the desk. Larson took a shuffling step into the room. The movement dislodged a pile of dirt which whirled madly through the air, sparkling in the sun's rays. Grit stung Larson's eyes and clung to the moist membranes of his mouth. Blinking and spitting, he motioned his companions back and waited for the debris to settle. The interior felt stifling compared with the late autumn coolness outside, and he doubted the warped windows could be opened.

Walking with more caution, Larson made a rapid circuit of the room. The desk supported the skeleton's arm and skull across a blank page of an open journal. Scraps of leathery skin still clung to the yellowed bones; the walls had protected it from insects and the elements. Too accustomed to death to concern himself with the remains, Larson removed a bound journal from the top of the stack and flipped to the title page. It read, "The Acceleration of Anti-muons to Super-relativistic Velocities and Its Applications to Time Travel by Galin R. . ." The last name was smeared beyond further recognition. ". . . and Gary Mannix." Though not discarding the potential significance of his discovery, Larson closed the journal and moved on to the shelves.

The books on the mantles fell into categories, many of their titles obscured by mold. The upper levels held psychology texts and guides to hypnotism, witchcraft, and other paranormal phenomena. Beneath it, a row of physics and history tomes stood in stately contrast. The historical references held a definite bias toward the Middle Eastern cultures. The last shelf consisted of a mixed batch of hardbound science fiction novels, a bible, and assorted medical and literary references. Many of the volumes held the same Library of Congress classification tags Larson had thought he recognized on the books of the current Dragonrank Master. A glance down the stairwell revealed a well-equipped kitchen and a bathroom. The remaining room appeared to be a bedroom.

The tour took only a few minutes, but the trapped, ancient air felt suffocating and centuries of grime burned Larson's lungs. Until he had a chance to identify the strange gadgets in the laboratory and kitchen, he knew that allowing his companions to explore might prove too dangerous.

Gaelinar stood in the doorway, blocking Bramin's entry. Only Taziar had followed Larson inside. Snatching up the half dozen journals on the lab bench, including the one wedged beneath the skeleton, Larson caught Taziar's arm and herded the climber to the exit. "I'm not sure what we have here, but I'd rather examine them where I can breathe and see." His brief inspection had also revealed overhead lighting. But even if Mannix had created a working system for electricity, Larson doubted the bulbs could have survived.

Larson led his companions back outside, leaving the door propped to air out the building. Scraping aside snow to uncover the sand beneath, they sat in their manufactured clearing. To Larson's relief, Bramin came, too; apparently the dark elf wanted to keep track of his quarry or else he assumed the journals in Larson's arms held more interesting information than the house itself. *And he's probably right. If these are, as I believe, Gary Mannix's private notes, they may hold a wealth of magical and technological data.* He shook his head, picking the first volume up in a hand which had begun to tremble. *The mind boggles.*

Taziar and Gaelinar seized later volumes as Larson flipped through page after page of formulas and calculations. The paper was watermarked, stout and sturdy enough to have survived the centuries. Tiny letters and numbers swarmed across each leaf in tight bunches, the mathematics punctuated by paragraphs of information, most of which made little sense to Larson: "The long-held theory that acceleration to light speed creates infinite mass is incorrect. No actual data has been previously available for particles traveling at or beyond light speed, only the extrapolation of Einstein's equations. We have shown that energy translates to mass up to a point. Beyond this threshold, energy will increase a particle to super-relativistic speed. Once the barrier of light speed is breached, a particle of insignificant mass liberates infinite energy. We have already determined time travel must be easier for energy than matter. Once the antiparticle mu was accelerated to super-relativistic speed, we might be able to store the massive energy this process would create in some alternate part of the Earth's orbit. If we can find the date of Nova, perhaps directly on our own sun.'' The text lapsed back into numerical incomprehensibility.

Larson looked up. Gaelinar and Taziar had lain aside their volumes in disgust, unable to interpret the English writings. Bramin stood behind Larson. Intent on his findings, Larson had not noticed the dark sorcerer reading over his shoulder. Apparently, however, Gaelinar had. The Kensei studied Bramin through narrowed eyes, his hand on his sword hilt.

Bramin broke the hush. ''Some sort of magical runes.''

Larson scooted around to face Bramin, annoyed by the abstraction which had kept him from perceiving an enemy at his back. ''English, actually.''

Taziar and Gaelinar exchanged glances. Larson's explanation held no meaning for them.

''I can read it,'' Larson clarified. ''It's written in a language I understand.'' He added belatedly, ''Elven, sort of.'' He hated to deceive his companions, but it seemed far less time consuming. He wanted as much of the daylight hours as possible to decipher the writings.

''Please, read, then,'' Gaelinar insisted.

''Aloud,'' Taziar specified.

Larson hesitated. His single semester of college physics had scarcely gotten him past the law of gravity and Newtonian mechanics. ''It's mostly numbers. They wouldn't have any meaning for you. If you give me a little time, I may find something useful.'' He opened to the first page again, taking note of details. The entry was dated 12/07/1988. Larson gawked until the numbers blurred beyond his ability to read them. *1988? Almost twenty years after I went to Vietnam.* He tried to picture his sister, Pam, more than forty years old, telling her children about their uncle killed in the war. But the image defied him. Absently, he fluttered the pages as he considered. *I destroyed the future, didn't I? Or changed it, at least. Then again, since Mannix apparently came back before I did . . .* His thoughts became incomprehensibly jumbled; time lost all relative meaning.

As pages flicked past him, Larson noticed a change in the quality of the penmanship. Toward the end of the journal, a darker handwriting replaced the chicken scratch of numbers. The discrepancy caught Larson's attention. He found the first entry of the newer author, a long treatise of words in letter form. "I think I have something here." Tucking his legs beneath his buttocks, he began to read.

"Galin R.," Larson glanced up to find Gaelinar watching him, a perplexed look on his wizened features. "Galin R.," Larson started again, and this time the incongruity clicked. "Galin R., Gaelinar." The names sounded too alike to attribute to coincidence. Despite the unfinished quest, an enemy close at hand, and multiple unsolved mysteries, Larson broke into laughter. Unable to read on, he lowered the book and roared.

Gaelinar and Taziar looked alarmed, which only made Larson laugh harder. He gasped between bouts, "Now . . . we know . . . where Silme . . . got your name." *The Dragonrank mages must have passed it on for centuries.* Several more minutes passed before Larson gained enough control to continue.

"Galin R.," Larson snickered, but managed to go on. "Well, I did it, at last. I channeled the stored energy and set off for . . ." Larson paused. The diary read "Egypt, 700 B.C.," but he saw no way to translate the place and era. He settled for a vague description of the location and indicated centuries back in time.

Taziar interrupted. "You must have misread. How could someone live for more than 1700 years?"

Larson held his place in the journal with a finger. "Shadow, I have a feeling it'll get even more confusing." He returned to reading.

"The explosion must have looked magnificent. I'm sure

you'll read about it in the papers long before you see this letter—if you ever see this letter. Certainly, there will be those who try to link my disappearance to the . . ." Larson skipped over the word "nuclear" which had no Old Norse equivalent. ". . . testing which went on here for the last fifteen years, but you and I and three dozen lab assistants know better. I thought we would never get past moving peach pits, books, apples, and cats short distances into the past and future. Now we've done it. I'm gone, and everything went with me: my research, yours, the . . ." Larson avoided the term "particle accelerator" which held no more meaning for him than for his companions. ". . . the equipment, the walls. Everything went exactly according to plan except one thing, dear Galin. The instant I arrived, I lost power. The lights went out, the . . ." Larson substituted "tools" for "machines" and continued ". . . went down, the . . ." He interposed "box for keeping food cold" for "refrigerator—" ". . . stopped running."

Larson continued reading, interpreting where possible, substituting descriptions for words when necessary, and paraphrasing as much as he could. "The air conditioner also quit working, but, oddly, it didn't bother me. It couldn't have been more than forty degrees outside, and the only desert sand was the stuff I brought with me from Nevada. Thank God for your paranoid insistence on contingencies—and your addiction to Pepsi. I lived off warm soda and canned fruit cocktail while the steaks spoiled in the nonfunctioning freezer during the two weeks it took me to establish a geothermal energy source. Boy, could I use a physicist. If you ever find yourself in ninth or tenth century Scandinavia, feel free to drop in for a visit, okay?

"By now, Galin, I'm certain you figured out what happened. Some miscalculation dropped me in the wrong place and time, not a tragedy in and of itself, except I'm apparently no longer in contact with our line of stored energy. I'm trapped, unable to tap the power and unable to move through time, stuck in a world of Vikings until you find me. Of course, I could start the process over again. I have the cyclotron and your notes. But without your knowledge or the patience to go over the long, complicated mathematics you did for me, I'd probably end up in the Pacific Ocean somewhere during World War II. Besides, I'm short a few pounds of plutonium and a handful of lab technicians. So, if you happen to come across any extra, please send them to Gary Mannix care of General Delivery, Old Scandinavia. I don't know the zip, but I can tell you I'm about six inches shy of hysteria.

"Galin, please tell Marsha and Jimmy I love them very much. I doubt my life insurance policy covers such a contingency. I trust you and your team. I know you'll come for me if you can. If you time it right, perhaps you'll arrive before I write this note. For the record, my watch says it's October 16, 1989 at 9:17 pm. According to the guarantee, it's not supposed to lose more than a minute a year. Think I can get my money back?" The signature at the bottom read simply "Gary." Larson lowered the journal.

An expectant hush followed, broken finally by Taziar. "Did that make any sense to anyone?"

"Not much," Gaelinar admitted.

Even Bramin looked perplexed.

The sun hovered directly overhead, creating short shadows beneath the buildings and the wall. Recalling the skeleton hunched over the lab chair, Larson reached for the final volume, labeled number six. *If someone spent his last moments of life writing, he must have had something urgent to say.* The binding was cracked, as if the book had remained in one position for quite some time. Larson separated the covers, and it fell open naturally to a blank page stained black with old blood. Larson backtracked to the final entry and read aloud in the same manner as before.

"Dear reader,

"Much of what I write may seem primitive to you. Unless the manufacturer greatly underestimated the life span of this paper, you must be a time traveler. Therefore, you come from a future I never had the opportunity to see. As far as I know, I am the first time traveler. Even if the technology I used has become outdated, my story may prove interesting to anyone who comes after me, if only to learn from my mistakes. I have no choice but write my story quickly. Today, almost certainly, I am going to die.

"My name is Gary Mannix. I am a parapsychologist, originally from Cherry Hill, New Jersey. More than once, a sneering skeptic has called my profession an oxymoron, but I don't find that comment any funnier now than when I became trapped in ninth or tenth century Scandinavia twenty-two years ago. Apparently, neither did the United States government. In their infinite wisdom, they gave me and my associates a grant to study ways to affect enemy alpha brain waves with oscillating magnetic fields, but they wouldn't give a penny to my friend, physicist Galin R., for his research on time travel.

"I have always had a special interest in the differences between the ancient mind and our own. Despite tremendous gains in technology, information and its processing, there has also been knowledge lost: the secrets of the great pyramids and Stonehenge, for example. I felt certain I could glean useful information from Egypt in 1000–500 B.C., an age when brain surgery was not only being performed, but the patients survived. Galin convinced me his project was worthwhile. By careful manipulation, I managed to work his research onto my grant. It worked out well for both of us. Galin got his money and a laboratory in the basement. I got a promise that I would be the first man to travel through time.

"Galin's research is detailed in previous volumes of his journal. To protect him, I've blotted out his last name, and those of our numerous assistants, everywhere they appear in his notes. I have no idea what impact my disappearance may have on him. Whatever happens, I want to give him the option of disclaiming his role in my mistakes. I take no credit for the brilliance of his project, but I deserve all the blame for the consequences my subsequent actions unleashed upon the world."

Larson paused. He knew Mannix's revelation lay beyond the comprehension of his companions, especially with the huge and myriad gaps lost to translation. But the word "Dragonrank" farther down the page seized Larson's attention. He continued reading.

"Our laboratory was understandably nonstandard. We needed modern living facilities to take with us on our hops through time and solid barriers to defend us from warrior cultures. The time travel required a huge cyclotron buried beneath the sand. Its ends pass through Galin's workroom in the basement. He used it to accelerate antiparticles to relativistic speeds, continuously feeding the generated energy back into the system. A single, contained nuclear fusion blast liberated enough additional energy to drive larger particles beyond light speed. Once the threshold was breached, the process became exothermic. By channeling the massive amounts of power thus created, Galin made an essentially infinite energy line which we tapped in small amounts to move through time and run the standard electricity in the laboratory. A series of complicated equations and experiments with inanimate objects determined the amount of energy needed to travel instantaneously to various times and places. That's how I understand it, but I'm no physicist. I have to rely on the simplified information of Galin's verbal explanations. I'm certain, friend reader, you could learn more from Galin's notes."

I doubt it. Larson's head was pounding already, and he made no attempt to translate the paragraph for the others. "Anyone for lunch?"

"I'll take care of it." Taziar opened his pack and set to the meal while Larson returned to Mannix's journal.

"A miscalculation brought me to ninth/tenth century Scandinavia rather than B.C. Egypt. I've reviewed Galin's calculations a thousand times without finding it. Over time, I've come to believe it's a mistake so small as to be within the natural error of the gauges. That would also explain why Galin was never able to rescue me. Regardless, I soon realized that if I was to ever see my wife and son, my friends, my home, my world again, I was going to have to find my own way back. In the meantime, I set out to meet the people of my new era.

"My Norwegian-English dictionary proved of little use in translating their ancient language, but desperation makes a damn good teacher. Eventually, I learned to communicate with them. They called me Geirmagnus. At first, I thought it was their accented pronunciation, but that didn't quite fit. Then I convinced myself it was a title of respect. Within a year, I met six other Geirmagnuses and realized it was simply a common name and the closest to my impossibly strange American one.

"No history text could describe just how filthy, foul-smelling, and diseased these people were." Larson looked up quickly, but his companions did not seem to take offense. "More than ever, I wanted to go home, but the same curiosity which pushed me into research drove me to gain their trust and experiment. It was then I discovered the fascinating truth. Not one of them could be hypnotized! I tried every technique I could think of, carefully adapting it to the culture of their time without success. Certainly, there are people from my own time who can't be hypnotized, and theories abound as to the reason. But, after due consideration, there was only one reason I could see for an entire primitive race, perhaps the entire era, evolving barriers to mental exploration. Protection. Apparently someone or something could meddle with minds, perhaps destroy them. And I was the only one defenseless against it!"

Larson ate the jerked meat Taziar handed him, feeling a sudden kinship with a parapsychologist named Gary Mannix. *But how did a man without mind barriers become a Dragonrank Master?* Understandably intrigued, Larson read on.

"Obviously, the people had little or no knowledge of their gifts. When questioned about mind-reading beings, most mentioned mythological gods. Nevertheless, my persistence won out. Eventually, I was told of a rare subculture of people known as "dream-readers." For a fee, a dream-reader would interpret dreams and thought obsessions, provided his client withdrew the mental barriers. As with all things not well understood, the dream-readers were looked upon with a mixture of fear, hatred, and respect.

"Scientist to the end, I couldn't let the discovery rest. I began a search which took me across Norway and parts of Sweden. I believe I interviewed and hired every dream-reader in existence. There were only eleven. More importantly, my efforts turned up Hosvir. He was a gawky youngster, not well suited to feats of strength or skill. After failing at multiple apprenticeships and on his father's farm, Hosvir was sent away from home. But Hosvir had the ability to perform tricks which I would have believed were simple sleight of hand were it not for the fact that he had the coordination and agility of an old plow horse. Because of his odd gift, he decided to try becoming a dream-reader.

"Hosvir did not fare well. He lacked the honey-tongued, used-car-salesmanlike sweetness which successful dream-readers use to relax clients enough to drop their mental barriers. Of course, I was no challenge. Hosvir read my thoughts. Then he read my memories. When I asked about his past, he didn't tell me. He showed me, with vivid images placed directly in my own mind. Hosvir was to other dream-readers what Harry Houdini's water tank was to my six-year-old son's card tricks. I thanked Hosvir for a unique experience. He thanked me for having flawed mind barriers. I took him back to the lab, and the first Dragonrank sorcerer was made."

Larson sighed, wishing his own experiences with Dragonrank mind powers had been equally benign.

"It didn't happen overnight. Through trial and error and good communication, I elicited the mechanism for Hosvir's ability. Some special difference in his internal makeup, I never discovered exactly what, allowed him to channel what I called 'psychic energy' and he referred to as 'Chaos.' In truth, his term was probably more accurate. He would summon this entropy as a scattered force and mold it into whatever he wanted or needed. It was the ultimate conversion of energy to matter, an alchemist's dream. Hosvir could turn lead to gold, but it was just as easy for him to create gold from nothing.

"It didn't end there. Strengthened by psychic exercises of my invention, Hosvir's powers seemed unlimited. He could create anything his mind could conceive, even life itself. He made Ingeborg, a large-boned, stout, and sturdy woman, beautiful by the standards of the era. Unfortunately, he couldn't conceive of antiparticles, nuclear fusion, or time travel. Even his exploration of my thoughts didn't help. Spanning epochs remained beyond Hosvir's abilities. And we soon discovered that we paid a great price for Hosvir's art.

"There is truth to the Chinese concept of yin and yang. Our world has two forces which must remain in relative balance: one, the natural entropy or randomness of the universe, the other, the ordered systems of matter. Hosvir's magic required him to summon large magnitudes of chaos-stuff from some source I never uncovered. The working of his spells would consume a certain amount of that energy, but there was always some left over. With time, the liberated chaos was becoming significant. Gradually, it took on a physical form. It looked to me rather like a small, European dragon. (Later, I learned this is the natural shape of huge volumes of banded entropy. Perhaps this opens a new area of research in Europe.) Unfortunately, the single purpose of the entropy-force was destruction.

"Initially, it was weak. It killed cattle now and again, uprooted a few trees. I left it alone, making the fatal mistake of believing that since I understood it, I could find a way to control it. Ingeborg turned out to have Hosvir's chaos-channeling abilities, and a search by Hosvir gained me two more magicians besides her. They reveled in the newfound power my psychic exercises opened for them. And the entropy-force grew."

Larson paused for a drink of water. Gaelinar and Taziar watched him expectantly. Bramin fidgeted with impatience. Larson gulped slowly, savoring a little power of his own before returning to Gary Mannix's narrative.

"Some ten years after I discovered Hosvir, a claw-shaped scar appeared on the hand of every sorcerer. Somehow, they knew it came from the entropy-force, but it was quite some time before we realized the creature was stamping its prey. We called the scars 'dragonmarks' after their source, and the sorcerers became known as my 'dragon ranks' or 'dragon troops.' The mark helped bring us all together. The first accidental channeling of chaos would cause the mark to appear on adults and children with the potential to become sorcerers. Frightened parents brought their marked sons and daughters to me. I took them all in, hoping one could learn the time travel 'magic' which would take me home.

"Luckily, the gift was rare. Over the next nine years, my dragon ranks swelled to eighteen. And the chaos force grew exponentially. It had begun to kill people, at first singly. Then it slaughtered entire towns. A few of the sorcerers attempted to destroy or contain it, but they were beaten before they started. The chaos they summoned to use for spells against it only added to its power. And the entropy-force grew.

"Eighteen years of training sorcerers gave me enough knowledge of their craft to finally realize how to reroute their energy and stop feeding the entropy-force. Rather than summoning an extrinsic chaos force, I taught the novice mages to tap only the psychic power within themselves. In good faith, the higher ranking sorcerers tried to do the same. But the change limited their powers to a tiny fraction, and old habits die hard. Hosvir and his earlier-trained companions frequently slipped back into previous patterns. Worse, the tapping of self-energy required keener judgment of the amount of summoned force needed for a spell. Bringing forth more life energy than necessary simply sapped their own strength, and depleting life force too far resulted in death. We lost six of my dragon ranks in the first week. Though more slowly now, the chaos force continued to grow, leaving a trail of death and destruction in its wake.

"Now in my twenty-second year in Old Norway, I have come to realize my dragon ranks will never learn to bridge time, especially with their power curtailed. Last week, desperation drove me to attempt something recklessly stupid. I gathered the remaining dozen sorcerers who still knew how to channel external psychic energy and brought them together in a cause. It occurred to me that, if the sorcerers were unable to control time, perhaps a god could. I had them create 'Thor,' describing him from my memory of the comics. Had I not been blinded by homesickness, I might have realized just how foolish this undertaking was. The Thor they created came directly from their own perceptions. With him, they brought the entire Norse pantheon. And the excess entropy was almost beyond comprehension."

Larson let the book slap closed over his finger. The implications seemed too far beyond reality to believe. *If Gary Mannix wrote the truth, we have the answer to the age old question, "But who created God?" I can't believe the gods were invented by a twentieth century American parapsychologist.* He reopened the journal and continued reading.

"The backlash was tremendous. Earthquakes swept Norway. Forests shattered to kindling, and death came in the form of a rampaging dragon. God only knows the ripple effect on the countries outside Scandinavia. The way Hosvir explained it to me, Law and Chaos are in a constant battle for control. There are advantages to being the stronger force, but too much power serves no one and destroys everyone. We were approaching that threshold. The world had become so skewed toward Chaos, it was rocketing toward oblivion.

"I'm convinced the entropy-force is nonintelligent, but somehow it knew it had grown too strong. The night we summoned the gods, Hosvir's dragonmark began to ache. By morning, the entropy-force had clawed him to death. It came for the sources of its excessive power. One by one, it hunted down and killed my dragon ranks, sparing only those who tapped exclusively internal energy sources. Then, tonight, the mark appeared on me. It hurts like an open wound, and I have no doubt the entropy-force will come for me soon. I've set a trap for it. I hope to contain it within the particle accelerator beneath this laboratory, thereby removing it and restoring the balance of the world. I have no choice but to use myself as bait. Likely, I'll die with it, perhaps deservedly. But I can't help wondering what will happen to this world that I've created. When time travel was only the realm of science fiction, people wondered if tiny changes in the past might multiply and radically alter the future. I've always been of the mind that, once time travel becomes possible, so many people will make so many changes, the mistakes of any one individual will go unnoticed. Let us hope, friend reader, my theory is correct. Judge as you will.''

The signature read ''Gary Mannix, 9th/10th century Norway on the equivalent of May 3, 2011.''

Beneath the signature, a brown discoloration covered words scrawled across the bottom of the page in shaky, unfamiliar handwriting: ''I believe only my rads will kill the monster. —GM.''

''Rads,'' Larson repeated in English, puzzled. ''I must have misread that. It has to be rods. Geirmagnus' rod.'' With this correction, he told the final sentence to his companions.

Taziar glanced at the page. ''Geirmagnus must have trapped the chaos-force in that 'thing you can't translate.' Otherwise, it would have destroyed the world a long time ago.''

The sun had slipped lower in the sky while Larson read, lengthening the shadows into slender caricatures. ''Apparently, it killed Geirmagnus, too. The handwriting, the bloodstain, and the skeleton convince me. Mannix must have staggered up the stairs, fatally wounded, to write that last sentence. It must have been pretty important . . .''

Bramin interrupted, casually sidling beyond range of Gaelinar's swords. ''More important than you know. What your so-called friends neglected to tell you . . .''

Gaelinar leaped to his feet.

Bramin met the threat with a sneer. ''I am protected by Allerum's vow.''

''Not if you break that vow,'' Gaelinar threw back. ''You swore not to hurt Allerum or hinder the quest for Geirmagnus' rod. If you say it, you will do both.''

''Say what?'' Larson pressed, annoyed at being talked around.

Bramin met Larson's gaze. Red eyes flashed in a face wearing an expression like iron. He addressed Gaelinar, but his reply was for Larson alone. ''Do I hinder him with knowledge or do you fetter him with ignorance? Would you send him to his doom unaware?''

''Stop right now,'' Gaelinar warned. He laid a hand on each sword hilt.

Larson tried to gain some control of the situation. "Quit it, both of you," he screamed. All eyes turned to Larson as he continued. "Bramin and I made the vow. We can revise it if we both agree."

Bramin remained still and silent. His features were placid, without triumph.

"Fool." Gaelinar spat. "Don't let him play you again. Do you really think Bramin would tell you something to help you?"

"No," Larson admitted. "But I do believe you would hide information to protect me; I know it for a fact. And right now, the more I understand, the better off we all are."

Taziar tugged at Larson's sleeve. "Trust us," he said softly.

Larson hesitated, recalling Taziar's pleas at the city border. *I have every reason to trust my companions, to place my life in their hands. Perhaps my ignorance may prove the best way to complete this quest.* As he came to the decision, a feeling of complacency settled over Larson. He had no doubt he had made the right choice. And yet, the certainty itself seemed tainted, foreign. Realization seeped around Larson's inner calm. *Vidarr! You influenced my thoughts. How dare you!* Anger exploded across Larson's mind. He lashed out in fury against Vidarr's presumed violation and the companions who would not trust him with the knowledge of his own life and death. "Damn it, I'm no child. I can handle the truth. I retract the vow, Bramin, only enough to allow you to speak."

Vidarr's voice wound through Larson's mind in startled accusation. *Allerum, I didn't . . .*

A smile curled across Bramin's features, grotesque as a stone gargoyle on a motel roof. Realization hammered Larson. *It wasn't Vidarr. My god! Bramin influenced my thoughts to make me believe he was Vidarr. He made me betray my friends. And I can't claim foul because it was my misinterpretation, not an attack.*

Bramin spoke quickly, before Larson could rescind his permission. "Allerum, *your quest is impossible.*"

"You idiot!" Taziar shouted, but Larson never knew whether the Shadow Climber addressed him or Bramin.

Gaelinar pointed a finger at the dark elf. "You know I have too much honor to interfere with your vows. But you had best hope the hero kills you. If he doesn't, I will."

If I don't get him first, Vidarr added.

"Take a number," Larson grumbled, surprised by his own calm acceptance. "But first, let Bramin finish. A little knowledge is a dangerous thing. Tell me why the quest is impossible."

Bramin's gaze passed over each of Larson's companions in turn. When no one protested, he continued. "My source is the Fates and therefore cannot be disputed. Centuries back, they released a trinity of fortunes concerning Geirmagnus' rod. All the gods know the prophecy, and every child born to Midgard hears the tale at his mother's knee. First, the retrieval of the rod will release a chaos-force of immeasurable power. Second, no matter the state of the balance, the release of the chaos-force will open a place for Baldur on Midgard. Third, and I quote, 'The weapon Geirmagnus planned to be used to defeat the chaos-force has not yet been made and may never be. The only weapon of its kind will not be used against it.' "

Gary Mannix's last scrawled words rang clearly through Larson's thoughts. *I believe only my rod will kill the monster.* Sweat rose on his temples. He fingered his own ear, bending it down until the point touched the lobe. *So I have to find this rod/weapon, thereby freeing a creature which destroyed cities and killed a dozen Dragonrank sorcerers. And the only weapon which will work against it is destined never to be used.* Frustration writhed through him, and Vidarr's echoing hatred in his mind served only to strengthen it. Larson stared down Gaelinar and Taziar in turn. "The quest is impossible. You led me into it, blindly, knowing we all would die. And you dare call yourselves friends?" Larson whirled.

Something slammed him in the back of the head. He staggered forward a step. On angry impulse, he drew his sword and spun to face Taziar. The comma of black hair had slipped into the Shadow Climber's eye, making his scarlet features seem almost comical. "You stupid, selfish bastard! When are you going to start thinking with your head instead of your sword? Sure, we knew the quest was impossible. But we chose to sacrifice our lives and come anyway. Gaelinar is here, prepared to die with a student who apparently doesn't deserve his loyalty. I came, ready to die to prove nothing is impossible. Silme's life hangs on your willingness not only to die, but to achieve the impossible."

Taziar tossed his head, freeing blue eyes cold as ice and deadly serious. "They said Loki couldn't be killed until Ragnarok, but he was. Not even the gods could find a way to raise the dead, but you've done that." He made a vague gesture at Bramin. "Sneaking into the Dragonrank school is impossible, right? But a man half your size did just that. Impossible has no meaning; it's a term coined by the simple-minded to explain tasks they're too weak or lazy to accomplish. If you would rather bow to the whims of gods and Fates and sorcerers, lie down and die here. I'm getting Silme." Quick as a rabbit, Taziar dodged between Gaelinar and Bramin and was halfway to the door of Gary Mannix's lab before Larson could think to reply.

CHAPTER 13:

Master of Time

"My rod holds the key to unlimited power.
Once freed, the future will be changed
And nothing will be impossible."
—Gary Mannix,
Dragonrank Master

Taziar's verbal attack swept raw fury through Larson. *Shadow and Gaelinar decided to come. I was never given a choice!* He charged after Taziar, boots crunching in the shallow layer of snow. Bounding up the concrete steps, he dashed through the open doorway just in time to hear Taziar's footfalls on the lower landing of the stairs.

Once inside Gary Mannix's laboratory, Larson's anger dissipated, replaced by a feeling of imminent danger. His acid retort died, forgotten. *Silme is my problem. I'm not going to let Shadow face the chaos-force alone.* As he stood debating in the entryway, Bramin and Gaelinar drew up beside him. *But what the hell is Gary Mannix's rod?*

Evening cast a gray haze over piled centuries of dust and the dark line of office furniture. From habit, Larson flipped a set of four plastic switches by the door. The first three had no visible effect. As the fourth snapped upward, pale light sputtered, dimmed, then brightened at the bottom of the stairs accompanied by Taziar's startled cry. *Fluorescent. Thank God for modern technology.* Shouting a reassurance, Larson plunged down the stairwell, a film of dirt coating his snow-wet boots. Gaelinar and Bramin clattered down the steps behind him.

The diffuse glow from an elongated, overhead bulb chased darkness from the quarter of the room at the base of the staircase. Beyond it, the light faded, revealing kitchen appliances as hulking shapes lining the western and northern walls. Air from the propped door had not circulated well; the lower level still felt stifling. A portal in the eastern wall opened into a bathroom. A rectangular table of plastic, constructed to appear woodlike, occupied the center of the room. It rested against a brick and mortar pole which supported the plumbing, a fuse box, and a conduit cable to supply power to the upstairs and basement.

Taziar had followed the right, southern wall, groping through grime-filled mist which had once been nearly total blackness. Not at all certain what to look for, Larson circled in the opposite direction, examining the western wall. He came first upon a wooden storage cabinet. Flicking open its hinged doors, he discovered its contents had fallen to dust. Atop it, a boxlike, glass and metal appliance sported buttons not unlike the ones which coded the gate. A list of temperatures and cooking instructions beneath the keys revealed it as some sort of oven, unlike any Larson had ever seen. Above it, the sand-covered, warped casement windows he had noticed from the outside admitted meager stripes of sunlight.

Next in line, Larson discovered a dishwasher and an electric stove with a conventional oven beneath it. He watched Bramin fiddle with the temperature controls. Burner coils glowed to red life, inspiring spiteful thoughts in Larson's mind. *It'd serve the bastard right if he burned his hands off.* After the stove/oven unit, the room came to a corner. Against the northern wall, closed cabinets of oak hung over a porcelain sink with a steel spigot and handles and an attached countertop of speckled, dingy formica. Beside it, a refrigerator towered nearly to the ceiling.

Taziar blurred into the shadows beyond the light, moving toward the southeastern corner. Gaelinar chose not to aid their search. Instead, he leaned against the table, gaze locked on Bramin with fanatical interest. The dark elf turned his attention to the sink, and Larson spun the stove dial to its off position to protect his friends. The burner dulled to orange, then faded to neutral black. Watching a process which seemed trivial and routine turned Larson's thoughts to the ridiculousness of an exploration for an undescribed item. Mannix's journals had given him no clue, and he wondered if his companions might have more knowledge they had not revealed to him. "Does anyone have the foggiest notion what we're looking for?"

Larson half expected someone to reply stupidly, "Geirmagnus' rod." But no one did. Taziar and Gaelinar remained silent. Bramin made a wordless sound, but offered no further explanation.

Larson pressed. "Bramin? You know what the rod looks like?"

Bramin did not bother to face Larson as he replied, regal as a king. "I have an idea."

"And?"

"And I'm not here at your convenience, to share my thoughts with a fool who has condemned himself and his friends to death. I never promised to help you, only that I wouldn't interfere."

Larson restrained an obscenity, glad Gaelinar had chosen to guard the dark elf. *If the rod has some sort of magical powers, I would as soon it not fall into Bramin's hands.*

Vidarr replied. *I believe it is a product of sorcery, Allerum. The description I've heard is "a rod of wood and iron, a weapon of unfathomable power."*

Anything more? Larson urged.

Vidarr lapsed into an aura of regret without attempting a verbal reply.

Bramin seemed preoccupied with the miniature waterfall created by twirling the faucet knobs. Larson ducked into the lane between the half man and the table. Nearly at the northeastern corner, he stopped before the refrigerator, his back to the brick pole which held the pipes. Scattered light from the fluorescent bulb dragged pale shadows across magnets in the form of metal hooks and plastic fruit. It appeared much like the refrigerator Larson remembered from his parents' apartment in New York City, except that his mother had trapped memos, school menus and scrawled children's drawings beneath the magnets. Recalling the odor of week-old leftovers green with mold, Larson wondered what effect a century or two might have had on stored refreshments. Only he and Bramin stood close enough to suffer the consequences of his curiosity. Holding his breath, Larson caught the metal handle and pulled.

The door swung open easily, but the bulb inside did not go on. Weak light from the farther corner filtered in, defining shapes into recognizable figures. Plastic containers lined the upper shelf. All were sealed, Larson noted in relief. A receptacle which had once held milk lay on its side, half-filled with a clear substance he guessed was water. On the lower level, a single can of Pepsi stood, pushed to the back. Its red, white, and blue emblem seemed different than he recalled; but so much time had passed since his last soda, the details escaped him. The flip top appeared more square and flat, laid into a depression. He grabbed the can. It felt flimsier than he expected, aluminum instead of steel.

Taziar's voice wafted to Larson from beyond the pole. "What's this?"

"The rod!" Bramin screamed.

Larson jerked his head out of the refrigerator. Bramin's sword crashed into its door, slamming it shut. Magnets showered to the floor, and a spray of broken chips rattled across the concrete.

Gaelinar sprang for Bramin, halted by the dark elf's snarl. "Fair fight, Kensei."

Reluctantly, Gaelinar retreated as Bramin thrust for Larson.

It seemed less than fair to Larson, who had neither time nor space to draw a sword. He dodged into the lane between the pole and the eastern wall, still clutching the Pepsi. Bramin's blade swept for Larson's head. Larson ducked. The sword struck the fuse box with a thin chime of steel. In the seconds it took Bramin to recover from his stroke, Larson slapped the bottom of the can against the conduit and pulled the tab. Soda geysered, splashing over the combatants and forming a foaming, brown puddle across the floor. Caught by surprise, Bramin hesitated. Larson used the opening to draw his sword and cut for Bramin's throat.

Bramin parried and riposted. Larson sidled, slipping in the spilled cola. Bramin's blade slit open the sleeve of Larson's cloak. Though too close for another sword stroke, the half man pressed his advantage. He caught Larson's chin in a sticky hand, and slammed the elf against the pole. Larson's head hit a pipe. A bolt of white slashed his vision, and his limbs went suddenly flaccid. The world swirled in sickening circles. He felt his back sliding down the bricks, and fought desperately for consciousness.

Bramin spun Larson and hurled him to the floor, creating the distance needed for a sword stroke. Impact snapped Larson to full awareness. As Bramin's sword plunged toward him, he rolled. The blade scraped concrete. Larson's back whacked against the solid stone of the southern wall. Dizzily, he noticed an empty gun rack nailed to the wall above his head, but its significance escaped him. Gathering his feet beneath him, he raised his sword and rushed Bramin.

Bramin scrambled back to avoid the bold commitment of Larson's attack. He caught Larson's blade on his crossguard, parrying the stroke aside. Bramin's riposte sliced the air before Larson's chest and bit squarely into the conduit cable.

Sparks blazed from the contact. White light flared like fire around the sword. The fluorescent bulb winked out, plunging them into darkness. Larson dove aside. Bramin's shout of triumph split into a scream, and his face went pale as bleached wool. The force hurled him, limp, to the ground; the sword stuck, embedded in the circuits. The ozone reek of electrical fire permeated the room, twined through with smoke.

Larson scarcely had time to register the scene before an explosion rocked the courtyard. Outside, chips of concrete rattled like hail from the walls and roof. One piece slammed through the window, hurling glass shards across the stove, Gaelinar, and the table beyond him with a soprano sprinkle of noise. Nearer to the stairwell, Gaelinar and Taziar responded first. They led a frantic charge up the steps with Larson close behind. As they burst into the fading light of evening, Larson's mind registered a number of realities at once.

Jagged blocks of concrete littered the courtyard around a hole the size of a mine crater. A section of the outer wall had collapsed. Snapped free at one end, its razor wire coiled to the ground. In the center of the carnage, a dragon thrashed in a spiraled wreath of copper wire with clinging slivers of cement. Scales of solid steel-gray made the evening look pale in comparison. Twice the size of the creature in Hel, its flailing jaws seemed to rake the clouds into the blood-colored streaks of dusk. Only its head and neck had emerged from the shattered ring of the particle accelerator, the remainder was still caught in wire now devoid of current.

Gaelinar covered the distance from door to monster in three running strides. His sword bit into the muscle of a tremendous foreleg, splitting wire like paper. With a roar, the chaos-force wrenched a claw partially free. It snapped for Gaelinar. The Kensei scrambled backward as Taziar came up on the dragon from the opposite side.

Larson scurried to the attack. He had covered only half the distance when Gaelinar bore in for a second strike. Again, his blade sliced flesh and wire. Black blood seeped from the wound, thick as syrup. The chaos-force bit for Gaelinar. Taziar dodged in. The Climber swung his weapon like a club, and Larson got his first glimpse of Geirmagnus' rod. *My god, I should have known. It's a fucking rifle!* The butt crashed against the monstrous head, and wood split with a crack. The dragon turned its jaws on Taziar. The Climber dodged, and knifelike fangs closed on empty air.

"Pull the trigger!" Larson screamed as he ran to help. "Pull the goddamned trigger!"

Larson's command fell on deaf ears. His words could have no more meaning to Taziar than the workings of a weapon not yet invented. And, with Taziar clutching the barrel, obedience would only have resulted in the Climber shooting his own foot.

Again, Gaelinar slashed. His sword plowed through flesh, opening another row of copper wire. As the dragon bit at Gaelinar, Taziar swept forward, gun poised for another blow. Larson dove. He seized the rifle butt, attempting to wrench it from his companion's hand. Mannix's last words pounded through his mind like a cadence. *I believe only my rod can kill the monster.* Taziar gripped tighter, stumbling in surprise.

"Give it to me, damn it!" Larson howled. "I know how to use it."

The chaos-force made a tremendous lurch which tore half its body free of the encumbering wire. The ground bucked and trembled. Taziar lost his footing, staggering backward. Larson fell to his knees. The gun twisted from their grips skidding forward to land beneath the darker scales of the creature's underbelly. Razor-sharp teeth gashed Larson's arm. He rolled aside as the beast whirled to answer Gaelinar's next attack.

Larson knew despair. *The Fates were right. Getting the rod did release the chaos-force; it caused the battle in which Bramin broke the electric current containing the beast. We've lost the gun "Geirmagnus" planned to be used to defeat it, so the only weapon of its kind will not be used against it."*

The rasp of Taziar's drawn sword punctuated Larson's thought. The Shadow Climber seemed to read his mind. "The Fates were right, but Geirmagnus was wrong. Look at the damage from Gaelinar's sword!" Without awaiting a reply, Taziar charged the chaos-force again. His blade rattled on scales like iron, drawing a superficial line across the flesh beneath them. The dragon swung its head around. Its bite fell short, but its muzzle smacked Taziar, toppling him to concrete-riddled ground. Before it could finish its attack, Gaelinar stabbed from its other side. The beast's neck arched back to the Kensei.

Larson drew his sword as Taziar clambered to shaky legs. *Shadow's right. It wasn't the Fates who surmised only one weapon could kill the chaos-force. Twentieth-century American parapsychologists can make mistakes.* He joined the battle with renewed vigor. Whipping forward, he plunged his blade into the dragon's side. It loosed a high-pitched scream. Its efforts jerked it fully free of the copper wire. Leathery wings large as tents flashed upward. One slapped Larson's chest and face as he dodged. The force hurled him backward. He hit the ground, biting his tongue hard enough to draw blood. It suddenly occurred to him that this dragon seemed to lack the fire-breathing ability of its smaller, more focused and agile cousins. For that, he was grateful.

Larson rose as the dragon attempted flight. It spun in an awkward semicircle. Apparently, Gaelinar's katana had taken its toll on the muscles of its opposite wing. Sword high, Larson rushed the beast. Before his blow landed, Taziar's blade gashed the scaled side, drawing blood the color of ink. The chaos-force whirled, moving its bulk with astonishing speed. It whisked toward Taziar.

Larson and Taziar broke and ran. A single step closed the gap between the beast and its prey. Hot saliva dripped over Larson. He stopped suddenly, hoping the change in momentum would throw off the creature's timing. Steel flashed behind the lumbering giant, and Gaelinar's swords stabbed into its flank.

The chaos-force spun, bellowing its rage. It turned on Gaelinar who ran, the creature on his heels. Larson and Taziar turned, hoping to gain the beast's attention long enough for Gaelinar to escape. But it outmaneuvered them, quickly widening the ground between them.

Larson sprinted after it. Losing one of his companions meant losing the battle. Without forces on each side of the dragon, there was no way to distract it from killing. So far, all the wounds inflicted on the chaos-force looked superficial. *And,* Larson thought with alarm, *once it finishes with us, it'll destroy the rest of the world.* Terror quickened his pace.

Gaelinar raced for the downed section of wall and the dangling corkscrew of razor wire. Too late, his plan became clear. Inches from the coil, he dodged aside. A dragon claw dug through the back of his cloak. Momentum carried the chaos-force into the wire, dragging the Kensei with it. Honed steel sliced scaled skin to bone. Animal screams of pain rent the air. The chaos-force floundered, reeling with an agony which only worked it deeper into the wire. Tarlike blood cascaded from hundreds of wounds, coating the snow and sand beneath it.

Larson drew up beside the thrashing dragon in horror. "Gaelinar!" His cry emerged as distressed as the dying beast's. Carefully avoiding the wire, he plunged his blade through the reptilian head. The chaos-force went still. The world went silent except for the ceaseless drip of blood.

A soft voice broke the hush. "Allerum."

Larson followed the sound to the opposite side of the razor wire and the great beast's corpse. Several feet from the carnage, Gaelinar lay in a red puddle, still clutching his sword in his right fist. Blood spurted from a gaping tear through his left armpit.

"Gaelinar!" Larson rushed to his mentor's side. He caught the wound between his hands, attempting to apply pressure. But the blood ran freely through the gaps between his fingers. Desperately, he readjusted his grip.

Clumsily, Gaelinar thrust the hilt of his katana toward Larson. His wrist struck Larson's neck so weakly, the elf scarcely felt the blow. The sword fell across Gaelinar's thighs. He fumbled for it with blinded, glazing eyes, apparently unaware he had caught the blade. Again, he jabbed the hilt for Larson's hand. "Hero," he said, his voice like the dry rasp of a drawing sword. "It begins again. Carry on."

Larson accepted the hilt. Blood pulsed in a spray across his hands, then dropped to a methodical wash. Still Larson clung to the wound and the image of Gaelinar's immortality. Somehow, his mind could not accept the demise of a man who had survived being crushed by a dragon, who had killed a god with his bare hands, who feared nothing, not even a Dragonrank Master in his own school. Larson had seen death often enough to recognize it, but, this time, his mind deceived him. He raised a hand, but his own irrational certainty would not allow him to check for a pulse.

"Allerum." Taziar knelt beside Larson and reached for Gaelinar's neck. "He's . . ."

"No." Larson lashed out in misdirected fury. His

blood-wet hand caught Taziar across one cheek. The force of the blow staggered the smaller man.

Immediately, Larson regretted his attack. He had hit Taziar to keep the Climber from stating something they both already knew. *Gaelinar is dead.* The revelation wrenched tears from Larson's eyes. The world blurred around him as he succumbed to the blanketing curtain of grief.

A sound pierced Larson's shrouded awareness, the metallic clack of a rifle bolt slammed into place. Bramin's sibilant voice followed. "Don't move, Allerum."

Cautiously, Larson raised his eyes. He blinked away tears to find himself staring down the barrel of Gary Mannix's rifle, now in Bramin's hands.

The dark elf sneered. "Did you forget about our fight to the death? Or did you believe a little jolt would kill me?" He laughed with the dignified arrogance which comes with great power. "Thanks for showing me how to use the rod."

"Wait," Larson pleaded hoarsely, praying Mannix had stored his gun unloaded. "This is between you and me. Let Shadow go first."

"And let him stab me in the back?" Bramin started.

Instantly, Larson realized his mistake. Taziar had made a charge for Bramin just as Larson drew the dark elf's attention to his companion. The gun roared. Taziar toppled forward into the snow. Blood trickled from a hole in his thigh. He struggled to his knees as Bramin chambered another round.

"No!" Larson screamed. Brandishing Gaelinar's sword, he plunged toward Bramin. Hovering at the half man's hip, the gun swung around to Larson again.

Larson halted, lowering the katana in a gesture of surrender. Bramin remained just beyond sword range. "Go ahead," Larson challenged, more boldly than he felt. "Shoot him again. I'll kill you before you can chamber the third round."

Taziar had slipped to his haunches, staring at the wound in his leg in startled awe. His features turned stark white, and Larson suspected pain was driving the Climber into shock.

Bramin simply smiled. "He's not going anywhere. I have time to shoot you first."

"Go ahead." Surprisingly, Larson knew no fear. "But you doom yourself as well."

Patient as a cat with a cornered bird, Bramin allowed Larson to elaborate.

Larson stalled, keeping his gaze locked on the gun. As long as Bramin held it low, he doubted the dark elf would pull the trigger. A hip shot from a beginner was unlikely to hit even a target at close range. "If you bring the great equalizer into Midgard, you sign your own death warrant. You have nothing to gain and everything to lose. Your magic and sword skill, gained through a lifetime of effort, make you more powerful than almost anyone, stronger even than some of the gods. Sure, you have the first gun. But you saw my world. They breed. They grow. *Bramin, if you put guns into your world, you open the way for any weak coward to kill you before you see him coming!*"

Bramin's head twitched.

Larson granted no mercy. *If I can distract him just long enough to make my move . . .* "Dragonrank magic is no match for bullets. Once you bring guns into your world," unintentionally, he parroted Vidarr, "there is no more glory in war."

Abruptly, the rifle arched toward Bramin's shoulder.

And Larson ran out of time. As soon as the barrel started moving, he charged. Bramin shot as he positioned. Larson's ears rang with the blast. The bullet ripped through his lower abdomen bringing white hot agony. He screamed. Oblivion crushed down on him, bringing with it Gaelinar's admonishments from a sword lesson which seemed centuries ago. *"Excuse me, O most worthy opponent. I banged my arm. Please don't decapitate me."*

From a great distance, Larson heard the ragged clatter of the rifle bolt. He swept Gaelinar's katana in a desperate, half-blind dive. The razor-honed edge bit into Bramin's shoulder and through his neck. The bullet bounced off the other wall, strewing chips of concrete. Larson rolled, tangled with Bramin's decapitated body, covered with blood of which very little was his own.

Pain quickened Larson's breathing to a pant. He forced himself to slow down, gathering enough strength to fling Bramin's limp arm away from his face. The effort drove dizziness down upon him. He lay still, not daring to move again. His vision narrowed to a tunnel which admitted only the clouds, and starred points of light threatened to blur what little of the world remained to him.

Allerum, Vidarr sent softly. *Are you . . .* He completed the query with an aura of sympathy and concern.

Unable to gather a coherent answer, Larson tried to force desperation from his thoughts. His gut burned like acid, but he believed he would survive the injury. At the moment, he did not feel fully certain he wanted to.

Vidarr kept his tone level, soothing. *I thought it might cheer you to know Baldur is with me.*

Shadows edged in on Larson. With effort, he questioned. *How?*

The chaos-force you loosed was more than powerful enough to repair the rift created when you destroyed Loki. The excess energy balanced Baldur's return from Hel.

But, Larson managed, *we killed the chaos-force.*

Not really. Distress leeched through Vidarr's aura of compassion. *You killed a physical manifestation of a chaos-force, dispersing it. Chaos is not an object, it's an energy. So long as it's not destroyed utterly, it remains around us to be channeled by its servants.*

Vidarr's reply seemed thinned as if by distance. Still, Larson could not help noticing the eerie resemblance between Vidarr's explanation and the Law of the Conservation of Matter and Energy. Pressed to the extreme edge of consciousness, he nearly forgot to force an issue far more important to him than Baldur's rescue. *Silme?*

Larson detected a trace of guilt beneath Vidarr's cavalier answer. *She's safe with me, Allerum.*

Larson's strength ebbed. Even breathing seemed too much work. Unable to gather mental words, he hoped Vidarr could detect his curiosity.

The hesitation in Vidarr's attitude was unequivocal. *Allerum, I must tell you something unpleasant. I hate to speak while you're hurt, but perhaps this is best. You have no choice but to listen. Afterward, I hope you won't judge me too harshly; and, first, I want you to realize Silme and I will get you through this . . . and Shadow, too. Rest easy.*

Larson did not speculate, afraid even that small endeavor might drive away the last spark of his awareness.

We have all long believed the quest for Geirmagnus' rod was impossible. I believe our own doubts kept us from achieving it, so skepticism was the one luxury I couldn't allow you. I hid the truth from you. Apparently guessing my motives, Gaelinar did likewise. My recommendation, that you take Shadow with you, may have seemed casual. It was not. After you met Shadow in the tavern, I made a detailed check of his background and discovered useful qualities. Despite his dishonest profession, his loyalty to friends was unquestionable. And to him, the terms "impossible" and "interesting challenge" were interchangeable.

I knew Bramin would tell you the task was impossible; I was only surprised it took him as long as it did. I tried everything to keep you from raising him. Failing that, you left me without option. I needed some way to force you to finish your quest. I had to find a cause so important to you as to preclude all doubt—to drive you beyond the impossible. That goal could only be the same which made you challenge me: Silme. When she left Hel, I met her; recall, she is pledged to my service. I brought her to my hall on Asgard. She asked to reunite with you, believe that, Allerum. I told her it could not be. I didn't explain the situation, but she chose to trust me. Then I cornered Shadow. By making him believe I was working against you in addition to your enemies, I fueled his allegiance to you. I knew his attitude could only help you succeed.

I always knew any or all of you might die, but I had no other choice. If you refused the quest, Odin would have slain you all, perhaps me, as well. I care for Baldur very deeply. I did not enjoy the deceptions any more than you, but I saw no other way. I plead the cause of brotherly love and hope you can find it in yourself to forgive me. Vidarr stopped, obviously awaiting a reply. His anxiety felt tangible.

Larson trembled in the grip of pain. He tried to search his mind for an answer, but he felt only the crushing weight of darkness. Quietly, he slipped into oblivion.

Epilogue

"The law that I have preached . . . and the discipline that I have established will be your master after my disappearance."

—The Pali Canon
Digha Nikaya, II

A quarter moon dangled above Hvergelmir's chasm, mirrored in the sluggish waters of the eleven rivers which formed the falls. Twisted as one, the streams crashed to Hel's entryway, whipped to foam by the force of impact on the rocks below. Spray rebounded, needling Larson and freezing on the metallic surfaces of the rifle in his hands. Winds from the rushing cascade ruffled thin, yellow-white hair into his eyes. With no regrets, he hurled the weapon. It spun through air, reflecting patterns of moonlight across the surface of water. Then Hvergelmir accepted the offering. Steel clanked against stone, and the rifle was swallowed beneath the boiling current. Larson knew the wild waters would pummel Gary Mannix's rod to splinters and beyond; he had learned from Loki's death that the cascade could bash not only a man, but also his soul, to irretrievable oblivion.

For some time after the gun disappeared, Larson stood watching, awed by the unbridled power of the waterfall. It held a vitality beyond man's ability to master, a strength he might capture in his mind and tap in times of need. Unconsciously, his hand fell to the hilt of the katana at his hip. Suddenly, Gaelinar was with him again, berating stupid questions, punishing inattentiveness with an unexpected kick during a practice, preparing to retrieve Silme's soul from Hel as if readying for an excursion to a farm village. Larson's eyes burned and his face felt moist; he blamed it on the pelting splatter of the falls. *Could we resurrect Gaelinar?* Larson answered his own question. *When Gaelinar first spoke with Modgudr, he claimed death would make his soul become one with the universe. Where would we look for him?* Larson realized something more. *Gaelinar was an old man, a warrior who lived and died by his swords. His deeds were his immortality. He would never have wanted us to steal him from his ultimate reward.*

Larson turned, shuffling through snow speckled with crushed, brown foliage, a chaotic pattern of stems and seeds, the timeworn mingling inseparably with the hopes of the future spring. *What goes around comes around. It seems strangely fitting Gaelinar would choose to say "begin again" rather than "it's over."* Grimly, Larson returned to the companions who awaited him by the cliffs which surrounded the clearing. Astryd sat cross-legged, propped against a boulder, Taziar's head cradled in her lap. The thief's eyes were closed. Tousled black hair fringed features oddly at peace; to Larson the notorious Shadow Climber looked more like an unkempt child. Larson could not banish a feeling of guilt, aware the risk of peritonitis had forced Astryd to focus her taxing healing spells on him. Taziar's limping gait surely required twice the energy of normal walking, but the little Climber had never complained.

Silme extended her arm as Larson approached. He accepted her hand, pulling her into an embrace. For the hundredth time in as many minutes, he felt like the luckiest creature alive. Side by side, they sat, touching in as many places as the position and decorum allowed. But a question still plagued Larson, and he realized Silme would have the answer. "Gaelinar told us how the two of you wound up together."

Silme rested a palm on Larson's knee. Her nod encouraged him to continue.

"Gaelinar said you met him in Japan. He didn't know why you came there."

"He didn't?" Silme seemed surprised. She stroked Larson's leg absently. "I came for him. When I realized I would need to contest Bramin's evil, I selected my repertoire of spells to counteract his, to protect innocents from his vengeance. He was always more powerful than me, both in magic and physical strength. I needed someone to even the odds. So, with the help of other Dragonrank sorcerers and Vidarr, I identified our world's most skilled swordsman. I met with Gaelinar's lord, a loathsome weasel of a man, and asked him to free Gaelinar from his service." Silme's features screwed into wrinkles at the memory, as if she had tasted something bitter.

Larson glanced at Astryd who was smoothing stray strands of hair away from Taziar's lids. "And?" he prompted.

"Gaelinar's lord refused, of course," Silme continued. "Then the old fool tried to force himself on me."

Larson winced, wondering how any man could be stupid enough to try to ravish a Dragonrank sorceress. With equal speed, he recalled the mages were a Northern phenomenon, nearly unknown outside Scandinavia.

"I didn't mean to kill him," Silme said with honest regret. "I think he had a weak heart and my spell simply propelled him a bit closer to Hel."

Larson put his hand over Silme's. "Gaelinar believed his master died of natural causes."

"A necessary lie." Silme stared off toward the horizon. "If Gaelinar had known I took his lord's life, he would have been obligated to kill me."

Wind hissed through the snow, tossing flakes in a gentle spray. Larson remained in silent contemplation, wondering if Gaelinar could have avenged himself on Silme. The Kensei's dedication to Silme, his willingness to serve her even after death seemed beyond the realm of normal loyalty. Though Gaelinar had tried to hide and deny his morality, it came through in a thousand different ways: his selfless dedication to causes, his ability to tolerate and even find humor in Larson's disrespect. Larson could not help but wonder whether Gaelinar's pledge to a repulsive master would allow him to act against Silme. He doubted it. *But we'll never really know.*

"Any other questions?" Silme prompted.

Just one, Larson thought. *But you can't answer it. I still don't understand why Gary Mannix wrote "rod" or rather, "rads" instead of "rifle" or "gun." But that's another thing I don't believe I'll ever fully understand.* Larson slipped an arm around Silme, drawing her closer. The warm reality of her nearness remained scarcely within his ability to believe. "No," he said. "That's enough." His words went beyond the reply to Silme's query. "That's enough," he repeated emphatically. "I don't care if I never see another dragon or hear from another god. We've saved mankind twice. Now, if the world doesn't mind, I'd like to forget about Law and Chaos, about hopeless futures and doomed pasts, and especially about performing impossible tasks. I've got some 'happily ever after' time coming, and I'm going to share it with the woman of my dreams." He pressed his cheek to Silme's breast.

Taziar spoke. "Happily ever after time, huh? I've never heard it put that way."

Larson glanced at his small companion to find Taziar's blue eyes wide and sparkling with excitement. "I know just the place. Did I ever tell you about a city called Cullinsberg? Its baron has a bounty on me, but if we're careful, we should be able to slip past. . . ."

Larson lost the remainder of Taziar's words to the distant roar of Hvergelmir. He studied the Shadow Climber for a long time before he laughed. *It's not over yet. Not by a long shot.*

An Exciting New Fantasy Talent!

Mickey Zucker Reichert

THE BIFROST GUARDIANS

☐ **GODSLAYER: Book 1** (UE2372—$3.95)

The war god Freyr has snatched Al Larson from the midst of a firefight in Vietnam, flinging him through time and space into the body of an elvish warrior to stand against Loki in the combat with Chaos. Torn from a world where bullets and grenades, not swords and spells, are the weapons of war, Al must adapt swiftly, or die. And his only chance of survival rests in completing the quest Freyr has set for him—a quest that will take him to the very gates of Hel.

☐ **SHADOW CLIMBER: Book 2** (UE2284—$3.50)

Here is an unforgettable tale of battles and betrayals, of magical spells and mythical creatures—and of the thief-hero Taziar Shadow Climber and his quest for vengeance on his father's slayer. Together with his comrade-in-arms, the barbarian lord Moonbear, he will face all comers in a world where death waits one swordstroke or evil enchantment away!

☐ **DRAGONRANK MASTER: Book 3** (UE2366—$3.95)

Here, at last, the characters from *Godslayer* are united with those from *Shadow Climber*, in a climactic conflict between the forces of Chaos and Order. Swinging from the legendary world of elves, gods, and magic to the bloody battlefields of Vietnam, and back again, this is a special brand of fantasy unlike anything you've ever read!

NEW AMERICAN LIBRARY
P.O. Box 999, Bergenfield, New Jersey 07621

Please send me the DAW BOOKS I have checked above. I am enclosing $________ (check or money order—no currency or C.O.D.'s). Please include the list price plus $1.00 per order to cover handling costs. Prices and numbers are subject to change without notice. (Prices slightly higher in Canada.)

Name ________________________________

Address ______________________________

City _______________ State ________ Zip ________

Please allow 4-6 weeks for delivery.